UNQUIET GHOSTS

—— A NOVEL ——

GLENN MEADE

HOWARD BOOKS
AN IMPRINT OF SIMON & SCHUSTER, INC.

NEW YORK   NASHVILLE   LONDON   TORONTO   SYDNEY   NEW DELHI

Howard Books
An Imprint of Simon & Schuster, Inc.
1230 Avenue of the Americas
New York, NY 10020

First Howard Books hardcover edition July 2017

HOWARD and colophon are trademarks of Simon & Schuster, Inc.

For information about special discounts for bulk purchases, please contact Simon & Schuster Special Sales at 1-866-506-1949 or business@simonandschuster.com.

The Simon & Schuster Speakers Bureau can bring authors to your live event. For more information, or to book an event, contact the Simon & Schuster Speakers Bureau at 1-866-248-3049 or visit our website at www.simonspeakers.com.

Interior design by Jaime Putorti

Manufactured in the United States of America

10 9 8 7 6 5 4 3 2 1

Library of Congress Cataloging-in-Publication Data is available.

ISBN 978-1-4767-9741-0
ISBN 978-1-4767-9775-5 (ebook)

FOR MY MOM,
CARMEL MEADE,
WITH LOVE

There must be those among whom we can sit down and weep and still be counted as warriors.

—ADRIENNE RICH

UNQUIET GHOSTS

PROLOGUE

_____

THUNDER MOUNTAIN, SMOKY MOUNTAINS,
EAST TENNESSEE
11:45 P.M.

Dwight McCoy liked to talk to God.

He sat in his front porch rocker—angry coal-black clouds on the horizon, lightning spits sizzling from the dark heavens—and stared out at the approaching storm. He always looked forward to his weekend talk with the Big Man, but this time the goats were ruining his conversation. They were going crazy, bleating their lungs out.

Dwight tried to ignore them as he took a drag on his joint and let the smoke fill his lungs. Usually he liked to pass a quiet Friday evening rocking in his chair on his shack's front porch, sucking on a joint, his Bible on his lap, indulging in a one-way conversation. But the goats were messing up his evening.

It would never have occurred to Dwight that in reality he was only three minutes away from meeting God personally. Or that all his prayers were about to be answered. But such was life, always full of surprises.

The two goats on the lawn were tied to the front porch and kept bleating, getting agitated, then charging toward the porch rails, slamming their stumpy horns into the wood.

"Easy up, boys. Easy, you hear?"

Dwight heard a thunderous growl. He stroked his greasy beard and peered out past the mess of junk and crushed beer cans that decorated his lawn. High in the inky night sky, way out beyond his rusted thirty-year-old Chevy pickup and the mess of an ancient ruined tractor, storm clouds bubbled.

A big one coming, by the looks of it. Dwight sipped from the mason jar, gargled, swallowed a mouthful of burning spirit, and let out a sigh.

Man, that was good.

Dwight always kicked off the weekend with some fiesta time—a mason jar of moonshine accompanied by a couple of really good joints. Relaxing on his front porch with a pair of goats and a banged-up old refrigerator full of beer for company was the perfect way to watch some dazzling summer storms. On the tar-black horizon, the show had already started: sizzling bolts of lightning, their volleys of thunder echoing in the darkness like cannon shot.

Chewing the cud with God was part of Dwight's enjoyment. Nothing too deep, mind, just the occasional whine about life or the kind of day he'd had on the ten-acre Smokies hill farm since Hilda had passed.

When the 'shine or the spliffs weren't up to scratch and it seemed as if God wasn't listening, sometimes his goats, Barack and Obama, just sat there, listening. Dwight liked to talk to his goats, but tonight neither animal seemed in the mood for social chitchat.

"Easy up, boys. Easy up, you hear?" he said again.

The agitated goats were acting kind of strange. Head-butting the porch railing, the *clack-clack* of their clipped horns chipping the wood. Being tethered to the porch never usually irked them. But for the last few minutes they had been bleating their hearts out.

"What you getting worked up about, fellas?"

The goats paid him no heed, just kept head-butting the post. *Clack. Clack.* Dwight reckoned it was the approaching storm. Bad weather often got them riled, but tonight it was so bad it was getting on his nerves.

"Settle down, old buddies. Settle down."

Dwight swallowed a mouthful of 'shine from the mason jar and wiped his beard with his grimy shirt sleeve. The homemade spirit burned his throat like a lit match but sure tasted good. He sucked deep on the spliff, savored the vapors searing his lungs. Saturday night fever, and all homemade, the weed grown in the woods behind him, the 'shine made in his own still.

A frightening rumble of thunder echoed in the night sky, but he felt so relaxed he barely reacted. The storm wouldn't hit here for maybe another five minutes, which gave him enough time to enjoy the fireworks. After that, the rain would hammer like bullets on the cabin's tin roof. He sucked again on the joint, held the smoke in his lungs, let it out slowly.

They said weed frazzled your brain, but Dwight didn't care, not since the day Hilda went to cancer. From then on he figured he was on the downhill slope anyway, and weed would change nothing. Hilda had slipped away in her sleep after a year of agony. One minute breathing, the next lifeless as he clutched her hand. He talked with God about that, begged not to let him suffer as painful a going as his wife's. Give him a heart attack, hit him with a Mack truck, whatever, just take him quick.

Dwight grabbed his walking cane. He flicked the hook end to open the porch refrigerator. The light inside came on. Cans of Bud, milk, some provisions. But mostly Bud. He hooked out a Bud, grabbed it in the crook of his foot, kicked it into the air, and caught it in his palm, then banged shut the door with the tip of his snake boot.

Not bad for an old guy. He hissed open the can, swallowed some cold amber. High in the Smoky Mountains, away from civilization, more thunderbolts sizzled, the storm coming closer. *Clack. Clack.* The goats took another bleating run at the rail post. Their distress was driving him nuts.

They said animals sensed imminent danger. That in fear they moved up into the hills when tsunamis or hurricanes hit. He reckoned the goats sensed the approaching thunderstorm.

"Settle down, fellas. Nobody's going to get crisped."

At that precise moment, a booming thunderbolt echoed around the mountains, and the goats went crazy. Dwight looked up at the sky as something caught his eye. Weird.

A spark of light spit out of the dark storm cloud. The spark blazed, like a glittering star. What the . . . ? Dwight squinted and felt his heart race. Was it his imagination, or was the object shooting toward him?

For a moment he wondered if he'd drunk too much. Sometimes the moonshine caused him to have visions or to perceive the real meaning of existence. Once he'd decided to keep a notebook and pen by his bed, and when he woke in the night, he'd write down his jumbled thoughts, hoping to decipher the meaning of life hidden in his dreams, and fall back to sleep. Next day, sober, he'd read his scrawled notes: oil change due Friday, pay wheel tax, buy a packet of smokes and a gallon of milk. Packet of butt wipes for sensitive skin.

Dwight rubbed his eyes and blinked. The spark blazed in the black sky dead ahead of him and got brighter, speeding out of the storm cloud. Whoever said drinking ruined your eyesight was lying, because Dwight saw the object glowing brighter and moving closer by the second. It was definitely coming toward him, whatever it was.

A UFO? Some weird light phenomenon? Now it sparkled brighter, seemed to break apart. A piece of the object fell away, a ball of flaming light. Now there were two objects. Then the smaller one disappeared, its light dying like an orange emergency flare as it dropped toward Earth.

But the bigger object kept hurtling toward him.

"Holy cow."

Alarmed, Dwight pushed himself out of the rocker and went to turn to his cabin, to grab his shotgun. His survivor's instinct was already telling him it was a total waste of time as the *thing* came screaming toward him like a banshee.

He heard a swish of air and then a mighty *thud* when something hit the forest floor with a sound like an earthquake, shaking the ground under him, as if some unseen monster in the bowels of the Earth had just given a massive growl.

The powerful impact blew Barack and Obama clear off the ground, sent the goats' exploding carcasses flying through the darkness, as if sucked skyward by a tornado.

The same force field plowed into Dwight like an artillery shell blast, shattering his cabin, turning it to matchwood, crushing every bone in his seventy-five-year-old body, and killing him instantly.

All in all, Dwight McCoy could not have asked for a quicker and less painful death.

I

I keep two photographs by my bed. They are my deepest wounds.

One is a snapshot of my parents at a party celebrating my younger brother's West Point graduation ceremony. Sweet, funny, twenty-one-year-old Kyle, his sapphire-blue eyes smiling for the camera, looking so handsome in his gray and white cadet's uniform.

In the photograph next to Kyle's stands my colonel father, tall and proud, every inch the Army man, his uniform creases so razor-sharp they could cut tomatoes, every medal buffed and polished. We're a military family, Appalachian settlers who come from a long line of battle-hardened Scotch-Irish warriors, the kind who seem to be born missing a fear gene.

And standing between my father and my brother is my mother, Martha Beth Kelly. I often remember her with a vodka grin on her face as she danced the evening away, her wild red hair tossed, one hand raised like a crazed rocker, in the other maybe a joint if she'd gotten hold of one, more often a cocktail glass kissing her smudged lipstick.

And always that look on her face, the one that told me there was no stopping her from making a drunken fool of herself, even as my father tried to coax her off the dance floor.

My father, the courageous six-foot-three colonel who battled his way across Iraq to the gates of Saddam Hussein's palace. Who fought hand-to-hand at Fallujah and lost his left foot in a grenade blast.

Kyle and I adored my father. He was our idol. Someone gave my kid brother a miniature soldier's uniform when he was six. He paraded up and down our backyard with his shoes polished and a stick in his hands for a rifle.

I asked, "What are you doing, Kyle?"

A smile lit up his face. "Playing cadet. When I grow up, I want to be a soldier just like Daddy."

Kyle was already into athletics, a stickler for competition sports, but easygoing with it. When my dad saw him marching solemnly in the yard, he said, "Cadet Kyle, what is your motto?"

Kyle stood to attention, held a salute, and recited the cadet's West Point code. "A cadet does not lie, cheat, steal, or tolerate those who do."

My father beamed at me and said, "Looks like we got another one for West Point."

My father, who always makes me feel safe, even though I am an adult. Once in a Florida bar a few years back while I was on vacation with my dad, two big, steroid-muscled guys drinking beer wolf-whistled at me and whispered a dirty remark as I passed them on the way to the restroom. My dad was over there in a second, right in their faces, his muscled arms bulging, his chest proud, spoiling for a fight, ready to beat the life out of anyone who taunted his daughter.

He insisted that the idiots apologize. They did and slinked off like a pair of sorry kids, abandoning their beers. He's that kind of father. He has his pride, takes no prisoners, and backs off from no one.

A man who was never truly afraid of anything—except the fiery-tempered little woman from Temperance, Georgia, whom he loved and married but was never able to make happy no matter how hard he tried.

And all because they could never share their deepest secret.

The two photographs I keep are side by side in a silver-toned metal frame. The second image is of my husband, Jack, and me and our two smiling, beloved children, Amy and Sean, then four and eight.

The photograph showed Jack not in Army uniform, as so often in the images I keep of him, but wearing a Jimmy Buffett tropical shirt while on vacation at Myrtle Beach in South Carolina one blistering summer. It was a vacation meant to salve my husband's mental wounds from a punishing deployment in Iraq—and it was three months before he and our children vanished, never to be seen again.

Three months before those "terrible events" befell us all, as my father refers to our tragedies, his anguished face like granite whenever he talks about our heartbreak, which is seldom. For a hardened veteran who witnessed many die in battle and who rarely flinched recalling the experience, any mention of our family's loss brings him to the edge of tears.

And so I keep these photographs by my bed and not in the rooms downstairs, well out of his sight. The photographs do not make me cry, or at least not the way they once did.

And although they will always be a reminder of my sorrow, my wounds are no longer searing but a healing scar. Grief is still my shadow, but now my world has changed.

I have a new life.

In time, I found a new husband and child to ease the pain of those I lost.

There are other photographs I hold sacred, of my kid brother and me growing up, enjoying holidays and vacations together.

Kyle and I shared the same manic Kelly sense of humor, the same sometimes short-fused temper, the same taste in food and movies. We were born within eleven months of each other, so my father used to call us his Irish twins.

Kyle was the perfect baby—blond, porcelain-skinned, good-humored. When I was four, for a time we shared a room together. On stormy winter nights when he was scared to sleep alone or afraid of the dark, Kyle would climb into bed beside me to seek refuge.

"Ats, Amy. Ats." As an infant, Kyle couldn't pronounce "Thanks"; it always came out as "Ats."

I loved the soft feel of his puppy-fat cheeks, the angel kiss of his infant lips, and the scared-tight arms around my neck after he'd crawled in to snuggle next to me. For me, there is nothing quite so heart-stirringly touching as the hug of a child clinging to you out of fear, as if it connects us to a thread gloriously human and yet divine woven into our souls.

For a long time, Kyle was the quiet one in our family. He'd tag along behind me, holding on to my sweater, head down and shy, hardly saying a word. One Christmas at a family party when he was eight, he shocked us with an amazing crimson-faced rendition of my father's favorite song, "Danny Boy." Kyle's sweet singing voice as angelic as that of a soloist in the Vienna Boys Choir.

It wasn't like Kyle to thrust himself into the spotlight, but someone discovered the reason: he was sneaking sips from my mother's Irish whiskey and soda. For every childhood Christmas party afterward, carefully monitored to make sure he hadn't touched the seasonal booze, he'd bestow his version of "Danny Boy" and bring everyone close to tears.

As he grew older, it became Kyle's shower song. Whenever he stepped under the steaming jets and the sounds of "Danny Boy" rang through our house, we would all stop and listen, for deep in his honeyed voice was a touching echo, a sound that my father teasingly used to say, like the bagpipes, "never failed to light a blazing bonfire under our Celtic chromosomes."

Other images I keep are in photograph albums of the day I got married at age twenty-one at Cedar Springs Church in Knoxville, Tennessee.

Snapshots of my children as infants and during their growing spurts, at treasured milestones in their short lives—vacations, weekends at the lake or the beach, the day a tooth was lost or when they'd dressed for Halloween or celebrated a birthday.

First came Sean, barely ten months after Jack and I married. Shy little Sean, always eager to please even as an infant, who loved to be read stories and have his back rubbed.

Three years later, I was pregnant again with Amy. She raged into our lives like a whirlwind, a spark plug of a girl, the exact opposite of her shy brother. A giggling rebel imp who never stopped talking, brimful of life, endlessly on the move.

"Ain't that girl got no off switch?" Jack used to joke.

She seemed to have a powerful furnace burning inside her, until she collapsed into bed at night. Even then, she could never sleep in the dark. I guess my daughter always gave me trouble at bedtime. She insisted on a light blazing or would instantly wake, become anxious, and call down from her room if the landing light was ever turned off. As if, like a flower, she thrived on light and sunshine.

So each evening, to ease her fear, I left a lamp lit on the landing.

Amy would see its golden light beyond her door whenever she awoke. And then she would fall back to sleep.

With children in my life, my existence felt complete.

These were days I wanted to inhale like fragrant air, each memory precious. And so I kept a diary. I hoped one day to be a writer, and I read somewhere that keeping a journal was important for an author, like a singer practicing scales. So I wrote about every tiny or meaningful experience I shared with our children, until another wicked tempest raged into my life and claimed my family from me, and they disappeared. From that day on, I never thought I would write another word.

Yet these images in the silver frame—my deepest wounds—are also my salvation. For when I feel the cool smoothness of the glass that covers their beaming faces and glide my fingertips over their outlines, it reminds me of the radiant spirits that once illuminated my world.

The lips I can no longer kiss, voices I can no longer hear, faces I can no longer touch.

And they remind me of the cruelest lessons life has taught me.

Write this down if you want, and never let anyone tell you otherwise: Love has a price.

There never can be—never will be and never has been—a single love that comes without agony. When loved ones die or leave us of their own choosing—when we stay but love no longer or when we shatter a human heart by our treachery or by our leaving—we pay the cost sooner or later.

As every sin has its own avenging angel, every giving and letting go has its day of reckoning.

Another thing I've learned: Sometimes those we worship harbor unimaginable secrets.

All families have secrets. Some are innocent. Some seep like poison through the veins of successive generations. Dark secrets that can maim and destroy as cruelly as any weapon. For just as the sweetest sounds can induce the greatest sorrows, so, too, can the purest love contain the seeds of the most malignant hurts.

Like the Celtic legend of the bird that sings just once in its life but more sweetly than any other creature on this earth. From the moment it can fly, it searches for a rosebush, and when it finds one, it impales its breast on the sharpest barb. In its dying agony, it sings a supreme hymn, a song so exquisite that every living thing in its orbit stops to listen and marvel at the beauty.

And so do we, each of us in our own way, seek out our own thorns to impale our hearts on. Not for the pained joy of some glorious hymn but because we cannot help ourselves. It's as if our fortunes are written in our stars.

And so they are.

Have you ever stopped and realized that if you had not met a certain person, your whole life would be different? For this, too, I've learned, that whatever love we encounter in our lives isn't just a chance meeting in a chaotic world.

It's a fate.

A thread in the tapestry of our existence that is more mysterious than any of us can understand, one that echoes across the ages. To rephrase another writer's words, you will find in each of us all the sums we have not counted. For every moment in our lives is a window on all time, as if the kiss that began four thousand years ago in Crete ended yesterday in Texas.

I believe that.

And that each heart and mind seeking and finding another is never the consequence of some accidental journey but a destiny, waiting to teach us a life lesson or ambush us with some terrible truth that the universe insists we must learn.

I know that because I have learned from my own bitter truths.

And my first lesson began on the morning I got married, when my mother arrived drunk at Cedar Springs Church with a loaded gun in her purse and murder in her heart.

2

THUNDER MOUNTAIN, SMOKY MOUNTAINS,
EAST TENNESSEE

If there was a hell on earth, then this swampy forest came close.

Brewster Tanner felt an icy shiver snake down his spine. Tanner hated wooded swamps.

Tanner was fifty pounds overweight, with a noble profile that would not have looked out of place on an ancient Roman coin. If he was a singer, he would have been Barry White. People said he sounded like him, too, when Tanner used to do karaoke. A bass voice, deep as a dungeon, the kind that resonated with certain women.

Except he didn't look anything like Barry White. Tanner was a light-skinned African-American, soft-featured, handsome-pretty. Folks often said he reminded them of that old-time actor Sidney Poitier but just, well, a little heavier.

He stared through the windshield as he drove his white Camry through emerald-green forest, the radio on. It was not Barry singing but Beyoncé blaring about "all the single ladies." Tanner always got a laugh when he heard that song. Beyoncé in concert, pocketing millions and going home to her husband and kids, leaving all those dumb single hos singing that song, dancing around with their handbags.

In the sultry heat, tangled green branches overhung stagnant pools of water the color of coffee grounds. A nearby stream had flooded, saturating the ground, covering tree trunks with at least a foot of water. The air was rich with the smells of damp soil and green plants.

Reporters, cameramen, and TV crews mingled on either side of the track, the crowd three deep. Tanner saw a man running with a camera and a brace contraption on his shoulder, as if he'd just stolen it. Nearby, a pair of TV vans, local affiliates for CNN, ABC, and NBC, swung their satellite dishes to point into the hot noon sun, ready to relay their news stories to headquarters in Atlanta and New York.

Tanner flicked crumbs from his size-58 chest, the flaky remains of a diabetic-friendly hazelnut cookie he'd eaten on the long stretch of dirt track that twisted through the swamp.

Bony tendrils of dead creepers were woven through the trees like petrified snakes, some of the branches covered in wispy spider veils that resembled Spanish moss. Tanner took a deep breath, and the brown, musty smell of decaying rain forest flooded his nostrils. He felt another shiver, more violent.

Swamps gave him the creeps, even one as full of activity as this. They made him think of alligators and snakes, reptiles and spiders. Things that bit you, killed you, or chewed you alive. Did they have gators in East Tennessee? He didn't think so, even if this particular landscape more resembled his hometown in Louisiana.

Bears and snakes here for sure. And crazy folks, like the ones he'd passed along the track. Shabby single-wide hillbilly trailer homes or pitiful shacks, their lots adorned with the rusting carcasses of old cars and pontoon boats, flower beds sown around them as if in a graveyard, planted in fond memory of their once-beloved transport. Didn't these people ever get rid of an old car, other than leave it to rot on their property?

The Smoky Mountains looked beautiful, draped in a thin veil of morning fog. But this place—this ugly, swampy creek below the side of a mountain—reminded him of something out of that old madcap survival movie *Deliverance*.

Along the way, Tanner saw muddy four-wheelers and ancient-looking rocking chairs on nailed-together DIY porches made of boxwood. A few grubby kids played outside the shacks near wire-run chicken coops and goats. Older faces peered from behind sun-bleached shutters, weathered with missing teeth, their owners with tattoos adorning arms, hands, or necks.

In one window, a sign said "Banjo Lessons."

Who in their right mind would want to come out here for banjo lessons, unless they were drugged or psychotic?

He eased his Camry past a TV crew. Yellow police tape blocked his path. Tanner flashed his ID at a pair of sheriff's uniforms, and one of them raised the yellow tape, indicating that he could park fifty yards along the dirt road, near a clearing. He coasted the Camry onto the grassy spot and hit the hand brake.

As he flicked off Beyoncé and stepped out of the Camry into a solid wave of heat, the sounds of the swamp exploded. An orchestra of crickets, frogs, and birds, all accompanied by the clatter of a pair of police helicopters up high.

His bulk had made it a struggle as he climbed out, the car floor and side pockets awash with crushed candy bar and gum wrappers. Sweat beading his brow—it was unseasonably hot for mid-March, not unusual in the South—Tanner stood there, taking the shallow breaths of a mild asthmatic, holding on to the Camry's door for support.

Up ahead, he saw something weird. A mangled mess. What it was he couldn't rightly tell. But it was some kind of structure, beaten to a pulp.

"What in the heck have we got here?"

Tanner shut the Camry's door and strolled forward. He halted after twenty yards. The mess appeared to be the remains of a cabin lot backing onto the forest.

What he saw shocked him. The cabin had all but disintegrated.

What remained was the wooden base and a jagged portion of one wall, as if some monster had taken a bite out of it. Bits of debris and siding were spread about the site. The relics of a refrigerator were flung to one side, parts of it crushed and shattered in the trees, with wood siding, part of a window frame, and a chunk of an aircraft wing entangled in the upper branches.

Farther on, through the forest, he saw the scattered remains of a small aircraft that looked as if it had shattered into a thousand pieces. Little yellow card markers with numbers on them were planted next to debris, and people in white hazard suits were sifting through the wreckage. He spotted a bunch of Park Services guys in uniforms. Tanner had to look twice to be certain; it appeared as if the property on the lot had been smashed into the woods by the force of the crash.

"Hey, Tanner!"

A bunch of men carrying clipboards huddled nearby, "NTSB" in gold lettering on the backs of their blue nylon vests—National Transportation Safety Board. Next to them was a muddied green Polaris Ranger buggy.

A little ruddy-faced man with wiry gray hair and glasses waved to Tanner and broke away from the others. Dale Dexter looked like a garden gnome, his oversized head way too large for his slender body.

"Hey, big fella. You made it."

"Dexter, how are they hanging, baby?" Tanner looked over at the crash site and made a face. "Looks bad. Dead?"

"At least three. The pilot and a female passenger and some poor unfortunate guy I reckon may have been out front of the cabin when the downed plane hit the porch."

"How's that?"

"We're scraping what's left of him off the Cessna's nose cowl."

Tanner made another face. "Ouch! Not a nice way to go."

"A word of warning. Watch out for snakes."

"You trying to ruin my day?"

"Cottonmouths are the most dangerous. You don't get an antidote in thirty minutes, you're going home nailed in a box."

"You're a good man, Dexter. Full of useful survival tips. Please tell me you're going to suck the poison out of my butt if I get bitten."

"I don't think we're that close, Tanner."

"Charming."

"Ask your buddy, Agent Breedon, though."

"He's here?"

"Arrived fifteen minutes ago. Big boy, muscular, chews gum. Doesn't say much, does he?"

"Naw, he's a mute."

"What?"

"Seems that way. Breedon's a man of few words. Scares the life out of me sometimes. You look over your shoulder, and there he is. Or else he creeps up on you, saying nothing. I try to let him work away on his own and out of my way."

Dexter climbed into the buggy. "Get in."

"Where we going?" Tanner squeezed his bulk into the passenger seat, and the buggy tilted to one side. The engine growled as Dexter hit the start button, turning the wheels away from the crash site.

"We've opened a second investigation a half mile away, where part of the aircraft landed. That's where the real action is. That's where we found something buried deep, right there in the woods."

"Don't tell me, Jimmy Hoffa, right?"

"Funny. But you ain't ever seen nothing like this, big fella."

3

KNOXVILLE, TENNESSEE

Some people remember their dead with mausoleums, stone-carved angels, elaborate tombs, or brass plaques.

I had no need of such things.

The gravesite I chose was on a rise, a simple granite stone shaded by a clump of cedar trees. I parked outside the cemetery and walked up the narrow path in the cold sunshine, carrying a bunch of yellow winter roses and tugging up my coat collar against the cold air.

It was one of those weird schizophrenic weather weeks in Tennessee that could catch you off guard. Twenty-four hours ago, it was in the mid-seventies. Today it was still sunny but a good thirty degrees less, chilly and cold. Some days in February and March it might snow, but within twenty-four hours a heat wave would split the stones. Like I said, weird.

The local cemetery dated back to 1796, but most of the graves were much more recent. Some of the city's first settlers were buried here. A few were victims of the early Indian wars, and a few others were well-known dignitaries or from notable families. But the rest, like all of us, were the mediocre dead, as my father liked to say.

I moved past tombs of worn granite and marble, past the uprooted earth of freshly dug graves and a group of mourners hunched in their own private grief.

An elderly man was sweeping away some leaves on the path, and he touched his baseball cap. "'Morning, Kath."

"Good morning, George." I didn't engage the cemetery caretaker in our usual conversation about the weather. I really didn't feel much like talking today, an anniversary on which I sometimes preferred to be alone.

On this of all days, I wanted to stand upon the earth that covered my husband, son, and daughter. To touch the stone that bore their names and to remember the sacredness of our lives together. That stone was pretty much all I had to remember the life we had shared and lost, eight years ago.

I came to the top and the two graves. My mother was the one on the left. The other was for Jack and our children. The bodies of my husband and children had never been found, but we all need to remember our dead with plaques or gravestones, so I chose to place a gravestone here.

There was a small bench off to the left, but before I sat, I laid the roses on the graves, split them equally, the yellow a flash of vivid color against the black granite slabs. I said the prayers and the words I wanted to say, the same words I always said—that I missed them so much, that I longed to have them back, that their passing had left such a terrible ache, an unending sorrow.

That nothing could replace them, *nothing,* not ever. Standing there, under the warm sun, my eyes swept over the smooth, dark granite, and I stared at the simple chiseled words that inscribed my pain:

Here lies Jack Hayes, beloved husband of Kath.
And their son, Sean, and daughter, Amy.
Until we're together again, you will forever be missed.

I still missed them. Sometimes I missed them so much I felt physically ill, my grief so huge it was hard for me to breathe. Of course, I had dreams and memories and photographs. But my dreams were sometimes disturbed, and photographs were always so inadequate, never capturing the real truth—the soul behind the image, the beauty behind the smile, the happiness behind the laughter.

They had never captured the real Jack I had known since we first met at Fort Campbell Army Base. I was an eighteen-year-old high school senior, and he was a twenty-three-year-old Army chopper pilot—warmhearted, tough, fun. A caring husband and father and the love of my life.

You couldn't see the real Sean behind the photograph, taken on his third birthday while on vacation in Myrtle Beach. You could see that he was a beautiful blond-haired little boy with a lopsided smile. He loved to run to my arms, be held and tickled. He was never the sort of child to get angry or throw a fit because he wanted more chocolate-chip ice cream.

And the other photographs—the ones of Amy, my sweet little girl, so brimming with energy, a passion for life so powerful that it used to take my breath away.

It was the manner of their passing that had troubled me most. A business trip eight years ago on a private company jet en route from New Orleans to Savannah that crashed in stormy weather. Jack was never even meant to take the children. It was a last-minute decision because of Amy's birthday. Busy with work, I couldn't free myself, but Amy and Sean were so looking forward to seeing Savannah, the ghost capital of the U.S.A., so looking forward to visiting a haunted house that Jack had organized a chauffeur to take them on a private ghost tour. Never did I think that they would become what they most dreaded— specters of the living, souls of the dead. That irony brought me to tears.

I always imagined that death in a plane crash would come instantly if the aircraft exploded in midair. But I could never cease contemplating the stark terror they would have felt if the aircraft was still intact as it sank through bubbling storm clouds, buffeted by extreme turbulence—their panic a living thing, death looking them in the face as they plunged toward the ground.

I shuddered every time I visualized that image. Sometimes I cried with despair—my beautiful daughter and son and husband having to endure the crushing, chaotic fear as their aircraft plummeted to earth. It broke my heart, shredded my soul to pieces.

And after their deaths, the hardness of my own heart truly frightened me. I no longer cared about the suffering of others. Music that had once stirred my heart no longer moved me. I became numb, unaffected. The loss of a child at any stage of life is so unnatural, so wrong, that purpose seems difficult to reclaim. But the loss of two children and my husband was a devastation I never believed I would recover from. I kept expecting to wake up and discover it was all some cruel joke and that everything was OK. But it wasn't.

You learn a lot when you lose someone you love. You learn even more when you lose your entire family. I learned that to come through the trials my husband had come through in Iraq, to get past losing friends and comrades in battle, he must have had incredible strength and fortitude.

And I had neither.

I crumbled.

Haunted by absence, I used to visit the cemetery at all hours of the day and night, lying down on the ground beside the graves. I would stretch myself out on the cold earth and feel it seep into my bones as it must have seeped into theirs, wherever they lay. For such a long time, my heart felt as brittle as charcoal, my soul as gouged as the earth covering the fresh graves of this burial ground.

Twice I actually thought I saw Jack in the woods behind our house, where he used to stroll and play with our children. I ran out, calling his name, following the mystery figure deep into the woods, but there was no one there.

People who knew me then must have thought I was crazy. And for a time I was. My doctor recommended antianxiety medication. I rejected the prescription. I wanted to feel the pain. It was all I had, all that allowed me to recall the happiness of my past life.

And now, though my dreams still reclaimed me briefly, especially on anniversaries, they came less often. *I miss you, Jack. I miss you, Amy and Sean.*

I would always miss them.

Standing there, lost in the limbo between the present and the past, I heard a noise behind me and turned. I never imagined who would be standing there, not for a second, and it sent a shock through me like a bolt of lightning . . .

4

THE PAST

Every cause has an effect; there's always a backstory. I learned that cliché my first year in college, when I took a course in fiction writing. And it's true, because when I look back on what happened at my wedding, I can see with hindsight all the signs that triggered my mother's fury, as clearly as if they were ablaze in neon.

She was in a bitter mood all week—I remember that—and stoked the fires of her resentment by sipping vodka from a hip flask during the wedding ceremony. To make matters worse, when we adjourned to the hotel reception, my mother made a drunken pass at the handsome pastor who had conducted our service. Unfazed by his mortified rejection, she hit on the band's cute young guitarist, grabbing his arm and urging him to dance.

"Come on, pretty boy. Let's see those feet burn the floor. I want to see *flames*, honey."

The horrified youth brushed her away as if she were a vampire trying to locate a neck vein. "Get the heck off me, you crazy old woman."

I don't know what may have hurt my mom more, "crazy" or "old." She sure wasn't old at fifty-four, although her love of alcohol had added a decade to her face. But I realize now that my mother was desperate for some kind of diversion that day, needed distraction from the drunken rage that consumed her and maybe her awareness of the cruel sin she was about to commit.

I remember my bridesmaid Courtney, my best friend, squeezing my arm when she witnessed my horrified reaction to my mother's flirting with the pastor and guitarist. Courtney was a man's woman, down-to-earth, vivacious, big into nails and hair. We called her Crazy C, because Courtney had a wild side, was forever up to mischief, partying, getting into trouble. But she always tried to ease my embarrassment by making light of my mother's drunken recklessness. "Hey, sweetie, look on the bright side. No matter what, you never can fault Martha Beth's excellent taste in good-looking guys."

Courtney, who fell in love with my brother, Kyle, and desperately wanted to marry him; the same Courtney I was to catch in flagrante delicto, locked in a passionate embrace with my father, their clothes half off on a warm summer night, as fireflies danced and sparked along the lakeshore where I found them, kissing like love-hungry teenagers. It was the only time I ever felt disappointed by my father.

But that was another story, way down the tracks, a bizarre strand in the tapestry of our family's unending theater.

Courtney and I had been friends since preschool. She was another base brat. Her father was an officer serving with CID, the United States Army Criminal Investigation Division, and he investigated crimes committed within the military's branches. It was a career Courtney would follow when she became a CID officer herself, even though I'd never thought I'd see her don a military uniform in a zillion years. I guess DNA's thread is stronger than we think.

Back in our base brat schooldays, even the razor-wire confines of a military compound could not contain our free spirits. My father liked to joke that if we were ever imprisoned, we'd be leading the escape committee.

High school was where it all happened for Courtney and me. She liked to party, thought nothing of stealing her parents' car and taking us dancing or to drink beer by the lake. With Courtney, I felt the thrill of being a gangster's moll. Once, when my folks went away to a weekend party, we held a party of our own in my parents' house, and it exemplified Courtney's chutzpah.

She organized more than forty friends, everything right down to the jars of plump maraschino cherries and the little colorful umbrellas for the weird cocktails she liked to make. And added to the mix was carefully chosen slow music for when Courtney turned the lights down.

Every boy I knew lusted after Courtney, but she only had the hots for my brother, Kyle, and he felt the same way about her. Sometimes I'd hear them singing together on the back porch, Kyle strumming a guitar my dad gave him one Christmas, and he and Courtney would usually attempt a duet, some country-and-western hit or an old Joni Mitchell or Bruce Springsteen song. If they couldn't reach the high notes, they'd always end up laughing their way through the song.

They laughed a lot in each other's company. They seemed good for each other. And Kyle may have been shy, but when Courtney was around, he became a prankster.

Once, when a carnival came to town, complete with a giant Ferris wheel and bumper cars, Kyle and Courtney drove to a hardware store and bought a six-inch threaded screw bolt. The Casey brothers ran the carnival—twitchy, hairy-backed men in grubby vests who carried oily tan leather tool bags on their hips. They chain-smoked like expectant fathers as they prowled around their ancient, creaking rides with watchful eyes, as if half expecting an imminent disaster to match the *Hindenburg*.

When Kyle and Courtney stepped off the Ferris wheel after a couple of rides, Kyle held up the screw bolt: "Excuse me, sir, but I found this."

The older Casey studied the bolt with the kind of bug-eyed horror reserved for a soldier who has just mistakenly pulled a grenade pin. Then he stared up at the Ferris wheel and screamed, "Stop the ride! Stop the darn thing now! Everyone off! Get 'em off, ya hear me? *Off*, for the love of God!"

Kyle and Courtney scuttled away to watch from behind a wall, bent double in laughter as the Casey brothers scrambled all over the big wheel, checking every nut and bolt.

Most girls wouldn't be overly fond of their brothers making out with their best friends. It didn't bother me. Courtney was loyal, never really drank too much, never smoked weed, and didn't put herself around— although she probably did pretty much everything else.

On the back porch on the day of our planned party, Courtney puffed on one of her daddy's best Panama cigars, coughed, and blew out smoke, offering me her best advice. "When I stick on a slow one, just remember to ignore that dumb warning the base chaplain gave us, OK?"

"Which warning was that?"

Courtney mimicked the pastor's Southern twang. "'Just you young ladies be cautious, y'all hear? When you're dancing slow with a boy, always remember to leave enough room between the two of you for Jesus.'" She giggled. "As far as I'm concerned, Jesus can sit this one out."

In case my parents came home early—a possibility if my mother wasn't being served hard liquor—we posted lookouts at the windows. A little before midnight, just when things were in full swing and Courtney had mixed another bowl of punch—one of her weirdly blended cocktails, complete with cherries skewered by tiny fancy umbrellas— someone saw the flash of headlights come up the drive and shouted, "Hey, it's them!"

Courtney and I screamed, "Red alert! Hide!" at the tops of our lungs, and the music died as herds of suddenly stone-cold-sober teens trampled all over one another in their rush to hide, as if a pack of marauding zombies were about to invade the house.

When my parents strode in, they were accompanied by my mother's boozing buddies: Courtney's parents, Captain and Mrs. Vicky Adams. It seemed the party hadn't been up to scratch, and my tipsy mother had decided they should all beat it back to our place for some "proper" drinks.

They lingered a little while in my father's study, with its Irish and American flags crossed like swords on one wall. My parents showed the Adamses photographs of their anniversary trip to Ireland—kissing the Blarney Stone, posing on the Cliffs of Moher and castle ramparts high above emerald-green fields, raising whiskies in an Irish bar, my mom with a grin on her the width of her face and a pint of Guinness in one hand and astride a donkey. And my mother's favorite memento of her Ireland visit: a six-inch bronze cast of a legendary Celtic bird sitting on the branch of a thorn tree.

But it turned out my mother also wanted to show Mrs. Adams our remodeled bathrooms. "Wait until you see the new baths and showers, Vicky!"

When my mother stepped into the main bathroom, a cigarette dangling between her lips with a long ash at its end, and pulled back the shower curtain, she found Courtney standing there with Kyle, both clutching huge mud-colored cocktails.

For a second or two came a stunned silence. My mother broke it, the instant her cigarette ash fell off. "What in the name of—"

"Hey, Mom. Welcome to the party." Kyle giggled, his face flushed crimson red as usual whenever he really got embarrassed. The cocktail probably didn't help, either, but soon Kyle's expression changed, and he looked as if his privates had just been caught in a mangle or he'd been found naked with an au pair.

Mrs. Adams wisely two-stepped it backward out the bathroom door. She was more than happy to let my mom deal with it.

"Mom!" Courtney called pleadingly after her mother, but Mrs. Adams departed with a tipsy, carefree wave to her daughter. "Your problem, honey."

Courtney tried a brazen smile on my mom. "Hey, Mrs. K. You're looking terrific. Did you have a good night?" She offered my mother a boozy, wide-eyed, blue-mascara stare.

"Kyle, get out and wait outside."

"Mom . . ."

"Do it!"

Kyle slinked out. You didn't argue with my mom when she was in her cups, unless you totally had a death wish. My mother snatched the glass from Courtney's hand, sipped the contents, and made a face. "What kind of crap is in here?"

"Soda."

"And *what*?"

"Whiskey."

"And?"

"Vodka. A little crème de menthe."

"With a *cherry*?"

"I figured I needed the vitamin C."

"It looks like something they'd mix in an asylum." My mother turned and raged at me, giving her best Bette Davis impression. "Get Courtney out of here and any other sissy little losers you've got stashed in the house, or I'm going to find your father's gun and start shooting."

Every high school kid I knew thought my mother was crazy, and they didn't need to hear gunfire for proof. Which is why dozens of kids came scrambling out of their hiding places and raced out the front and back doors, like rats deserting a sinking ship.

My mother drained the glass and tossed it into the washbasin, where it shattered to pieces. "And y'all don't come back in this house until you learn how to mix a proper cocktail, ya hear?"

5

My father's blue Ford Taurus pulled up near the cemetery gates. I saw him climb out with a little difficulty, a difficulty he'd never admit to, his prosthetic foot dragging as he moved past the caretaker. For a man who had faced death all his life, my father had a deep dislike of graveyards. I put it down to the fact that he'd probably seen enough death in his career. He rarely, if ever, came here.

"'Morning, Colonel."

"'Morning, George." My father gave the caretaker a mock salute. People still addressed my father by his military title, although he'd been retired now for years.

As he came toward me, I saw a brown-wrapped parcel under his right arm. It looked heavy.

Despite his false limb, Dad walked erect. Or at least he tried to. Two years ago, he was diagnosed with the onset of Parkinson's disease. It hadn't progressed yet to a point where it was a serious problem, but he still suffered with the symptoms on occasion—tremor of the hands, jaw, and face, slowness and stiffness of movement that sometimes seemed to affect his balance. And now and then his memory got sluggish. Medication helped, and being a soldier, having all that Celtic blood in his veins, he fought it, as he had fought everything in his life.

He wore immaculately creased slacks, leather loafers, and a brown leather flying jacket. What made him stand out even more was his signature hat, one of those goofy lumberjack ones with ear flaps, tied together with string and with plaid flannel lining. I used to joke that he looked like Goofy in that hat. "Yeah, maybe, but at least my ears are warm."

At sixty-seven, he was grayer and more bushy-browed with each year, but he was still a powerhouse of a man, imposing the moment you laid eyes on him. He had that familiar craggy Celtic face, skewed but handsome. The same kind of look that had freaked my mother out when she first visited Ireland, because, she said, whenever she looked over her shoulder, she kept seeing "that darned actor Spencer Tracy."

Dad joined me. He took my hand in his big palm, and squeezed. "Those flowers look good. Thought I'd call by before I hit the road. Say a prayer. Kind of chilly out."

Yellow roses were my mom's favorite. My father wore a beige scarf around his neck, his breath fogging in the cold air. He tugged down at his hat flaps, rubbed his hands, and blew air into his fists. "Even colder up north. Snow in parts."

"You'd better take care on the roads."

"You know me. Like the best of criminals who evade the law, I never do more than sixty." He winked.

I managed a smile. "So it should take you about three days to reach Michigan."

"Day and a half, tops, with the wind to my back. Should be there by tomorrow noon."

For a man who'd jumped out of airplanes in his military career, my father had a strange aversion to flying, and he drove everywhere. His hatred of flying became even more pathological after Jack and my children disappeared. His excuse: "Driving gives me time to think."

About what, I wondered? He was retired. Aside from tinkering in his workshop in the back of the barn, hiking, devouring books, some occasional travel, and his lady friend Ruby, what did he need to think about?

He was always close to Amy and Sean, to Sean in particular. I recall not long after he retired, my dad was lying on the couch in his study, reading yet another book while recovering from a bout of prostatitis, a blanket over his groin. Sean was snuggled up to him.

"Why do you read so much, Grandpa?"

"Because reading is good for your brain, son. Keeps you alert."

"Any other reason?"

"Yeah." I remember Dad picked up a golf ball from a mug on his study desk. "See this golf ball, son?"

"Yes, sir."

"Well, as a man gets older, his prostate enlarges, to about the size of a golf ball. At the same time as his prostate enlarges with age, his brain shrinks. When the two are about equal in size, that's when a man starts to take an interest in historical novels. You'll get that one when you're older, son."

Sean had a bemused look, but Jack cracked up.

Now my father's face became more serious as he rubbed my arm. "You doing OK, honey?"

I wasn't—visiting the graves always troubled me—but I nodded. "You called Ruby? How is she?"

"They'll operate tomorrow. Depending on how it goes, they'll start chemo. But she's a tough lady. She'll hang in there. And come out the other side fighting, you wait and see."

"It'll help, you being there."

It seemed a total irony. A year ago my father went online to a seniors dating site and met a woman from Michigan, the first real relationship he'd had since my mother's death. There had been occasional dates he picked up at the bridge club. The ones he discovered to be serious drinkers he ditched. The wacky ones lasted a little longer, but Dad didn't tolerate troubled women for long. I guess he'd had enough of it in his marriage.

But Ruby Alice was just what he needed—sweet, sane, vivacious, a widow with a grown family. Ruby was good for him. Her husband was ex-military. They shared interests—hiking, movies, books, travel. Best of all, she had a sense of humor and was able to handle my father's occasional Irish moodiness.

Then, four weeks ago, just when they were talking marriage and she was getting ready to move down south to join my father, Ruby got the crushing news that she had ovarian cancer. I saw the weariness and anguish in my father's face. As if he'd run a long race and the course wasn't getting any easier—first his wife, now a prospective wife. But once a fighter, always a fighter. Colonel Frank Kelly wasn't the kind to ever give up.

I loved him for that. He'd always been a good father, loving, sup-
portive, tough but kind, a no-nonsense man but with a soft heart. In
Iraq, he always insisted that his unit carry gum, candy, coloring books,
and pencils to hand out to Iraqi kids, not only to win hearts and minds
but because he felt for those kids, trapped in a war zone and a battle
not of their making.

"How's the writing going?" Dad asked, changing the subject.

Dad knew my writing habits. He knew I was struggling right now.
He ought to know. My home was my father's ten-acre farm on Lake
Loudon. There were lots of reasons I'd moved back into the family
residence, not just because of his Parkinson's, but we'll get to those.
"You've heard of writer's block?"

"Sure. Like hitting a wall, huh?"

"Well, I think I haven't just hit a wall, more like a mountain."

I'd gone and done the unthinkable, given up teaching at Bearden
High School, where I'd taught full-time for almost six years. I had
enough money saved and figured I'd take a year off to try to write a
novel. I needed to get writing again. Not just because it was bugging
me to finally attempt to write a book but because I hoped—prayed—
that writing would in some way help me to come to terms with my
ghosts. They say writing is like taking off all your clothes in public,
and by so doing you in some way purge yourself. I hoped so. My soul
needed it.

My father half smiled. "The block, it'll pass."

"I hope. What's in the package?"

He took the heavy parcel from under his arm, weighed it in both
hands. "Something I made."

He unwrapped the crinkly brown paper. It was a heart-shaped gray
marble stone, about a foot long and an inch thick. Inscribed in the center were some words that look like Latin: *Dilexisset, numquam oblivi-
one delebitur.* Whatever that meant. But I could see he'd put a lot of
work into it—cutting, shaping, chiseling, polishing.

"That explains all the screeching and squealing noises I heard from
your workshop."

"Yeah?"

"I thought you were torturing a cat."

"My stone grinder. Sounded like it, huh?"

"Close."

He held up the marble heart. "The Latin inscription means 'Always loved, never forgotten.' Archaeologists sometimes found that inscribed on the tombs of respected ancient Roman nobles. If it was good enough for ancient nobles, I reckon it's good enough for us Kellys. I've been meaning to do it since I mastered that chisel and grinder."

I felt touched. "Thanks."

"You bet." Taking his hat off, he went to lay the inscribed piece on the white marble chips between the two graves.

As he leaned over, holding on to my mom's gravestone for balance, with a tremor in his hands and jaw, I saw the crown of his head, his gray hair thinning on top. I noticed the raised veins on his outstretched hands as they placed the marble, the skin on the backs of his hands starting to take on that crepe-paper look. The strong-man father I adored was getting older. That day in Florida when he faced off against those two macho idiots seemed a lifetime away. Yet I knew he'd still protect me with his life if he needed to. He was still my shining knight.

My father was no pushover. He kept a loaded .45 in his nightstand and an array of weapons around the house. "Be prepared, honey. That's one thing the Army always taught me." He kind of reminded me of Clint Eastwood in *Gran Torino,* the same lean but tough look. You don't mess with Grandpa, even if he had Parkinson's.

It's hard watching a parent grow old. You see your own mortality in theirs. An entire life and your shared past receding, the brightest days gone, certain death and your own future looking you in the face. Dad was still fit and able, but you could see the cracks beginning, hear the wheels starting to creak.

He laid his handiwork down between the two graves, lovingly touched the marble of both gravestones, and then said a prayer and stood, tugged on his hat again, and tightened the string of his hat flaps. "Guess I'd better go if I'm to make good time."

"Call me on the way."

Dad never liked lingering long here, even when it was just my mom's grave. And we never talked about our loss. But we both know how deep the void is and how cruel. That was another thing about my dad, maybe a Celtic flaw—he tried never to show pain if he could help it.

"You bet."

But then I saw his shoulders hunch and shake, and I heard it, a whimper that sounded like an agonized cry. He suppressed his pain. His eyes teared. He wiped them. I hugged him, kissed his cheek hard. I loved the smell of my father. Soap and workshop oil, all maleness.

Dad kissed me so hard on the cheek it hurt, and his big arms went around me, smothering me in a bear hug. When he let me go, he looked over at the graves.

"I loved her so much, Kath. Loved her like crazy. I've never stopped. Loved them all. Jack, Amy, Sean." There were tears on his cheeks.

I met his stare. There were tears on mine, too. "We both did."

I sat there alone after Dad left.

It must have been half an hour, maybe less, of getting lost in memories, the kind that only those who remember their dead can understand. I remembered Amy's birth, how she came eleven weeks early, and in the hour after she was delivered, when things were touch and go, Jack was pacing the hospital room like a madman. Chewing gum, reeking of the cigarettes he smoked outside the hospital lobby, and worrying that Amy was not going to make it.

Until I begged him to stop pacing, my own nerves frayed, and he stopped, sat beside my bed, held my hand tightly with tears in his eyes, and told me that somehow everything would be OK. His reassuring smile and the grip of his hand told me that he really loved me.

I recalled Sean's first day at school and my son turning to wave at me one last time before he entered the classroom, beaming uncertainly as he said good-bye.

I mentally pushed Sean's and Jack's smiles away. They were too painful. Too deep. I was ready to leave. I touched the gravestones one last time, felt their glacial coldness seep into my fingers.

That's when I heard the whisper of a car engine somewhere behind me.

I turned and saw a gleaming silver chauffeured Bentley glide up to the cemetery entrance.

I recognized the man who climbed out, talking on his cell phone. Handsome, wearing a long black tailored overcoat, his dress shoes polished like porcelain.

My pulse went wild.

Because the moment I saw the man's face turn toward me, I knew there was trouble.

6

You never really fall out of love with a face you fell in love with.

It can still lure you, twenty-odd years on. And sometimes I still felt the lure of Chad Benton. You could smell power and money on him. Old money. The kind that never goes out of fashion and never gets squandered, because there's so much of it.

Chad was West Point and Vanderbilt. His grandfather had been a Supreme Court justice. His father was once a senator for North Carolina, before his passing from a heart attack at fifty-eight. The newspapers said he'd died in the ER while on a business trip to Miami. The rumors said he'd suffered a cardiac arrest in a brothel with an eighteen-year-old Brazilian girl for company.

They said Chad's family had serious presidential ambitions for their golden boy. I knew that wasn't just a rumor. Chad ventured into politics five years ago and languished a little, not making much headway in the polls. But it was still early days, and he was still young at forty-two. And most of all, his family had connections, and the vitally important requisite for any electoral ambition: a truckload of money.

I once heard the rumor that his family were gangsters, classy gangsters, and that the old riches weren't all that old and mostly earned illegally.

I also knew that Chad's maternal great-grandfather made a fortune during Prohibition, running whiskey and rum from the Caribbean. "Thugs with money," I overheard someone once call the family at a party. Which was kind of ironic, because the first time I ever saw Chad, I thought he looked like Gatsby in the old movie when Gatsby was played by Robert Redford. Chad was that kind of handsome.

Chiseled jawline, a perfectly shaped nose, thick fair hair graying attractively at the sides. He could have been an actor if his life had not been mapped out by his old man. Kind of a bad boy with a good streak, the kind some women can't resist.

And when I was sixteen, he was the first guy I ever had a serious crush on, when I saw him on parade in his lieutenant's uniform at Fort Campbell. Even then, I knew he was out of my league.

Now he slipped his cell into the pocket of his overcoat. With a wave of his leather-gloved hand, he strode toward me.

Chad didn't seem his usual confident self. Maybe that was what alerted me to trouble.

Overconfidence and arrogance were qualities in men that never usually attracted me. But Chad's self-assurance, his powerful family connections, his striking looks, and his strong sense of personal destiny always made him an exception to any rule. Not that he was arrogant—well, maybe he could be—but the general aura he gave off was that he was a man of importance, in control, the kind who always earned your attention.

Even today, as he walked up the rise to join me, and as distracted as I was by my family's graves, Chad wrenched my focus from the past.

President of Brown Bear International, Chad ran a lucrative empire that specialized in corporate security and risk-management consulting. He provided military and law-enforcement training to governments worldwide, and his company logo was an enormous grizzly bear, rearing up on its hind legs, wielding its claws. The company's slogan—"A Trusted Ally. Ultimate Training. Elite Protection"—was always right below the grizzly.

Chad's company operated in places like Iraq, Afghanistan, Yemen, and a dozen other hot spots around the world. He had served for twelve years in the military before resigning his commission and taking over running the firm his father had started.

Chad and Jack were comrades in the 101st, and after Jack left the military, he went to work for Brown Bear as a security adviser. So did my dad for a couple of years. Jack was working for them at the time of his death. He was good at his job and traveled the world, usually on short assignments.

Brown Bear was a good employer. It had a reputation for looking after its personnel and for generous pay scales. Health plans, pension plans, payouts to family in the event of an operator's death on active duty were far from tight-fisted. For a year after Jack's disappearance, Chad made sure to check up on me, phoning or visiting, to make certain I was OK. He had his secretary do it sometimes, but more often than not, he called me himself.

His daughter, Julie Ann, was the same age as Amy. They often played together, and they liked each other. Julie Ann reminded me so much of Amy. After the plane went down, she brought me comfort.

Exactly when my relationship with Chad morphed from him comforting a widow to a physical thing I still don't exactly recall, but it kind of sneaked up on me. About a year after Jack and my children disappeared and the aircraft had not been found and it was obvious my family was not coming back, Chad started to get more serious. I figured later that he was being proper about it, giving me time to grieve. Besides, he had just come through a divorce.

Then, two years after Jack's death, Chad asked me to marry him. I took a long time to think about it—a month—and finally said yes. We were married in a small, quiet ceremony in Key West. My dad seemed happy for me, but I knew by his reluctance to talk about my marriage that he was uncertain about whether I was doing the right thing.

For two years it was intoxicating. A lot of good memories, fun times, trips abroad, and building a relationship with Julie Ann. And then—well, then it just seemed to fizzle out. Or at least it did so on Chad's part. Too many overseas trips and business meetings. He seemed to have little time for me or even for Julie Ann.

One weekend I got a call from Courtney. "I'm e-mailing you a pic. You're not going to like this."

"Of what?"

"Just take a look."

I opened her e-mail. It was a snapshot from the *New York Daily News*, taken at a gala political fund-raiser. A pic of Chad and a mid-twenties glamour model with her arms wrapped around his neck. I called Chad.

"It's nothing, Kath. The woman was just a guest. It was a fund-raiser."

"What else did she raise?"

"Not funny."

"I need more commitment, Chad. We hardly see each other."

That's when I heard the silence, and I knew we were doomed. "Kath, I just can't seriously commit more time to us right now. I've too much business to take care of."

I knew by his tone that the dance was over. In Courtney's words, when a man says he can't commit, there's just one word you need to answer him with. *Good-bye.* We split, amicably enough, in the end. Once we did, I decided to revert my name to Hayes.

All in the past, as they say, even if the past keeps knocking on your door now and then.

But in fairness, Chad had helped ease my pain. He was just what I needed at the time. He had been a rock, caring and patient, and helped bring me out into the world again. And being around his daughter, Julie Ann, had made me feel what it was like to be a mother again, and I had cherished that feeling. I didn't have any real bitterness at our parting, just sadness. No, actually, that's a lie. I did feel bitterness. I was angry that Chad cheated on me, although he always swore he hadn't. But all men will swear that. In the end, we remained civil to each other. No point in hurling bombs in a war that's over.

He walked up the rise to join me. "Kath. Good to see you. It's been a while."

Chad had put on a little weight in the few months since I'd last seen him, his shirt collar was a little strained, and there was a touch more gray hair at the sides. Rarely did he look uncomfortable—Chad was a calm, composed guy—but today he appeared uneasy, rubbing one gloved hand with the other. There was no kiss on the cheek—that would have been too much, too intimate, in a relationship that was dead—but he touched my arm.

"How are you? I tried to get you on your cell."

"I left it off." I usually did when I came to the cemetery, not wanting the jingle to intrude. "What brings you here?"

Chad gave a fleeting, unhappy smile. "I . . . I need to talk about something important."

His hesitancy set off alarm bells in my head. Chad's voice was deep, Southern, alluring, but with a hint of New York, where he'd spent some time running his father's various other business enterprises. To be honest, Chad sounded like one of those news anchors, the bass-voiced, tight-lipped macho brigade I always suspected had a third testicle. With that kind of throaty, masculine tone that had an instant effect on women.

Before he could say another word, my eyes drifted over his shoulder. I saw the Bentley's rear door open. A striking dark-haired woman was seated inside the limo. She looked Middle Eastern. I glimpsed a tanned leg, a spray of well-cut hair, and then the rest of her. Perfect figure, pretty face, about thirty. It made sense. Chad was a single guy again.

Then a thirteen-year-old girl with almond-brown hair climbed out of the back of the Bentley and ran toward me. She was all smiles, a beatific face, like a Botticelli angel, gushing with excitement and energy.

Julie Ann was Chad's daughter from his first marriage. For a rich kid, she was the sweetest thing you could imagine. Kind, well mannered, fun, energetic. She so reminded me of Amy. But it wasn't all sweetness and light. Adolescence is a battlefield, no matter what part of town you live in. Wealth might cushion the blows, but it doesn't let you avoid them. Once in a while, Julie Ann threw blazing tantrums that were like an array of rockets going off, but usually they were over quickly. Chad said she got her fiery temper from her mother, who had died in a Jet Ski accident in Key West.

"Kath!" Julie Ann threw her arms around me.

She hugged me hard. I kissed her. "How are you doing, sweetheart?"

"Good, and school's OK. What will we do for our next weekend?"

She was smart and pretty. I could see her being a boy magnet very soon. "We'll figure it out."

"Manicure and pedicure, movie and dinner?"

"Sounds good."

"And a little gossip?"

"Why not?" I smiled back. Julie Ann delighted in gossip the way an adult Southern woman did. After our divorce, Chad still obviously had prime sole custody of his daughter, but I had her overnight two weekends a month. A prenup drawn up by his family's lawyer meant that I agreed to only a modest settlement, but that didn't bother me. I was never into Chad for his money. It made life interesting for a few years, that's for sure, but the truth was, he reminded me of Jack in many ways. Except with more class and polish, as much as I hated to say that.

Chad touched Julie Ann's arm. "Can you give us some privacy, honey? Kath and I have some things to talk about."

Her face tightened a little, as if she'd rather have stayed but knew this was adult time. "Sure. See you on our next Saturday, Kath."

"It's a date. Take care, honey."

A final kiss, and she was gone, back to the car, waving at me as she went.

"She loves you so much, Kath." Chad met my eyes as he said it. I held his look. Something seemed to pass between us. Attraction or simply familiarity? Probably the former, I thought. Was the spark still there a little between us? Or was I fooling myself?

"You know the feeling is mutual. What brings you here?"

He glanced at his watch, as if there was some kind of urgency. "Actually, I drove out to your home first. I've been looking all over for you. I knew this was the anniversary, so I figured I'd drive by. I saw your car. Your dad isn't here?"

"He's on his way to Michigan. A lady friend is having medical treatment, and he wanted to be there. Why, what's up, Chad?"

The clatter of helicopter blades seemed to erupt out of nowhere, like a volley of gunshots. I looked up, shielding my eyes. I recognized one of the private Bell helicopters belonging to Chad's company. A white-and-burgundy-striped logo on the tail, "Brown Bear" beneath an upright grizzly bear, the chopper polished and gleaming. It descended, hovered. The pilot, wearing sunglasses, deftly landed in the field beside the cemetery, the blades dying to a dull *swish*.

Chad raised his voice above the noise. "I need to take you someplace." He held out his hand for mine and nodded toward the helicopter. "It's pretty inaccessible, but the chopper can get us there."

I felt a strange flutter in my chest. "Take me where?"

He glanced over at the grave of Jack, Amy, and Sean, a lingering look before he turned back to me.

"They've found them, Kath. They've found Jack's aircraft."

7

THE PAST

Kyle was always my mother's favorite.

I know she loved me, too, but Kyle reminded her of her young brother, Tom, who died of TB in childhood and whom she nursed in his illness. Kyle had the same sandy-blond hair, sapphire eyes, and freckled grin. Familiar features passed in memoriam through DNA, in what can either be a cruel trick of nature or a comfort. It's sometimes hard to tell.

My mother was never keen on Kyle joining the Army, wary of the dangers. But the Army was in our blood, and Kyle had only one ambition after he graduated from West Point: to join my father in the 101st Airborne, be posted to Iraq as a second lieutenant, where my husband-to-be, Jack, was also serving.

Five years older than me, Jack had followed in his own father's footsteps and became an Army helicopter pilot, much later transitioning to fixed-wing aircraft, flying transporters, and then back to choppers. I'd known Jack since I was seventeen. We had the same base brat upbringing, laughed at the same wacky jokes and movies. We loved the outdoors, going hiking in the iciest of winters or canoeing on the lake in summer. We didn't date until I was eighteen, but we sparked instantly, became soul mates, best friends, and lovers. Marriage was the logical next step, but we were in no hurry.

Before my brother deployed, Kyle bought Courtney a silver engagement ring from Meyer's Jewelry. They had kept their relationship going all during Kyle's four tough years at West Point. They were a good match. I had a feeling they would start a family once they married. Kyle loved kids; he was a kid himself. Put Kyle with a bunch of kids, and he was in his element, joining in the horseplay.

I was happy. Courtney was delirious. My mother was uncertain. She liked Courtney, even if she thought my best friend was a tad slutty and no stranger to a cocktail, my mom being pretty well qualified to judge the latter.

But my mother's worry came to nothing. Late in January, Kyle flew to Iraq to join my father's battalion. Jack, a captain by now and with the 101st, promised to look out for Kyle, to keep my brother safe. My dad thought it would be better if they could both keep a protective eye on Kyle.

Courtney and I read and watched the news reports, always fearful. The word from the base was that both sides fought like dogs in Fallujah during the spring offensive, the fighting so intense against Iraqi insurgents that many combatants lost limbs and minds in the savage battles that raged for four long months, until the ancient Persian city resembled the ruins of a mini-Stalingrad. The bombing was so intense that even dogs and cats lay down and died during the massive, thunderous blasts of heavy shelling.

But when it was all over and the dust cleared, Jack had kept to his word, and he and my father and Kyle came home.

Except they really didn't.

They were all different.

My father lost most of his left foot to grenade shrapnel when he encountered resistance clearing a building. He had shown extraordinary valor that day by personally leading a platoon to wipe out a unit of insurgents directing withering rocket fire at his men.

Ten months later and not even fully recuperated, he was back in the fray in Iraq. The Army wanted him to help train new commanders and tidy up some loose administrative ends. My dad used to say, his satisfaction obvious, that the Army needed him, and in a way it did. He prided himself on being a counterinsurgency expert. But he also needed the Army. It was his lifeblood, his anchor, all he'd known since he was a seventeen-year-old cadet.

There was even talk of him being awarded the Medal of Honor for the valor he'd shown when he lost his foot. Recipients are presented with the award personally by the president of the United States at a White House ceremony. My father was intensely proud.

But it all came to nothing. When Kyle's tour ended, my father's ended at about the same time, and he returned home. But I got the feeling that my dad was bitter about something, that maybe he was forced into retirement and didn't resign voluntarily. Whatever the truth, he never spoke about it, and he was never the same afterward.

As a consequence of his wound, he became gruffer and sterner and developed a bitter edge, angrily hobbling around the house on his prosthetic limb.

When the Medal of Honor was being talked about, my mother was extremely excited for a time. She anticipated the trip to the White

House, the respect accorded her for having a husband as a recipient, and living on that promise seemed to imbue her with a new sense of pride and self-importance, but when that hope withered, she seemed to become bitter, too.

Jack was never the same, either. Moodier and quieter, he started to drink more often, to spend more time alone, fishing on the lake or blindly watching TV, feeding off it as if it were an infant's bottle. The glass nipple, Mom called the TV.

But Kyle, the baby of our family, seemed affected the most. Courtney said he seemed "forever distant" after he returned from war. He told her he'd seen too much bad on his tour of duty ever to believe in good. Kyle started a Xanax prescription the week he got home. And he started smoking marijuana, something my sports-mad brother had avoided like crazy under the peer pressure of high school. Now weed seemed to make his lethargy worse and to induce an edge of paranoia.

Melancholy ran river-deep in him. He avoided driving and crowds. He never talked about his battle experiences or what he witnessed, even though I tried many times to discover what the trigger was that changed him.

A bloody moment in combat? Being shot at and shelled daily? Or was it more than that? What bad had he seen "over there" that shattered his mind? Jack said they once came across an insurgent safe house they had shelled; inside, to their horror, they found the mangled bodies of six children. I asked Kyle if that was it. But the brother I loved refused to talk, closed up tight as a clam, like the keeper of some terrible secret.

I had the feeling he could not trust anyone, could not get close to anyone again because of what he'd seen.

He walked the house morosely, in grubby pajamas that he never seemed to launder. The cotton stank of stale sweat and skunky weed, and he hardly bothered to shower or bathe. He left a malodorous wake around the house that was impossible to ignore. Often he kept his stubble for weeks. He piled on sixty pounds, drinking too much beer, eating junk food, and confined himself to the separate visitor's cottage on my parents' farm, which became his home.

He looked older than his twenty-one years. A weird detachment clouded his face, an empty stare that told me my brother was lost to us and maybe never coming back. My father sought help for Kyle from an Army psychiatrist. Kyle saw him twice but never went back. He didn't want help, I think because that kept him from having to think or talk about the events he witnessed.

"There's something really wrong with Kyle," I told Jack, who was going through his own hell. After Iraq, Jack experienced nightmares that woke him in a drenching sweat, and he became obsessive about the children's safety. He said he saw too many dead children in Iraq not to worry.

"What did it, Jack? What happened to you all? What did Kyle see or do that made him like this?"

Jack wore his poker face, the grim mask that tightened his features whenever we talked about battle. "The same unpleasant stuff we all saw. Dead, wounded, the aftermath of bombing. Some guys are more affected than others. I guess they're more sensitive. Kyle's one of them, Kath."

"I read that people who suffer trauma when they're young are more prone to PTSD."

"What's that got to do with it?"

"Kyle almost drowned when he was ten, but my dad resuscitated him. It happened in the lake at Admiral Farragut Park, where we played in the woods as kids."

We all tried to persuade Kyle to keep seeing the Army psychiatrist, but he just said, "Sure, I'll call him."

You just knew by Kyle's tone that talking to a therapist meant about as much to him as talking to a pet rabbit. We had no answers. All we could do was love Kyle, be there for him. Except you can't always physically be there.

One day, three months after Kyle returned, I was at home with my mom when her cell phone rang. It was my father. I knew the second I saw my mother's face screwed up in pain that something was terribly wrong. I saw her grip go loose on the phone and her mouth fall open in a silent scream of horror. She faltered, could barely stand, her eyes filling with tears as I rushed to support her.

At Admiral Farragut Park, by the lake, on Knoxville's pretty North-shore, in the same woods where we often played in summer as kids, Kyle had pulled up in his ten-year-old white Nissan. It was one of the few times I knew of Kyle driving his car since he returned—he always avoided driving.

A woman walking her Labrador said she saw Kyle sitting in his Nissan for several minutes. She said he appeared to be talking to him-self, until he started to cry, tears streaming down his face. Why he was upset she had no idea, but in her opinion—she was a registered nurse—the young man she observed seemed disturbed.

Kyle took a fold-up sports chair he used to use for football games from his trunk, along with a blue nylon tow rope, and walked into the woods. There, in the soft, warm heat of that April afternoon, my beau-tiful Kyle threw the rope over a tree, tied one end, made a noose around his neck with the other, and stood on the game chair. He stepped off.

The alarmed nurse had followed him into the woods, already calling 911. When she found Kyle, his body was hanging limply. She screamed, and a male jogger came to her aid. Between them, they managed to cut the rope with a penknife. Kyle's face was blue, but he was still breathing. By the time the paramedics got to him, his heart had stopped. They hooked him up to a defibrillator and got it going again. It was touch and go all evening.

Kyle lived. If you can call it living. The rope cut off the blood supply to his brain, causing a massive cerebral stroke.

At twenty-one, my kid brother was condemned to dribble and drool and be pushed around in a wheelchair, fed liquid foods and needing 24/7 medical care for the rest of his days. He could talk and communicate, but it was all basic stuff, nods and grunts along with a few intelligible words. His head lolled from side to side like a sluggish ball bearing in a pinball machine.

We found a well-run nursing home near Sevierville. Serenity Ridge was a twenty-mile drive, close enough to visit every day. These homes always have names that contain words or symbols of comfort and renewal—Serenity, Harmony, Spring, Meadow—as if to offer relatives a kind of hope, when really there's often none. Five weeks after he went into the woods, Kyle was transferred to Serenity Ridge by ambulance.

The first time my father visited, he came home looking as bleached as marble. He withdrew into himself for months. My mother barely seemed able to cope, even though she drank more. But the truth was, we all felt relieved that Kyle was still alive, that we still had him in body if not in mind. That we could still love him and not have to bury him in some cold patch of rust-colored earth in a Knoxville cemetery.

But the young man we knew, the sweet and sensitive Kyle who enriched our lives with love and humor, the crimson-faced boy who made us laugh with his silly pranks or made our eyes wet from melancholy whenever he sang "Danny Boy"—that Kyle was lost to us forever.

8

The past

Whatever happened in Iraq seemed to have cast a wicked spell over all the men I loved—Jack, Kyle, my father.

After Kyle's suicide attempt, Jack, the man I was to marry, was a rock—comforting, loving, caring. But Jack was also drinking, moody, and nervous, which was so unlike him. Before Iraq, he was the calmest, most grounded man I knew. After Iraq, he was still loving, still attentive, but he wanted to spend more time alone, and he talked less, too.

Sometimes Jack would get a faraway look in his eyes, a look that told me something disturbing was going on inside his head. Just as with Kyle or my dad, any mention of war was a no-no. I never saw or heard any of them sit around over a beer and shooting the bull about their combat experiences. Nothing. They never even went to veterans reunions. What awful event had changed them? What had they seen or done? Why did I get the feeling that there was some shared secret that none of them ever wanted to talk about?

As for Kyle, I couldn't stop crying about him for weeks.

I cried for the blond-haired little boy I shared a bed with on winter nights when he was too scared to sleep. Cried for the memory of his puppy-fat cheeks and the hold-me-tight hugs. For the little boy who said "Ats" instead of "Thanks." For the lost brother who suffered an invisible wound that took him to a place from which he could not return. Some days I'd just break down, in the middle of driving or at the mall or out on a date with Jack.

I read and reread every newspaper report I could about the battles fought against the remnants of Saddam's army, the various insurgent groups, tracing their names and their locations on maps: Fallujah, Najaf, Ramadi. I watched hundreds of YouTube clips on the same subject and googled a whole bunch of veterans blogs.

Some claimed they survived total hell during their Iraq deployment; others said it was a walk in the park. I guess it depended on whether you were behind the front lines or up close to the action having your nerves shot to hell. I read lots of threads about roadside bombs, bloody skirmishes, and repeated deployments taking their toll, causing the dreaded four letters PTSD.

Long before it was ever properly diagnosed as post-traumatic stress disorder, they called it shell shock. It could cause depression, sleeplessness, anxiety, paranoia, hallucinations, drug dependency, and a raft of mental-health issues and illnesses that sometimes caused once sane and sensible men to put guns to their heads and blow their brains out. Others withdrew into themselves like hermits.

But it was impossible to know what it was that had wounded Kyle's mind and spirit so badly that I could not reach him again.

I recall my last moments of closeness with Kyle, three days before the Admiral Farragut Park incident.

We sat in two rocking chairs on my parents' back porch. Kyle was smoking a joint and stared out at the lake, a faraway look in his red-veined eyes.

"What are you thinking about, Kyle?"

He kept staring ahead vacantly. "Know what the West Point motto is?"

"'A cadet does not lie, cheat, steal, or tolerate those who do.' Why?"

He nodded and just kept staring out at nothing.

"Talk to me, Kyle. What's on your mind?"

As I tried to break down the wall yet again, he took a deep drag before he slowly let it out, tossed down the tiny butt, and crushed it with his flip-flop. "Drop it, Sis. You really don't want to know."

It was as if he couldn't trust anyone. Couldn't get close to anyone again because of whatever he'd seen in battle that so destroyed him. I rubbed his arm gently, but he moved away, as if he was at risk of catching a deadly disease. Courtney told me they'd "lost it" as a couple. That Kyle never talked to her much anymore and that the slightest intimacy seemed to scare him.

I persisted. "But I do, Kyle. I want to know what makes you feel the way you're feeling. I'm trying to help. We all are."

I'd spoken those words so many times they were a worn script. Kyle's far-off stare didn't shift as he said tonelessly, "Some things you're better off not talking about."

"Not even to Dad? He served with you, Kyle. He just wants to help."

"Help? Our father? Sure he does." He grunted, cut it short, and I saw it then, the slit of his angry mouth, shut tight. It was so unlike Kyle. Once he and our dad and Jack went hunting together or to ball games. But Kyle hadn't spent much time with our father since he returned. Whenever Dad asked him a question, Kyle would barely grunt a reply. And when Dad asked Kyle to join him duck hunting, my brother didn't even answer. I had asked Kyle about it, but he just said, "I've seen enough blood to last me a lifetime."

"What do you mean?" I asked him now. "What was it you did in Iraq, Kyle? What brought you to this?"

He looked out at the lake like a zombie, slowly shaking his head. "What I saw . . . what I saw . . . was like a stopover in hell. One village . . . near some cedar woods . . . it was a massacre . . ." He shook his head, tears welling in his eyes. His voice trailed off, as if the memory was too painful.

"What village? What did you see?"

I saw his hands tremble. Now his mouth twisted in irritation, and he wiped his eyes with his sleeve. "You need to drop it."

"You need to talk about it someday. Can't you just trust me?"

Behind us, I saw our father through the open blinds in his study. He got up from his desk and peered out at us before he left the room, as if coming toward us.

Kyle saw him and stood, zipped up his grubby fleece hoodie, and stabbed me with a look before he headed for the lakeshore alone. "Leave it," he said.

I watched him go.

My father came to stand in the doorway, twirling his reading glasses in his hands, his craggy Celtic face tense with unease. "He worries me."

His warrior demeanor had mellowed with the years, and he'd found it easier to show affection. Without a word, he came over and put an arm around my shoulder. I leaned into him. He hugged me so tightly I could hardly breathe. It made me feel so secure, despite everything.

I loved to feel the strength of my father. He was always my hero. His mere presence was often the only reassurance I sought when trouble loomed or danger threatened. Dad was the man I always looked up to. And as a child, I felt there was nothing my father couldn't protect me from. But as we watched Kyle down by the lake, head hunched down, hands in his pockets while he kicked stones into the water, I knew that my father was helpless.

"Kyle's like his mom, honey. Not one for showing his feelings. We love him so much, and it's killing us all."

"How can we help him?"

My father's face tightened. "Pray for him. Stay close to him. Let him know we love and care for him. Nothing else we can do." He hugged me again and turned to go, looking forlorn.

"Dad?"

His bushy eyebrows rose in a question mark.

"What happened to Kyle in Iraq?"

"God only knows. We saw action in so many places."

"But what do you think happened to him?"

He stared back at me as if I'd peeled off a scab. "I'll tell you a true story about Kyle. A bunch of us are in a burnt-out apartment building in Fallujah, a lookout post, and we're watching our guys a mile away taking machine gun fire. The guy next to Kyle, a sniper, hands him his rifle with a powerful scope, points toward the streets below, and says, 'Take a look at the kid.'"

My father paused. "It's a seven-year-old girl who hangs around outside our base. Pretty, dark eyes, always friendly. She often wears a purple gown. We call her the flower girl. She gives us flowers, and we give her hugs and candy.

"But we also know that in a street fight, she carries weapons and ammo for the insurgents. The rules of engagement say we can shoot her. But nobody does. Kyle likes her. She likes him. They're always high-fiving and smiling at each other, and he always gives her extra candy. You know Kyle and kids. He's a natural with them. But that day, the sniper says bitterly to Kyle, 'She's been back and forth across the street at least a dozen times. She's been getting a whole load of ammo to her people, and our guys are getting killed.'"

My father sighed, shook his head. "Nobody shoots her. We can't do it. But a few days later, Kyle's in the same lookout and peers out through his binoculars. He sees the little flower girl's body in the street. Next to her bloodied corpse are a bunch of loaded AK magazines lying in the dirt. A kid of seven. Shot dead."

"Our . . . our troops shot her?"

"Or she got caught in a crossfire. Or was shot deliberately by her own side to make it look like we were war criminals. Anything is possible. I've no idea. But Kyle was convinced one of our snipers killed her. He went crazy after that. Wasn't right for weeks."

My father's mouth was tight as he looked at me. "People just want to hear the *Band of Brothers* stories. The rousing, heroic stuff. The average American doesn't want to hear about our soldiers seeing and doing evil things and coming home with it weighing on them. They don't want to know about killing kids and old people. They really don't want to know about the stuff that destroys your soul."

"You think that was what sent Kyle over the edge? The little flower girl?"

"Maybe. But in the end, it's always the same thing that happens to everyone who goes into battle, honey."

"What?"

"The soldier who goes to war is not the same soldier who comes back."

Courtney visited Kyle at Serenity Ridge every day for the first two months.

Then her visits tapered off. After a year training as a beautician while she tried to figure out what to do with her life—"I don't want to jump into some pool I'll want to climb out of after a few months, honey"—Courtney decided to join the military, and she received a CID posting in her father's unit. CID was the Department of Defense's prime investigation organization, responsible for conducting criminal investigations into crimes for which the Army was, or might be, a party of interest.

"Here's the thing, honey. I love it. You get a good case, and it's like a mystery, a puzzle to solve. If they could just give us some decent heels to go with the uniform, they could really sex up this outfit."

Courtney was smart, good at her job, the rumors said. During her training at Quantico, Virginia, she would often drive all the way to Tennessee—eight or more hours through the night sometimes—just to visit Kyle. But after her military career took off, her visits dropped to three times a month and then two.

"Kyle never talks, never reacts, Kath. When he wants to, he'll let me hold his hand, but mostly he just seems to want to be left in whatever world he's in. I can't get through to him, honey."

That's how it was most times when I visited Kyle, too. Tiny, muted sparks of reaction once in a while, but mostly his head lolled to one side, his eyes locked in a thousand-yard stare. Or he'd focus blindly on the TV as if attracted just by the light and not the action on-screen. He'd sit there, often in total silence, as I wiped dribble from his lips.

I used to ask myself, was it the brutal sight of the little flower girl's body that sent him over the edge? I had no way of knowing. I could try talking to him about Iraq, show him videos or photos of the dead and the street battles, but to me that was risking far too much. I knew from past experience that kind of thing disturbed him so much he might try to kill himself again.

The doctors said his mental perception was about twenty percent of normal. He had physical therapy, but it was as if Kyle was going through it all in a trance. I felt saturated with pain every single time I drove up the oak-lined driveway to Serenity Ridge. With every yard, it felt as if a six-inch nail were being hammered into my heart.

"I still love him, Kath, and always will," Courtney confessed. "But I'd be fooling myself to believe it could work out. I mean, I want a husband, I want kids someday . . . I . . . I want a life."

She broke down, crying into her sleeve. I was angry at her. I had expected Courtney to be loyal to Kyle, to devote herself to his care. But when my anger washed away, I knew that was just wishful thinking. I couldn't have kept a relationship like that going, either.

Besides, I felt mixed up about my own impending marriage. Jack and I had been due to get hitched in June. Because of what happened to Kyle, we'd postponed our wedding until August. It might as well have been two years, not two months, because it made not a shred of difference to my mother's grief or her state of mind. Kyle's affliction hit both her and my father hard.

But when my mother's grief turned to anger, she began to blame my father—for being a soldier, for Kyle's joining the military, for allowing him to be posted to Iraq. She even blamed my father for the warrior genes in our family DNA, which she claimed "crippled Kyle's mind with the lure of war."

But in the end, the terrible crime she committed on my wedding day told me that she really just blamed herself.

9

The next twenty minutes in the helicopter went past in a blur.

A blur and a welter of emotions wrenched my heart in every direction. My mind went into a tailspin so severe I wanted to throw up. Fear and helplessness overwhelmed me. Chad's words ricocheted around inside my head.

"They've found it, Kath. They've found Jack's aircraft."

My insides felt hollowed out, yet I still managed to ask a barrage of questions. How? Where? When? How had the aircraft crashed? Was it intact or scattered in pieces? Did they find . . . did they find *bodies*?

I hated even saying that word. It was so brutally final. Sometimes I used to almost convince myself that maybe Jack and my children didn't die that night. That maybe they somehow survived and lived on without me in some alternate universe. My mind never figured out the exact details. But it's weird the things a troubled mind will convince you of.

The very thought of bodies turned my stomach. My husband's and children's remains scattered among wreckage. Bleached bones at this stage. I couldn't get my head around that. Even after eight years of not knowing exactly what happened to my family, I guess I still could not grasp the finality of their deaths.

Until now. Now it began to seep into me like rot. I felt tormented, gripped by a kind of madness. I saw that I was wringing my hands, yet I could not stop. I was locked into a loop of desperation, wanting to know everything at once.

"They found the wreckage in a remote part of the Smoky Mountains." Chad spoke softly. "An area called Thunder Mountain. Apparently, the crash site was covered by years of debris, and the aircraft is reasonably intact."

I remember reading somewhere—maybe in the *Knoxville News Sentinel* or some local tabloid—that there are still aircraft wrecks they have never found in the Smokies. It is a vast area, many hundreds of square miles of sometimes dense foliage and forest, some of it subtropical.

"But . . . but Jack wasn't supposed to be flying in that area, was he?"

Chad looked down at his black shoes, polished like glass, then back up at me. He gave a tiny shake of his head. "Not that I'm aware of, Kath."

"Then . . . then why there?"

"I don't know. The company wasn't aware that the aircraft would be in that area at that time. I'm hoping the investigation may solve the mystery."

"Oh, my God." I put my head in my hands, feeling overwhelmed again. "What about remains?"

Chad touched my arm, squeezed it. His other hand went around my shoulder to comfort me. "I don't know about any remains, Kath. The site's still being investigated."

"How? How did they find the wreckage?"

"I'm not sure. I guess they'll explain."

I looked out at the landscape drifting by. We were beyond Knoxville's sprawl and the wide Tennessee River, maybe a couple of thousand feet up, the vast mountain range that made up the Smokies not far ahead. The helicopter banked, rose higher, and my stomach sank in response.

"If you need me to stay with you for a while when we land, I'll stay," Chad offered.

I didn't respond.

"But the police are probably going to want your full attention, Kath. They'll likely want to talk with you alone. But just know I'm there if you need me. You still have my number."

Of course I still had his number. I still saw Julie Ann fairly regularly. I think Chad knew that being in her company was good for me, even though seeing her made me think about Amy and what she might look like now. Getting braces on her teeth, going to middle school, hanging out with friends, cruising the mall at weekends, having crushes on boys.

I don't know why I said it, but I did. "I think I want to be alone."

"Are you sure, Kath?"

"Yes . . . yes, I'm sure."

But I wasn't sure. I wasn't sure of anything, but I had a sickening sensation in my stomach that had nothing to do with the helicopter ride and a lot to do with the truckload of fear and dread that was rioting inside my head.

I felt Chad squeeze my hand again. I wanted it to feel reassuring, but it didn't. Right that minute, nothing would reassure me.

The Smoky Mountains were all around us now, their vast, rugged majesty drenched in misty sunshine, snow on top of some of the highest peaks.

Jack and I used to bring the children up here in winter and summer, to ride down the river in rubber tubes, picnic, visit Dollywood or Gatlinburg or sometimes Cades Cove to see bears in the wild.

One memory stuck out above all others.

When I was pregnant with Amy, I'd had preeclampsia, and she came almost three months early. A preterm birth can sometimes signal problems for a child's physical and mental development. Lung problems, brain development, and eyesight problems are all risks, but we were lucky; aside from a left-ear abnormality, Amy was perfect. A final operation at age three to correct the problem with her cochlea, and she was as good as new. A month after she left the hospital, all the medical reports were clear, and Jack and I decided to celebrate.

We drove up into the Smokies with Sean and Amy early one evening, brought a homemade picnic, and joined thousands of other visitors on the field outside Gatlinburg who came to watch the annual fireflies dance, a symphony of light like no other, which happened in only two places in the world, Southeast Asia and the Smoky Mountains.

When darkness fell and the stars appeared, we were treated to the sight of hundreds of millions of fireflies dancing in weird synchronous displays that took our breath away. We watched, astonished.

A wide-eyed Sean said, "Wow, Mommy, Daddy, look at all those twinkling lights!"

Amy was in a trance. "It's . . . it's like a lot of Christmas trees, Mommy."

At first, she and Sean tried to catch the errant fireflies that strayed our way, giggling and chasing them this way and that, before they gave up, exhausted. Sean attempted to count the winking lights and got stuck at "twenty and one hundred."

It was such a special moment, sitting on that hillside. One of those times when you look at your children and you know they are your whole life, and it moves you so much it frightens you, because you realize you are a hostage to fortune. Your existence would be meaningless if anything happened to your kids. It makes you wish that time could stand still.

It was the kind of glorious memory everyone should experience once in his or her lifetime. My mother used to say that there should always be one bright, shining, happy incident in our lives that we remember above all else. That evening was surely ours.

I looked down now at those same mountains, in sunlight now, not darkness. It was such a cruel irony that the bodies of my husband and children should lie here, in a place that was always so special to us.

I felt besieged by my memories, my eyes wet.

Chad held on to my hand. I felt its strength as he clasped it to his chest.

Our eyes met. I got the feeling there was a lot more he wanted to say to me. But this was not the time.

And then below, I saw a splash of activity appear in the forest. Police cars, TV vans, and figures scouring the forest in all directions.

My heart swelled, feeling as if it were going to explode.

The helicopter started to descend.

10

The rotors tossed branches and sent rippling air across the brackish, swampy waters in the forest below.

As the helicopter came in to land, my stomach clenched with pain. Below, I could make out a crush of TV crews and reporters, held back by uniformed sheriff's deputies. All around there was nothing but patches of swamp and thick forest, speckled with what looked like bits of aircraft wreckage. I spotted a big central mass of it off to my left, but as the helicopter banked, I lost sight of it. Next to me, Chad squeezed my hand again, even tighter. "You hanging in there?"

"I . . . I'm not sure."

"Kath, are you sure you don't want me to stay with you?"

"I'm sure."

It was true. This was about my family. This was about me and Jack and Sean and Amy. No one else. I felt my eyes become wet.

The helicopter landed with a solid bump. The swish of the blades died, and then a man slid open the door. Big, handsome, light-skinned African-American carrying too much weight.

He slipped off his Ray-Bans, and I saw green eyes flecked with gray. He flashed an ID. "Ms. Kelly, thanks for coming. I'm Brewster Tanner. I'm with the FBI."

I barely nodded, still in a daze.

Tanner gestured to a tall, muscular dark-haired man who was chewing gum. The man didn't speak; he looked remote but made eye contact with me as his jaws moved. "And this is Agent Breedon," Tanner added.

Breedon barely nodded.

A hundred yards away, I saw a bunch of SUVs parked near a pair of canvas walk-in tents, a half dozen sheriff's deputies standing around. Men and women in blue nylon zip-up jackets with large yellow NTSB lettering on the back were gathering up the bits of debris, tagging them before removing them to the tents. Some areas were marked off with yellow tape or red tape.

The next thing I knew, I was out of the chopper, and Chad was lost somewhere behind me. The FBI man seemed to be studying me, as if trying to size me up.

"Are you familiar with this area, ma'am?"

"No."

Tanner jerked his chin toward a mountain nearby. "We're at a place called Thunder Mountain, southeast of the Great Smoky Mountains National Park. This particular area is actually pretty dense, kinda looks like rain forest. An elderly couple from Louisville, Kentucky, died last night when their private aircraft came down in a bad storm."

When I looked closer at the central mass of wreckage, I realized what it was: the remains of a cabin, scattered in a zillion pieces all around the forest. Bits of a white refrigerator and a chunk of an aircraft wing were stuck in some branches. Little yellow flag markers were planted next to debris, people in white hazard suits poking around whatever interested them.

I understood none of this, none of it at all. I felt a strange fluttering in my chest. A muddied green Polaris Ranger drove up, the buggy's engine sounding like an angry garden mower. A small, ruddy-faced man with wiry gray hair and glasses climbed out of the seat, leaving a clipboard on the dash.

He offered his hand, and Tanner said, "This is Dale Dexter. He's with the NTSB. That's the National Transportation Safety Board. It investigates aircraft crashes, Ms. Kelly."

"I know what they do." I recalled two men from the NTSB who came to talk to me, accompanied by a pair of sheriff's deputies, after Jack's aircraft disappeared. They bombarded me with all kinds of questions, everything from if I'd ever heard my husband express any concerns about the maintenance of the corporate aircraft to his knowledge of flying, even his drinking habits and mental state.

Jack was a qualified pilot when he served in the military, but he'd allowed his license to lapse. And on the night his aircraft disappeared en route from New Orleans to Savannah, a corporate pilot was in command of the flight.

Now I stared over at the tents. "I don't get any of this."

Tanner gestured to the Ranger, as Agent Breedon and Dexter jumped in. "Climb aboard, ma'am. Mr. Dexter here will explain. I guess what he has to say may come as a shock."

Dexter gripped the steering wheel hard as the Polaris bumped and jolted its way along a rutted track. "Did you ever hear of the term *synchronicity*, Ms. Kelly?"

"Yes. I think so."

"Simply put, synchronicity is when there's an apparently meaningful coincidence in time between two or more similar or identical events that appear unrelated. It's a term that's often used to explain when paranormal events occur simultaneously. Kind of an unnatural coincidence, really. Not that I'm suggesting any paranormal significance here, but in this case, there is a commonality. A storm, we believe. But a bizarre synchronicity kind of links the events."

I felt muddled as I stared back at Dexter, but I stayed silent.

"Let me explain. Last night, a Cessna twin-turboprop aircraft crashed, carrying a retired couple from Louisville, Kentucky. Those are the remains of the collision you just saw. The Cessna plowed into the cabin back there, killed a guy, probably the owner. We're still trying to figure that one out."

I said nothing, just listened.

"The craft went down about midnight during a bad storm. Aircraft crashes are not uncommon in this area in very bad weather, especially light aircraft. But here's the thing: one of the Cessna's engines sheared from the wing structure."

"You mean it broke off?"

The NTSB man nodded. "Yes, ma'am. The separation may have been caused by the g-forces as the plane came plummeting out of the storm. The engine may have already been damaged and on fire. It hit the ground and tumbled away from the main body of the aircraft—almost four hundred yards away, to be precise. And that's the strange part."

Dexter shot me a quick look. "Not far from where the engine was embedded in the ground, we found the wreckage of *another* aircraft. It was probably on much the same flight path as the one that crashed last night. Synchronicity of a kind. Except that this wreckage had been there a very long time. Eight years, in fact."

My blood iced up. Dexter slowed. Up ahead I saw a clearing, a forest behind it. An NTSB crew in white disposable suits was working away, probing the ground near the woods and what looked like a solid chunk of an aircraft engine. Bits of aluminum were scattered about, the ground plowed up for about eighty yards before it hit the solid wall of forest.

Despair overwhelmed me. Jack, my children—were their bodies here, in this remote, swampy forest? Is this how it had ended for them? Anguish thudded in my chest with a powerful jolt as Dexter halted and stepped on the parking brake.

"I ought to tell you that the fuselage identity markings match your husband's aircraft. It's the wreckage of a small business jet, a Beechcraft Premier, Ms. Kelly. We're pretty certain it's his missing plane."

11

The Polaris buggy snarled along a track overhung with tall trees.

Finally, we burst out into a clearing and came to a stop. Fifty yards away, I saw what looked like a mangled aircraft engine. More people in white forensics suits were using sifters and trowels, and others hefted bigger parts toward a blue canopy erected thirty yards away.

I held my breath until my lungs hurt. My heart swelled with fear.

Near the canopy I saw what looked like blue windbreaks propped up here and there. We all followed Dexter, cautiously leading the way along a trampled-down path through grass and ferns.

"Watch out for snakes. We had to warn our people. One of them almost got bit by a copperhead. So holler if you see anything."

I barely registered the warning, my eyes fixed on the crash site ahead. I saw a tangled mass of metal and aluminum that had plowed into a slowly rising hillside. In its wake, a six-foot-wide streak was gouged into the rich red earth. About eighty yards farther into the woods, I spotted another crew moving under a huge green tarpaulin. A few more National Park rangers stood around chatting. Dexter led us past the tangled ruin of an engine.

I felt barely able to stand, my legs shaking violently.

The NTSB man said, "Air crashes are not all that unusual in this region, with so many mountains, Ms. Kelly. Less experienced pilots can wander off course in the haze that you often see all over the Smokies."

He jerked his head toward the wrecked engine. "And sometimes they get disoriented and crash. Maybe they lose contact with the nearest airfield, too, which wouldn't help. They've had a good number of crashes in the park in the last decades. A few of the aircraft have never been found."

"Never?"

He pushed aside an emerald-green fern on our path and shook his head. "Never. Have you got any idea how big an area we're talking about? The Great Smoky Mountains National Park is more than five hundred square miles. That's more than half a million acres."

Tanner added, "Here's the thing. The park rangers say that two inches of natural debris covers the woodland here every year—leaves, soil particles, and so on. If a plane crashed and wasn't found immediately or it wasn't known that it crashed in the park area . . ." Tanner spread his huge hands. "And if it's lying there eight years, well, by then we're talking about over a foot of debris covering the wreckage. Ain't nobody going to find that, except by luck or chance."

Dexter said, "In this case, a part of the separated engine from last night's crash slammed in there." He pointed into the woods, where the crew was working. "It hit a tree. When we were searching for that wreckage, one of our guys exposed the fuselage of an older aircraft, covered in debris. The two aircraft were probably on the same flight path. Maybe bad storms in the area took them both down; only time will tell."

It was all becoming chillingly clear to me now. I felt tightness in my chest as we got closer to the canopy. My heart was racing so fast I could hardly breathe, my legs still shaking.

"Can you confirm the ages of your husband and children when they went missing, Ms. Kelly?" Dexter trod through the long grass.

"Jack . . . was thirty-five. Sean was eight. Amy . . . my daughter, Amy, was five." I felt my eyes well up. "Did you find . . ." My question trailed away. I couldn't finish it.

Dexter said, "It's early days, and we're just starting to excavate the site, but yes, we found human remains, Ms. Kelly. It's undetermined for sure as yet whose remains they are. That's why we needed you here. There were some personal belongings we hoped you may be able to identify."

I felt afraid, afraid to look at any remains. My heart was stuttering, and I had an ache in my breastbone, as if a knife were stuck there. All I could think of was Jack and my beautiful children, Sean and Amy, their bones rotting in this moist silt. I felt a hot flush ripple inside my body, a weakness again in my legs. "Whose . . . whose remains did you find?"

My voice must have sounded hysterical—I registered the pitch of it becoming higher. I felt Tanner gently put one of his huge hands on my shoulder. "Ms. Kelly, I know this is difficult, but try to stay calm. We'll get through this quicker."

In the tangled undergrowth, I saw two little yellow cards. They marked two objects, one a shred of gray corrugated leather that may have been part of an aircraft seat, the other a small, cheap black plastic comb. A powerful memory jolted me. My son, Sean, age six. We were in a Target store one day, grocery shopping, and Sean wanted me to buy him a comb. He was to have a class photograph taken in school the next day, and he wanted to "Make sure I straighten my tornado, Mommy."

We used to joke about Sean's "tornado," a little clump of hair on his crown that he would nervously work into a twirl whenever he got fretful or anxious. Sometimes I'd catch him unaware, in the middle of a store or among his toys, standing with one hand behind his back and the other twirling his hair. It was an image of Sean I never forgot.

It may not have been the same comb, but the sight of it brought the memory of my son back. My legs felt shaky, and I seemed to lose it, my body heavy as if I were moving in water. Everything was in slow motion, and I felt I was about to collapse. I was taking shallow breaths.

A man's hand gripped my arm. "Ms. Kelly? . . ."

And then my head started to spin and I slumped. Tanner and Dexter held me up. Someone brought a fold-up chair. I took a deep breath.

"Ms. Kelly? Ms. Kelly, are you OK?"

No, I wasn't OK. I felt cool water splash my face. Someone must have grabbed a first-aid kit, too, because there was a sharp scent, like smelling salts, and all of a sudden my lungs jolted and I snapped wide awake.

I sat forward in the fold-up chair. Tanner and the NTSB man were beside me. A woman, too. She had a first-aid kit.

Tanner knelt, but I could see that it was an effort, and he had to put a hand behind himself to keep from falling over. Close up, I saw that he had pitted skin, and his breath smelled bad—not terrible but not pleasant, either, kind of sour.

I felt groggy, but I still had my senses. "You never answered my question. Whose remains did you find?"

"We don't know yet for sure," Dexter said. "We found a skeleton, or at least most of one. It may be your husband's. Only tests will tell for sure."

"Why . . . why haven't you found Amy? . . . Sean?"

Dexter didn't answer. Neither did Tanner. Both men looked uncomfortable.

"Why?" I repeated.

"Ms. Kelly, in this area . . ." Tanner shrugged. "Well, forest creatures roam wild here, including bears. The remains could have been carried off."

I felt faint again, my entire body shaking. Dexter saw my reaction and added quickly, "But we're not sure that occurred, Ms. Kelly. As I said, it's early days. And more than likely, the remains were *not* taken by animals."

"Why?"

Dexter gave Tanner a quick look before he answered. "Because there's something odd about the crash scene, something that just doesn't add up. Can you walk, Ms. Kelly?"

I struggled to my feet with Tanner's help. My legs still felt rubbery, but I knew I had to face whatever lay ahead in those woods. "Odd in what way?"

"Let me show you."

12

The day of my wedding, my mother cut a pathetic figure—a once-pretty woman of fifty-four, her face deeply wrinkled, her alcohol addiction and the mental ruin of her only son's affliction aging her at least ten years.

Skew-eyed with booze, she did the Hokey Pokey alone around the dance floor, looking like a sad, middle-aged victim afflicted by palsy. I watched her trampling all over one of the most important highlights in my life, and I felt a terrible hurt inside—not from anger or shame but from knowing the suffering she was trying to hide. If I'd had some knowledge of the horror she planned that afternoon, could I have intervened? I was to wonder that for years afterward. I blamed myself for not deciphering a hint of the misfortune that was to come. But would it have changed everything that happened? Would it have saved the lives of those I loved?

Maybe.

Or at least, that's what I sometimes tell myself.

I certainly sensed my mother's resentment. She often had a vicious streak when drunk. But I didn't realize how the volcano of despair and anger boiled inside her. I did, however, hear it in her tone of voice when I got up the courage that day to beg her to behave.

"Behave? You're telling me to behave? Don't tell me how to behave, missy. This family doesn't know the meaning of good behavior, and certainly not that father of yours. Who does he think he's fooling? He needs to pull that head of his out of his rear end."

Her cruelty blazed back at me through drunken eyes. "And don't think he's the officer and gentleman he pretends to be! He's a sham, a pathetic liar, a fraud!" She fled the room.

I had no idea what my mother meant or where she disappeared to. Probably the restroom, I guessed. She often did that after her drunken outbursts. Sobbing into a tissue, shouting insults that made no sense, sounding like a high-strung Southern belle from a Tennessee Williams play.

Jack, familiar with my mother's ways from years of knowing her at Fort Campbell, usually offered the wisest advice. "Leave her, she'll sober up. Then you'll see the real Martha Beth again. The kind woman with a good heart."

I'd touch Jack's face with the back of my hand, and then he'd kiss me. Nobody kissed as well as Jack or could hold me the way I wanted to be held when I felt vulnerable—tight and close and safe.

My mother was kind and good-hearted when she was sober. But drunk and roused, red-haired little Martha Beth was a snarling panther. That afternoon of my wedding, my father and I tried to plead with her, but when she was in her cups, she never listened to anyone. And so we endured the tongue lashings and backed off, hoping she'd tire herself out and sleep it off in a corner somewhere. Besides, what bride needed a wedding album with a photograph of her mom being dragged into a squad car in handcuffs?

But I know now that I should have tried to sober her up, talk sense to her, anything but leave her to drown in her own pool of booze and bitterness.

But I didn't, and I didn't know about the gun in her purse.

And that was my big mistake.

13

Tanner moved toward the canopy. It covered most of the wreckage.

Under it, behind one of the windbreaks, I saw two stainless-steel tables side by side. One was bare, the other covered by a white sheet, a lumpy form underneath. I felt my legs shake again, emotion welling in me. I could see a corkboard on a trestle and what appeared to be photographic images tacked to it, but someone had covered them with a light-blue tarp. The woman who had tended to me with the first-aid kit joined us, and Dexter said, "This is Carole, by the way. She's one of our forensics techs."

The woman gave me a sympathetic nod. "Ms. Kelly."

I shook her hand. "Can . . . can you tell me more about the remains?"

Carole guided us toward the tables, past a jumble of plastic and aluminum storage boxes. I felt overcome by a terrible feeling of dread. As I stared at the table with the white sheet, my breath caught in my lungs. Were these Jack's remains?

I wanted to weep aloud, to collapse again. I fought my emotions. And then I thought of Amy and Sean. What if forest creatures had savaged them or dragged away their bodies? That kind of horror was too revolting for any parent to contemplate. I felt my stomach churn, tears welling.

"It's a male," the woman said, and she consulted a chart. "Your husband was thirty-five when he disappeared? Six foot one, I believe. A tattoo on his right arm."

"That . . . that's right."

"We haven't identified the man yet, Ms. Kelly. He had no ID that we could locate." Carole gently touched my arm as if to prepare me before she lifted back the sheet.

I must have let out a gasp, because I felt Tanner's hand tighten on my other arm. I pulled my right hand away to cover my mouth.

Laid out on the table were muddied bones that formed most of a human skeleton. The bones had a tint of green, as if oxidized or stained by forest lichen. I saw that parts of the right arm were missing, as was the left leg below the knee. I felt my stomach heave and wanted to retch. Was this all that was left of the man I had loved, even still loved?

I felt bile rise from the pit of my stomach. I kept my hand on my mouth.

At the bottom right of the table was a pathetic-looking collection of corroded items. What looked like a belt buckle, scraps of clothing, and a messy bunch of clothes fibers, mostly dried out. Lying next to them was a big set of stainless-steel tweezers.

Dexter said, "Is there anything here that you recognize among the items, Ms. Kelly? Some scraps of clothes? A belt buckle, perhaps?"

"Is . . . is that all you found?"

Tanner gave Dexter that look again. "No, but we'll get to that later. Do you recognize anything here, ma'am?"

The clothing fibers were dark gray or black. The belt buckle was gilded, a simple, plain design; it was badly tarnished. A piece of a blue shirt, maybe the collar. I had packed Jack's bag the night before he left with Amy and Sean. I didn't have to struggle to remember what their three suitcases contained or what they wore.

In eight years, I replayed that list over and over in my mind. Jack's bag contained a Brooks Brothers business suit in dark blue. Tan corduroys and two pairs of cargo shorts. A half dozen pairs of Old Navy underwear in dark blue and black. Two white cotton business shirts, a blue silk tie, and a pink one. Three pairs of black business socks, three pairs of white cotton crews, and two old, faded Nike T-shirts he loved, one red and the other sepia-brown that matched his eyes. A brown leather belt.

But Jack's belt buckle was silver-toned and embellished with the shape of a hawk. He'd had the buckle specially made as a memento of his air unit.

As for Amy's and Sean's clothes, I could remember every single item I packed. And what they wore when I kissed them good-bye for the last time on the front porch. Sean had on beige chino cargo shorts and a pale-green T-shirt and Tikka sandals. Amy was dressed in a pink tank top and a white skirt, pink socks, and matching tennis shoes, and she carried a Barbie backpack. They both looked so cute, so clean and tidy. That was unusual for Sean, because he was going through a messy phase.

I felt confused now. "I'm sorry, but nothing looks familiar."

Tanner consulted his notebook. "The pilot was a man named Felipe Hernandez. A former military pilot, like your husband."

"Y-yes. They knew each other pretty well."

"Did you know Mr. Hernandez?"

"Not really. I only met him a couple of times, socially."

"Were he and your husband similar in height and build?"

"Hernandez wasn't as tall, and he was stockier. Why? Do you think the remains are his?"

Dexter didn't seem to want to commit to anything just yet. "Too early to say. The remains were out of the aircraft but near the pilot's seat. The flight that night was from New Orleans to Savannah, and you were to meet your family at Knoxville's Tyson Airport at eleven p.m. the following evening when they returned from their Savannah day trip. Isn't that right, Ms. Kelly?"

I nodded. "Yes. But I don't understand. The night Jack's aircraft disappeared, it wasn't supposed to be in this area, was it?"

"No, ma'am. You got the call from Jack's company when?"

"Nine the next morning. A colleague of his phoned to say that they feared the company aircraft may have crashed or crash-landed somewhere because of storms that night, en route to Savannah. Maybe this is going to sound crazy, but are you certain this is my husband's aircraft?"

"No question. The tail number's correct." Dexter consulted a notebook he picked up. "The plane was registered to Benton Enterprises and flew under the logo of Brown Bear International, your husband's employer." His eyes stayed on me. "What line of work was your husband in exactly, Ms. Kelly?"

I forced myself to distract my gaze from the bones on the table, the feeling of nausea never leaving my stomach. "Corporate security and military training. He was a security adviser."

Tanner spoke up, filling in the rest. "Brown Bear provides bodyguards and protection consultants to American and foreign businesses operating in hostile overseas environments. They employ mostly U.S. former military. Right, Ms. Kelly?"

I nodded.

Dexter plucked through the objects lying on the bottom of the table using the big metal tweezers. "And you're certain none of these items looks familiar?"

"Positive."

"Weird. I would have thought you would recognize at least some of them. But then I guess there's a lot about this investigation that's strange." Dexter tossed aside the tweezers and shot Tanner a quick glance before his gaze settled on me. "I need to show you something that deepens this mystery."

14

Dexter moved off to whisper some words with the white-suited crew. They all stopped working and stepped aside before Dexter led us toward the wreckage.

The Beechcraft's main cabin looked intact except for the missing tail, but the fuselage was dented and crushed in places, and one half of a wing was completely sheared off. Weathered aluminum was eroded to a dull gray-black, and the white and blue paint was flaked. Inside the fuselage, I could see nothing beyond the filthy Plexiglas windows, streaked with black and mossy green lichen.

"Please don't tread outside the colored markers. Those areas haven't yet been thoroughly examined." As Dexter moved closer to the wreckage, he stayed within a path of red tape on either side.

"Your husband's aircraft departed New Orleans at eight-twenty p.m. We estimate it would have reached this area around about eleven p.m., local time. It's possible the pilot tried to pick out a landing spot once he hit trouble, and it looks like the plane came down at a shallow angle. All things considered, it landed pretty intact. This part of the forest is relatively flat, with some clearings."

"Do you know what caused the crash?"

"Not yet, and it'll likely take some time to find answers. Crashes are usually caused by a combination of events like weather, mechanical failure, or pilot error."

"I thought the aircraft would have exploded when it hit the ground."

"Not necessarily. The pilot could have ditched fuel before the crash, or maybe they were losing fuel, or ran out of it. And stormy, rainy weather would not have been conducive to a fire. But we'll know better when we remove the wreckage to our facility in Knoxville for a thorough investigation."

I dreaded setting my eyes on the place where my family had perished. But I needed to, even if it was freaking me out. I felt a shiver go through me and swept my arms around myself. Close up, I saw that some of the undergrowth around the aircraft had been excavated to a shallow depth, with a few trowels and sifters lying in the soil where the accident investigators were busy. "We've still got a lot of work to carry out, Ms. Kelly. But I'm hoping you may recognize some of the items we've already found."

As we stepped toward the fuselage, a powerful stench of mold and decay hit my nostrils.

Dexter guided me to the open cockpit door, its aluminum crinkled from the impact. He gently gripped my arm, whether to prevent me from moving in closer or to brace me for a shock I didn't know.

"If you could just look inside. And please be careful not to touch anything."

The closer to the fuselage we got, the more powerful the stench got. Part of the cramped cockpit was smashed in at the front, the nose cone either missing or flattened, I couldn't tell which. Everywhere there were torn-out panels, tangled cables, corroded wires, and smashed instruments, their shattered glass as jagged as shark's teeth. The cockpit floor was covered in a carpet of damp mud and forest debris.

I felt overcome. This was the last place my family was alive. I figure everyone was strapped in their seat belts in the storm, but in my mind's eye, I imagined their bodies tossed about violently as the aircraft smashed into the earth, their limbs mangled, their bones cracking, blood everywhere. I closed my eyes, whimpered, felt my body shaking. The image was too raw, too heart-wrenching.

When I opened my eyes, they were so wet I could hardly see. I wiped them with my hands. I noticed a folding table off to one side with some items on it, marked with identifier tags. Mostly aircraft parts. But one item stood out: an old aluminum briefcase. It appeared to be the same weathered color as the exposed fuselage, a dull gray-black. Dexter saw me notice the briefcase.

"We found it deep in some undergrowth about a hundred feet away, next to some metal debris from the other crash. I reckon it was thrown from the Beechcraft with the force of the crash. We've tried to pry it open, but it's wedged solid. Do you recognize the briefcase?"

"No. My husband used an old tan leather case he had for years."

Dexter pursed his lips in thought. "It's unlikely to be part of the aircraft's emergency equipment. It looks more like something personal. But we won't know until we get it open."

As I stared into the cockpit, I noticed one part of the inner wall low down had crumpled. Parts of the aluminum were crinkled like an accordion, and what looked like a cover of some kind had burst open, revealing an empty recess in the aircraft wall.

Dexter saw me notice it and said, "That's pretty weird."

"What is?"

"What you're looking at is some kind of nonregulation private storage area. It wasn't fitted by the manufacturer. It's after-factory and frankly kind of puzzling."

"A storage area for what?"

"Your guess is as good as mine."

I studied the scene again, trying to see if I could make out anything familiar in the muddied debris on the floor. And then something snagged my gaze. The air chilled ten degrees.

The object was half encrusted with a layer of soil, and the other half looked as if it had been cleaned away. I recognized the plastic cover from an old Pokémon Gameboy. Two Pokémon figures on the front, mud masking half of the images. It was Amy's favorite game. I'd packed it in her overnight bag myself. And then I saw it. A Barbie backpack. The color so faded and the material so stained and crumpled that it was hardly recognizable. Grief slashed like cold steel claws inside my chest, my distress so intense that I cried out with a whimper.

I went to touch the backpack. My hand seemed suspended in mid-air as Dexter grabbed it.

"Ms. Kelly, please remember. This area hasn't been completely forensically examined. You can't touch anything. I'm sorry."

Dexter let go of my hand. I scanned the cockpit for several more minutes, seeing nothing else, until my eyes made out on a mass of rotted wool on the left, near a doorframe. I knew that gray color. I could make out a woolen fold. Sean's beanie hat. This time I could not help myself and reached out to touch it. Dexter's hand fastened on mine once more, grasped it hard. "*Please*, Ms. Kelly. We have a job to do."

I started to cry. Dexter's other hand gripped my shoulder. I couldn't stop weeping. My shoulders heaved. I felt hands laid on me for support, and Dexter pulled me in close to his shoulder.

"I'm sorry. Truly I am. I know this must be difficult for you."

When I finally stopped crying, I wiped my eyes, and Dexter said gently, "The video game, the backpack . . ."

"They . . . they belonged to my daughter."

Tanner said, "Could I ask you to look inside again, please? It's important. Dexter, you have the light?"

Dexter took a penlight from his pocket, flicked it on. An intense, icy-blue light came on, the same color ultraviolet light pen I'd seen on TV programs like *CSI*. Dexter knelt so I could see over his shoulder. He shone the light on the muddied hat. The ultraviolet light circled over the hat, covering it in all the same color, except for one area where it revealed two black spots, no bigger than dimes, maybe four inches apart.

Dexter indicated the seating area behind the pilot's seat. "The children would have sat about here. Next to your husband, perhaps. The dark stains you see are traces of old blood."

I felt that stabbing pain again in my breastbone.

Dexter moved the blue light over the aircraft's interior walls, panels, and roof, then the leather seats. The panels had lots of black spots on the left-hand side, where the pilot must have sat. But there were no more black spots elsewhere, just blue light. The penlight moved to Amy's Pokémon game. A couple of very small black specks.

I felt myself gagging.

"We've scraped off some samples to have analyzed and will need to verify your children's blood types. There will have to be DNA tests. We'll need a blood sample from you to make a comparison. And from the pilot's family, too. The tests can take several weeks to complete. Three if we're lucky. But here's the thing." Dexter made a circling motion with the pen, over all the areas he'd just examined. "Apart from the pilot's area, what's remarkable is that there's so little blood."

"What . . . what do you mean?"

"A violent crash like that, I would have expected more blood. We know somebody's dead, likely killed by the blunt trauma of the crash. So I really would expect more blood and to see other remains. Some of the blood traces could have been weathered away by the elements in such an exposed environment, for sure. It's just that I expected to see more."

Dexter shone the beam all around the cockpit, upholstery, and seats, as if to prove something. "In fact, it makes me wonder."

"Wonder what?"

"No other bodies on board or in the undergrowth, at least that we've found so far. We've searched for three hundred yards' circumference. We've looked at the topography from the air. This area is desolate enough but not *that* desolate. There are maybe a dozen homes and small farms scattered within a couple of square miles."

He paused. "Actually, there's an abandoned wood shack maybe a hundred yards from here. Look that way, you may get a glimpse of it."

I followed the line of Dexter's finger. Beyond the trees I thought I saw the blackened and bleached wood of a ruined shack that looked as if it was barely standing.

"We found a little blood residue there, too."

"What are you saying?"

I looked at Dexter, waiting for something, but I didn't know what, except that I felt the moment was pregnant with a weird kind of expectation, like a rain cloud about to burst.

"Here's what's weird, Ms. Kelly. No more bodies and no excessive blood in the rear area to suggest serious injury to the passengers. Sure, your family could have wandered off into the forest and perished there, but we've searched and found no remains."

Dexter paused, pursing his lips. "If need be, we can even call in experts who would use ground-penetrating radar. We may well do that. But here's the clincher. Carole, could you fetch the evidence bag we looked at earlier?"

The forensics woman disappeared toward the canopy and returned carrying a clear plastic bag. Dexter took it and shone the blue light on the contents inside. It appeared to be a flashlight made of some kind of pale plastic material, discolored by the years, a small LED indicator on the shank.

Dexter said, "This here's the aircraft's emergency flashlight. All aircraft usually have them by law. We brushed off the debris and some dirt and managed to find this." He shone the blue light through the plastic bag. Faded but visible, I saw more black spots.

"Blood?"

"Yes, ma'am."

Dexter gave me a look. "We found the flashlight almost two hundred yards from the aircraft. The switch was in the on position. Somebody used it, maybe until the battery power ran out. We searched thoroughly around where the flashlight was located, but nothing else has shown up so far. We even did a rough search way out to the nearest main roadway."

"Where's that?"

"About a half mile away. It hooks up with a main highway. But the searches produced the same results, zilch. And something else kinda odd."

"What?"

"The aircraft's onboard first-aid kit is not there. I had a copy of the plane's certified inventory e-mailed to me, from the investigation back when it first went missing, and it lists that the kit was on board. But it's definitely gone."

He let it hang. I felt my heart pounding even faster and stared back at Dexter, waiting for the bombshell I sensed he was about to drop.

"Here's what we've got in my estimation, Ms. Kelly. Somebody—maybe more than one person—survived this crash eight years ago. I'm pretty certain of that from the lack of blood and remains. They not only survived, but I figure they could have made it out of these woods alive."

15

KEY WEST, FLORIDA

It was raining hard, a torrential downpour that lashed the streets, swaying the palm trees along Smathers Beach.

The tail end of the hurricane was hammering his Explorer's roof as the man pulled up at the Bayou Tavern in the Florida Keys. He ran inside the bar, trying to beat the rain, and pushed in the door.

It was a noisy place, a TV blaring, a dozen craggy-faced drinkers and a few tourists glancing around to eye the guy who entered.

He wore an old Tommy Bahamas shirt, creased cargo shorts and Nike flip-flops. He was starting to show his age, somewhere in the forties, with a three-day beard stubble and deep wrinkling around his eyes. In the dim light you had to look closer, but you could see the thick pink scars on his left hand and on his throat around his Adam's apple, where he wore a slim back bandanna. But even more noticeable was the left side of his face.

It was missing, along with his left eye and a good chunk of his jaw-bone. In their place was a false eye and a latex prosthesis of a color that looked like human flesh. He wore a Passy-Muir speaking valve attached to his throat with Velcro strips, most of it discreetly covered by the black bandanna. But the scars on his neck were a telltale reminder of where part of his voice box had been removed by surgeons. He was used to people trying not to notice, and he saw the bartender's eyes flicking to his prosthesis.

"What'll it be, buddy?"

"Miller Lite, from the tap." The man ran a hand through his wet hair.

"Sure."

The speaking valve helped make his voice sound normal, if a touch husky. The speaking valve didn't seem to faze the bartender, who ran a damp cloth across the countertop. "It's hitting pretty hard out there. They say it'll close the airports for a few days. You like to see a menu? Cajun shrimp is good."

"Yeah, why not?"

The bartender tossed aside the damp cloth and pulled an ice-cold Miller Lite, placed it on a mat on the counter, and slid across a menu.

The man lifted his beer to his mouth, his gaze drawn to the pretty woman on CNN. A slew of images flooded the screen—guys in jackets with NTSB lettering on the back, news-channel vehicles, cops, several small aircraft.

". . . The site of an air accident is being combed by NTSB staff for clues to a crash that occurred last night in severe weather in Tennessee's Smoky Mountains. A Kentucky couple was killed when their Cessna crashed in the area south of the national park. In a bizarre twist, it's understood that the forest where the downed aircraft was located turned up a grim discovery: yet another airplane crash, this one a mystery that has remained unsolved for almost eight years. Jack Hayes, an employee with international security company Brown Bear, vanished on a corporate flight from New Orleans to Savannah, along with his two children, ages five and eight, who were also on board. More about this story in our main newscast . . ."

The man stopped sipping his Miller Lite. Gaping at the screen, he felt his breath go stale in his lungs, until at last he exhaled.

The bartender said, "Weird one, huh? Been on the news all morning. Missing eight years, and now it shows up in some redneck backwoods. You want to try the shrimp?"

The man kept his stare on the screen, mesmerized.

"Mister?"

No response.

"Mister, hey, are you OK?"

The man was pale now, and he looked blankly at the bartender.

"If you don't like the shrimp, I can recommend the crab, sir."

"You're sure the airports are closed?"

"That's what the weather channels say. Wherever you want to get to, you're either going to have to wait until the storm passes or drive, mister. Shrimp or crab?"

"I'll pass." The man slapped a ten-dollar bill on the table and hurried out the door.

16

KNOXVILLE, TENNESSEE
3:06 P.M.

There are deep inlets in the human heart.

Deep rivers that contain our most savage hurts, our most painful wounds. The important word is *contain*. My mother used to say that this helps us submerge our grief, immerse our agony. Help us sink it for a while until we're strong enough to deal with whatever we need to deal with. I needed the calming waters of those inlets now.

Dexter's words were still ringing in my ears: *They not only survived, but I figure they could have made it out of these woods alive.*

I convinced myself that it was true.

I needed a soft place to fall and swallow me up as my mind raged with a million questions and a million thoughts. I felt my blood pressure rise. My head ached, as if a steel band were crushing my skull. The trauma of that morning was almost too much to take in. My mind was on a treadmill, my thoughts like a mantra.

Jack is alive. Jack is alive. Jack is alive.

And if Jack was alive, where were Sean and Amy? If they survived the crash, why did they disappear? Why? Where were they now? What did my children look like? How had they coped in the last eight years? Did they miss me, remember me, and still love me?

Had they really somehow survived? My temples pounded with rushing blood. My head hurt so much from thinking and fretting that it felt like a dam about to burst. I was convinced by now that my family had survived.

As Tanner accompanied me home in an unmarked police car, my body was rigid with shock. Tanner hardly spoke, his jaw stiff, as if he was mulling things over. I didn't feel much like talking, either.

Home was now my father's ten-acre farm. When Jack and I first married, when he was home from West Point or on leave, we moved into a cottage not far from the farmhouse. We loved it there. My father could babysit the kids whenever Jack and I wanted to go to the movies or out for dinner or I needed to go shopping.

We had planned on building our own home, had bought a lot with a lake view. But my father encouraged us to stay at the cottage. He even had an extra bedroom and play room built on. So we moved in and decorated. Pastel straw-yellow walls, lots of wood and stone, and to complete the cozy look, Jack fitted a potbelly woodstove. My father loved having the kids nearby, cherished the company. If we had moved, he'd have been alone on the farm, and he didn't seem to want that, and neither did Jack and I.

We kept promising ourselves we'd move someday. But Amy and Sean loved the farm, loved the space, the lakeside dock. For a time, my father kept a pony, a goat, and some chickens, until a coyote broke into the coop and feasted on the chickens. He kept an old motorboat, and the kids loved going out on the lake fishing with him.

After the "terrible tragedy" when Jack and Amy and Sean were no longer there, I moved back into my father's house, partly because he insisted on it and partly because I felt safer, needed his company, again needed the reassurance of his presence in my life. My father was all I had now.

Then, for two years, I lived with Chad, but after our divorce—you guessed it—my father insisted that I move back in with him. I did. I found it hard being alone in the cottage. Memories of Jack and Amy and Sean would crowd in on me. For a time, the lows got so low that I took Prozac. I found it hard just entering the cottage again. I didn't even clear it out after Jack and the children disappeared. I couldn't face that chore. Just couldn't. Besides, a part of me always wanted to believe they would come back again.

So I left everything as it was. For a time afterward, whenever I opened the front door that led straight into the living room, I would feel weak at the knees. My body would crumple. There was so much pain. So many good memories had become such a searing burden of grief.

My mom had kept a big old zinc bathtub from when I was a kid. I kept up the tradition by bathing Amy and Sean in the tub in front of the potbelly woodstove in the cottage's living room. I could never forget Amy's giggles as she played with an old shampoo bottle filled with sudsy water. She would spray it all over the tub and on me. And Sean, already bathed, playing with his Legos by the blazing stove, would be laughing at Amy but then complaining when she got too boisterous and started spraying him with the shampoo bottle.

Once, Sean was playing a game after supper and posed the question, "If our house was a dog, what kind of dog would it be, Daddy?"

Jack answered, "Easy. An old, comfortable Labrador."

He was right. Our home had that kind of feeling.

I remember us all having dinner in front of the stove some evenings. My father would stroll over from the farmhouse and join us for the chicken and dumplings and corn bread I'd cook or a pot roast with mashed potatoes and greens. In summer we'd sit out on the small patch of garden in front of the cottage, eating ice cream and watching the fireflies ignite the air by the lake. I cherished those days, ached at those bittersweet memories.

For a long time, whenever I stepped out onto the farmhouse's back patio and glimpsed the cottage, I would turn my head away. The memories were too agonizing. I couldn't even face going though my family's belongings. It was too much. Apart from cleaning out and unplugging the refrigerator and removing my own possessions, I left everything as it was—clothes in closets and in drawers, personal effects wherever they lay.

And then one day, I took six old pieces of two-by-four wood, grabbed a rusted hammer from my dad's barn, and nailed up the front and back doors. I couldn't bear to step into the cottage again.

My dad saw what I had done, but he said nothing. He had figured it out. He understood that love is sometimes a crucifying pain. The cottage had become like a mausoleum. A mausoleum I could not enter, unless I wanted to kill myself with remembered grief. I knew the consequences; if I entered it, I would be morbidly depressed for weeks. For a time—six months—I even leased an apartment in one of the many rental blocks in Cedar Bluff, just to give myself some space.

But after that, I came home to the farmhouse and my father's reassuring company and began to accept my plight. I never even considered that living in my father's house in my thirties would mess up my social life, cramp my style. Because I didn't really have a style for it to mess up. I lived in one end of the house, he in the other. We shared a kitchen and the living room. He had that male refuge, his study. And he would visit Ruby or friends a lot or go on hunting trips with buddies. I often had the farm to myself. I could have friends over anytime I wanted.

Now the mantra that had haunted those early days began to echo again in my head. *Jack is alive.* An inexplicable impulse raged inside me. I wanted to open up those cottage rooms once more. Wanted to but felt afraid and uncertain. Could I face bursting open those nailed-up doors? Could I step up to my fear?

Tanner finally broke the silence and broke into my thoughts. "I'm going to ask the local sheriff to post a couple of his men at your house in case the news media bother you. We'll keep it that way until we figure this thing out, if we can."

He looked over at me. "You can be pretty sure the news reporters will be on your case as soon as they start putting things together, but we'll keep them away until you're ready or willing to talk. Really, you don't have to say a thing."

"There—there's a private back road that leads to my father's farm. It's quicker."

"That's where you live?"

I nodded.

"Is your father home?"

"No." I explained about Ruby's illness and gave directions.

Five minutes later, as Tanner chatted with the police driver and just as I checked the time on my cell—3:15—it rang. The jangle of music wracked my shot nerves. I didn't recognize the number. I was half tempted to ignore the call, but then I wondered if it was a friend or a relative. I flicked it on.

"Hello."

There was a pause for a second, and then a firm, husky male voice spoke. It sounded distant, almost otherworldly, like a hard whisper. "I'll call you in exactly thirty minutes. Make sure you're alone when you answer."

I felt something ice-cold clutch at my chest. "Who . . . who is this?"

"You know who it is, Kath. Don't talk to the police. Don't tell them about this call. Don't tell anyone, or this will be the last time we talk."

There was another pause.

"I mean it—it *will* be the last time. You tell no one. I can't emphasize that enough. In thirty minutes, be ready to take my call. If there's anyone listening or if you tell anyone I contacted you, we'll never talk again. And believe me, I'll know. Thirty minutes."

The line went dead.

I glanced at Tanner, who was staring out the car window as we approached my home. I felt a chill as frigid as a Siberian wind cut into my heart. There was no mistaking the husky voice I'd just heard.

Not in a million years.

It was Jack.

17

MACON, GEORGIA

The man ended the call.

Rain still hammered down, slamming into the concrete, relentless thunder rumbling, as he turned into the Love's gas station off I-75.

He paid for his gas and grabbed a coffee to keep awake, and when he'd filled up his tank, he jumped back into the Explorer, shaking rain from his shirt and pushing back his floppy wet hair. He turned on the Garmin and was impatient for it to fire up. "Come, on, come on!" He wanted to scream.

The screen came alive, and he punched in his destination in Knoxville, Tennessee. The Garmin offered two routes. He chose the first, having the shorter time. Almost five hours. Three hundred miles, most of it on I-75.

A lot more driving, and bad weather and traffic delays might make it even longer. But he had to do this before things got out of control. TV images of the crashed aircraft raged through his mind. Eight years. Eight years had gone by in the blink of an eye.

His hand was already searching under his seat, making sure he had the Kimber .45 automatic. He felt the loaded gun and slid it back beneath the seat. The Explorer's engine throbbed as he hit the ignition.

He turned out of the gas station with screeching tires and sped north onto I-75.

18

KNOXVILLE, TENNESSEE

"Everything OK, Ms. Kelly?"

I couldn't breathe. I fought to keep my voice steady, to hold my emotions in check. My hand clutched my throat as Tanner shot me a look in the back of the unmarked cop car. "Y-yes."

But everything wasn't OK. My heart was beating so wildly I thought I was going to have a heart attack. I felt as if the ground could give way beneath me at any second.

"Who just called?"

"A . . . a friend. I didn't feel up to talking."

I desperately wanted to tell Tanner the truth, but in my heart I knew Jack meant what he'd said. Tanner looked skeptical, but my distress may have convinced him, and he gave a nod. Ten long minutes later, we pulled up in the farmhouse driveway and climbed out. I checked the time on my phone. It was 3:25. Jack's call came at exactly 3:15. I had twenty minutes before he called again. I felt so anxious that my legs were shaking, my throat dry. We went up onto the back porch and into the kitchen.

I usually wrote at a small desk in a corner of the kitchen. It held my laptop and a notepad on top and some pens stuffed into an old Starbucks mug. A comfortable old study chair completed all I needed, apart from the shelf full of books on my right. Novels, nonfiction works, old books of my mom's, all stuff I'd read over the years. A Hewlett Packard printer and some loose pages.

Tanner gave it all a glance. "You work from home?"

"Yes."

"What do you do, Ms. Kelly?"

"I'm a writer. Or at least, I'm trying to be."

"Yeah? You been published?"

"Not yet."

Tanner gave me an arched eyebrow as if to say, *Dream on, baby.*

"Could I impose and ask you for a coffee?"

"I . . . I'm really stressed out, Mr. Tanner. I need to rest."

"I know, ma'am, but this won't take long."

"Can't it wait?"

"Not really. It's important."

"Can you help yourself?"

"Sure."

Tanner was already moving to the Keurig coffee machine to make a cup. I must have looked so numb he figured he'd be faster doing it himself. He fiddled with the machine and popped in a fresh pod.

When I glanced at the kitchen clock again, I noticed it was one minute out of sync with my watch, the wall clock being ahead. Sixteen minutes left. I was starting to panic. What if Tanner wasn't gone in time? What if Jack rang back and he was still here and overheard or sensed my unease?

"Coffee, ma'am?"

"No. No, thank you." I found the creamer and the sugar and handed them across, with a spoon.

My eyes kept flicking to the wall clock as the Keurig gurgled and Tanner's mug filled with coffee. He added a spoonful of creamer and a half of sugar. "If Dexter is right, well, we'll need to go over a lot of stuff. Including all the questions you were asked back when your husband and children first disappeared. Tedious, I know, but it has to be done."

"What kind of questions?"

"I'm looking for motives, Ms. Kelly. Reasons why your husband may have vanished and not come back. Putting aside the possibility that he may have suffered head injuries that affected his thinking and maybe caused memory loss . . ."

Tanner sighed. "Then there's the whole big question as to what the aircraft was doing in an area it wasn't supposed to be in that night. It was supposed to be flying southeast toward Savannah and two hundred miles away. We'll be checking that with your husband's former employer. But what about you? Are you sure you've no idea why that was?"

"Of course not."

Tanner coughed into his fist, as if he disliked having to say what he said next or it was delicate. "That's why I'll need to ask you some personal questions. I don't necessarily want to ask them, Ms. Kelly, but they need to be asked."

This was no time to encourage conversation, but I didn't want to seem even more on edge. "I'm listening."

"What can you tell me about your marriage to Jack?"

Alarm bells started going off inside my head. "You think the state of my marriage has something to do with all this?"

"Maybe it has nothing to do with it. Or maybe everything. That's what I'm trying to figure out."

"My marriage was good," I lied. "Very good."

It's easy to fool ourselves. I used to do it all the time. When I was a child, I knew my mother drank too much. Whether because of an errant strand of addiction in her DNA, the stress of my father's rootless military life, or her deep unhappiness at the way her life had turned out, I have no idea. But I used to pretend the problem wasn't so bad. Until one day, when I was nine and I found a dead jaybird lying by some hedges in our back lawn.

I wondered about that jaybird. Had it simply died of old age? Was it hit by some kid firing a BB gun, or had it struck an electric pylon? Nearby I spotted an empty vodka bottle lodged in a nest in the hedges—the bottle's trajectory on a clear path from my mother's bedroom window—and the case was solved. There was no more pretending. Even to a nine-year-old, my mother throwing liquor bottles recklessly out of windows smacked of a disturbing problem.

I lied to myself about Jack, too. We were destined to meet, I felt sure of that and that our children and our love for them were part of that destiny. Sometimes I think the universe knows better than we do, and it conspires to arrange certain events within our lives. But things were not perfect between Jack and me. While our relationship may have had some celestial purpose, our marriage wasn't made in heaven. The last six months were truly lousy. But I didn't want to dwell on that now.

"OK if I come by later or tomorrow and we talk some more?"

"Y-yes. Tomorrow might be better."

"Are you sure you're OK, Ms. Kelly?"

"Yes . . . yes . . . no . . . I don't know. I'm just stressed out. Confused."

"I understand." He nodded and sipped his coffee. "Coffee's good."

"Thank you. If you like, you can take the coffee with you."

"Ma'am?"

"There are some Styrofoam cups somewhere."

"No, I'm good. I'll just finish it."

"It's just, I'd really like to lie down." The wall clock in the kitchen told me I had eight minutes. *Please, just go!* I wanted to scream. *Just go, and leave me alone to take Jack's call.*

But Tanner didn't seem inclined to go anywhere just yet. He jerked his chin toward a photograph hanging on the wall. My father in his colonel's uniform, taken in Iraq, standing in front of a Humvee with a bunch of his men. "What about your dad?"

"I'll . . . contact him."

He took a closer look at some other photographs. "You sure you don't want me to do that for you?"

"No. No . . . I'll do it." The wall clock said five more minutes.

Tanner pointed at one of the photos. "That's a lot of ribbons and medals your old man's wearing."

"Yes. Is there anything else, Agent Tanner?"

"Yeah. If Dexter's hypothesis is right, then Jack may still be alive. This is all over the news. He's bound to see it. And as the story pans out, they're going to have shots of you up there on the screen, with him and the kids, just wait and see."

"What are you saying?"

Tanner shrugged. "Who knows, maybe it'll play on his mind. Maybe he'll get the urge to contact you."

"*What?*"

"The news is out there now, in the public domain. I've known it to happen with missing person cases that once a story gets a lot of air time, the missing person gets in touch. It may be a possibility in this case. So if there are any calls or any kind of contact from Jack, you let me know at once. You got that?"

More alarm bells should have gone off with statements like those, but I already felt so dazed, I barely took them in. "What reason would he have to contact me?"

Tanner gave a tight smile. "I've no idea, Ms. Kelly. I'm just thinking out loud. Telling you my experience in missing persons cases I've worked. There could be all kinds of reasons. Regret, grief, curiosity. Who knows?"

I still desperately wanted to tell Tanner, *He just has called me.* If only because my mind was raging with the news and I was so deeply perplexed. What would happen *after* the call? Would I see my children? Had they even survived? What would happen if Jack didn't call back? My anxiety level was through the roof.

Tanner laid his cup down on the kitchen table.

The next time I looked at the clock, I had four minutes. My heart beat even faster, my blood pressure boiling. "I-I'm really stressed, Mr. Tanner. Please, I need to lie down."

"Sure. I need to head back to the site. See if they got that aluminum case open yet or found anything else."

He wrote another number on the back of his card. "If you need me for any reason, you can get me on my cell. I'll give you my other number, too."

I walked him to the front door.

"You're sure there's nothing you didn't tell the first time around, Ms. Kelly?"

"I'm sure. I don't understand any of this."

For some reason, Tanner didn't look like he believed me. "So you've really got no idea why he might have vanished? Something in his past? Secrets and lies he kept?"

"Not a single one."

I meant it. But I could tell by Tanner's face that he was unconvinced. He still wasn't in any hurry, either.

I put a hand to my forehead. "Look, I'm sorry. I need to close my eyes and rest. It's been difficult. . . ."

"Sure. Take care."

I let him out the front door. I watched him walk down the pathway, climb into his car, and drive off. I stared at my watch. I had one minute.

I felt it hard to breathe, my adrenaline soaring in anticipation. I began to doubt that I'd even received the call. Was I going crazy? Was it all in my mind? Was I so distressed that I'd imagined it?

Thirty seconds later, my cell phone rang.

19

It rang again.

The number was unlisted.

I answered on the second ring.

"Kath?"

The voice I heard sounded distant, otherworldly. Or was that just my imagination, part of the trauma of hearing Jack's voice again? For a moment, I didn't reply. My own voice was gone. I was in deep shock, my reply strangled in my throat.

"Kath, are you there?"

Oh, my God. Jack. Back from the dead. That voice I knew so well. It was him. It was *really* him. I had not imagined it. Eight years. Eight years, one month, three days.

"Yes."

"Are you alone?"

"Yes."

"Are you sure?"

"I promise. Is . . . is it really you, Jack?"

"You know it's me. And if you're lying about being alone, I'll find out."

"Jack, I'm not lying. I'm telling you the truth. Why would I lie?"

"I want you to listen."

"Amy and Sean. Where are they? Where?" I sounded frantic, like a crazy woman. I heard the wild panic in my own voice, like someone on the verge of a breakdown.

He didn't answer.

"Jack, please . . . don't do this to me. I need to know. I need the truth."

"For now, just listen to me. Listen carefully. This is really important."

I knew I seemed deranged. I *felt* deranged. But my senses were still sharp enough to sense something in Jack's voice, something rare.

I sensed fear. Raw fear. What was he afraid of? Or was my imagination haywire?

"For God's sake, Jack, I need to see my children. Don't you get it? I *have* to see them." My pleading was so pitiful, my voice a cry.

"We've got thirty-three seconds left."

"What?"

"That's how much longer it could take to trace my call. Then I'm going to switch off."

"Jack, no one's tracing the call. I told no one."

A tight pause. "Just listen. You'll see Sean, you'll see Amy—"

"When, Jack? When?" I felt tears scald my face. "When? Oh, God, I . . . I'm still in shock."

"Twenty-three seconds left, Kath. You need to listen to me right now, or I'll end the call."

I fell silent at the threat.

"Two p.m. tomorrow. I'll call you. Two on the nail. We'll talk then, and you'll know everything."

That was twenty-two hours away. "What . . . what if you don't call?"

"I'll call. When I do, you answer. If you need proof it's me, I've left proof."

"Where?"

"The Fifth Lock. Bottom of the black trash can by the park bench, you'll find a brown paper bag. I left it there an hour ago. Until then, the same rules apply. Tell no one, and be alone."

"Jack—but Amy and Sean . . ."

"Do exactly as I say, and you'll see them."

"Jack, why? Why did you do it? Why? Why did you cut my heart out? Why?"

My words sounded like an echo in my own head, the last "why" ringing in my ears.

I heard the faint click.

And the line went dead.

20

I stood in the kitchen, feeling strangely numb.

Numb but alive. I felt the weight of eight years of grief and anguish lift from me like the heaviness of a massive stone. My heart was thudding against my breastbone. I couldn't speak, even if I wanted to.

Eight years.

After eight years of believing my husband was dead, he called. No explanation, no reasons, no answer about why he was a dead man walking again. Nothing about what happened to my son and daughter.

Was it really Jack? But he mentioned the Fifth Lock, a stretch of waterway three miles away, with public moorings, where we used to take Jack's bass boat out when we were engaged, heading out to the islands or an isolated bank to picnic and smooch. It was our place, a special place, for private times alone.

I felt frantic.

I hurried outside to the barn. The Polaris Ranger that my dad used to drive around the farm was parked there. The Fifth Lock was less than ten minutes away. The key was in the Ranger's ignition. I climbed in and turned it on, the little engine sputtering, and I reversed out of the barn.

My heart thudding, my breath shallow, I drove onto the bumpy track that led down to the lake.

It was the longest ten minutes of my life.

I followed the rutted track until I came to a lakeside walkway. Some benches, a wooden pergola. A black metal garbage bin on a metal stake.

I drove up to the bin, braked, and frantically jumped out.

This part of the lakeside was remote. No one about.

I reached the trash can. It had a black plastic liner. The thought that Jack had actually been here an hour ago freaked me out. I looked inside the bin. A few Coke cans, blackened banana peel, some junk-food packaging. A brown paper bag at the bottom.

I reached in, plucked it out.

The bag was bulky, but it felt light. Something hard at the bottom, metallic maybe.

My rib cage felt tight with anxiety.

I opened the bag and looked inside.

A jumble of blue and purple cloth.

My chest felt even tighter.

I tossed the contents out onto the damp grass and sat down beside them.

I recognized a blue sweater. It was Sean's.

A purple hoodie. Amy's.

I'd packed them in their go-away bags before they vanished.

I wanted to cry.

I gathered up the clothes, pulled them to my face, as if I could smell them, touch my children, by touching these clothes.

They smelled faintly of lavender, as if freshly washed. A set of keys fell out of the garments.

Two keys on a metal key ring, with a big silver-toned *J* on it.

I recognized Jack's old keys to our home's front and back doors.

I felt light-headed. My throat spasmed, and I almost choked. I couldn't breathe. The same haunting questions echoed inside my head. *Why? Why? Why? Why? Why?*

And my children. *Where are my children? What's happened to them?*

My cell phone rang, loud and sharp. It was an old friend of mine from college, Lois Snow, calling to chat as she sometimes did. I had neither the strength nor the inclination to answer it. It was as if I were anesthetized.

It was all too much. And then I felt it, a wave of fear and shock that roared in on me like a violent, crashing wave. As I tried to stand straight, I lurched toward the Ranger.

All I remembered after that was that my head started to swim, my legs collapsed from under me as if made of rubber, and everything turned to darkest black.

21

I don't know for how long I was out cold, but the dizziness was still there when I became conscious again.

It lasted a few minutes, until the fog finally cleared. I sat there on the grass until I felt I could get up. My head still felt light as I picked up the clothes and the keys and the bag. I placed them on the Ranger's passenger seat, and then I drove back to my home as fast as my muzzy head would allow.

I didn't recall a single second of the drive. At the barn, I parked the Ranger and moved into the front room. I sat on the couch, staring at the clothes. I smelled them again, inhaling the lavender scent.

I felt elated. I felt lethargic. My mind was too frazzled to think about anything else, but in moments of panic mundane ideas sometimes strike you. One struck me now. It was Wednesday. My day for getting things ready to visit Kyle on Thursday morning. I had to get his clean clothes together, other stuff. It's crazy the things you think of when you're in shock.

I tried to compose myself, but I felt as if I was falling apart. I tried to tell myself I was OK. But I wasn't.

I was far from OK.

Like a sleepwalker, I climbed the stairs to my bedroom, undressed, and showered. After I toweled myself dry, I put on fresh jeans and a T-shirt and went to lie on my bed.

I felt numb, confused.

I couldn't help but stare at the two photographs on the nightstand. Every night before I slept and every morning when I woke, they were there. I reached across and picked up the silver-toned frame.

As I focused on the faces of Jack and Sean and Amy, the same questions raged. Could they *really* be alive? The haunting question was like an ache.

I recalled the raw fear in Jack's voice.

Or was I picking it up wrong, my senses frazzled by everything that was happening? Was it just anxiety on Jack's part?

I couldn't be sure, but it *sounded* like fear. I looked out through the window.

The cottage was fifty yards away. I saw the white door, the paint flaking in places. Three pieces of old two-by-four were still nailed into the door's wood and frame. Another three were nailed into the back door. The curtains were closed, as I had left them. The last time I went in there was five years ago, after Chad and I split. It almost killed me. Everything was just as it had been the day I boarded up the property, and the surge of grief that hit me almost smothered me the moment I stepped inside the hall.

Inexplicably, I still wanted to go in there. I had a weird feeling in my gut. It was as if the rooms still held some as-yet-undiscovered secret, some clue I had not discovered. I was afraid. Afraid of another tidal wave of emotions. But the urge still niggled and persisted.

I would try to psych myself up to do it.

But not yet.

Not just yet.

I shifted my gaze toward Loudon Lake and the graceful weeping willow that I planted twenty years ago, its branches dripping over the water. Memories came in a torrent. Times we enjoyed together— distant days, but I remembered them like yesterday. Picnics. Birthdays. Special times on the lake when the children were small. Lazy Sundays, holiday weekends.

I recalled Buddy, a black border collie with white paws that we had for two years until he got run over by a truck. Amy and Sean were inconsolable. Jack buried the dog under the willow tree I was looking at now.

Amy wanted the dog buried there. "Because I'll always be sad that Buddy died, and weeping willows are like sad trees, aren't they, Mommy?"

No more dogs after that. It was too painful. A hamster and a gold-fish fit the bill.

I recalled other moments: Jack's thirtieth birthday when I bought him a David Gray CD and we made love in the dark that night as the Stairs played softly in the background. I felt so complete that night, so totally complete—so loved and part of a loving, healing family. I felt like crying.

I ached to feel them near me again, to smell them, to touch them. But if I was honest, my mind couldn't really handle Jack's seeming treachery. I had such mixed feelings that I was sure I hated him. After hearing Tanner's news, I'd felt a fearful sense of joy, but now a fero-cious, vehement anger was seeping in. How could Jack have done this to me? How could he have kept the children we both cherished and loved from me? And why? I wanted to scream the questions aloud.

My headache started again. I had a desperate urge to talk to my father. I fumbled for my cell and called him. He answered on the second ring.

"Kath? Are you home yet? Are you OK, honey?"

"Yes. Where are you, Dad?"

"Two hundred miles from Michigan. I was just about to call you. I stopped at a Comfort Inn for the night and just saw the news. I saw the wreckage. I-I'm dumbfounded."

I heard the distress in his voice, the Parkinson's tremble. "Did you take your meds?"

"No. I'll take them now. This is more important."

"Dad, there's stuff we need to talk about."

"Did . . . did they find Jack and the children?"

"Not yet. They're not sure. They're still examining the site."

I heard what sounded like a cry, an exclamation of grief. "Not sure? I don't get it."

"I'll explain once I have more information, Dad."

"I'm coming home. I'll get back on the road first thing in the morning. Tonight, if you want me to."

"No, Dad, your place is with Ruby right now. She needs you. At least see her first."

"*You* need me."

"I'm doing OK, really."

I was desperate to tell him about Jack's call. It ate inside me like a cancer. But I dared not. Knowing my father, he'd jump into his car and drive straight back, right through the night. I didn't want him to do that. I didn't want him to get tired and total his car.

But I wished he wasn't so far away. He was the rock I always leaned on when things got rough. I felt I needed to lean on his broad shoulders now and be comforted by him. Sometimes nothing can replace the sense of solid security a father can impart. "Don't do it, you hear me, Dad?"

"Can't you tell me anything at all, honey?"

"There's nothing more to tell. They may have more news tomorrow."

He must have heard the tired upset in my voice, because he didn't pursue it. "Are you coping OK?"

"Strangely, yes. But I promise I'll call you if I need you."

"Kath, I don't know . . ."

"I promise. Please believe me. Get a good night's sleep, see Ruby, and then we'll talk tomorrow."

He sighed.

"*Please*, Dad."

There was a long pause. It was getting late. I felt tired. He must have heard the fatigue in my voice.

Finally, he gave in. "Hang in there, baby. And remember, I'm just a phone call away, no matter what the time. Just pick up that phone if you need me."

"I will."

22

THE PAST

There's a Hooters T-shirt logo that kind of sums up the South: "Delightfully tacky, yet unrefined."

The South has a kindness and a charm that are warmly eccentric, a touch wacky, jagged around the edges. As my mother used to say, a Southerner will bless your soul and then slap you six ways from Sunday, gossip about your deepest secrets on the grounds that "we need to pray for them," and still come by with a smile and a home-baked pie.

Although I come from a military family, I wish I didn't.

I used to aspire to a normal existence, one where my father's armed-forces background didn't intrude on every facet of my life because we often lived on or near a base. I'm more of a dreamer, a reader of books, not the spit-and-polish parade-ground stomper.

But my father's ancestors saw service in every major battle since the War of Independence, and as a consequence, my early life was spent as a military brat at Fort Campbell, on the borders of Tennessee and Kentucky.

As lives go, it was rich in drama.

Maybe the wild, Celtic DNA in our blood had a fatal taste for it or maybe it was just bad luck, but the drama was about to go off the clock when my mother arrived at Cedar Springs Church for my wedding.

And what was to unfold in the wicked heat of an August day in Knoxville—what was to forever maim my soul with a festering scar— seemed to set the tone for everything bad that came after.

23

After I ended my father's call, I got my handgun from a drawer in the kitchen.

I really don't know why. Maybe I felt safer. I'd had a handgun conceal-carry permit for years, which allowed me to carry a loaded firearm on my person. I was no great gun lover, but when I was in my late teens, my dad insisted that I learn how to defend myself. My silver-toned Taurus .38 revolver gave me a feeling of security when I was home alone or when I traveled. I often kept it in my car's glove compartment or in a drawer, by my nightstand, or in my purse.

Now I took it with me. I felt a strange, inexplicable instinct to protect myself. My gut, a fear of the unknown.

I left Jack's old keys on the kitchen table, but I could not let go of the blue sweater and the purple hoodie. I clutched them as tightly as a drowning man might clutch a life buoy.

I sat in my room and picked up the two photographs by my bed. I held them close to me, as if they were delicate lace. After I finally laid them down again, I took two pillows and padded into my mother's bedroom. I hated this bedroom. Hated it with all its associations of grief and pain and tumult. This was the place where she'd faced her final moments, where she took her life. But for some reason, I needed to be here, to be comforted by my mother's long-gone presence, as troubling as it so often was to me. But not now. Now she was that soft place to fall.

I looked toward the far wall. The safe was still there, behind my mother's portrait. Her eyes looked out at me. Those thin, unhappy lips seemed to emphasize her unhappiness, and those deep brown eyes forever guarded her secrets.

And her dress.

Red.

That word again.

What did it mean?

I stared out at the lake and the view my mother looked upon on her last day. The waters calm, an occasional motorboat passing, a single white sail in the distance. Probably the same last images my mother saw before she pulled the trigger.

Eight years. Eight long, agonizing years, and I was going to see my children again.

They say death is the cruelest blow. The hardest cross to bear. But it's not. Hope is harder. And when you live with it for months and years, when every day it worms its way into your heart and eats it away from the inside, it leaches your energy. You cannot stop it. You cannot reconstruct your life. In a way, that hope becomes no hope. You are a prisoner who can never be free. Not until you have proof positive.

Now I had proof.

Not proof of death but proof of life.

At least, that's how I perceived it. A door had opened.

And while I was filled with hope, I was obsessed by fear.

What revelations lay ahead? What shocks? As my mother liked to say, when one door closes, another one opens. But it's the hallways in between that kill you.

I pressed the blue sweater and the purple hoodie to my face and inhaled. Overcome again, I felt I was breaking down, a floodgate was opening, drenching me with memories. As if something inside me was starting to tear apart. I recalled a hot July day by the lake with Jack and Amy and Sean. I made a picnic, and Amy played and giggled in the grass next to me, a powerhouse of life as usual, wearing that purple hoodie, until the heat finally got to her and she fell asleep in my arms.

Sean and Jack were by the water, pretending to be bears, fighting and rolling in the grass, Sean's laughter saturating the air. He wore the blue sweater that day, until his child's body was drenched in sweat and he peeled it off and went bare-chested. I recalled the smell of Amy's hair; I'd washed it that morning in apple-scented shampoo. They were achingly wonderful memories, yet these were the ones that hurt most of all, because of their simplicity and beauty. I felt beyond tears, and yet I wanted to cry, but then the numbness I longed for suddenly washed over me.

Why I had no idea, but perhaps it was because I was being pulled by two polar emotions at once: hope and dread. Hope that my children might be alive and dread that they might not.

I stared at my watch: 5:55 p.m. I had just more than twenty hours before Jack called again. It seemed so far away. Could I bear to wait that long? As quickly as I felt numb, I felt raw again, brittle, fragile as a reed. And exhausted. As if a tiny whisper of wind would knock me down.

Still, I opened a window. Darkness was falling, the light in the western sky an aching burnt amber. There was a slight breeze. It brushed my face.

Moments later I laid my head on the soft pillows, closed my eyes, and wept, deep, violent convulsions that racked my body, and every wicked part of my life seemed to flash before me.

24

Dusk. The smoky amber sky the color of fire.

Lights blazed around the crash site. The hum of electric generators sounded like a zillion angry mosquitoes.

Brewster Tanner emptied the last of the peanut M&M's from the bag as he watched the NTSB crew finish up their work for the evening. He crunched the candy, swallowed, and crumpled the empty packet, slipping it into his pocket.

The dizzying sugar rush came seconds later.

He fumbled for the hypodermic pen in his other pocket and lifted his shirt to reveal the rolls of stomach flesh. Slapping the pen into the fat, he depressed the plunger. When he took the pen away, a faint speck of blood stood out against his dark flesh. He started to feel better.

"Hey, you're back. My wife swears by a vegetarian diet, by the way. She's got the curse, too." Dexter came out of the tent, his shirt patched with sweat.

"Yeah?" Tanner stared over the NTSB man's shoulder, past a crack in the tent flap. He glimpsed the aluminum briefcase from the cockpit laid out on a table. It was unlocked, spread open, a black plastic garbage bag laid over it.

Dexter took a cloth neckband from his pocket and wiped sweat from his face and throat. "For dinner and lunch, use a teaspoon of oil to stir-fry all the vegetables you care to eat, add some soy sauce, a little ginger or spices if you like. Helped her lose fifty pounds, got her blood sugar right down. Ever try a diet like that?"

Tanner tucked in his shirt. "That and a million others. Story of my life. Lost three pounds a month ago. Put on four this week."

"Exercise?"

"Hey, keep that dirty word to yourself. You done for tonight?"

"Yeah, we'll keep a watch crew on-site, to keep the local sheriff's deputies company. It's getting late. We'll carry on tomorrow and try to wrap it up as fast as we can. You eat lunch or dinner?"

"Yeah, earlier. Saw a Subway ten miles back on the main road. Got me a meatball sub the size of a small torpedo. I reckoned I needed to put on a nose bag before I passed out." Tanner jerked his head toward the tent. "So, you find anything interesting?"

"You sure could say that." Dexter finished mopping his face, tucked the neckband into his pocket, and glanced up at the burnt-orange sky. It was really quite stunning, with the darkening outlines of the Smoky Mountain peaks. "That's an awesome sunset. You from around here, Tanner?"

"Naw. Hometown's a place called Jameson, Louisiana."

"Never heard of it."

"Man, you wouldn't want to. Lived in a neighborhood that was tough as a jockey's hide. The German shepherds used to go round in pairs, just to stay safe. Home sweet home was a trailer at the end of a dirt road."

"Happy times."

"You kidding? I never really knew my dad. My mom's sister helped take care of me for a few years when I went through a rebel phase. She was a teacher. Made sure I got my grades."

Tanner stared at the remains of the shack.

"I used to dream of living in a shack like that. Inside toilet, a piece of land to do some growing. Not have to share a room with three female cousins."

"Sounds like some guys have all the luck."

"Not if you have to wait in line for an hour to get into the bathroom. So, I see you guys got the aluminum case open. You find anything inside?"

"Something weird, Tanner. Mucho weird, in fact. Let me show you."

25

Tanner followed Dexter into the tent. Two techs in white boiler suits were finishing up examining part of an aircraft engine.

Dexter stood over the black plastic sheet covering the briefcase and grabbed a fresh pair of forensics gloves from a box.

Tanner said, "You find any more remains?"

"Nope."

"What about personal effects?"

"Nada. But you know my theory."

"Yeah, I know it, Einstein."

Dexter slipped on one of the forensics gloves. "One or all of the remaining passengers survived."

"A crash like that?"

"A small aircraft. Low undergrowth with a clearing. No fireball. I've seen enough crash sites in my day. I reckon it's possible."

"How many you think survived?"

"Maybe all of them. But I figure at least one survivor walked out of here, for sure. By the way, we've searched the entire site pretty thoroughly and still haven't found the aircraft's first-aid kit."

"Yet."

Dexter shrugged a *whatever you think*.

Tanner said, "Could it have been stolen?"

"You mean, did someone scavenge the site?"

"I guess."

"If that was the case, they would have taken more than just a first-aid kit. I've known scavengers to strip a crash site to the bones, like piranhas. But there's no evidence there's been any tampering."

"You sound pretty certain, Dexter."

"Bet my pension plan on it."

"Yeah? I wouldn't care to bet mine. The feds ain't that generous."

"We also found more small blood smears. We can have those checked against the family DNA."

"And why here? What was it doing near Knoxville? The pilot was supposed to be on his way to Savannah. He wasn't due in Knoxville until the following evening."

"You got me there. I checked. The flight plan the pilot filed would have put the aircraft almost two hundred miles away, heading toward Savannah, when it vanished."

"Ain't that weird?"

"Mucho."

"Didn't radar pick it up or something?"

"Yeah, it had a transponder identifier."

"A what?"

"Aircraft have a unique code pertinent only to that aircraft during its flight. It's transmitted to ATC—air traffic control—by something called a transponder. That way, air traffic control knows where the aircraft is, relative to altitude, speed, and direction of heading. Atlanta records show that the transponder signal vanished off ATC screens about forty-five minutes before the aircraft was due to land in Savannah and about a hundred and sixty miles south of here."

"Which tells us?"

Dexter shrugged. "It could tell us that there was a catastrophic event on board and that the aircraft was lost. But we know it didn't disappear in that area or disintegrate, because we found it here. The aircraft was still flying."

"Anything else the vanished signal could tell us?"

"Yeah, that the transponder simply became unserviceable. Or it could have been deliberately switched off."

"On purpose? Why would that happen?"

Dexter made a face. "If a pilot wanted to fly a route or land without air traffic control knowing about it, maybe."

"For what reason?"

"Your guess is as good as mine. But illegal activity of some sort would be high on the motive list."

"You think that could have been a likely scenario?"

Dexter gave a fleeting smile. "Hey, you're the law, baby. I guess anything's possible. I mean, what's your definition of illegal? That's a broad beam, my man."

Tanner considered and ran two fingers over a part of the mangled engine. He saw that the techs were heading off, heard the sound of vehicles starting up.

"You look like a man with something on his mind, Tanner."

"You know much about the missing husband?"

"Nothing."

"Interesting past."

"Yeah?"

An edge of bitterness crept into Tanner's voice. "Eight years ago, when he vanished, I was on the case."

"Why didn't you say that before now?"

"Wasn't important."

"So, you're still looking for him?"

"This is between you and me, OK?"

"Sure."

"I mean it, Dexter."

"Won't tell a soul."

"A month after Jack Hayes vanished, my house was burned down one night. My wife died in the blaze. I hit the bottle. Had to take six months off work on health grounds."

Dexter's face showed alarm. "Gee, heavy stuff. You have kids?"

"Naw. There was just me and Lorrie. I reckon someone tried to put me off the scent. Tell me it was personal."

"What scent?"

Tanner didn't answer.

Dexter said, "You're saying there's more to this than I know?"

"Yeah, a lot more."

"Can you tell me?"

Tanner shook his head. "We're straying into the realm of case confidentiality, bro."

Dexter raised an eyebrow. "They get anyone for the arson?"

"Never. Case is still open but no suspects. That's why I need you to give me your all on this one. Help me in every way you can. No matter how small the details seem, I want to hear them. And I want to hear them first. Will you do that for me, please, Dexter?"

"Sure, man. I'll do my absolute best."

"In a way, it's why my gut's telling me the guy's former wife may be in serious danger."

"From what?"

"Her husband. If he survived the crash, I'm betting he'll turn up."

"For what reason?"

"Can't go into that. This case has a lot of confidential stuff. Fact is, CID is involved on this case with me, but the feds have supremacy."

"You mean the military Criminal Investigation Division?"

"Yes, sir."

"But you sound sure about the threat," Dexter said.

"If he's still alive, yeah, I feel sure."

"Why did he disappear?"

"That's a whole other story for another day. But it's a weird one."

"Yeah? Which brings us back to the aluminum case. Let me give you a cherry on top of that weird, a cherry with a dollop of whipped cream."

Dexter's eyes were wide open, mimicking an expression of surprise, as he slipped on the second glove and lifted the plastic cover over the briefcase.

"Just feast your eyes on this."

26

It's easy to lie to ourselves.

As a child, I knew my mother drank too much, but I pretended she didn't.

I also knew she tried to stop drinking. I'd find little notes, written to herself. "Start Monday. Only water, lots of exercise. I *will* do it." "*Please God, please help me stay sober.*" "I beg you to give me the willpower, Father, to fight this terrible, evil addiction."

She tried, and when she failed, she'd smoke an occasional joint to calm her down, a habit that horrified my father. Sometimes I witnessed her smashing bottles of liquor with raging frustration, and when her temper burned out, she would go to her bedroom and cry herself to sleep.

Although she seldom talked about it, my mother came from a dirt-poor family of nine. A grinding, bleak struggle on a twenty-acre holding made her dream of escape, hankering after a more fertile soil for her dreams than the dry red earth of her father's farm and a momma so impoverished that she could not even afford a decent purse.

My mother was a pretty girl with a good figure, and she longed to be the lady of a mansion with a rich husband to support her, but she was neither classy enough nor smart enough to attain either. Her dreams would always lie beyond her. Like Gatsby, she believed in the green light, the promising future that always seemed to recede before her.

She fell in love with my father after meeting him at a dance in Athens, Georgia. She fell in love with a West Point graduate, the status conveyed by my father's crisp white dress uniform, and the promise of his promotion. The fact that his father was a relatively wealthy doctor with a busy practice who owned a substantial farm and that my father was one day likely to receive a decent inheritance probably influenced her, too. I know my father loved her. I know he worked hard to give her some of the status she craved.

But in every relationship there is the lover and the loved, and my father was the lover, and he never stopped trying to please. He wasn't five-star-general material, although in my mother's delusional moments she was convinced he belonged on the Joint Chiefs of Staff. The peak of my father's military promotion was colonel, but that would never be enough for my mother.

She would rail after a few drinks. "That idiot Maguire they made two-star general is dumber than a half-breed ass. You're a smart officer, Frank. Why not *you*?"

My father would simply shrug. "It's not for me to say, honey."

"It's all about connections, Frank. We need to make more connections! Ask General Hogue to dinner. I'll make supper, some drinks. We'll show him what a smart, capable officer you are."

The social grid my mother longed to plug into somehow always revolved around booze. And I have a suspicion that any chance my father had of further promotion was ruined by my mother's love affair with the juice.

Yet it wasn't always that way.

I still keep pictures of her wedding day, and I see a happy young woman of nineteen with dreams bright in her eyes. Yet for whatever reasons, her life was not to become the one she imagined, no more than her marriage to my father was the upwardly mobile vehicle she sought to propel her youthful hopes.

My father's inheritance would come to little. At a late stage in life, his doctor father, my grandfather, a wonderful, kindhearted man, lost his mind a little. He was grieving the death of his wife from ovarian cancer and turned to playing rich man's poker—as a stock-market investor. He lost all of his life's savings and the title deeds to most of his land in a tech crash—four hundred acres of prime real estate in Knox County—except for the modest family home on a ten-acre gentleman's farm out in Loudon, near Knoxville, Tennessee.

I think it was on that account my parents often fought, argued, and had pitched battles. Much of it was incited by my mother's angry drinking. First came small barbs, then metaphorically the guns were drawn. If the battle got worse, the cannons were rolled out, and then it was full-scale war, one the soldier in the family could never win. Once combat began, my mother could sustain her mood for weeks or even months.

"I hate you, Frank Kelly. *Hate* you. Just keep out of my way. I don't want to see your wretched face. Do you hear me? *Are you deaf?* I said, do you hear me? You're a loser, a no-good, rotten loser."

Yet despite her brittle addiction, my father still loved her. Even if his letters or notes to her often went unanswered when he was deployed or the cards and flowers he sent were left untouched because of my mother's alcoholic moods. I know that every letter and note my father wrote to her—from a posting abroad or if he simply wrote a "love you" note—was kept in my mother's personal bedroom safe, behind a portrait of her in a scarlet chiffon dress that my father had had painted of her the year before I was born.

When I was eighteen and my father retired at fifty with a military disability pension—and "the parting gift of a gammy prosthetic left foot," as my mother liked to remind him—we left Fort Campbell for good. But my father didn't move us far, just to the modest ten-acre gentleman's farm he inherited from his father and where he grew up, a few hundred miles away in Knoxville.

It was a simple basement rancher built by his grandfather in 1918 after he came back from the First World War. My father remodeled it, adding a sunroom and a boat dock to complement the beautiful views of peaceful Loudon Lake. It had a two-story guest cottage that looked out onto the water. We had once lived in the rancher for four years while my father was seconded to army recruitment, soon after my mother became pregnant with Kyle. We had fond memories of the house.

Knoxville is a sports-mad, compact Southern city that straddles the Tennessee River, mostly beautiful in a Norman Rockwell kind of way. Aside from the slum areas off Magnolia Avenue, the wrong end of North Central, and the gritty east side with its shabby rental units and ethnic ghettos, Knoxville is pretty idyllic. Rolling hills, forests and lakes, parklands galore, granite mansions nestled among immaculately landscaped wealthy subdivisions. Refinement is there, with ladies clubs, church clubs, rich socialites swanning it in their walnut-paneled parlors, but it's still down home.

It's Dolly Parton country, my mother used to say—vivacious, welcoming to strangers, a touch redneck eccentric, but darn nice with it. Banjo music might waft from a trailer home out on Knoxville's hillbilly edges, which might be enough to convince some migrant idiots from up north that there are still shades of the homicidal feuds of the Hatfields and McCoys.

The jagged majesty of the Smoky Mountains adds to the beauty. The Gatlinburg mountain resort does a pretty good impersonation of a displaced Austrian ski town, minus the yodelers. For fun, throw in Dollywood and the glittering carnival canyons of tacky neon at Pigeon Forge that stretch for miles. It's no wonder some people call their city Knox Vegas. And it was here that a ray of hope began to shine in our lives.

I started college, first at Pellissippi State, and then I transferred to UT after two years, setting my sights on an English degree and becoming a high school teacher. It seemed the sensible thing to do, giving me summers free to learn to write, a path I longed to pursue.

Meanwhile my mother did her best to decorate the remodeled house as she would have wanted her very own Southern mansion to look.

Antique furniture belonging to my grandparents was combined with chintz curtains, a big plastic faux chandelier in the hall, wingback loungers, a polished walnut dining table and chairs, and white porch rockers on the veranda. She was in her element. Her drinking seemed to subside.

It appeared she felt at home in Knoxville, a city with what seemed like a thousand different houses of worship—Methodists, Presbyterians, Greek Orthodox, Jews, Catholics, Church of God. Name a religion, and Knoxville had it. Signboards outside churches announced that everybody seemed to be recovering from something; there were classes in divorce recovery, bereavement recovery, marriage guidance, overcoming substance abuse. Preachers sometimes lured you in with a smart joke. "The Dollar Store isn't the only saving place in town." Or my own favorite: "Eternity. Smoking or nonsmoking?"

I graduated from UT and got a temporary English teacher position at Bearden High School, while I thought about attempting my master's in education. For a time, my mother managed to ingratiate herself into Knoxville society by joining several ladies clubs. But when her bingeing started again, her few new friends faded. I know that her failure caused her to be unhappy again.

Sometimes I'd find her sitting alone and staring out at the lake, her eyes fixed intently on the water, as if she was looking for something.

"What are you looking for, Mom?" I'd ask.

And she always gave me the same answer. "Peace, honey. I'm looking for peace."

There was a kind of pain in her voice, as if the peace she sought truly eluded her.

Something else I remember. Once, while my father was away, I passed her bedroom and heard her sobbing.

I eased open her door. "Hey, Mom. Are you OK?" I said it lightly, with a smile on my face. "You still looking for peace?"

When she looked around, I saw tears wet her face. She wiped them away and looked back out at Loudon Lake with a vacant stare. "You're home early, sweetie."

She struggled to show a fragile smile when she finally turned back. "What do you dream of most, Kath?"

"What do you mean?"

"You have dreams—or daydreams. All girls do. Don't you dream about what you'd like to do with your life or how you'd like it to turn out? About meeting a good man, a Prince Charming?"

"Sure, Mom."

"Dreams like those are dangerous. Don't ever entertain them."

"Why?"

"When I was your age, I had those dreams all the time. Dreams so vivid that I knew I was going to leave my parents' home one day, and I was never going to come back, not until I was rich and famous."

"Tell me more, Mom."

"There's nothing to tell. I didn't want my family to hear from me, I wanted them to hear *about* me. Except our dreams often mislead us. Most times they just fade to smoke and don't come true, honey. They just don't come true."

And then she came over and hugged me, harder than I ever remember being hugged by her, even since I was a child. The familiar aroma of alcohol and stale cigarette smoke wafted from her.

When she drew back, she held my chin, looking into my face with moist eyes. "Kath, you have to be prepared for that, you hear? So never pay too much heed to those kinds of dreams. Or they can mess up your life. You've got to be careful, honey. Remember that story I told you? About the bird that looks for a thorn tree?"

"Sure, Momma." The bronze cast my mom brought back from Ireland of a legendary Celtic bird perched on a thorn tree took pride of place on our mantelpiece.

"Don't go looking to put no thorns in your heart, you hear? Those thorns are going to find your heart anyhow. So you be careful of that."

But then that was what she always told me, to be careful, and then she wiped her eyes and was gone.

Late that night in my room, I thought I heard her crying again.

When I finally went in to see her, she was lying on the bed, fast asleep, one arm stretched out as if to reach the vodka bottle on her nightstand, her glass heavily smudged with lipstick. There was always a pile of books by her bed. Novels mostly—we shared an interest in books. They were now scattered on the floor by her bed as if she'd knocked them over.

I noticed how frail she looked, how loose the skin around her neck had become. She was getting thinner and looked more sallow. Her once-raven hair was flecked now with so much gray that a cheap dye job couldn't hide it. Makeup did little to mask the corners of her heavily wrinkled eyes.

I pulled up the bedsheet, kissed her cheek, and felt overcome by her alcohol breath and the smell of cigarettes and cheap perfume. She'd sometimes used the perfume to mask the fact that she urinated on herself but was too tired or too drunk to change her underwear.

That night, as she sometimes did, she called out in her sleep, a muttered word or two. This time it was a mumbled cascade. "Frank, Frank, no, please . . . you have to take this further . . . you have to tell the authorities. But who? Who'll kill us? No, that's absurd."

What did she mean? I was sure she said "kill." Were her words merely the hallucinations of a drunk woman or something else? I suspected the former, could never have imagined otherwise. It was a threat that made no sense. Besides, at that moment all that mattered was dressing her in fresh nightclothes and cleaning up her mess. I placed a towel under the damp bedsheet and threw her soiled garments into the washing machine. I left her, closing her door, and went to sit on my bed.

I bent my head and cried. I wasn't sure why.

Perhaps I was crying for the mother I wished I'd had. I know that sometimes people drink because alcohol is their mistress, a substitute lover, or a crutch to help them cope with life's harsh ways. Or to flee some unbearable truth they cannot face. In my mother's case, I would eventually learn that there was another reason, deeper and much darker. There were many truths and lies she could not face, and her slurred, drunken words that night hinted at them.

But the next day, when she was sober, I asked her about her talking in her sleep. She looked at me askance. "I . . . I said that?"

"You said, 'Who'll kill us?' Who would, Mom? What were you thinking?"

"I've no idea what I was saying. I . . . I had a slip, that's all. A drink or two too many last night. Forget it."

I sensed the lie in the anxious quiver in her voice.

But she never spoke about it again.

27

SEVIERVILLE, TENNESSEE

8:00 A.M.

"Kyle, can you hear me?"

I stared at my watch. I felt as if I was looking at it every few seconds, and I knew I'd have to stop. I had slept badly, tossed and turned in a half-wakeful state all through the night, and I felt exhausted. Every waking minute, I felt expectant, desperate to see my children, to touch their faces, anxious to hear from Jack again. I tried to imagine what they might look like now. It drove me crazy. I still had six hours before he called again.

I seemed to be the only visitor at Serenity Ridge that day, which was hardly surprising, considering I arrived there at seven-forty-five a.m. after waking at five a.m. Mostly, Serenity Ridge catered to patients with mental-health and drug issues. A range of types, from those who appeared pretty normal to those who looked like they could be extras in the movie *Crazy People*.

These days, Kyle looked somewhere in the middle. Withdrawn as always, staring into nothing, and only in a presentable state because the nurses made sure of it.

I was totally distracted and didn't even feel I was in the room with Kyle. Throughout the drive to Serenity Ridge, I kept the blue sweater and the purple hoodie on the seat next to me. Every now and then I picked them up, held them to my face, inhaled the new-washed scent as I drove. Same when I finished parking my car. I felt like I was going crazy.

I forced myself back to the present, tried to focus.

I looked around Kyle's room. It was just like in a hospital—a metal bed, no protruding edges anywhere so he couldn't harm himself if he fell or, worse, tried to self-harm. Gray rubber-tiled floor. Family pictures pasted neatly on the straw-colored walls—Kyle, my dad, Mom, me. A bunch of greeting cards from Kyle's last birthday that I'd tacked on a string behind his bed.

Kyle sat in front of me in a wheelchair, not making eye contact as usual, his head rocking from side to side and his mouth dribbling a little. I leaned across to dab his mouth with a tissue from my pocket. He smelled of soap and sweat. I brushed flakes of dandruff off his dark sweater.

So many times I hoped and waited for his beautiful voice to sing, but he never sang. Kyle still liked music. He wore a pair of earphones, attached to a new-looking iPod, lying in his lap. I could hear the music playing through the earphones. Opera—Kyle liked opera. Or Taylor Swift or Adele or the Dixie Chicks or pretty much anything that wasn't hip-hop or rap, Snoop Dogg or P. Diddy. Play the wrong kind of music, and he vamoosed out of the room as if his wheelchair was on fire or he had a rocket attached, for he had a gritty determination to avoid what he didn't like. I hadn't seen the iPod before. Kyle still got gifts now and then, on birthdays and at Christmas, from old friends.

I took a deep breath, let it out. The thing that drove me nuts about Serenity Ridge was that it was über-clean, nothing out of place, everything exactly where it should be. The smell of disinfectant wafted in the air like poison gas. The bedclothes were virginal white. You could lick gravy off the floors. I hated it. There was no happiness, just a neutral state that seemed sterile and soulless and, well, drugged, I guess.

If Kyle made a mess of his bib at lunch, it was quickly whisked away a second after he ate, and he was tidied up and buffed and polished again like new. It should have been comforting that the nurses at Serenity Ridge did their job. But it wasn't home, and it never would be. It seared my soul, thinking that Kyle was never coming home. Or ever going back to any real home. Sure, we took him to stay at home for the occasional night, but he needed full-time care. Serenity Ridge was where it was at.

My dad and I took turns visiting, or sometimes we came together. Today was my turn, with my dad away. Despite all the turmoil in my head—the crash-scene visit, the news about Jack and my kids, and my thoughts doing cartwheels—I couldn't miss it. I had brought fresh clothes and the treats Kyle liked—Reese's Peanut Butter Cups, Snickers bars, fruit gums, Saltine crackers, Mountain Dew. Kyle looked at me, so there in body but not in mind. As terrible as it sounds, I often wondered sometimes if we were being cruel to him.

Would it have been better if he had died that day in the park? It was a harsh thought. But I sometimes mused about it. My brother's hollow, sad blue eyes always got to me. There was a heart and a soul and a life trapped inside his lackluster body, but they were forever entombed in the past and bound by its chains. He had no present life, other than Serenity Ridge, which was just death's waiting room.

I leaned across the wheelchair and gently removed the iPod headphones from Kyle's ears. I hadn't bought it. I spotted an open Apple box in the garbage bin and a scrunched-up ball of gift-wrap paper. His birthday was last month. Thirty. He looked eighteen. I'd found a few birthday cards in his room. One from Courtney—I recognized her handwriting. "Love you, Kyle, always will. Happy Birthday, honey." Courtney had visited. Had she left the iPod?

"Is that new, Kyle? Did someone give you a gift? Who was it?"

Kyle said nothing, as usual, just gave me the familiar thousand-yard stare that had meds written all over it. Sometimes he'd grunt, gesture to things, utter a whispered word or two, smile, laugh. But mostly—well, mostly nothing. Finally came a brief nod. *Yes.* He got it. It just took a while. You had to have patience with Kyle.

There's another patient, Raymond, childlike, the kind it pained you to ever see hurt in a world this harsh. Severe brain damage from a car accident when he was twelve, and he was now forty—but still twelve, forever trapped in a mental time warp. He liked to take it upon himself to speak for Kyle sometimes, and he would sit with us when he felt like it. Raymond liked cake. Whenever anyone left some for Kyle, Raymond was never far away, angling for a slice.

Once I asked Kyle what he liked to do. It was a rhetorical question, just to fill the silence, but Raymond was right there, hanging loose, wearing Batman pajamas that were two sizes too small for him. He was scratching his crotch the way he always did, as if he had a bad case of fleas, hoping for another slice of Bavarian chocolate cake.

"What do you like, Kyle?" I asked again when I got no answer.

"Boobies," Raymond said, scratching himself as if he were on fire.

"Excuse me?"

"He likes to watch the nurses' boobies. I see him watching them sometimes. I watch them, too. Especially Janice."

"Janice?"

"Nurse Janice. She's got the nicest." Raymond giggled.

Thanks, Raymond. Of all the answers. It was one of the few laughs I got in this place. I knew Kyle still had feelings; I saw his eyes wet a few times. Mostly he never showed them. I guessed the meds he was on to stop the seizures that he sometimes suffered didn't help.

I embraced Kyle and blinked away the tears. Then I wheeled him out to the sunroom, the doors open, a cool breeze blowing into the room. Kyle sat in the wheelchair, head to one side. "So, how are you doing, bro? All right?"

It was very peaceful, the lawns beyond the glass rolling away to a thick forest, the Smoky Mountains beyond. A breeze blew in across the glazed cream tiles and ruffled Kyle's hair. I leaned over and patted it down.

Kyle nodded again. *Yes.* He began to rock back and forth in his wheelchair. He liked to rock. It seemed to comfort him. He looked so boyish, with his blond hair and pale, milky skin. Sometimes I thought about all the things he might have been if his life hadn't turned out the way it had.

Right now he'd probably be married, have kids, be living a life full of highs and lows like us all—but above all, living. I so often had to push such thoughts away; they disturbed me. Then I always told myself that Kyle was alive, that was what was important, and we still had each other. "You miss me, Kyle?"

He nodded and rocked.

"Have you been eating right? Is everything good? Tell me some news."

Kyle just smiled back at me, a brief smile that vanished as quickly as it came.

My mind drifted back to the crash site. I wished I could tell Kyle my news, that I was filled with hope and elation and a powerful curiosity. But Kyle would understand none of it, or if he did, he would say nothing. Nothing more than a grunted word or two at best.

Raymond sauntered by, scratching his crotch, and peered in. "Got cake?"

"No cake today, Raymond."

"Oooh, OK." And he was gone.

I sat there, talking as always while I held on to Kyle's hand and rubbed his arm. Talking about nothing, really, just filling the void with meaningless small talk, until a good twenty minutes later I heard footsteps behind us and looked around.

A graceful black lady—a nurse's aide named Deesha—stepped into the sunroom.

"The iPod—where did Kyle get it, Deesha? Was it from Courtney?"

"No, ma'am. She was here yesterday. But another visitor gave him the gift. He was here yesterday, too."

"Who?"

"Old Army buddy of Kyle's, I believe. Amputee, in a motorized wheelchair. Didn't you ever see him before? He visited Kyle last week, too, when you were here."

Come to think of it, on my way in to see Kyle on my last visit, I passed a guy in a motorized wheelie in the hallway. Grizzled, with a beard, a real mountain man type, one leg amputated above the knee. He gave me a silent nod, as if maybe he knew me, and then he was gone, powering his way down the corridor.

"Guy with a beard, a leg missing?"

"That's probably him. He's left stuff for Kyle before. Nice gifts, expensive. That really good bathrobe he got a few years back, I think that was the same guy. And the new TV he got in his room last winter."

"I thought that the home replaced the old one?"

"No, ma'am. The same guy. Been coming here for years, I'd say. You've never seen him before?"

"Maybe I have." His face looked kind of familiar. "He's not a patient here?"

"No, ma'am. But I've seen him here before, visiting Kyle. Sometimes he brings his kids." Deesha gave a dazzling smile. "He calls his boy Elvis. The girl's name is Marilyn, after Marilyn Monroe, I believe."

"You get his name?"

"No, ma'am, but it'll be in the visitors book. Everybody's got to sign in, or they don't get past Agnes."

Agnes was bulletproof, with a hide as hard as Kevlar. Mountain-tough, she manned the reception desk with a mullet that had gone out of style decades ago everywhere but in the Appalachians. Not that you'd dare tell Agnes that to her face, unless you wanted to die a painful death.

"Thanks."

Deesha said, "Sure seems like it's a day for visitors. There's a man outside asking to see you."

"Me?"

"Yes, ma'am. Asked for you by name. I think he's foreign. Sure looks foreign. He's waiting out in the hall."

28

He looked Arab, Persian, Mexican—it was kind of hard to tell.

Tall, meaty, around thirty, black mustache, square head, no neck. He was waiting at the end of the hall, pacing up and down. Dressed in a dark business suit, white shirt, and black tie. His shirt was a size too small, so that his gut strained at the buttons.

Our eyes locked, and we met in the middle of the hall. I had the weird impression that he looked like a butler of some kind. Stiff and formal. His coarse skin made him seem even more sinister.

"Ms. Kelly?"

"Yes."

He offered his hand, his accent faintly Middle Eastern. "It is good to see you."

I shook the offered palm, which was limp and moist. "Do I know you?"

"No. I was asked to deliver a message to you."

He handed me a business card.

I looked at the gold-embossed lettering, and I wasn't surprised.

Tarik Funeral Home.
Licensed embalmer and crematorium
We care for your loved ones
With compassion and respect.

There was an address, off Kingston Pike, Knoxville's main commercial drag, the alpha and omega where every direction began and ended. "From Kingston Pike, go east . . . or west." Whatever.

"What has this got to do with?"

"Your deceased loved ones, Ms. Kelly."

"There must be some misunderstanding. If it's about the air crash, my family's remains haven't been found."

No-Neck totally ignored my reply. It was as if I hadn't spoken. He offered a weird half grin that looked kind of creepy. "Mr. Tarik thinks it is very important that you see him today." He pointed to the address on the card. "He is expecting you soon. He would appreciate if you called by the address on the card."

I stared back at him, waiting for him to explain.

"Mr. Tarik has an important message to deliver to you, about your family."

I felt a catch in my heart. "What . . . message?"

"Mr. Tarik will explain. Good day, Ms. Kelly." And without another word, the man turned and exited by the reception's front door.

Just like that. Wham, bam, thank you, ma'am.

I stood there, puzzled, looking down at the card, before I stared out at the parking lot. The man climbed into a gleaming black Mercedes and drove off.

Weird.

What message about my family?

Deesha came up beside me. "That man who visited Kyle and gave him the iPod?"

"What about him?"

Deesha nodded over to Agnes at the reception desk, granite-faced and with mullet hair, busy on a phone call.

"Agnes thinks she knows the guy."

As I climbed into my car, my cell phone rang.

I didn't recognize the number. But it was Courtney. "Hey, Kath, how are you, honey?"

Courtney was larger than life, even in a military uniform. But today her tone sounded more muted than usual. Had she seen the news on TV about the crash site? If she did, she never said. She also seemed to want to keep the conversation brief.

"I'm at my aunt Jean's place in Seven Oaks? My mom's staying in Knoxville a few days, and I called by to visit. She and Jean are just leaving to go shopping and have lunch. The place will be free, we'll have some privacy. Could you meet me there?"

"Sure. Is everything OK?"

"Yeah, just wanted to catch up." Courtney was keeping it brief. She usually kept you talking for an hour. I had the feeling she wanted to talk but not over the phone.

"Courtney . . ."

I almost said it, but I didn't. Courtney beat me to it.

"I know, honey, I know. I saw the news. Keep sane until I see you, OK? You doing OK? You can't be."

"It's crazy. Can . . . can you give me an hour or two? I've got something to do first. Someone to see."

I checked my watch. Eight-fifteen a.m. I had almost six hours until Jack's call.

"Get here as soon as you can, OK? It's kind of important. And honey . . ."

"Yeah?"

"I just don't want to talk about it on my cell, OK?"

"Why? What's up?"

"Just don't. I'll explain when I see you."

29

Knoxville, Tennessee
9:10 a.m.

The girl's body lay naked on the metal gurney.

She was ravishing, with long blond hair, barely seventeen.

Fazil Tarik thought, *What a total waste.* He heard a noise outside the mortuary building and stared out. Through the blinds, he saw a black Mercedes pull into the red-brick courtyard building's lot off Kingston Pike. It parked next to the hand-painted wooden sign that said "Tarik, Undertakers, Licensed Embalmers and Crematorium."

Tarik turned his attention back to the corpse. He was busy that afternoon, applying his skills to the victim of a drunk-driving accident. A tall man of sixty with a neatly trimmed and pencil-thin mustache—dyed black, unlike his shock of gray hair—Tarik wore a dark suit and had an actor's well-practiced, sorrowful expression. His dour look gave him the appearance of a demanding man used to getting what he wanted.

On a wooden table next to him lay a selection of mortician's implements, the familiar tools of his trade: a rubber mallet, a jar of formaldehyde preservative, and pots of brushes and makeup pads. He studied the girl's body that lay before him, her head bandaged.

He smiled, and his smile was an unpleasant thing, his teeth too small for his wide mouth, like some kind of rodent's.

Such a terrible waste of youth and beauty, Tarik reflected with a sigh, but then traffic deaths were all too common in America. And some hillbillies drove even more crazily than the lunatics back in his native Iraq.

In Knoxville, as in most of the South, you had to forget traffic rules you learned elsewhere. Southerners had their own version. The Trans-Am with the loudest exhaust goes first at a four-way stop, and the truck with the biggest tires goes after that.

If you stopped at a yellow light, you would be rear-ended, cussed out, and possibly shot. The minimum acceptable speed on the interstate was eighty-five. Anything less than that was downright sissy. And the scariest of all, drugs and alcohol were a frightening and frequent reality on the highway. Hence so many road deaths, like the one in front of him. Drive hammered, get nailed.

When he finished applying a touch of rouge to the young girl's cheeks, Tarik stared down at his handiwork. He enjoyed working on young females—it gave him a chance to admire their bodies. He studied the girl's full breasts, her silken legs, her splendid curves. Her left breast was still badly bruised from the crash. Tarik dabbed on more makeup, touching the breast with a pad. It felt hard. Rigor had set in.

He kept his fingers there for a few seconds too long, massaging the pad into the dead flesh, until he stepped back to admire his work. It looked acceptable. His hand reached out, and his fingers traced all the way down the dead girl's flat stomach to the rift between her legs. Tarik sighed again. A ravishing body squandered, headed to the worms.

As he finished his work and soaped and rinsed his hands in a basin of warm water, the wall intercom buzzed.

Moments later, a bulky man with a squat neck appeared, wearing a dark suit a size too large for him. Kiril Tarik was endowed with a dour look as experienced as his father's.

"Well?"

"I told her. She came straight here, Pop. I kept an eye on her in the rear mirror. She's parking in the lot."

"Excellent. Finish the young lady while I see to her."

"Sure, Pop."

As Tarik Senior turned away from the washbasin and toweled his hands dry, a doorbell buzzed from somewhere out in the hall. He stroked his pencil-thin black mustache and smiled at his son.

"Time to see if we can bring the dead back to life."

30

She was seated in the chapel, facing a coffin on the dais.

Tarik crossed to her, offering a flicker of a sympathetic smile. She was pretty, with blond hair, wearing jeans and a pastel blue top with a casual woolen jacket.

"Ms. Kelly. How good of you to come." He shook her hand, letting hers rest in the gentle grip of both of his, before he slowly released his grasp.

"I explained to your colleague—"

"My son, Kiril."

"Yes, I explained that you made a mistake. No bodies were found at the crash site. But he said you had a message for me?"

Tarik nodded politely, taking in her figure, her face, forcing a sympathetic smile. "Yes, I saw the report on CNN and several other stations."

"Then what's this about?"

"I wanted to tell you that if you have need of my help, please know that I am at your service. I am aware also that the TV news mentioned that your husband was a veteran. We offer special services for veterans—"

"Let me stop you right there, Mr. Tarik. Did you really call me here to make a sales pitch at a time like this?"

Tarik felt the sting of the remark and tilted his head a touch sideways, gave that *I understand your grief* look he often practiced. But really he was trying to see through a crack in one of the chapel's window blinds. Kiril was kneeling down next to the woman's car and slid something under the rear driver's-side wheel well. Kiril stood up at once and walked away, out of sight.

Tarik's focus returned to the woman, and he put the palm of his right hand on his heart. "Dear lady, please, I beg your pardon. That was not my intention. I simply wanted to help. You see, I have a long tradition of dealing with members of the military and their families. We offer special concessions, a complete range of additional services at no extra cost to veteran families. I thought you would like to know that. Your military did so much for my country. For that I'm always grateful."

"Where's your country?"

"Iraq. You helped rid us of that dictator, Saddam Hussein. I once worked with your army as a translator. Many of us who lost loved ones, who suffered during his cruel reign, are forever grateful to America. I simply want you to know that I am here should you require my help. That I would be honored to handle your needs with the greatest of sympathy and compassion."

"Yes, I saw that on the card."

The woman sounded touchy, impatient to go.

Tarik reached out a hand and touched her arm in a sympathetic gesture. It had about as much sincerity as a hooker's kiss, but he liked to think that a soft touch and a practiced look of sympathy calmed those in need of it.

The woman gently drew her arm away. Tarik slipped an embossed business card from his breast pocket. "My cell number is on my personal card if you need me. Your husband has been missing a long time, I believe."

"Eight years."

"My dearest hope is, of course, that you will have no need of my services or those of any others in my profession. That they find your family still alive. The TV news seemed to suggest that may be a possibility?"

"Did they? I'm not sure what they said."

Tarik gave her the look again of fake compassion. "We all have our unquiet ghosts, Ms. Kelly. I honestly pray that you find yours safe and well."

The woman looked back at him as if he'd just made an odd remark.

Tarik said, "A saying in Iraq. During the bad times in our country, so many people lost loved ones who disappeared. We called them our unquiet ghosts. They would never be at peace until we found them. Just as you won't. I do understand that." He placed a palm on his heart again. "But forgive me, I won't detain you any longer. Please accept my best wishes in your endeavor."

Her face showed no response.

"Good day, Mr. Tarik."

Tarik watched as the woman left.

Then he stepped into an office down the hall. It was neatly functional, with a desk and chairs, a big, sturdy Centurion safe, gray rubber-tiled flooring, and the American flag standing on a plinth in the corner. Peering through the curtain blinds, he watched her drive away.

When the car disappeared, Tarik stood there a few moments, thinking, before his gaze shifted to the American flag. His fingers reached, and he clutched the material, crushed it into a ball, until his knuckles turned white with rage.

The door opened, and Kiril came in.

He was joined by two other men. Mehmet, short and aggressive, with a flat face like an angry bulldog. Abu, tall and robust, with hands like iron lump hammers and a muscled body beefed by steroids.

Tarik said to Kiril, "Well?"

"It's done. Babek did his work well. The device is fitted to her car. Another is planted in the purse she left on her car seat. With luck, we'll know where she is at all times."

Tarik smiled and let go of the flag. "Good."

"Did you really need to have her come here and see us? She'll be curious about why you wanted to see her."

Tarik placed his open palm on his heart once more. "And she has her answer. A believable one. I kindly offered her my sympathy and my services."

"But we could have put the tracking devices on her car and belongings elsewhere—at her home or in the mall."

"True. But learn this lesson well, Kiril. Know your enemy. Find a way to look them in the eye, to appraise what you are up against. In this case, the woman won't be a problem."

Tarik took a slim cigar from his top pocket and lit it with a gold lighter. "I'm certain she will lead us to the others." He gave Kiril a look of steel. "And once she does, you know what must be done."

31

THE PAST

By the end of my wedding day, the question of what had led to Kyle's suicide attempt was not the only mystery I couldn't solve. I also wondered what was on my mother's tortured mind when she left my wedding reception.

When she vanished, she didn't go to the restroom as I thought she had. Instead, witnesses saw her leave in a Knoxville cab that she called from the hotel front desk.

Someone else claimed they saw my father leave, too, saw him drive out of the lot in his car in a hurry and return thirty minutes later. He admitted this. He said he went looking for my mother in a bunch of nearby restaurants and bars, places she often vanished to after a tirade, but he said he couldn't find her and returned.

She was still drunk, that much I know. I also know that when she arrived at our family home, she went to the wall safe in her bedroom, swung back the portrait of herself in the red dress, and removed a diary and some envelopes. It must have been at this point that she saw no hope or was consumed by drunken rage.

I believe that because she burned the diary and the papers and all my father's love letters to her in the bedroom fireplace. The blackened ashes and the remains of the diary's cover and the envelopes were testament to that. All that remained unburned was a single discarded piece of paper, part of a page from her diary, lying under her bed, on which she had once written in black ink: *Red.* There was another illegible word scrawled next to it.

But what secrets the pages contained or what *Red* meant I had no idea. My father didn't know, either, and always said my mother's behavior that day was brought on by her distress at Kyle's hopeless mental state. That she had lost her baby boy. The enigma of what my mother might have kept locked in that steel safe or in the envelopes remained a mystery.

I know she set fire to the diary and the papers in the fireplace using the same cheap plastic Bic she used to light her Marlboro Golds, her cherry lipstick staining the cigarette filter, as always. And that she took a handful of antidepressants from a pill bottle she kept in her safe. The investigating detectives mentioned those things—and the discarded paper—in their report.

My "terrible event," as my father called it—the loss of my husband and our beloved children—was still to come, to alter my life forever with its cruel, heart-wrenching mystery, but even if I'd known, I could never have imagined how they were linked to the envelope bearing the simple word *Red.*

The police questioned me about my father's movements being partly unaccounted for in the thirty-eight minutes after my mother vanished. His claim that he searched for her in the nearest local bars and restaurants that she liked to haunt could not be proven. I always thought it seemed weird that they might even vaguely suspect my father in any way. That aspect of the case came to nothing in the end, but there were still questions left unanswered about the tragedy that unfolded that day.

Why would my mother do what she did during such an important event in my life, unless her motive had some deep personal significance? I could not fathom it. I would often ask myself that question afterward, but I found no answers.

I can only imagine what might have happened, that my mother may have looked out over the view of Loudon Lake from her bedroom window as she smoked her cigarette, that lake view being her favorite ever since she nursed Kyle and me on her lap as children.

And maybe she thought about those days or the way she had ruined my wedding but not intended to and of her sad, screwed-up life that she had made worse with alcohol and pot or Kyle's shattered life or her youthful dreams of riches that lay far beyond her grasp. Faded now, they were wisps of dying smoke in a distant sky.

But the tragedy of my wedding was so disturbing that it would forever haunt my memory, for my mother's senseless act seemed to set the tone for every bad thing that followed from that day on.

That evening, after leaving my reception, after burning the diary and the envelope contents from her safe, after smoking a cigarette and looking out at Loudon Lake, I think she must have made up her mind to seek the peace and solace that had so long eluded her but to seek it in a different place.

Martha Beth Kelly drew a Smith & Wesson revolver from her purse, put the barrel to her temple, and blew her brains out.

That was my mother.

And as flawed as she was, I loved her.

32

LOUDON LAKE

The man heard the GPS *ding*, and a metallic voice announced, "You have arrived at your destination."

Not that he needed to be told. He knew the house. A white-painted sign in wrought iron above the mailbox announced the name: Lakeview.

It was set back from a minor country road that hardly saw any traffic. He could just make out the two-story home through some tall pine trees, built of brown cut stone and gray-painted siding. A lake and a private dock lay beyond. A calm expanse of water beyond the trees, with a few sailboats and motorboats.

He drove past Lakeview and at the end of the road did a U-turn, kept the engine idling, and stared out. Two more properties lay farther along the road, but he saw no one. No sign of any external security cameras, either. Thick woods lay to the left and right. He figured he could walk up to the house through the woods and approach the rear without being seen.

The neighborhood was mostly small farms and multiacre lots. Tons of privacy, which was perfect for what he had in mind. He'd already checked on Google Maps, wanting to make sure there were no changes since the last time he was here.

Eight years was a long time, and he wanted to be certain of the layout.

Lots of tracks and narrow roads snaked off in every direction, a public walkway and park nearby that wound its way down to the lake. He knew which track to take.

He shifted into gear and drove until he turned the Explorer into a heavily wooded parking lot for lakeside walkers. A track veered off, thick woods on either side. He drove the Explorer along it for another hundred yards, then reversed the vehicle into the track, careful not to rev the engine. After reversing twenty yards, he turned off the ignition and jerked on the parking brake. His car was masked by trees now, and it couldn't be seen from the road.

He rolled down the window and listened. Silence, except for the birds. He glimpsed the brown cut stone and gray-painted house through the trees. No cars were parked outside in the driveway. He knew from Google Maps that it could be approached through the woodland from two sides.

He'd go the rest of the way on foot, taking care not to make too much noise. The damp ground was strewn with dead leaves and rotted wood, the smell of forest mold drenching the air.

His jaw hurt, and so did the gaping wound that the prosthesis covered. It happened now and then, a deep seething pain that seemed to begin in the bone. He took a couple of OxyContin painkillers, swallowing them with some water from a plastic bottle on the passenger seat.

Then he pulled on the black pigskin gloves. Removing the Kimber .45 from under his seat, he found the Taser in the glove compartment and slid both into his jacket pockets. Next was a set of locksmith's skeleton keys on a steel ring that he kept in the CD compartment. He stuffed them into his jeans.

The last thing—a black woolen ski mask—he tucked inside his jacket.

He grabbed his black leather jacket and climbed out of the Explorer. He locked it with the key instead of the remote so as not to make any noise.

A jolt of dread slammed into him, knowing what he had to do.

But first he needed to watch the house, check things out before he made his move.

Taking a couple of deep breaths, he filled his lungs, then started to walk into the woods.

33

Four hours until Jack's call.

I drove up into the Seven Oaks subdivision, off Kingston Pike. The place was heavily wooded, like a forest in places.

Courtney's aunt Jean lived in a rancher built in the seventies, a butter-colored brick-and-siding that looked a little dated by now. Courtney's Toyota convertible, scarlet with a brown top, was already there.

I kept the sweater and hoodie on the passenger seat. Just seeing them made me hopeful.

Courtney came to the door when I rang, looking glamorous as always. And even without the helping hand from a Nashville plastic surgeon and a regular Botox fix, the years had been good to her. Just saying.

Her last husband—there had been two—had been a well-off but slightly dodgy haulage company owner named Sammy Frisco. A divorce settlement from Sammy kept her in a little extra comfort. Kids never seemed to be part of her plan. "They looked great on paper, honey, but I want a life, not servitude. Got enough of that in the military."

Her current beau—she never told me much about him except that she was lukewarm about the guy—was a divorced colonel, and he wanted her to quit the service. He planned on retiring to the Florida Keys and wanted her to come with him. Courtney claimed she'd be taking off the harness in eighteen months and was thinking about taking up the offer. Daiquiris and ocean sunsets and Jimmy Buffett appealed, even if the guy didn't exactly ring her bell. "Even so, when the time comes, I'll be out of the trap faster than a greyhound on speed. I've had me enough of military life."

When she came to the door, Courtney wore her captain's uniform, with the CID flashes, everything crisply pressed, with a white shirt.

"How are you doing, honey? I know that's a dumb question, you've got to be in turmoil." She hugged me warmly, holding my hand tightly, her eyes showing her concern.

I was glad to feel the comforting embrace of an old friend, and when we finally let go of each other and I wiped my eyes, we moved into the kitchen. "I'm still in shock, Courtney. My mind's a riot."

I so wanted to confide in her about Jack's call. Wanted to show her the sweater and hoodie. But I couldn't, not after Jack's warning. We sat at the kitchen table. Courtney poured us coffee.

"I can't see how it could be any other way. I had some time before work intrudes and wanted to let you know I'm here for you. Saw the story on the news."

"It . . . it all seems so crazy."

"I can get that." She shook her head. "After eight years, then for things to turn up like this and to have to deal with it all over again, why, that's mind-wrecking. *Twilight Zone* stuff."

On a table lay her belt and holstered sidearm. Her civvies were on a hanger on the kitchen door—a pastel-pink sweater with a string of sequins across the top, designer jeans, and heels, to be topped off by a couple of expensive rings and a diamante bracelet. Her blond hair was cut shoulder-length, her nails expertly manicured. On summer holidays she always put tiny glitter sprays on the cuticles, but on duty it was Plain Jane stuff. She was still sexy, vivacious, a looker.

And here's the weird thing: Chad saw Courtney for about six months after his first divorce. She did a single tour of duty in Iraq, and that's where they "hooked up," as she liked to put it, in Courtney-speak meaning they had a fling. She liked the idea of the high life.

"I should have found me a millionaire a long time ago. Money can be an aphrodisiac, honey."

I guess I knew what she meant. And I think for a time Courtney thought she had found her millionaire with Chad. But once or twice after a few vinos too many, she told me she always felt she was punching above her weight. "Old money and West Point, they set a kind of high bar, you know. A high one to keep reaching for."

I knew what she meant. When the fling ended, there were no hard feelings—or as Courtney claimed, "Chad and I can still be friends."

We never talked about it. I guess our individual relationships with the same guy were a no-man's land between us, a territory we never really explored—or wanted to. Maybe there were mines we were afraid would go off? Especially when Chad and I started seeing each other. But I never sensed any animosity from Courtney when I started seeing Chad. And I could understand that Chad would have found her attractive.

Any guy would, money or not.

She held my hands in both of hers. "You look tired. Did I disturb you? Were you trying to sleep?"

"No, I was visiting Kyle. I slept badly last night. Just lay on my mom's bed, got to thinking about the past . . . all the bad stuff that happened."

She stroked my cheek with the back of her hand. "Hey, you don't want to do too much of that, not right now. It's not good for you. I wonder if Jean has any wine."

"I couldn't drink, Courtney."

"Hey, I'm not talking about you, it's for me, honey. I need something to settle my shocked nerves."

She found a bottle of cabernet in a cupboard, poured herself a large glass, and looked at me. "Sure you won't have one?"

"If I start now, there's no telling when I might stop."

"Tell me everything."

I told her. My eyes were wet.

Courtney meshed her hand with mine. "It's all so weird. But the one shining ray of hope is that they may all be alive. Do they honestly think Jack and the children could have survived? I guess they wouldn't feed you bull on something like that, give you false hope."

"It's what Dexter, the NTSB guy, is saying. He seemed certain. They're still looking, searching the undergrowth for evidence."

Courtney massaged my arm. "Did you tell your dad?"

"Yes. I think he's already on his way back."

"Sweetheart, that's good, you need him around right now. Me, I'm still reeling. Even to think they could have somehow survived and yet Jack never contacted you. I just can't get my head around it. It's . . . it's like something you'd see on TV, in a movie."

I could feel the empathy, her voice warm with concern. She was such a good friend.

"Your poor heart . . . I don't know what to say, Kath. I really don't. Except I'm sure that everybody involved will do everything they can to get to the bottom of this."

"You know what's bizarre, now that I think of it? Something I never told anyone."

"What?"

"Twice in the months after Jack disappeared, I thought I saw him in the woods behind our house. I was sure it was him. So sure I thought I was going crazy." I looked at Courtney. "And there was another time. It was kind of scary."

"Yeah?"

"I'd started seeing Chad. It was maybe eighteen months after Jack disappeared. Chad and I came out of a downtown restaurant one night. It was winter and cold. He put his coat over my shoulders. Just then, I saw a car start up across the lot. An old Ford pickup."

"So?"

"The driver lit up a cigarette. That's when I got a shiver down my spine. The guy behind the wheel wore a baseball cap, and his collar was pulled up, but he still looked so much like Jack that my breath caught in my throat. I was stunned."

"You should have told me, honey."

"The Ford drove off. I said nothing to Chad. But that . . . that image stayed with me for a long time. I told myself it couldn't have been him. He was dead, I felt sure. But now . . . now I'm not so sure."

Courtney hugged me again, patted my back. "Like I said, you don't want to do too much of that kind of thinking right now. It ain't good for you."

The back of her hand touched my face. "Hey, you mind if I change out of uniform? I'm on a case, and I've got a meeting to go to."

Courtney often swore civvies on a job. "Sure."

In uniform, Courtney reminded me of the contradiction of some convent girls I knew, demure on the outside but smoking hot and wild on the inside. She slipped off her tunic and skirt, stripping down to her panties and bra. Once she pulled on her civilian clothes and let down her hair, the transformation was immediate. Gone was strait-laced Courtney, all professional and somber. Now she was a woman who'd catch your eye in the mall or on the street. It was easy to see why men found her attractive.

After that time when I found Courtney and my father kissing, their clothes half off on a warm summer night along the lakeshore, we never talked about it. A couple of times we tried, but neither of them had much to say about it, and I stopped bringing it up. I didn't like to think about it.

She grabbed her sidearm. Out of uniform, she was addressed in civvy street as Agent Adams, not by her military rank. "Would you like me to come over later tonight? We can talk, if you feel up to it?"

"I think I'm going to have an early night. Take a pill and sleep. I feel all talked out. Do you mind?"

"Mind? No, hey, whatever helps, honey. Just call me if you feel you need me, no matter what the time, promise?"

"Sure."

"Better get going."

"What's the case?"

Courtney hesitated. She looked me up and down. Finally, she said, "This one."

34

I stared back at her, jolted by the words.

Courtney said, "I've been assigned, with another CID officer. The FBI out of Knoxville has the lead in the case. We've set up a task force, and we're hooking up with the Park Services guys, too. I'm headed now to view the wreckage. We're to liaise with the FBI guy, Tanner. Very cute black guy. He'd be even cuter if he lost fifty pounds."

She had that kind of distant, sparkly look in her eyes, the kind that told me she liked a guy. I knew she liked big men, tall and beefy. Being around military types all her life probably colored her choice of men.

My voice sounded hoarse. "Why?"

"Why me, or why is the military involved?"

"Both."

"I guess the fact that I knew Jack and you might have something to do with it, because I've got an inside track. But other than that, I can't tell you, Kath. You know the rules. They tell me to keep my mouth shut, I clam it."

"What's going on?"

Courtney sighed and sat at the table again. "Look, Fort Campbell has an interest in this one."

"They didn't when Jack went missing."

"Actually, they did."

"CID was investigating Jack?"

Courtney clamped her lips, until a single sentence escaped, as if reluctantly. "And a bunch of other people."

"Why didn't I hear?"

"You wouldn't have if the investigation was covert."

"Why was it covert? What or who was being investigated?"

"I can't say, honey. I'd love to put your mind at ease, but I can't. And on that, please don't ask me any more. That's sorta why I wanted you to meet me here. I didn't want to risk us being seen together in public or anyone thinking I might be giving an inside track."

"The inside track on what?"

She shook her head, a firm no, but patted my hand. "There's not an answer I can give right now. But I'm pretty sure you'll learn in good time."

"This is driving me insane."

"I'm sorry, Kath. You know if there was any way, I'd tell you everything. But the feds have primacy in this case. They decide who's told what."

"But there's more to it? A lot more?"

Courtney's lips were firmly shut, but her eyebrows arched. Which really told me nothing.

"What's that supposed to mean?"

She shrugged. "If CID *and* the feds are involved, that ought to tell you it's something serious."

"How serious?"

Courtney shut her mouth tight.

My head was aching, my curiosity powerful. I needed to know—anything, the tiniest morsel—but Courtney was saying nothing that offered me help or solace.

The doorbell rang, startling us both.

Courtney said, "That's probably Sergeant Stone."

"Who?"

"My partner on this case. He's here to meet me. Let me deal with him."

Courtney went out to the hall, and I heard her open the front door.

A muted conversation drifted back in, but I couldn't understand much more than a word or two, and then the door closed. I peered through a doorway to the front room. Past the window I saw a young man in civilian clothes walk out to a white Chevy Impala and climb in. He looked baby-faced, barely out of his teens. He did a U-turn in the street and drove off.

Courtney came back in. "I told him to go grab a coffee at Chick-fil-A on Kingston Pike and I'd meet him in the parking lot."

She sat down again, held my hands in hers. "Look, I don't want you to worry, Kath. Easy to say, but the heartening news is that Sean and Amy may well be alive. That's so terrific, so incredible. So . . ." She shrugged. "Hopeful, I guess. You have hope, where you've had none. Worries and fears, too, I know, but I'll be doing my best for you, honey, you know that. My very best. I'm on your side."

I was silent. I wanted to tell Courtney everything I knew, but a warning voice in the back of my head told me to keep my trap shut. I still felt a powerful need to share my fears and frustrations. I guess I even hoped that my doing so might make Courtney open up a little more about what it was that CID was investigating about Jack.

"Courtney, I think I should tell you, something else weird happened right before I came here. A guy showed up at Serenity Ridge and asked me to meet with someone. Turns out he was a weirdo."

"Who?"

I took Tarik's business card from my purse and showed it to Courtney. "An undertaker named Fazil Tarik. He gave me the creeps. He's got a funeral home off Kingston Pike. Ever heard of him?"

I saw a sudden reluctance in Courtney's face as she examined the card. "Yes. Yes, I have. Why . . . why did he want to talk to you?"

"He said he wanted to offer me his funeral services. That he knew Jack was a veteran, and he offered special services for veterans. But I got the feeling there was more to it. He seemed to be probing me, trying to check me out in some way. How do you know Tarik?"

"It's a long story."

"He's from Iraq."

Courtney nodded, handed me back the card. "Yeah, I know that. For a time, he worked as a translator and a liaison guy between his Sunni tribe and U.S. forces. A fixer, really. That's partly how he ended up in this country. He was awarded immigrant status for services rendered. But the guy's a weasel. Don't trust him an inch."

"You going to tell me more?"

"I'm running late, Kath. Let's talk another time, but make it soon."

"You're not exactly inspiring me with confidence here. Should I be worried about Tarik? Like I said, he seemed a little creepy."

"I don't want you to worry. Let me check him out some more."

Courtney squeezed my hand, offered a tight smile, then checked the time. "I'd better go, or the sergeant may have an epileptic. Remind me when I get bored down in the Keys and need something to do that I can't open a boutique, just an Internet business. Click-click and you're done. No face-to-face hysterics with accused suspects or military brass. They just kill me."

She drained her wineglass and stood, still holding my hand.

"You'll be OK driving?"

"Honey, you know me. I could drive blindfolded after a bottle." Courtney hugged me again and kissed my cheek. "You take care, you hear? Call me if you need anything. Bearing in mind I may be in the company of other uniforms and may have to call you back. But I can't answer stuff about the case. I know you're clear on that."

I decided to prompt her a little more, to see what she knew. "A guy called DJ Spears, a vet. Did you ever hear of him?"

"Why are you asking?"

"He left an expensive new iPod for Kyle. Birthday present, I guess."

"Yeah?"

"Yeah. He's left other gifts over the years. The nurse said he was an Army buddy of Kyle's."

"What's your drift?"

"If he knew Kyle, he probably knew Jack."

Courtney shook her head. "I'd give DJ a miss, honey. I doubt you're going to learn anything there. And leave finding Jack to Tanner and me."

"You know DJ?"

"Yeah. He served at Campbell. The guy had a few brushes with military police. He's trouble."

"What kind of trouble?"

Courtney half smiled. "The troublesome kind."

Our dads both liked to watch old *Pink Panther* movies. The corny gags cracked us up, too. Like when Inspector Clouseau engages an old man with a cute dog. Clouseau goes to pat him, and the dog snarls. "Does your dog bite?"

The old guy says, "No, sir, my dog doesn't bite."

Clouseau pats the dog, and it turns savage. "I thought you said your dog didn't bite!"

"It's not my dog."

Or the Clouseau bomb gag that used to crack our fathers up. "It was a bomb." "What kind of bomb?" "The exploding kind."

Now Courtney said, "DJ Spears lost a leg. Took a rocket-propelled grenade and a shrapnel hit. I reckon some of the shrapnel's still lodged in his brain. He's a crazed hillbilly."

"Why'd he buy Kyle all that expensive stuff?"

Courtney shrugged, led me to the door, and kissed my cheek. We hugged. "Only DJ knows. He and Kyle were kinda buddies, so I'm guessing he means well, but you need to avoid a guy like that."

"Like what?"

"Trust me, honey, DJ's missing a few tracks off his CD."

35

KNOXVILLE, TENNESSEE

I took I-75 north toward Lexington, out into the sticks.

I sniffled as I drove, popped a Zyrtec into my mouth, and swallowed half a bottle of water, then waited for the pill to take effect. Knoxville is allergy central—lots of trees, grass, flowers, weeds, and air pollutants that sweep down from the Ohio Valley. On windless days like today, they lingered in the atmosphere. My allergies were bothering me. A throbbing sinus headache, my eyes and nose running.

The sweater and hoodie still lay next to me. I touched them now and then, felt the comfort of their texture.

Deesha was right; Agnes knew of DJ Spears. Her cousin was a vet, too, and she called him. He said DJ lived out in the sticks, about forty minutes from Knoxville, by Norris Lake. I needed something to do, to keep my mind from going crazy fretting about my children, so I thought I'd see what he could tell me. Agnes's cousin said Spears was a mountain man and used to be big into game hunting before he lost a leg in Iraq. He also said that Spears and his wife were a bit wacky-tacky.

As I drove, something weird distracted me. I noticed a dark SUV behind me, and behind that was a metallic-gray van. The van looked a touch old, but on its roof were a couple of aerials and a satellite dish. The windows were blacked out in both vehicles.

I got the feeling I was being followed.

Or was I getting paranoid?

The SUV and the van stayed behind me for about twenty minutes, until I finally turned off the interstate and lost sight of them in the rearview mirror.

I didn't see them again after that.

Past Rocky Top, I turned off the highway and followed a forest road that went up into the hills and then dipped down again onto a track on the far side of Norris Lake. Rondo Avenue wasn't on the GPS or any map, but once I saw it, I didn't really expect it to be. It was a dirt road littered with single- or double-wide trailers and a few deserted-looking log cabins, most of them on overgrown lots. The lakeside homes looked mostly abandoned. I guessed some of them were seasonal properties, used more in spring and summer.

Parts of East Tennessee have the unpleasant habit of reminding me of those bleak black-and-white 1930s Depression-era photographs that accompanied journalist James Agee's famous series of articles for the *New York Times*—bleak images of ragged, poverty-stricken sharecroppers, moonshine makers, and their families. A grim existence you occasionally saw echoed in their descendants, except that these days, the human spirit was sometimes sapped by a reliance on government welfare checks or cooking meth to make a living.

I turned down a lane and saw a sign scrawled in black paint on a piece of siding nailed to a board: "Rondo Avnue."

Someone hadn't bothered with the *e*, or else it was shorthand in these parts. The double-wide sat on a property that couldn't have been much more than a few acres. A playful young hound with a mustard-colored coat was tethered to a metal stake in the ground and whimpering like crazy. Strewn about the lawn were a couple of rusted old cars, stuffed toys lying wet in the grass, and a pink Dora the Explorer tricycle covered in dirt and mildew.

A newish blue Dodge van with a disabled veteran sticker on the license plate was parked hard up against the side.

I noticed a rusted metal sign nailed to a piece of two-by-four, stuck right in the middle of the lawn: "Is There Life after Death? Trespass Here and Find Out."

I decided to stay safe and pulled up on the edge of the main track. I took the keys with me and walked up a cracked stone path to the home. It was shabby, needed a paint job, and one of the windows was cracked. All the curtains were closed.

The hound tried to reach me, but the rope didn't stretch that long; then it stood on its hind legs, begging for my attention. I rubbed its head. That was a mistake, because it tried to lick my hand to death.

I wiped the moistness on my sweater, went up to the front door, and rapped hard. A grubby, food-stained child seat was in the back, and the vehicle's floor was covered in scrunched-up McDonald's and Burger King cartons and discarded greaseproof bags for French fries. There were a few crushed chicken nuggets mashed into the carpet.

After a few seconds, the door opened and a weird-looking freckle-faced kid about ten or eleven peered out, his nose dripping yellow mucus. "Yeah?"

He wore a silver-toned earring, and his hair was cut Mohican-style. The back trailed off into a kind of weird mullet with a pigtail in the center. He wore camouflage shorts and a grimy beige T-shirt with a logo on the front that said "Born to Be Wild." I could believe it.

"Is your daddy home?"

"Which daddy?"

That kind of freaked me out. "I'm looking for Mr. DJ Spears."

"What fer?" The kid slid the palm of his hand up his nose.

A woman came around from behind the door. At least fifty pounds overweight, she was squeezed into a crumpled pink fleece lounge suit and bulged like an overinflated tire. Food spots blotched her top. Her greasy hair was cut straight in a fringe. She was missing a couple of teeth, the rest of them darkly stained. Dentists don't get a ton of work in parts of rural East Tennessee, although they probably would if a dental visit didn't require a bank loan.

The woman rested the knuckles of one hand on her hip, flicking a look at the boy, before she stared at me hard. "What's up here, Elvis?"

"Lady wants Paw."

The woman ran her eyes over my clothes, then out at my car, trying to make up her mind, her jaws munching on gum or candy. "You from Social?"

"No, ma'am, I'm not."

"That's all right, then. What you want, lady?"

"Does DJ Spears live here?"

"Who's asking?"

"My name's Kath Kelly."

"DJ know you?" She gave me a look that suggested she'd be kind of amazed if he did.

"He served in the military with my husband."

"In I-raq?"

"Yes, ma'am. I was hoping to talk with DJ about my husband."

"He come through I-raq OK?"

"Excuse me?"

"Your husband. My DJ, he lost a leg. He still gets night sweats with the PTSD. Never can sleep right. Lots of his buddies are the same."

"I'm sorry. Yes, my husband came through."

"He had his problems afterward, I bet?"

"Yes, yes, he did."

"They all do, the ones who were there. Saw some mean stuff that wrecked a lot of minds." She offered me the kind of bug-eyed smile I usually associated with religious fervor, as if she'd met a kindred sister.

Then she thrust out a sweaty palm, wiping it first on her grimy top. "I'm Vera, DJ's wife. Come on in, honey."

36

The double-wide was a mess.

Toys were scattered everywhere, along with a few scrunched-up fast-food bags. A pretty dark-haired girl of about seven, who I guessed was Marilyn, didn't speak but glanced at me once, looked bored, then turned back to stare at a wide-screen TV in a corner, a sixty-inch that seemed to take up an entire wall end of the home.

The room stank of human sweat and dog dirt, and the curtains were stained tobacco-yellow and smelled of cigarette smoke. On one wall was a big framed color photo of Dolly Parton, with her mountain of big hair and that amazing smile that could warm the dead. There was a garland around the photo frame, as if it were decorating a religious shrine. I noticed a couple of uncashed welfare checks on a table, next to a half-finished red-velvet cake on a split-open cake carton. Paper plates were scattered next to it, chunks of icing and crumbs spilling over onto the table.

Elvis dipped a finger into the icing, then grabbed a big chunk of cake in his soiled hands. Vera patted his head a little too hard. "Hey, manners, Elvis. Leave some red-velvet cake for everyone, you hear? DJ's not had none yet."

A hunting rifle hung on the wall—an expensive Steyr like one my father had, with a polished walnut stock—held in place by a deer's antlers. Surprisingly, most of the furniture, like the van outside, was good-quality and expensive. The double-wide near the lake seemed to be doing OK on welfare.

At the far end of the room, a thin, unshaven man with red hair was lying stretched out on a leather La-Z-Boy recliner in front of an electric coal fire, one that made those wispy fake flames. He had a tartan blanket half over his hips. He was in his mid-thirties, I guessed, and his right leg was missing. His prosthetic leg was off and stood upright by the end of the La-Z-Boy.

He looked as if he'd been dozing, his hair askew. He scratched his stubble and dragged himself up in the chair and immediately started chewing. I saw a tin of tobacco on the side table. Next to it was an empty Coke bottle with about half an inch of brackish liquid at the bottom, which I figured from experience of seeing tobacco chewers was probably spit. My stomach churned.

"Ma'am."

"I'm Kath Kelly, Mr. Spears. We've never met before, but I think you knew my husband."

"Yeah?"

"Major Jack Hayes. He was part of your unit when you served in Iraq. Do you remember him, Mr. Spears?"

"It's DJ. Yeah, sure, I knew the major."

I noticed a bunch of family photographs on the wall. A trip to Disney World, Vera pushing a smiling DJ in a wheelchair. Another of the family at the Grand Canyon, with what looked like an RV in the background. Yet more in Vegas, all glittering lights and slots, and a pic of them outside the five-star luxury Bellagio—wow—Vera giving it full throttle with a bad-toothed smile. Her daughter was blank-faced in every shot, impressed by nothing, and little Elvis with his weird haircut was wearing a Mossy Oak camo top and short cargos, offering a thumbs-up.

I'd bet after that visit the hotel concierge was still receiving therapy. In another pic, DJ's face grinned up at the camera lens with what looked like two palmfuls of slot tokens. Not too many folks on welfare could live this high on the hog.

"You knew him well?"

DJ dipped a finger into the icing, scooped a dollop, and sucked it into his mouth, smacking his lips. "As well as most he served with. Kept to himself a lot. But a good guy. A guy you could depend on, respect, too."

"You were a sergeant?"

"That's right."

"You knew my father also and my brother Kyle."

"Yes, ma'am, I sure did."

"I know you know Kyle, because you left him some neat presents. You're very generous. Thank you."

"My pleasure, ma'am."

"Why did you do that?"

"I never forget my Army buddies. Kyle was a good guy. Always liked him. Real tough what happened. But then a lot of guys came back not right in the head. I like to go see him now and then, make sure he's getting by. That's a nice home he's staying at. But it's kinda, well, lifeless and cold." He grinned. "Colder than a well digger's ass, I say, if you know what I mean."

"You must be doing OK, giving Kyle nice presents like that?"

"I get by. Got a small business on the side selling firearms at gun shows. Man's got to take care of his own family and needs. I mean, what does the federal government ever do for us?"

I heard the hint of anger and played devil's advocate, hoping it might reveal something about DJ. I shrugged. "Build roads, enact laws, protect the citizens, fund education and the military, and organize welfare, health care, social security. There's probably a lot more."

"Yeah, well, aside from all of that. What do they ever do for vets? Gimme a new leg every few years? Well, hot dog. I could whittle one out myself."

DJ sounded as if he was on his favorite hobby horse. "You ask me, all they do for vets is give 'em the finger when they've done their duty. Thanks for fighting for your country, moron. But truckloads of beaners enter this country illegally, and they get every darn thing going. Government's only short of wiping their rear ends for 'em. Don't make sense. Ain't fair."

I didn't answer, just looked sympathetic. DJ seemed to need an ear to listen to his gripe.

"A guy's got to take care of his own business, stand on his own two feet, ma'am."

"You're right." And with that, I couldn't help flicking a look at the prosthetic leg. DJ locked eyes with me when I looked up.

"My last duty. Got blasted outside of Fall-u-jah by an RPG."

"I'm sorry."

"Way it goes. Know what's funny? A buddy I served with was standing right next to me when the rocket tore my limb right off, but it didn't even scratch him. One minute I was standing there, the next I'm toppled over and my leg's gone. I said to my buddy, I said, 'Dwayne, I've lost my leg.' Dwayne's a smart one, likes to make jokes. He said, 'No, you haven't, DJ. Hey, look, it's right over there hanging outta that tree.'"

DJ laughed, an infectious kind of giggle that rolled on and on until it came to an abrupt full stop, and he shrugged. "I guess a man's gotta laugh at adversity, right? We all got crosses to bear or bears to cross."

Whatever that meant. "I'm sure it's been tough."

Vera came back, pulling on an old wool jacket, car keys in hand. "I gotta run some errands. Want me to take the kids with me, DJ?"

"Yeah. May as well."

"It's no trouble," I told Vera. "You don't have to leave on account of me."

"Hey, ain't no trouble for me, either. But Elvis here needs his Chicken McNuggets fix, and Marilyn, too. Want me to bring you back something, DJ?"

"Mac, large fries, and a Dew. Git me some 'baccy while you're at it."

"You care for something, ma'am?" Vera politely touched my arm.

It was a kind offer, but the trailer with its dog-doo smells was a dining experience I'd rather skip. "No, but thank you for asking."

"Why don't I get an extra Big Mac anyways, just in case you change your mind?"

With Vera, I figured it was easier to be polite than to argue. "Thank you, that's very kind of you."

"Nice to meet you, ma'am."

"You, too, Vera."

The kids spilled out after her, and I heard the car move off.

DJ said, "The eldest one ain't mine, he's Vera's. Likes to call me Paw since his daddy went out for an oil change and never came back."

"Your girl's pretty."

"Like Vera often says, I may have lost my leg, but ain't nothing wrong with my dongle." DJ gave that infectious giggle, and sure enough, it hit the buffers again, came to a hard stop.

"I'll have to take your word on that, DJ."

He grinned, showing a missing right molar. "You're a funny one, ma'am. So why you here?"

"Why do you visit Kyle?"

DJ shrugged. "I reckon he needs visitors. That place might be good and all, but it's the pits. Stiff as a dead horse. Besides, I reckon Kyle likes to see my kids."

"Yeah?"

"Yeah. Especially Marilyn. She always gets a reaction out of him. He likes to look at her and stroke her hair. You can see he likes kids, they make him happy."

That made sense.

"I always wondered what happened to Kyle in Iraq. What made him different when he came home. What traumatized him. Do you know what it was, DJ?"

DJ's eyes started shifting, as if he was looking for an escape route.

"What's wrong, DJ?"

"To tell the truth, I don't like going back there in my mind. It wasn't a good time. A lot of bad stuff went down that wasn't pleasant."

"You mean like buddies being shot or killed, post-traumatic stress from all the IEDs? Long tours of duty? Civilian massacres?"

"Yeah, I guess all of that. Men do strange things in wartime. I guess that's 'cause strange things happen to them."

"You know what traumatized Kyle, don't you?"

"No, ma'am."

"Are you sure? DJ, can I be honest here? I'm not trying to cause you trouble, but I saw your reaction. I believe you know. I believe you can tell me the truth."

"No, ma'am, I don't know. But a lot of what happened there was disturbing."

"Like what, precisely? Please, I know it must be difficult, but I am trying to understand what happened to my brother. What was it that you and Kyle might have participated in that could have distressed my brother so much that he came home and tried to kill himself?"

"I . . . I can't really say. Nothing in particular comes to mind."

I eyed him closely, but he didn't seem to want to meet my stare. "I'm not sure I believe you. It would mean so much to me to find out. You said strange things happened. What things do you mean?"

DJ started scratching his stubble again, as if he had a bad itch, looking uncomfortable. "I ain't got no idea what you're talking about, so back off, lady."

"Why did you react the way you did?"

"React how?"

"Please don't take me for a moron, DJ. You looked like you wanted to head for an exit door, pronto. So quit pulling my chain, and tell me the truth. I'm begging you."

I saw his lips purse. Soft at first, then tight, as if he was intent on not saying another word, but surprisingly, he did. "Look, I heard rumors."

"What rumors?"

"It was just a mission that went badly wrong, that's all."

"In what way wrong?"

He seemed to stall, then said, "People got killed."

"Soldiers?"

He shook his head. "Iraqi civilians. Women and kids, too."

"Are we talking a massacre?"

"I don't know . . . no. Look, these things happen in war, so listen, just back off. You don't want to go there. You really don't."

"Why not?"

"You just don't."

"What kind of answer is that?"

"The only one you're going to get."

"I need to know, DJ."

"Ain't you listening?"

"DJ, I've lived with this for years. I need an answer."

He fell silent. I felt a cold chill, a kind of creepy sensation that my intuition was trying to tell me something. That's when I heard the loud click of a firearm being cocked.

I spun around. Vera moved quietly for a big lady. I hadn't heard her step in through the back door, but I did notice the gun she clutched in both hands. A big, ferocious-looking stainless-steel revolver with a barrel that looked as long as a broom handle. It was pointed straight at me.

"You want fries with that Big Mac?"

37

"That's a big gun, Vera." It was all I could think of saying. It was true. The revolver was massive.

"Five hundred Smith and Wesson. You could take down a bar with a gun like this."

"You mean a bear?"

"Yeah, go ahead, poke fun. Except I'm the one with the firearm."

Which was true, and Vera didn't look as if she found it all that hilarious.

She jerked her chin at DJ. "I dumped the kids with Cousin Ruth. They're still whining they ain't got their nuggets."

"Let 'em whine."

"I took a look in her car as I drove out. She's got a gun in the glove compartment."

"You opened my car and messed with my belongings? That's against the law."

"You can't talk, so shut your mouth. You're a trespasser, lady."

"You invited me inside."

"Yeah? And how would the cops know that if I shot you? It could be more like you forced your way in. A home invasion. If you think we're dumber than dirt, you need to think again."

"No, but I think you're forgetting your kids are witnesses. Unless you mean to kill them, too?"

Was I imagining it, or did Vera let loose a tiny grin. "You trying to tempt me? They'll say whatever they're told to."

I decided not to hit her with a reply along the lines of *I guess you get full marks for parenting*. Vera didn't look like the kind who appreciated sarcasm. "Is there really any need to point that gun?"

"I'll point it anywhere I want in my own home. You're harassing my family, lady. DJ asked you to back off, but you keep stepping on his toes. You don't listen, do you? Maybe I ought to blow out those tires of yours and you've got to walk all the way back to I-75. How would you like that?"

When Vera said "tires," it sounded like "tars." But I didn't point that out. DJ grabbed his prosthetic leg, pulled it on, and almost toppled as he stood, using the La-Z-Boy for balance. "Here, give me that darn gun."

He sounded irritated, and Vera handed him the revolver. He grasped it and limped over to me, a gap-toothed grin spreading across his face. "Know what Vera sometimes says?"

"I wouldn't even hazard a guess."

"She says after what happened to me in I-raq, I've gone a little funny in the head."

I kept my mouth shut. DJ limped closer.

"That I'm capable of just about anything if I'm riled. She says I go nuts now and then, which is probably true. Know what really riles me?"

"You mean you've got a list?"

"Yeah, a short one: nosy parkers."

The gun barrel's tip came up, touched my nose. It was cold and smelled of old cordite. Then he slid it down to my lips, then my neck, and went lower until it brushed against my right breast. The grin never left his face.

"That's sexual assault where I come from, DJ."

"Yeah? Not around here. Besides, you ain't got no witnesses, aside from Vera here, and she's seen nothing. If I was you, I'd get going. Before I go all deranged and start plugging the walls."

"You know why I'm really here, don't you?"

"Yeah, I saw on the TV about that plane. I figure it's something to do with that."

"How do you figure that?"

DJ shut his mouth tight as a clam, as if he regretted his reply because it said more than he wanted to say. I didn't pursue that line right now.

"You know what happened during the incident with Kyle in Iraq. You were there, weren't you?"

"What makes you think that?"

"It's written all over your face, DJ. Not only that, but somebody talked."

"Who?"

"My husband," I lied, but I figured I'd go whole hog and try to wheedle something out of DJ.

Nothing. He didn't flinch.

I looked at Vera, hoping to elicit some kind of maternal sympathy or just touch their hearts. "DJ's right. I'm here because of the air crash. My husband disappeared eight years ago, along with our two children. Now it turns out he never really died. I'm hoping my children didn't die, either. You may be able to help me. I need clues. I need to figure out why my husband never came home."

I waited for a reaction. It never came on DJ's face or on Vera's. Steely-eyed, both of them.

"You know what it's like to lose your kids, Vera?"

"Naw, but if someone took Elvis for a few months, that would be real peachy. I'd thank them for the break." She stepped closer, her voice a threatening whisper. "You need to leave us in peace. There's nothing more DJ can tell you aside from what he already said, you got that?"

"I lost my family."

"I heard you. But you're squirreling up the wrong tree."

"Just tell me what you know, and I'll be gone."

"You're going anyway. Trouble is, you're picking on the wrong man. I don't know much about your husband. But maybe you need to talk with your daddy. Ask him those questions."

"I'm asking you."

"And I'm telling you to git lost. Sassy, ain't you? I told you, better ask your daddy. Because this conversation is over."

Vera took the Smith & Wesson back from DJ, using both hands. She stuck the heavy silver barrel right up against my chin. It pressed into my skin again.

"Now, git. I want to see a quick two-step out that door."

I moved to the door, lingered, looked back. I went to speak, to try one last time, but Vera beat me to it, her face closing like a steel gate.

"And don't bother coming back, you hear? Or next time, lady, you better have booked an ambulance."

38

As I drove home, I felt more bewildered and frustrated than ever.

Why was DJ so reticent? What or whom was he protecting?

He and his wife were definitely missing a track or two, but I felt there was more to this, a lot more. But what? I had absolutely no idea.

Something else troubled me. Vera said I should ask my father. What did she mean?

Half an hour later on the interstate, I thought I glimpsed the metallic-gray van again, way behind me. No sign of the SUV, though.

I slowed deliberately, pulled onto the side of the road, and turned around in my seat to look out the rear window. The van had no choice but to drive past me. The side windows were tinted, but I saw the driver. He looked foreign—Arab or Mexican, I couldn't be sure. He kept staring ahead, focusing on the road, not looking at my vehicle. I started my car and pulled out again, following the van. The rear license plate was muddied and unreadable. Two exits ahead, the vehicle turned off. I thought about following it, but that began to seem absurd. Was I losing it?

I kept my eye on the rearview mirror for the rest of the journey, but I saw no sign of either the van or the SUV again.

When I had parked the Nissan in my driveway, I took the sweater and hoodie with me and stepped onto the back porch.

I brushed past the brass wind chimes by the back door, the sounds of the tubular bells echoing around the garden. I slid the key into the lock and moved inside, and the first thing I did was check the kitchen wall clock: 12:05 p.m. Jack had promised to call at two p.m. I had just under two hours.

Just under two hours of going crazy with worry, apprehension, and downright confusion. Worse, I couldn't get Amy and Sean out of my mind, not for a second. What did they look like now? Would they remember me? What had happened to them in all those eight long years? Who or what had taken the place of my love?

I was driving myself insane.

I looked at my writing desk in the corner. I hadn't written in at least a week. Right now I didn't think I could ever write again. I had absolutely no interest.

In despair, I pulled up a kitchen chair, sat at the table, and put my head in my arms, the sweater and hoodie beside me. I wanted to weep aloud, to scream my frustration. When I finally looked up, my eyes drifted past the window and over to the cottage. I frowned.

Was I seeing things?

I was used to seeing those three pieces of two-by-four nailed to the door and the frame. But one of the wood pieces was hanging loose, as if someone had tried to remove it to open the door.

My .38 revolver was still in my glove compartment. But my father's shotgun was in the kitchen. I got up, opened the pantry door, and removed the shotgun. It was an old Remington pump-action, the varnish worn off the wooden stock. My father usually kept the shotgun loaded. I slid back the pump slide a little and saw no round in the chamber, but the safety was on.

Gripping the shotgun, I moved out onto the back patio.

I looked over at the cottage. The piece of two-by-four was definitely hanging loose.

I racked the shotgun, putting a cartridge in the chamber, then moved slowly down the patio steps and started to walk toward the cottage.

After a dozen steps, I saw something on the cottage's patio.

A rusted, discarded claw hammer. I recognized it from my dad's barn workshop. He often used the hammer when doing fixes. I felt my heart beat faster. I stepped up warily onto the cottage porch. There was no mistake—the piece of two-by-four was hanging off but still held in place by a couple of nails I had hammered into the wood. The other wood pieces looked as if someone had tried to loosen them, or else they had already been removed and then hammered back on again.

Who did it?

My father would never have done such a thing. It looked as if someone had tried to break in.

I took another step on the porch. The wood creaked.

I listened but heard nothing from inside the cottage.

I put a hand on the doorknob and turned. It was unlocked. I had left the door locked. When I looked closer, I saw that the wood near the lock, on the door and the frame, was splintered in places. Someone had broken in. There were few break-ins in the homes around here. Everyone had a gun in Tennessee. It didn't stop burglaries, but it probably lessened them, because the burglars risked ending up in a pine box for their trouble.

"Is there anybody in there?" I called out.

Silence.

"If anyone's in there, come out now. I've got a gun."

More silence.

Still holding the shotgun in one hand, I picked up the claw hammer with the other and wedged it between the last two wood pieces. The nails creaked and bent as I yanked one end of each two-by-four off the doorframe. Now I could open the door.

My heart was racing with apprehension, and a morbid fear seemed to slap me in the face.

More than six years. It had been more than six years since I had last stepped inside the cottage. The last time, I was so overwhelmed I didn't feel right for weeks afterward.

The window nearest the door caught my eye. A cobweb veil was stretched in the space between the fly screen and the glass and was mottled with black spots, the remains of dead flies. Every now and then, Dad had his housekeeper, Mrs. Bridges, vacuum and dust the cottage. He'd remove the two-by-fours to let her in and nail them back afterward. But I figured it had probably been a year or more since her last visit.

I forced myself to grip the doorknob. I twisted and pushed.

The door yawned inward with a rusty creak.

And that's when I got my first shock.

39

The cottage had been ransacked.

Drawers lay open, and personal belongings were all over the floor. The cushions from the sand-colored corduroy couch that Jack and I sat on to watch movies were tossed about the room. The couch material was ripped in places, like a gutted animal, clumps of the white polyester stuffing scattered about like sheared wool.

I let out a breath and covered my mouth with one hand, the shotgun loose in the other. Our old TV was still there, covered in a veil of dust. The same with the DVD player underneath. Whoever broke in, it didn't look as if they came to steal electronics.

I knew from Courtney—one of her nuggets of observation about crime-scene work—that sometimes criminals defecate on their victims' property during a burglary. It's not necessarily a crude snub to their victims but out of visceral fear as they carried out the theft. Usually, it's kids or young adults who have to drop their pants. But I saw nothing to suggest that this break-in had been carried out by delinquent teens. They would have taken the DVD player and the TV, as out-of-date as the electronics were. Someone would always give them a few bucks for an old TV, even if just to use it as a screen for computer games.

Nothing like that happened the first time the cottage was broken into, either, about three months after Jack vanished. Dad was in the house when he heard a noise and went out with a flashlight and his .45 to investigate. He found the cottage door's lock forced and broken. He called the cops.

Now a thought struck me. What if it was Jack who broke in back then?

Nothing appeared to be stolen, the would-be burglar probably frightened off by Dad's vigilance. After that, we kept the cottage locked, Dad had a driveway alarm installed, and we got a dog. The dog strayed within a year and never returned, and the driveway alarm often went without its batteries being replaced.

Moving among the mess now, I spotted some of Amy's and Sean's old toys—a boxed Lego helicopter set, a yellow Teletubbies doll that Amy loved, the stuffing burst out.

It was hard to breathe, as if a knife were stuck in my chest. Any break-in is a violation. To break into a place as precious as this shrine . . . Yes, it was a shrine, I admitted it. As borderline crazy as that might sound, I kept a shrine. They can either be a comfort to lessen your grief or a way to perpetuate it, depending on the state and strength of your mind. For me, knowing the cottage was there, as it had been when I lived there with my family, brought me a bittersweet kind of comfort. There was still something tangible from my past, something I could touch, feel, see, smell, if and whenever I wished. Even if it often frightened me to do so.

Right now I felt overwhelmed. I felt that something treasured had been desecrated. This was my property, and it had been broken into.

I picked up a cushion and coughed. The dust was getting to me. I put the cushion down. A corner cabinet was overturned near the bottom of the stairs. Papers lay strewn about, some on the stairs, along with some old CDs. The trail seemed to lead up to the landing.

Gripping the shotgun, I began to climb the stairs.

40

I reached the landing and looked around.

The cottage ceiling wasn't high. It had a half-mansard roof, French-looking, and in the three bedrooms the roof crawl spaces were turned into storage cupboards, accessed by doors.

All the cupboard doors were open, and you could see the old clothes and junk items crammed inside the spaces, along with a couple of boxes containing Jack's "bug-out" gear, everything we'd need in the event of a civil emergency. Jack was something of a hoarder. He used to buy emergency stuff at gun shows, including first-aid kits, survival items like water purifiers and emergency rations, maps, compasses, flashlights—he had stashed at least a dozen flashlights all over the house. He also used to buy amusing progun posters at those shows.

One that he got a particular kick out of was stuck on the cupboard door. It showed a bunch of Native Americans on horseback, armed with rifles, pistols, and bandoliers full of cartridges. Underneath it said, "Hand over all your guns—we will take care of you. Signed: The Government."

Jack used to laugh at that one. "Trust no one but yourself, and always be prepared." That had been his motto since his Army days. Another nugget he liked to repeat: "When disaster happens, and Walmart's shelves are empty, we're only one meal away from anarchy."

I wandered around all the bedrooms. Amy's and Sean's, hers pink and his blue, with a Spider-Man poster on one wall, where I had pinned it up for him. With every familiar object I saw, I felt a catch in my heart. A toy, Amy's Barbie bedside lamp, Sean's Batman sneakers.

I began to feel overwhelmed. The same kind of feeling I had when I last entered the cottage.

And I felt angry, violated. I slumped down on the dusty bed and felt like crying.

My eyes were drawn to a clutch of discarded clothes just inside one of the crawl-space cupboards. It was a cupboard I remembered opening only once, to store some of Kyle's stuff, an old CD player and TV, a game console, books, a bunch of clear plastic storage boxes full of clothes. Jack had cleared it out for me after Kyle moved to Serenity Ridge, because I couldn't face that chore. Whoever ransacked the cottage had to be looking for something specific; no one went to this much trouble. I'd have to call the police and make a report.

As I got up off the bed, I spotted Kyle's old exercise bike poking out from among the cupboard's junky darkness. And then I saw something stuck in the rafters, hidden out of view. I peered inside the crawl space. It looked like some kind of plastic food-storage box with a red lid. Wedged next to it was what appeared to be a thin black book, hidden between the rafters and the roof insulation.

I reached in and yanked the box out of its recess. It had a couple of old rubber bands wrapped around it. When I tried to remove them, the fatigued rubber crumbled and broke. I opened the box.

The skunky smell of weed wafted out. Inside was a glass marijuana pipe and a yellow plastic pill bottle with a white twist cap. I opened the cap. The aroma of marijuana was still there, and it drenched my nostrils. I saw a bunch of screwed-up plastic bags. Kyle's old hash stash.

I put down the box and its contents and focused on the black book.

What was it doing in there?

Did it belong to Kyle, or had Jack stashed it there? As I reached out to dislodge the black book, my cell phone rang. I jumped, my nerves frazzled. I didn't even check the number as I hit the answer button.

"Ms. Kelly?"

I recognized Tanner's voice. "Yes."

"Sorry to trouble you, ma'am, it's Agent Tanner. I wonder if we could meet."

"When?"

"This afternoon. I know it's pretty soon after what you've just been through, but it's important."

"Can you tell me why?"

"I'd really rather not discuss this over the phone."

"Did . . . did you find . . . ?"

"Remains? No, Ms. Kelly, not yet."

"What is it that's so important?"

"I'd prefer we talked face-to-face."

"If it's so important, I want to know about it *now*."

"Ms. Kelly, there's some lab work to be completed. I'm waiting for forensics to get back to me as we speak. And I'm waiting for some information I requested. I'd prefer not to discuss anything until it's confirmed."

"Until what's confirmed?"

"Ma'am, please, if you could bear with me. May I call back later?"

I felt a desperate urge to tell Tanner about the break-in. But what if it was Jack? What if they investigated and found his prints or something? Would Jack hold that against me and keep up his threat? I decided to hold off for now, but I felt confused and desperate.

"I've waited eight years to know the truth. *Eight years.* After seeing the crash site and hearing Dexter say that my family may be alive, I can't wait any longer, or else I think I'll go crazy."

Tanner said nothing.

"Can't you understand that? Please, I beg you, tell me *something.*"

A long silence. I heard Tanner sigh and then take a deep breath. "There have been a couple of developments at the site, Ms. Kelly. Like I said, I'm awaiting lab results."

"You're waiting on lab results for *all* of the developments?"

"No, not all of them."

"Then *please* tell me what you can."

Another long silence, as if Tanner was trying to decide something. "Maybe it's important, maybe not."

"And?"

"They managed to open the aluminum briefcase. Among . . . well, among some other stuff they found in there was a notebook. Some lines scribbled inside. But the handwriting is hard to decipher. I'd like you to take a look at it."

I felt a cold hand reach in again and grasp my heart. "Jack . . . Jack's handwriting was almost impossible to read. We used to joke that he should have been a doctor."

"I could only make out one word, just a single word on the first line. Maybe it means something to you, maybe not."

I hung on, Tanner's silence ominous down the line. My impatience was turning to anger. I wanted to scream, *Tell me, for heaven's sake!* "What's the word?"

"Red."

I stood there after I put the phone down.

In total shock, Tanner's answer ringing in my ears.

Red.

The same word my mother scrawled the day she killed herself. I felt mystified.

I heard a noise and stiffened.

A distinct noise like a footfall, a shoe or boot hitting wood. I spun around. It seemed to come from outside the cottage. Then I heard the wind chimes ringing on my father's back porch.

I peered out the window. I could see that the pipes of the chimes were moving, but I saw nothing.

I saw no wind stirring the tree branches; there wasn't a whisper of air that day.

My heart quickened.

Clutching the shotgun, I flicked off the safety and moved downstairs and out onto the cottage's front porch. I looked toward the house. Still I saw nothing, but I heard the wind chimes dying away.

A stray wind gust, or had a movement set them off?

I crossed the lawn to my the rear porch of the main house and edged my way across the decking, the wood creaking under my feet.

I had left the back door open. It was still open. I stepped back inside the kitchen.

The second I did, a man in black, wearing a ski mask, lunged at me. His left hand grabbed the shotgun barrel and tore it from my grasp with a force so violent it felt as if my chest had been ruptured. His other hand stabbed at my throat, and I was stung by a jolt of pain like an electric shock.

A split second later, my muscles went into violent spasm, and everything faded.

41

I awoke with a killer headache. It made me feel as if an elephant were sitting on my head. I was tied to a kitchen chair.

Pain spasmed in my throat, and it felt on fire, every muscle in my body raw. My mouth was taped up. I was breathing through my nose, and I couldn't move. Silver duct tape bound my wrists tightly to the armrests. I heard heavy footsteps.

I saw the man in black out in the hall, descending the stairs, still wearing his ski mask. In his right hand he held a black pistol. He stopped at the bottom of the stairs, peered out though a crack in the hall shutters, then turned toward me and strode back into the room.

Bloodshot brown eyes stared at me from behind the mask. His left hand held the Taser—a stun gun—that he'd used to immobilize me. He didn't speak but held up the Taser for me to see, a warning, before he laid it on the kitchen table. He placed the pistol next to it. Above his black pigskin gloves, I glimpsed angry red wrists, horribly scarred. He pulled up a chair and sat facing me.

Fear made my body shake, and my mouth went dry. Was the intruder going to rape me? Kill me? Jack used to warn me about break-ins and to be careful when I was alone in the house. A few nearby homes were burgled over the years, including the cottage, and once an intruder shot a woman during a neighborhood home invasion. It was why my father insisted I always keep a firearm handy. But my hands were bound, and there was no way could I free myself and use a gun, even if I could get my hands on one.

The man in the ski mask said nothing, but I heard his breathing. It had a rasp like that of an asthma sufferer. He pulled a bandana away from his neck to reveal some kind of speaking valve inserted into his throat. It appeared to be attached to his neck with two lengths of slim white Velcroed material. "Can you understand me? Nod if you do."

The voice sounded a little husky, like Jack's voice usually sounded, and it shocked me. I thought I saw knotted scar tissue staining the man's neck when he pulled away the neck bandana. It was such a momentary glimpse that I could have been wrong. But if I was right, the scars and the speaking valve told me his voice box was damaged. Unless—and this was when a weird thought struck me—unless in some way the intruder was trying to disguise his voice?

"I asked you a question. Answer it."

I nodded.

"Don't struggle, don't attempt to scream or flee, because you won't get far."

My fear ratcheted up. The electronic voice sounded tired. His bloodshot eyes made me wonder if he was drugged.

"Keep still. Behave and don't scream, and I'll take off the tape. Do exactly as I tell you, and you won't be harmed. We clear on that?"

Too terrified to answer, I managed to nod.

"Enjoy the free waxing, honey." He leaned across, and his glove touched my face. He gripped the tape and tore it off quickly. The shearing pain in my upper lip made my eyes water.

He laid the tape on the table, next to the pistol and the stun gun.

"Please . . . there . . . there's no money in the house, except what's in my purse. About . . . about eighty dollars." Words tumbled from my mouth, which was becoming weirdly numb.

"Shut up."

"There's . . . jewelry in the main bedroom."

"I said shut up and listen. This isn't about that. It's about your husband."

Wide-eyed with confusion, I stared as the intruder sat back on the table, his hands supporting him on either side. He looked down at me with a tilt of his chin.

A weird chill shot though me. I recalled how Jack often used to sit on the table's edge the same way and regard me with a tilt of his head. Was it a coincidence?

Or was it Jack?

I studied the intruder's physique. He looked about Jack's build, just stockier. That could have been with age. It hit me like a baseball bat—the scars, the surgery. Were they from the plane crash?

I stared at the bloodshot eyes, going through my mental checklist. Jack had brown eyes, too. "Who . . . who are you?"

"My name's not important. But what I have to tell you is."

He leaned in close, so close that I could smell his body odor, an outdoorsy scent that seemed like a mix of woodlands and unwashed clothes. "I'm here to give you a warning. Heed it, and you'll live. Don't, and you're going to die."

42

I felt an icy-cold hand reach in again and clutch my heart.

Panic smothered me, my chest pounding so fiercely I could hardly breathe. *I'm here to give you a warning. Heed it, and you'll live. Don't, and you're going to die.*

I stared back at the intruder, could feel my body tremble, my voice hoarse with fear. "Who—who are you?"

"I told you, just listen."

Was this Jack? The speaking valve made it impossible to tell exactly. My imagination was running riot, every instinct telling me it was him. But how could I be certain? Jack had a livid scar on his right wrist from a shrapnel blast he suffered in Iraq. He also had a small tattoo in red and black of the American eagle just above his left wrist. The intruder wore gloves, and I couldn't see his wrists. I looked for scarring or the eagle tattoo, but the gloves covered all of his hands.

Would you mind taking off your right glove?

Sure, lady.

It made me wonder, were the gloves deliberate to cover the scar or to leave no fingerprints or both? On a shelf by the window were several photographs of Jack, Amy, Sean, and me. Another of Julie Ann and me on Broadway, when we visited New York to see *The Lion King*. The intruder picked it up, studied it, and looked up.

"Nice-looking kid."

I was so rigid with fear I couldn't even nod.

"You like her?"

Was it my imagination, or was the intruder's tone mocking? I was becoming convinced that this was Jack masquerading as a burglar. Was he trying to taunt me?

"I asked, do you like her?"

"What . . . what does it matter to you?"

My fragile defiance earned me a steely look, before he put the photograph back. "You lost one family. That was a tragedy. You don't want to lose someone else you care about. That would be pretty careless, don't you think?"

The intruder stared at me, then picked up the pistol from the table.

"The TV news said that remains were found at the crash site. Whose?"

"They . . . they think they found the pilot's."

"They think?"

"They have to do an autopsy. They're not sure."

"What about the passengers?"

"They don't know if they perished or survived. They're still searching for remains. They found blood traces . . . and things were missing from the aircraft."

"What things?"

"A . . . a first-aid kit. A flashlight that they found a few hundred yards away . . ."

"They're suggesting somebody made it out alive?"

I nodded.

The intruder pursed his lips and sighed, as if considering my replies. When he spoke again, his electronic voice jarred the silence. "I'm here to give you a piece of advice."

He pointed to the snapshots on the shelf with the tip of his pistol's barrel. "Forget about your old life. It's over, done with. Accept that you've got a new one. Live it."

"My . . . my children."

"Are you listening? That part of your life is over. Bury it. Leave Jack that way, too. Because if you don't, it'll cost you your life."

He stood, pushing back the chair with a scraping sound as he stared down at me. "Ignore my advice and try to find your husband and kids, and you'll be digging your own grave. Guaranteed."

The warning seared like a branding iron. My blood pounded in my veins. "They . . . they're alive. All of them are alive, aren't they?" I blurted.

The intruder thrust his left hand into his pocket, he flicked out a big penknife, and the blade flashed. He brought the knife down and sliced through the duct tape binding me to the armrests.

"Remember my warning. One other thing. This didn't happen, understand? Tell anyone, including the cops, and I'll come for you— and the girl." He nodded to the photo of Julie Ann. "Got that? You'll pay the price."

I nodded.

He folded the knife and tucked it back into his pocket.

"You're Jack, aren't you?"

He moved toward the back door.

"No! Wait, you have to tell me. Please, the children . . ."

The bloodshot eyes bored into me. "Don't try to follow me. It would be a big mistake, Kath."

Something about the way he said my name—his tone softer—suggested that he knew me. It *was* Jack. I knew it in my heart. He reached for the door handle. Amy's sweater and Sean's hoodie were still on the kitchen table.

I was about to say, *You left them for me, didn't you? You left them as proof,* but as his fingers touched the handle, the sound of the door buzzer echoed throughout the house.

It was like an electric shock. I jerked my head toward the front door. A bulky dark figure appeared behind the frosted-glass panel. My heart panicked as the intruder's pistol gave a soft click. He touched the cold barrel against my cheek.

"One sound, you're dead."

43

The buzzer rang again.

A long, persistent, ten-second burst.

Then silence.

I sensed the intruder's unease as he stared at the front door. The figure on the porch shifted behind the frosted glass. The buzzer rang a third time, for maybe another ten seconds, and then stopped.

"Are you in, Ms. Kelly? It's me, Tanner."

A sharp rapping pounded the door, then ceased.

"Ms. Kelly?"

I felt the gun press against my throat as the man said, "Who is it?"

I could endanger Tanner's life if I told the truth. "It . . . it's a repairman," I lied. "Come to fix the air-conditioning."

"Get rid of him."

"How?"

"You've got his number in your phone, right? Call him."

But I didn't have Tanner's number stored in my cell phone. I had his card in my purse. If the intruder saw the card, it could give Tanner away. "What will I tell him?"

"You've got a migraine. Tell him to come by again. Just get rid of him. Where's your cell?"

It lay next to my purse on the kitchen worktop. I nodded to it. The intruder tossed my phone across. "Be careful what you say, or you'll both be sorry."

My hands shook as I fumbled with my cell phone. I made a pretense of scrolling through the contacts list. The doorbell sounded again, and then came more impatient knocking.

"Ms. Kelly?"

"Come on, hurry it up," the intruder said.

I sensed his panic. "I . . . I can't find the number."

"Why not?"

"I can't see it here anywhere."

Tanner's voice, louder. "Ms. Kelly? Can you hear me? I saw your car in the driveway. Are you OK?"

A couple of seconds of stark silence, and then the phone was wrenched from my hands. "Find that number."

I realized Tanner's number would be in my call log. But my phone suddenly rang, shrill and loud in the intruder's hand, startling us both.

He shoved the illuminated screen in my face. "Who is it?"

I couldn't recall Tanner's number, but I figured it was him. My ringing phone echoed all over the house. "The repairman, I think."

"Answer it, and remember what I said."

He hit the speakerphone button and thrust the phone at me.

"Ms. Kelly?"

I recognized Tanner's voice at once. "Y-yes."

"It's me, Tanner. I'm outside your home. Where are you, ma'am?"

"I-I'm inside."

"Inside? I've been ringing your doorbell, ma'am. Didn't you hear? Is everything OK?"

I was afraid Tanner would say something that would give him away. How could I stop him? I thought desperately. "Yes, yes, everything's OK. I'm sorry, Mr. Tanner. I have a migraine. I know when we spoke earlier, you said you'd come by, but could you fix the air-conditioning another time?"

A bloated silence.

I guessed Tanner was stumped by my answer. But if he had any sense, he'd figure it out. "Another time, ma'am?"

"Yes, please. If you don't mind."

Pause.

"And when exactly would suit?"

"Would tomorrow be OK?"

Another pause. "Yeah, I can do tomorrow. Same time?"

"Yes, thank you."

"You sure you're OK?"

"Yes, I'm sure."

"All right, I'll take care of the problem then. Hope you're feeling better by tomorrow."

And then the line clicked, the shadow disappeared from the glass, and Tanner's footsteps faded off the wooden porch.

44

I heard the intruder let out a sigh.

My own hands were shaking, my entire body in convulsions. Tanner was leaving but going where? And what would he do? Try to tackle the intruder alone? Or call for help? Outside, a car started up. The engine growled, the car drove off, and it faded to silence. I felt more worried by Tanner's disappearance, not reassured.

The intruder rubbed his left hand to his face. The movement revealed a small portion of his wrist. I tried again to see Jack's eagle tattoo but couldn't. "Don't move, not an inch, got that?"

His eyes stayed on me, and I nodded. Then he padded down the hall and peered through the curtain crack.

I prayed Tanner wouldn't go far. I had no idea what was going to happen next or what he might do, but right at that moment, I felt wracked by fear. And I sensed the absolute certainty of trouble.

Tanner was armed, and so was Jack; I was now more certain it was Jack. Someone could get shot or killed. I didn't want anyone to die. I was desperate to know where my children were, what had become of them. And why was Jack doing this? Why had he betrayed me and kept our children from me all these years?

He took my cell phone from me and tossed it onto the table. "Get up." He dragged me to my feet. "Move, toward the front room." He shoved me down the hallway and then peered again through a crack in the hall curtains.

I figured Tanner might park farther along the main road and walk back, his car hidden beyond the woods. I tried to squint through the curtain crack, but I could make out nothing but trees.

"Get back into the kitchen."

We reached the table, and he had me sit in the same chair. He laid his pistol on the table once more, then unrolled about a foot of duct tape and began to wrap it around my arms, binding me to the chair again. Where in God's name was Tanner? Had he driven a short distance away and doubled back or gone for help?

And then I almost gasped.

Across the kitchen, through the half-open wood blinds, I spotted Tanner. Alone, approaching the porch with his gun in his hand.

He saw me through the crack in the blinds—the intruder was still taping my arms—and Tanner put a finger to his mouth, urging me to stay silent. I wanted to scream, to let him know about the creaky floorboard on the back patio, but Tanner was already moving toward it.

No!

Creak.

The intruder spun around and spotted Tanner through the blinds as the agent's bulky frame came rushing like a bull toward the kitchen's back door, his pistol aimed.

Before the intruder could shoot his own weapon, Tanner fired two rapid shots through the door, shattering the glass.

The intruder ducked and wildly returned fire as he slammed me to the floor, my scream drowned by gunfire. "No, don't hurt him, don't kill him, Tanner!"

And then a hail of bullets exploded, and rang around the kitchen walls.

45

The gunfire died.

The stench of gunpowder choked my lungs, and I coughed hard.

I lay on the floor, and Jack lay beside me—I hadn't changed my mind that it was him. He was breathing hard and coughing, his gun aimed toward the kitchen door. Then came silence.

I couldn't see Tanner. He could have been out on the porch somewhere, only yards away, behind the cover of a couple of old floral patio couches. Or else he had retreated into the back garden. What if he was wounded or dead? Jack shuffled to his knees, just as Tanner's voice shouted, "Whoever you are, don't harm her. Help's on the way, you hear me? Ms. Kelly, are you there?"

"Yes."

"Are you hurt?"

"No."

Jack coughed, his back hunched as if he was injured. "Shut up and move. That way."

Grunting, he gripped the neck of my sweater and propelled me toward the kitchen table. I saw a crimson streak on the floor and felt a stab of torment. He was wounded. How badly I couldn't tell. He lurched toward the kitchen table and laid a hand on it for support. I noticed blood seeping from a wound in his chest.

"Please, let me help." I went to touch him, but he raised the gun to point at my head.

"You lied. The guy's a cop?"

"FBI."

He spoke loudly, projecting his voice toward the back door. "Can you hear me, Tanner?"

A few moments of silence. I figured Tanner was mulling over the situation, and then he said, "I hear you."

"I'm leaving and taking her with me. If you or anyone follows me, I kill her. We clear?"

"Don't hurt her, man. You do that, you're in big trouble."

"You didn't hear me."

"I heard you."

"Is there anyone out front?"

"Not yet, but they're coming. Minutes, maybe less."

"I'm leaving now. Put your gun on the ground in front of you, kick it away. Do it now. Remember what I said. Follow me or try anything, and I'll kill her, Tanner, for sure."

We heard something heavy drop onto the wooden patio. Jack seemed reluctant to move forward and check for certain. Panic seemed to light his eyes. He had minutes, maybe less, to get away. He backed us toward the front door but kept looking over his shoulder, as if expecting Tanner to burst in.

Jack peered through the blinds, then cautiously turned the handle and cracked open the door. The woods beyond the front driveway looked deserted. He pushed me out first, holding on to my sweater. But after a dozen steps, I saw Tanner's car through the trees, blocking the road. I could feel the tension rise in Jack.

"Is that Tanner's car?"

"Yes."

He seemed to think it better not to go out the front way and turned toward the barn, watchful in case Tanner appeared. The farm's green Polaris Ranger was parked in the barn's open doorway, the keys in the ignition. "Get in."

Jack pushed me into the Ranger's passenger seat. He slid behind the wheel, brandishing his gun. His shirt was drenched with crimson, his face beaded with sweat.

He turned the ignition, and the Ranger roared to life. He shifted into gear, and the engine snarled as we sped out of the barn.

I looked back and saw Tanner running out of the cover of the woods like a man possessed, his gun raised, moving fast for a big guy.

A shot rang out, then another, and the rounds zinged wide of Jack like crazed hornets. Then I lost sight of Tanner as Jack swung a hard left, accelerated hard, and we bumped onto a forest track that led toward the lake.

46

I always remember my father telling me that from Loudon Lake you could reach the Gulf of Mexico.

More than a thousand miles of waterway snaked its way down along the Tennessee River toward Mississippi and Louisiana. People traveled the waterway all the time on private boats, and there were masses of tributaries and canals you could get lost on.

I didn't know what Jack was planning, but Loudon Lake was where the track eventually led. Loudon's dam was a massive structure built during the Roosevelt years, a gateway to the Mississippi and the Gulf. Jack kept his foot on the accelerator, the Ranger moving fast, cool air rushing past.

The track was rough in places. Jack seemed to feel the pain whenever we hit a deep rut, but he kept glancing back to make sure Tanner wasn't following us. He couldn't have—there wasn't another all-terrain vehicle on the farm, and a car's suspension would never make it over the coarse track. I figured Jack would make a getaway unless Tanner got a chopper up.

My heart jackhammered. Five minutes ago, Jack was about to leave me unharmed, but after the shootout everything seemed up in the air.

"Why are you doing this?"

No answer. Behind the mask, Jack grunted in pain as he leaned forward, resting both hands on the steering wheel. A little later, the track came out near the lakeside marina and the massive dam up ahead.

Above the dam spanned a bridge, busy with traffic. Jack sped toward a metal stairway that led up to the dam's walkway, braked to a stop, and stumbled out. We had reached a dead end. There was only rough ground ahead that led nowhere except a grassy riverbank.

The stairway led up about a hundred steps to the bridge. A few boats were berthed along the far bank, and I could hear the roar of the lake, the sluice gates open, a thick waterfall gushing into the other side of the dam.

Jack gestured with the gun. "Move up the steps."

It occurred to me that he may have left a boat berthed on the lakeshore, on the other side of the bridge. "Please . . . Jack . . ."

He pushed me, and I led the way up the stairs. Jack grunted with effort as he climbed the metal steps, and I thought he might collapse, but somehow he managed to summon the strength to keep going, and we reached the top.

Traffic roared across the bridge as we kept moving. We were halfway across the walkway when we heard the banshee scream of police sirens. Jack froze. A hundred fifty yards away, two sheriff's cars came speeding down the far side of the bridge, the direction we were headed. More sirens, and another sheriff's deputy roared up behind us, on the near end of the bridge. The vehicles skidded to a halt, and police uniforms climbed out, waving all bridge traffic to a stop. In the distance, I heard the sound of helicopter blades. Tanner staggered from the rear of the last car, wielding his gun.

Then I saw Courtney clamber out from the other side of the car. She was armed and pointed her gun toward me as she shouted something to Tanner. Courtney's buddy Sergeant Stone and Tanner's soberfaced sidekick joined them.

We were trapped—no way out. If Jack had a boat berthed on the far side of the lakeshore, he couldn't reach it now. All the life seemed to go out of him, and his body sagged.

Every siren died, and then there was only the thunderous sound of the powerful jets of water gushing through the dam's sluices. Jack lurched against the walkway railing. He seemed in pain. I reached out to help him, but he waved me away with his gun.

"That was dumb of you, getting the cops involved—real dumb. I didn't come to harm you."

He slumped back against the railing. Blood dripped from his wound.

"What are you talking about?"

"I came to save you. Save you from what's about to happen . . ."

And then his left hand reached up, and he tore off the mask.

47

I opened my mouth for a scream, but it stuck in my throat.

The face I saw was disfigured. The left side was covered by a prosthetic made of some kind of flesh-colored latex. His neck was badly scarred. The man had once suffered horrific injuries or burns. He didn't look like Jack. Or if he was Jack, the injuries made him unrecognizable.

That's when I noticed that the leather glove on the man's left hand was folded down a little at the wrist. I recognized a tattoo—the American eagle in red and black—and I felt totally bewildered.

"If you and your family want to live, you'd better listen." His hoarse voice burned with pain. "Don't, and I guarantee you're all dead."

Farther along the bridge, I glimpsed Tanner grabbing an electric bullhorn as he and the deputies moved toward us. Courtney was right beside him, both hands on her gun.

I met the intruder's laser gaze, but then his eyes began to swim, to lose focus.

I felt a welter of shock and confusion. That was Jack's tattoo on the back of the man's hand. He had the same physique, the same cocky walk. He saw me stare at the tattoo.

"You really thought I was Jack, didn't you?"

"Yes."

"Jack's alive, all right. Alive and kicking. You can bet on it."

I stared back at him.

"He and I go back a long ways. Jack's a born survivor. But you need to do yourself a favor and forget about him."

"Why are you telling me this?"

The disfigured face looked grotesque. I could imagine that hideous wounds lay beneath the prosthetic mask.

"Let's just say I'm returning a favor. Know what you're dealing with here? Powerful, desperate people."

He snapped his fingers, a weak gesture that barely made a sound. "Anger them, and they wouldn't give it a second thought to snuff out your life and the lives of every living person you love. Kill them, just like that."

His body swayed, and crimson droplets spattered the ground at his feet. "When I saw the TV news and heard they'd found the pilot's body and no one else, I figured there was a chance Jack had made it. As sure as snakes crawl, Jack's going to come out of the woodwork and try to contact you. Once he knows you're aware that he's not dead, that's a certainty."

"Why would he contact me?"

Behind him, I saw Courtney, Tanner, and the armed cops clamber up the metal steps, two of them aiming rifles. I looked over my left shoulder. The other armed cops threaded their way along the far walkway. We were hemmed in on both sides.

"No time to explain. But do yourself a favor. Keep as far away from Jack as you can. You're chasing a ghost, even if he did survive."

"Where is he?"

"I've no idea."

"And my children?"

"Ditto."

"Why did you break into the cottage?"

"I didn't break in. You've got the wrong man, lady."

"I don't understand. I don't get any of this."

"You don't have to. Just pay attention to what I say. Your old life with Jack, it's over, done with. Be happy with what you've got."

He moved toward the cascading water. We were at least a hundred feet up, and water churned wildly below the dam. If he jumped, he could kill himself. The cops and Courtney aimed their firearms.

"Why did you come to warn me? Who are you?"

"You don't need to know that, either."

Tanner's voice roared on the megaphone, "This is Agent Tanner, FBI. Put down the gun. Put it down now, and no one will get hurt."

The man ignored the command and climbed over the metal railing, holding on with one hand. He looked back at me, with a weird kind of resignation. And then—then he actually smiled, holding the gun, his palm up, showing it to me. "I brought this along hoping it would scare you into seeing sense. But now it's got another purpose. So long, Kath."

The pistol came up, and the barrel slipped into his mouth. He squeezed the trigger. His skull jerked back as it exploded, and his body toppled into the deluge of dam water below.

I screamed.

48

It took twenty minutes to retrieve the body.

It disappeared into the churning water, until the cops spotted it floating a hundred yards from the dam. Two of them ran to the marina to commandeer a boat.

Courtney stayed beside me, holding my hand, trying to calm me down. "Take deep breaths. In and out. That's it, honey. Get that pulse down."

By the time the paramedics and the fire tender arrived, the cops had returned with the body aboard a boat. Courtney and I watched from fifty yards back as they laid it on the shoreline. I saw Tanner kneel and search through the man's pockets.

Courtney moved to join him. "Hang in there. I'll be back, OK?"

I nodded, still shaking.

A sheriff's deputy did another search of the man's clothes, and then a paramedic placed a brown blanket over the corpse. Tanner and Courtney came back to join me.

Tanner said, "Dead as old wood. Can't expect much else when you blow a chunk out of your skull."

"What about ID?"

Courtney shook her head. "He's carrying none."

"You look pretty shaken," Tanner remarked.

I stared down at my trembling hands. "Someone shooting himself in the head right in front of you isn't exactly an everyday event."

"Yeah, it freaked me out, too. Think you could tell us what happened, right from the top?"

Courtney and Tanner listened, Tanner gazing out at the water as I told them, as if he had difficulty taking it all in. "Weird. And you're certain you never saw the guy before?"

"Never. But from the way he spoke, he seemed to know me. I . . ." I looked to Courtney. "I thought he was Jack. That he was going to kill me."

Tanner stared back at the blanket-covered body. "Yeah, and instead he killed himself. Doesn't make a whole lot of sense. But there's always got to be a reason."

"This morning, I got the feeling I was being followed. A dark-colored SUV and a metallic-gray van tailed my car. The van had what looked like a couple of antennas on top and a satellite dish. It looked like some kind of communications vehicle. It could have been my imagination playing tricks on me, but I thought I was being followed."

"Where was this?"

"On I-75."

"How long were you followed?"

"Hard to tell. Maybe twenty minutes the first time. No more than a few minutes the second time."

"What were you doing out on I-75 at the time, ma'am?"

"Running errands."

Tanner gave Courtney a look as they seemed to consider my answers, and then his eyes met mine. "We'd like you to take another look at the man, Ms. Kelly. Or would that be asking too much?"

The paramedics were stashing away their equipment, and Tanner nodded to one of the deputies, who pulled back the blanket.

The man's face was grotesquely distorted, the bullet hole drilled out near the top of his skull. The prosthesis was tilted askew, exposing an ugly hollow in the face. Gruesome scarring stretched from the left side of the man's forehead down to his jaw.

I put a hand to my mouth. "Oh, my God."

I was trying not to gag. There was hardly any blood after he'd been in the water, and the electronic voice box was still strapped to his neck. I saw a spider's web of thick scarring on the man's throat.

Tanner said, "Freaked me out, what happened back at the farm. Couldn't figure it out at first."

He took out his camera phone, tilting his head as he stared down at the guy. "I'm guessing mid- to late forties. Somewhere along the line, he suffered pretty severe wounds to his face and neck, which probably damaged his vocal cords."

He leaned forward and clicked off a half dozen or more shots of the man's face from different angles with his camera phone. Courtney did the same with her own. When she finished, she noticed me staring at the tattoo on the man's left wrist, the leather glove peeled back. We exchanged looks.

"What is it?" Tanner said

"Jack . . . Jack had an eagle tattoo on his left wrist."

"Any other noticeable marks?"

"Some scarring on his right arm below the elbow."

Tanner pulled away part of the right glove and the man's jacket sleeve. I saw severe scarring.

"I don't remember Jack having as much scarring. This seems a lot worse."

Tanner took more shots of the tattoo and the scars, and then he stood, scratching his jaw. "But you're pretty sure your husband's tattoo was exactly the same?"

"It looks to be."

"But he ain't Jack, for sure?"

"No."

Tanner positioned himself, then snapped a couple of close-ups of the tattoo and several more shots of the man's face from different angles. "Apart from who he is, the humdinger question is, why'd he show up like he did?"

Courtney added, "What was his motive? Easy to understand why he covered his face—it would have frightened the bejeepers out of you if he came knocking on your door. But then so would a black mask."

"Don't look at me like that. I'm totally lost."

Tanner stared into my face. "You're absolutely sure you never saw him before, Ms. Kelly?"

"I've no reason to lie, Tanner."

"Never said you did." He held out a hand to touch the grass and balanced himself as he rose. "We'll see what his prints and photos turn up."

"Tanner, I think Kath needs to get home," Courtney said. "She's pretty shaken."

"One other thing, Ms. Kelly. The cottage looked like it was ransacked."

"Was it?"

"You know anything about that?"

"No. It was broken into years ago. We just left it as it was."

"Anything in there that someone might want?"

"No, nothing. Just clothes and old junk." I tried to look confused. I felt uncertain whether to tell the truth. What if that *had* been Jack? So I decided to play dumb.

Tanner looked at my hands, still trembling. "We can do a prints check, but the intruder was wearing gloves, so that may get us nowhere. That's if he did ransack the place."

"Are we done, Agent Tanner?"

"Not quite. We can take a statement on the way. And we need to talk about your husband's secret life."

"Secret life?"

"Yeah. We've got an air crash he disappears from with your kids. Next thing, out of nowhere, a stranger shows up at your home and ends up killing himself with a bullet to the head. But first he warns you that your life is in danger if your husband shows up. That you need to back off and forget you ever had a husband and kids. Kinda weird, don't you think?"

I put my fingers to my lips, felt them quiver with shock.

Tanner stared at me. "Then there are the contents of the aluminum case." He waited, his eyes searching my face, as if he was half expecting me to know what the case contained.

"What was in it?"

Tanner gave Courtney a look, then focused back on me. "We'll get to that. It's kind of bizarre, to say the least."

His mouth pursed, and his bottom lip curled, exposing the shiny flesh. "Ms. Kelly, I've been in law enforcement in some form or another for almost two decades. If all that ain't telling me the guy you married had a hidden life, I don't know what would."

His stare never left my face. "You ask me, your husband's been keeping some big secrets from you for years."

49

I saw five sheriff's cars parked at the curb when we reached my street.

As we passed the entrance to a lakeside walkway that ran by my dad's property, I noticed a black Explorer was about to be raised onto a tow truck, supervised by a couple of deputies.

The woods around the house were being searched by more deputies. Neighbors' kids rode by on their bikes, craning to look at all the activity. A scattering of reporters hung around, and two news vans plus a bunch of other cars were parked on the street.

Courtney sat beside me, and Tanner was in the front passenger seat.

Baby-faced Sergeant Stone and the serious Agent Breedon were in a car behind us.

As we approached, Tanner said, "Sit back and keep your head down, Ms. Kelly. We'll stop briefly while I find out what's been happening, and then we'll take the private back road to your place."

We pulled up near the tow truck, and Tanner climbed out. "Let me go check things out."

Courtney patted my hand. "I'd better go join him. Try to keep it together, honey. I'll be as quick as I can."

"Thanks, Courtney."

"You bet."

She hugged me and climbed out after Tanner. They walked close together, Courtney's head leaning in, as if they were whispering.

I sank lower in the seat so no one could see me, but then I realized the Dodge had rear tinted windows and there was probably no need. Yellow police tape kept the media way back. Tanner went over to the sheriff's deputies and walked around the black Explorer. He peered inside and into the cargo area before they lifted the vehicle onto the tow truck.

I sat there waiting, the media too far away to spot me. What I couldn't help thinking about—all that kept rattling around in my head—were Tanner's words: "You ask me, your husband's been keeping some big secrets from you for years."

I was convinced Tanner was right.

But what secrets?

I looked at my watch. Jack was due to call at two p.m. It was 1:36.

Twenty-four minutes. Would Courtney and Tanner be gone by then? I had to make sure. I couldn't risk them even suspecting that I was talking with Jack. Tanner and Courtney strolled back together and climbed into the Dodge.

"Did they find any clues in the Explorer?"

Courtney shook her head. "Nothing that jumps out, but forensics is still working it."

Tanner tapped the sheriff's deputy in the driver's seat. "Take the next turn right."

As we drove, Tanner said, "We're having the pilot, Felipe Hernandez, checked out. His parents are dead, but he's got a half brother living in Boca Raton, Florida. He'll give us a blood sample for a DNA comparison."

"Could his brother help in any way?"

"He claims they hadn't seen much of each other in the years before the crash but they still kept in touch. He said Felipe was just a normal guy, loved flying, and loved working on the corporate aircraft. It was his dream job after he left the military. Hernandez had no criminal record, not even a speeding ticket. He was a reputable, upstanding guy."

Courtney said, "We're going over Hernandez's file from the last investigation after the flight disappeared, in case there's anything we missed. And we'll talk again with his half brother."

The front door of the farmhouse was open, and a white van was parked in the driveway. A guy in a white forensics suit and wearing surgical gloves was taking something out to the van.

I saw no TV or media—I figured they probably didn't even know about this heavily wooded track through the forest. Lots of private roads snaked all over the neighborhood, and most had "No Trespassing" signs. In these parts, people meant what they said—you trespassed, and you risked getting shot. Privacy was usually respected.

Another tech in a white lab suit was searching my garden, and yet another was finishing up on the porch, packing up a bag. Tanner and Courtney went to talk to them, and then Courtney came back alone and guided me inside, leaving Tanner deep in conversation with the tech.

"You doing OK?"

I nodded but felt dazed.

I checked my watch: 1:42. I had eighteen minutes until Jack's call. I could still hardly believe I'd heard his voice. My hands were shaking, my throat dry.

"Tanner said you found a notebook."

"We can talk inside, Kath."

Sergeant Stone followed us into the house, but Agent Breedon remained outside, by an unmarked Dodge.

The kitchen looked in disarray, with overturned chairs. Spent cartridge casings no longer littered the floor, but the forensics techs had dotted the Spanish tile with round chalk circles. They looked like something Amy would have once drawn while playing at my feet in the kitchen.

My throat felt parched. I grabbed a bottle of water from the pantry.

Courtney said, "We'll get the mess cleaned up once we're done here. I'm hoping it won't be too long." She helped me tidy the chairs.

"I really need to rest, Courtney."

"I got you. Tanner ought to finish up soon, once he goes through a few things."

Tanner appeared just as one of the techs came over and indicated the blue sweater and the purple hoodie. They were still on the table where I had left them. "Ma'am, are these yours? Did the intruder touch them?"

"Yes, they're mine. No, he didn't touch them."

I picked them up and saw Tanner watching me, as if demanding an explanation. "Sean's and Amy's old clothes. I . . . I keep them in my bedroom. I simply want to feel them near me. They're a comfort."

He nodded as if he understood. "Could I impose and ask you for another coffee?"

I glimpsed the sweeping second hand. Sixteen minutes left. I shot a look at Courtney. She gave a tiny shrug that seemed to say, *Just go with it.*

I folded the hoodie and the sweater and laid them in a cupboard drawer in the kitchen. "I'm really worn out, Mr. Tanner. Can we just get to the briefcase and the notebook?"

"Sure." But Tanner was already making himself at home again, moving to the coffee machine, popping a fresh pod into the Keurig.

He looked at Sergeant Stone, who was standing there with his arms folded, trying to seem tough and older but in reality looking like a kid fresh out of college. "How old are you, Sergeant?"

"Twenty-four, sir."

"Anyone ever tell you that you look nineteen?"

Stone gave a sulky shrug, which made his jacket look a size too big, and he seemed to take the remark as an insult. "I guess it's been said."

"Don't look so unhappy. You'll take it as a compliment as you get older, sonny. Hey, how about you go join Agent Breedon outside, keep my buddy from getting lonely? We'd like a little private time with the lady."

Stone looked at Courtney for approval. A tiny nod from her, and Stone moved out without a word, the kitchen door closing quietly after him.

I glanced at the wall clock. Fourteen minutes. I was starting to panic again. What if Tanner was still here when Jack called back?

He hit the button on the machine, and the coffee drained into a mug. "Any incidents or calls, anything that troubles you, just holler for the sheriff's deputies outside, and you get in touch with me immediately, OK?"

"OK."

"Is your house alarm working?"

"Yes."

"You usually leave it on or off?"

"It depends. Sometimes I disable the chime if it bugs me opening and closing the patio door."

"Keep the alarm on at all times, whether you're in or out. Have you got a gun?"

The kitchen wall clock told me thirteen minutes. I wanted to scream at Tanner, *Please, just show me the briefcase and go! Just leave me alone!* I was desperately curious about the case but even more desperate to hear from Jack.

"Yes, a thirty-eight revolver I keep in my purse or my car. And my dad has several firearms. There's a shotgun in a cupboard in the corner." I had put it back in the cupboard when I'd tidied up the kitchen.

"Can you use it?"

"Yeah, she sure can," Courtney interjected.

Tanner said, "I'm asking her."

I jerked my head at the photograph of my father in uniform. "I've been around firearms all my life." I didn't mention the fact that they gave me the creeps since my mother's suicide. No point.

Tanner said, "Keep a firearm by you at all times. Leave the shotgun downstairs, maybe. But maybe out of the cupboard so you can reach it in a hurry."

I looked from Courtney to Tanner. "You make it sound like I could be in danger." The man in the mask had said as much.

Tanner pulled up a chair, sat. The wood creaked under his weight. "Always better to be safe than sorry."

"You didn't answer my question."

"The danger's real if I take the threat seriously. And I do."

"I just don't get any of this."

"Join the club. But we're back to Jack's secret life, whatever it was. Right now, you need to protect yourself and not take any chances. Another thing. Any calls or any kind of contact from your ex-husband, you let me know at once. You got that?"

"Yes."

"I can have the house phone tapped so we can trace any calls. And we can have your cell phone monitored. I'll need your permission for that. I'll call you later and bring by the paperwork."

Tanner laid down his cup on the kitchen table. "Keep your doors and windows locked, and try not to go out alone. We clear on that?"

"Yes."

"Good. The sheriff's deputies will check on you intermittently."

Next time I looked at the clock, I had less than ten minutes. I felt as if a giant hand were pressing down on my chest, making my heart hammer even faster. "Can . . . can you tell me about the briefcase?"

"Let me go get it."

Tanner stepped out toward the front door, and I heard it open.

I looked at Courtney. She seemed uncomfortable as she came over, unease on her face as she put a hand on my back, rubbed it. "Won't be long. Then you can rest."

"What's wrong, Courtney?"

She shook her head. "Nothing, honey."

But for some reason, I didn't believe her. Why was she uncomfortable? I stared at her.

She faltered. "Look . . . there's a bunch of sensitive stuff we need to discuss. Some of it is going to seem weird. And we need to talk about that guy, Tarik, the creepy undertaker."

"What about him?"

"We'll get to that, just as soon as Tanner comes back."

I glanced at the wall clock.

I had eight minutes.

50

"Do you know what's in the case?"

I spoke to Courtney as I moved to the front window and saw Tanner step over to the unmarked Dodge. Sergeant Stone and Agent Breedon were standing there with folded arms, talking, or, rather Stone was talking while Breedon chewed gum and looked as bored as a blind man in an art gallery.

"Yeah, I do, honey."

"What is it?"

"Honey, it's best if you wait for Tanner."

As Tanner approached the Dodge, he said something, and I saw Agent Breedon raise the Dodge's trunk lid, grab something, and hand it to him. I kept looking at my watch and then the wall clock, the seconds ticking away.

Tanner returned, carrying a bulky blue zippered plastic evidence bag. He laid it on the kitchen table and took a pair of surgical gloves from his pocket and slipped them on. He unzipped the bag and carefully slid out the corroded aluminum briefcase.

"You told me Jack hardly ever talked much about what he did in Iraq."

"Hardly ever. It was a no-go zone. Why?"

Tanner shrugged and undid the clasps on the case, and they clicked.

He didn't open it yet, though. Inside the large evidence bag was yet another plastic bag, but clear. I saw a leather notebook inside, maybe eight inches by six. I recognized it as the kind of notebook Jack often used to make business notes.

Tanner slipped it out of the plastic bag and opened it.

I saw lots of figures. Scrawled words. Illegible, all of it, pretty much. Jack often couldn't read his own writing. Tanner flipped to a page near the beginning. Both sides of the page had a series of figures written in blue ink. But at the top of the left page, above the figures, was the one word I could make out, the unmistakable three-letter word, *Red*, underlined with a single stroke.

"That notebook look familiar?"

"Jack often used a similar kind. He used to buy them at Staples."

Tanner gave Courtney a look and said, "We're not done examining it yet, but it's mostly figures in there. Very few words, it seems."

Courtney said delicately, "That word, *Red*, does it mean anything to you, Kath? I mean, aside from the obvious?"

By the obvious, I knew she meant the scrawled word my mom had left the day she died. Courtney and I had talked about that in the past.

"No."

She pursed her lips and jerked her head to Tanner, as if they'd discussed this moment in detail beforehand.

Then Tanner nodded, and he lifted the case's lid . . .

51

I gasped, took a step back.

Inside four thick protective plastic bags were thick wads of cash—hundred-dollar bills—a sheaf of water-stained business envelopes, and something . . . weird.

A face mask, evil-looking. Like some eerie Inca god or devil. Bulbous eyes and an ugly, sneering expression. The mask was inlaid with gold and turquoise. I looked from Courtney to Tanner. "What . . . what's that?"

Tanner took out his cell phone and wiggled it in front of me. "I took a pic, downloaded it, had it checked it out by headquarters in D.C." He jerked his chin at Courtney. "Agent Adams had it confirmed by CID."

"What is it?"

Tanner pointed to the money and the stained envelopes. "First, just in case you're wondering, there's a quarter million in cash. Looks kosher, not counterfeit. The envelopes contain what appear to be bonds originating in the Cayman Islands, with a value of more than three million dollars."

"Three . . . million?"

His rubber-gloved finger pointed to the mask. "Nothing compared to this thing. Could be worth maybe ten times that, even more."

"But what is it?"

Courtney said, "One of a collection of three Persian death masks from the fourth century B.C. that once belonged to the National Museum of Iraq. This one was made for a senior officer in a special battalion of the Persian Army called the Immortals. I guess you might say the battalion was like a special forces, a bodyguard unit, with a religious aspect, secret rites of initiation, that kind of thing."

Courtney studied the mask. "The Immortals fought against Alexander the Great, the Byzantines, the Mongol hordes of Genghis Khan that invaded Persia. They earned a mystical, fearless, aggressive reputation. Mystical because every time one of their number was wounded or killed, another took his place, no matter how depleted their ranks."

Tanner rubbed his jaw with one hand and with the other pointed to the inlaid turquoise and gold. "The turquoise comes from the historical Khorasan Province of Persia. The gold is said to have come from King Solomon's mines. We know this thing used to sit among Saddam Hussein's private collection when it wasn't displayed in the museum. Sometime after our troops invaded, the three masks were plundered and went missing. Who actually took them is anyone's guess. They're probably priceless."

"What happened to the other two masks?"

"Good question. After I close this briefcase up, this one's going into a safe at FBI headquarters until we find out who rightfully owns it. At a guess, probably the National Museum of Iraq."

"Jack . . . Jack stole the artifact?"

"Don't know if he did. But the mask wasn't his, that's for sure. Let me show you something else."

Tanner removed an envelope from his pocket. He opened it, spread out maybe a dozen colored photographs as if they were a deck of cards. The objects in the photos looked no bigger than a human hand. Some were miniature human figures made of silver and gold, and others were of some kind of gods, with rams' horns on their heads or men with strange-looking beards or headdresses. They looked like images I'd seen before, at a guess from ancient Persia. A couple were photos of gold amulets, earrings, and bracelets.

"What we've got here is just as valuable," Tanner remarked. "And I mean all of them. Every one of these objects is irreplaceable."

Courtney said, "A lot of priceless artifacts like these went missing during the Iraq War. They're small and transportable. We know some of the missing objects were sold to private collectors on the black market, and some of them are probably hidden in private vaults all over the world. It's not the only thing that disappeared. Estimates suggest about eight billion in U.S. dollars disappeared back then."

"Did you say eight *billion*?"

"Yeah, you heard me right. Much of it was U.S. money meant for funding the rebuilding of Iraq and to buy off tribal chiefs, get them on board against the insurgency. Except a lot of dirty, crooked hands dipped in and helped themselves."

"Jack's, too?"

"I don't know for certain, Kath. The suspicion persisted that one or more of the men in his unit were involved." Courtney nodded to the briefcase's contents. "So that's a problem right there that raises a big question mark. And it brings us to our undertaker friend, Tarik."

Tanner said, "Courtney tells me you met him?"

I nodded. "What about him?"

"He and his family were given refugee status and admitted into the U.S. He was part of the Iraqi insurgency but switched sides to help our military by informing on a couple of Al-Qaeda cells in his own tribe. Later, the U.S. rewarded him with a fistful of dollars and a green card. Next thing you know, he's running an undertaking business and a bunch of others. He's set himself up pretty nicely. Bottom line is, Tarik's a rat who'd sell out his own mother and probably did."

"What do you mean?"

"Soon after he informed on the Al-Qaeda cells, a whole bunch of his relatives got totaled in a car-bomb revenge attack. Then a convoy he was in got ambushed by our troops, and a truckload of the tribe's money went missing."

"How much?"

"I can't talk about details, but besides the money, there were a bunch of priceless artifacts from the Baghdad museum. Suspicion fell on Tarik, and there were rumors that he had help from someone in the American military. But no one could ever prove a thing. The word from military intelligence was that Tarik's as slippery as a snake and cunning as they come. The truck that vanished that day, he could have driven it over the border into Iran and stashed it away with relatives or arranged for it to be banked abroad. His tribe had relatives there, some of them involved in banking. Or he could have headed west to Syria and done the same thing. CID suspects he did the dirty deed or played a big part in it, but no one can prove it."

Courtney continued, "Most of what we've told you falls under the category of classified information. You repeat it to no one. Got that, Kath?"

I nodded.

Tanner said, "What you probably don't get is why they let people like Tarik into this country." He shrugged. "Why did they ever let all those Nazi scientists into the country at the end of World War Two to work at NASA? Tarik's no scientist, but I guess in politics, the end always justifies the means."

Tanner rested his hand on his jaw. "The real question is, what's all this stuff doing in a case in an aircraft that Jack was on?"

I stared at the death mask's ugly, evil face. It seemed to stare back at me.

Tanner broke the moment, closing the lid and snapping shut the clips. "Jack may want it back."

"What?"

"It may be important to him."

"I don't get it."

"Just my gut, again. And like my old grandma used to say, always trust your gut. And right now, it's heaving." Pause. "*Has* he contacted you, Ms. Kelly?"

"No," I lied. I tried to make it sound convincing. I think I did.

I looked back at Tanner, his eyes searching my face. Then he let his stare go. "We'll be checking out the pilot, Hernandez, too, in that regard. In case this stuff has anything to do with him. We'll check it for prints."

This time, it was Tanner who looked at his watch. I shot a glance at the wall clock. Distracted by the aluminum case, I had forgotten about the time.

1:56.

Four minutes until Jack's call. My nerves felt raw, scoured with steel wool. *Please leave.*

To my relief, Tanner slid the case into the evidence bag and zipped it up. He shot Courtney a look before he said to me, "We've got to go. We'll talk again soon."

Courtney said, "Try to get some rest. You need me, holler."

I walked them to the back door. Tanner said, "I think the guy on the bridge was right. Jack will try to contact you. The big question is why. You've really got no idea what any of this is about? Something in his past? Lies and secrets he kept?"

"Not a single one."

I meant it. But I could tell by Tanner's face that he was unconvinced. "Take care, Ms. Kelly. Remember, the deputies are right outside."

Courtney squeezed my hand. "Call me if you need me. And even if you don't."

"Thanks."

"That's what friends are for." She kissed my cheek and followed Tanner out.

I watched them walk down the gravel pathway, climb into their car, and drive off. I moved back into the kitchen, expecting the phone to ring any moment. Sixty seconds. I watched the second hand sweep past the minute.

My phone didn't ring.

I waited, clutching it in my palm, looking at the screen, ready to answer the call. Two more excruciating minutes, and I was still waiting. I checked the volume—twice. It was set at max.

Five minutes more, and fear burrowed into my chest.

Still no call.

Seven minutes past the deadline.

I sat there, wringing my hands, fidgeting, until five more minutes had passed.

I felt on edge, hanging by a thread.

And then I had the most awful feeling slam into my heart like an Arctic chill.

Jack wasn't going to call—ever again.

I felt like throwing up at the thought. I didn't care about any price-less Persian death mask, money, or Cayman Islands bonds. Didn't care a rat's about Alexander the Great or Genghis Khan. I cared about my children. I cared about Amy and Sean. I felt a growing rage, a weird kind of rage.

Rage at Jack, for making me vulnerable again, for sending my life spinning out of control again. For putting me through all this uncer-tainty, this anguish.

I let out a cry of frustration as I picked up Tanner's empty coffee mug and threw it against the wall. It smashed and shattered into a cas-cade of white pieces, scattering on the kitchen floor in all directions.

A split second later, my cell phone rang.

I expected to hear Jack's voice.

Instead, I heard Chad's.

"Kath . . ."

Chad was the last person I expected to hear from. He had barely crossed my mind since we parted ways at Thunder Mountain. I knew I needed to thank him for the helicopter ride and the offer to be there for me, but there had not been time in the madness since Jack's phone call. "Chad . . . I'm expecting a call. I'm sorry, can you call back?"

"This won't take a second, Kath. I'll keep it short."

His voice had its usual deep, commanding tone. "Chad, I—"

"Kath, I didn't hang around at the crash site because I knew you wanted to be alone, but we need to talk. We need to meet."

"Why?"

I heard a sigh, then a sharp intake of breath. "There's . . . there's something . . ." He paused, as if he was wary of discussing it on the phone. "Could you come over to my house? I've got an important business meeting in a minute with some Middle East customers. But I should be free in just over an hour."

"Why? What's it about, Chad? I'm really busy."

"It's about Jack."

I heard the pause, the pregnant beat.

And then Chad dropped his bombshell. "I think I know the real reason he vanished."

52

I waited another thirty minutes, anxiously pacing the kitchen.

No call from Jack.

I felt so on edge, as if a bomb were about too go off next to me.

I had the terrible feeling that Jack was never going to call again.

If there was one thing you could always take Jack's word on, it was time. If he said he'd call at a certain time, he called. He was a stickler for timekeeping, ever since his Army days. He saw not keeping a deadline as a sign of disrespect. I used to get tired of hearing that line if I was a minute late getting ready.

"Disrespect, Kath. You're showing disrespect. We've got to leave now, honey."

"I'll be showing disrespect if I turn up half dressed, looking like a deranged woman with my hair in a mess and wearing no makeup. Give me just five more minutes, Jack, for Pete's sake."

"You need to plan better. Get yourself organized. Why's that so hard? Plan. Prepare. Otherwise you panic, and we're late, every time."

Jack was right, of course, but I was disorganized at the best of times. My weakness. I should have been better, coming from a military family, but there you go. Offspring don't always fit their parents' mold.

When I felt I could wait no more, I made up my mind. If Jack was going to call, he'd call me on my cell phone, so I moved out to my car parked by the barn.

What Chad meant I had no idea. But the moment I heard his words, my body had stiffened. He had me hooked, on edge again, my curiosity on fire. What did he mean? What could be the real reason Jack vanished, other than a whole lot of money, as I now imagined? This whole thing was getting murkier by the minute. My head was throbbing. I took three ibuprofen, and as I knocked back a glass of water, a thought struck me.

I remembered the thin black book I'd found in the cottage, hidden between the rafters and the roof insulation. I'd left it there. With all the drama after the intruder Tasered me, I'd put it out of my head.

I felt a powerful urge to see what was inside the book.

But equally powerful was my reluctance to enter the cottage again.

I could feel my body tremble at the mere thought.

I fought the fear, tried to steel myself.

Then I slapped the glass onto the kitchen table, left by the back door, and hurried over to the cottage.

I reached the front door. I couldn't recall if I had closed it behind me, but it was closed now. I turned the knob, pushed in the door, and stepped into the ransacked cottage.

I moved past the open drawers, scattered cushions, and Amy's and Sean's toys. I tried to keep my eyes half shut, not to see the wreckage all around me, but it was no use. My mind felt tormented by my desecrated precious memories.

I was finding it hard to breathe again as I raced up the stairs, the pain stabbing at my chest.

I turned into the bedroom; the door into the storage space was still open, clothes and junk strewn about. I couldn't bear even to look into Sean and Amy's bedrooms—that would have been too much. Jack had not called back. I wondered if he ever would. To have my hopes raised and now to worry that they'd be dashed totally crushed me.

I looked inside the crawl space. The open plastic food-storage box with the red lid lay on the floor, along with Kyle's small plastic bags. The stench of stale marijuana drenched the air.

I saw the thin black book still wedged between the rafters and the roof insulation. I reached in and yanked it out.

The book looked like a journal or a small art book and was closed with a studded clasp. I flicked it open. A blast of must hit my nostrils. Most of the pages were blank. A folded piece of paper fell out.

I picked it up and unfolded a copy of a newspaper clipping. The black-and-white photocopy was frayed and flimsy at the creases. It showed a convoy of U.S. Army Humvees and trucks.

They passed under a symbol I knew well: a pair of triumphal arches in Saddam Hussein's Baghdad known as the Hands of Victory. Each arch consisted of an enormous hand holding a giant sword, and the two swords crossed in the middle of the arch.

The original newspaper photo had been trimmed so it didn't denote any newspaper or magazine, and the article itself, if it existed, had been cut away. All I saw below the picture was a headline in bold black ink: "Operation Babylon Well Under Way."

I put down the worn paper and flicked through the journal. For a time when Kyle lived at the cottage, I had witnessed him sketching in notepads. I once picked one up and was shocked to see pictures and squiggles that seemed to reflect a kind of childlike torment.

The writing in this notebook was Kyle's, I was sure. Near the edges of a few of the ripped pages, I could make out some letters—*t*, an *i*, maybe an *m*—and a complete word—*if*—but little else. Had Kyle ripped out the pages, or had someone else? I flicked to the front of the journal.

And for some reason, my heart quivered.

On the inside cover was a drawing in red ink that looked like a doodle. Kyle had an arty side, and he used to sketch. He often used to fill his art books with secretive little doodles when he was drawing, stuff that meant something only to him. This drawing looked like a boulder, a rock, or a stone.

It could have been doodling, but the image looked pretty defined and deliberate. Was it meant to be cryptic? Something of significance to Kyle? My mind ran through the permutations of what was the image might suggest. Red stone? Or maybe just a boulder? Rock? Mountain?

Was it just a harmless sketch that meant nothing at all? I was perplexed. But I realized why my heart quivered: that word again, *Red*. It felt as if alarm bells were going off in my stomach.

I was conscious of the time passing. I glanced at my watch. I had twenty minutes to make it to Chad's.

I closed the notebook and snapped shut the clasp. After taking one last, shuddering look around the ransacked bedroom, I hurried down the stairs.

53

The sheriff's deputies were still out front. They might hear me if I started up the engine. So I walked out to where one of them sat in his car. A big old guy with prominent ears, a red-veined nose, and a beer gut. He got out as I approached. I wasn't going to tell him about the break-in; that would just complicate things right now. "I've got to go out for a short time."

"Where to, ma'am?"

"Just a neighbor's nearby."

"Let me go with you."

"Why?"

"Agent Tanner said we were to watch over you."

"I'll be fine. And I don't want to alarm my friends with the police in tow. I've got my cell. I can call 911 if I need to."

"I understand, ma'am, but—"

"Am I under arrest? Or house arrest, whatever that it is?"

"Arrest? No, ma'am."

"Then let me be the judge of where I can go."

I turned and walked back to my car. As I slid in, I saw him get on his radio.

I started my car. I knew something was weird immediately.

A big white business envelope lay on the passenger seat. I knew I hadn't left it there. My father was out of town, and besides, he never left stuff in my car; he never used my vehicle. My car had been locked. My first thought was that someone had broken into my car.

I picked up the envelope.

There was something hard inside, filling the flat space, like a photograph.

No postage, no address. The envelope was sealed. I heard the crackle of a radio.

I looked back. The deputy had his radio to his mouth.

I started the car, reversed, and drove out along the back garden track that led toward the main road.

After three hundred yards, I reached the main road. No one followed me.

No police cars in sight. I drove on another few hundred yards and pulled over, keeping the engine running. It occurred to me that Tanner might go ape if he knew I'd left. The last thing I wanted was a posse. I decided to call Courtney. She could square it with Tanner. As I fumbled to tear open the envelope, I called her. She answered on the second ring.

"Hey, glad you called. I wanted to give you a heads-up. We got an ID on the bridge shooter."

I put down the envelope. "Who was he?"

"His photograph and prints match a guy named Quentin Lusk. Ever hear of him?"

"Never."

"He's a former corporal who served in Jack's unit in Iraq."

"Is that all you've got?"

"He suffered from PTSD after he got blasted in an explosion and lost part of his face. Seems it tore out part of his voice box, too. Last known address was down in Florida. Had a small farm there and kept to himself. He was seeing a Miami shrink to deal with his PTSD but hadn't been keeping his appointments in quite a while. Quentin had developed a reputation for being odd, eccentric, a loner."

"What about violent?"

"No mention of that. But his shrink said Quentin had tipped over the edge since Iraq and was prone to chronic paranoia."

"Any other link to Jack?"

"We don't know yet. We've got some people on their way to conduct a search of his property, to see what more we can learn. I'll get back as soon as I have more details. You OK?"

"For now. Look, Courtney, I've got to go out for a little while. It's no big deal, but I don't want a sheriff's posse following me."

"Going where?"

"To see Chad, among other things."

There was a definite beat, a complete silence, before Courtney said, "Why Chad?"

"Didn't I tell you? He arranged for the company helicopter to take me to see the crash site. He's been kind and good and helpful. I wanted to thank him." I didn't want to tell her the truth about Chad's call. Not yet, at least.

Another silence, and then Courtney said, "Don't tell me Chad's on the scene again?"

Was it my disturbed imagination, or did I sense a hint of jealousy? I had to be wrong. Courtney and Chad were over and done a long time ago. OK, Courtney would probably claim that they remained friends. But I was assuming that friendship was just a distant memory at this stage—unless it was recently rekindled—and whatever sexual or romantic allure they once had for each other was by now long gone.

"There's no scene, and he isn't on it."

"Sure?"

"Sure. You don't still like him, do you, Courtney?"

"Heck, no, honey, I just don't want your heart broken again."

"It's bulletproof at this stage."

"Yeah, mine, too. Solid Kevlar."

It was strange. We still never talked much about our mutual love of the same man. As if it was a taboo subject. I don't know why I said it, but I did. "You ever miss him, Courtney?"

"Chad? He was a little rich for my peasant blood. Too rich, too good-looking. I didn't grasp it at the time, but I guess we all get blinded by desire." She laughed. "You ever think how gullible we women can be sometimes? How we can fall for looks and physical attraction just as easy as men do?"

I was tempted to smile.

Courtney said, "OK, keep in touch. And remember what Tanner said. We'll talk later. Call me if you need me."

"Thanks, Courtney."

I ended the call. No mention of me leaving my home. Had Tanner not known yet, or had he told her? I picked up the envelope and tore open the flap.

I spotted a couple of color photographs inside and pulled them out.

Ice ran through my veins when I saw the images. One of my mother and father taken years ago, another of my father in military uniform.

I frowned. What was this?

The photo of my father showed him in combat fatigues, seated at one of two big wooden tables. On each table was a mountain of cash, in what looked like U.S. currency. The hills of money totally dominated the room. There must have been hundreds of millions there. My dad was smiling and had a wad of notes in each hand, showing them off for the camera.

On the table in front of the cash was a pile of what looked like artifacts. One of them looked just like the Persian mask that Tanner showed me.

The ice in my veins felt even colder.

I looked at the other photograph. My parents at a function, maybe twenty years ago. My mom with a cocktail glass in her hand. Smiling. Dad smiling, too. A happy shot of the two of them. No one would have had this photograph except someone in my family. But what disturbed me most, what chilled me to the bone, what made my heart leap into my mouth, were the words scrawled in black indelible marker along the bottom of the shot:

Nothing is what it seems.
He killed her.

54

The written note made me quake. Totally unsettled me. I had the pics on the seat beside me all during the drive to Chad's. I kept shifting my eyes to the black marker note every now and then—I didn't recognize the block handwriting—and then a horn blared at me on the interstate, and I almost crashed. After that, I kept my eyes on the road.

Nothing is what it seems.

He killed her.

Killed whom? But I knew. I knew what the note meant. My father had killed my mother. There was no other meaning my mind would entertain. But who had typed the note? And why? Was it the truth? Or meant to mislead me? The money, the same Persian mask. What did it mean? I couldn't get the words out of my mind.

My mind even returned to that most disturbing of memories. For some weird reason, I recalled when I caught Courtney and my father half clothed and in an embrace by the lakeshore. Had my father and Courtney ever had a long-term affair? Was there more to it than Courtney always claimed?

Had my father been seeing other women during his marriage? Might he have killed my mother because he wanted to be free of her in order to pursue another relationship? But my father never had another relationship that I knew of, nothing really until long after my mother's death.

As I turned off the interstate, heading to Chad's, my cell phone rang.

I looked at the screen. The number was private. I felt a thud in my chest. I answered as I slowed and pulled the car onto the shoulder. *Please let it be Jack.*

"Yes?"

"There's been a change of plan. I'll call you soon."

It was Jack.

"Wh-why?"

"It'll be safer, for everyone."

I sensed it again. Palpable fear. Was it Jack's PTSD acting up? A kind of paranoia?

I also felt a surge of relief that was overwhelming, knowing that I would see my children. I wanted to ask him if he'd left the note in my car, but he didn't even give me time.

"Same rules apply."

"Jack, please don't treat me like this. I've been in a limbo for eight years. I need to know about Amy and Sean, and I need to know *now*."

"Six o'clock. Six p.m. on the nail. Then you'll know everything."

And the line died with a click.

55

My hands shook as I drove to Chad's home.

At least Jack had called. I felt elated. Hope surged through me like an electric current once again.

But it didn't stop me from keeping my eyes on the rearview mirror.

I saw no sign of the SUV or the metallic-gray communications van.

I began to figure either my imagination was in overdrive and I wasn't really being followed, or whoever it was, was being careful. The latter seemed more probable. But I couldn't help thinking that Jack might be experiencing one of his PTSD episodes and rampant paranoia was at work.

It was possible.

But I still felt vigilant.

I hated the thought that some faceless creeps might be stalking me, watching me. It drove me crazy, and I felt my heart pounding.

It also scared the life out of me.

*　*　*

To call Chad's home a mansion would not be doing it justice.

It was one of those big, picture-perfect manor houses, all expensive oak and granite, with a huge bubbling water fountain in front and a quarter-mile-long entrance driveway lined with maple and elm trees. It always kind of reminded me of Hugh Hefner's Playboy crib but a touch smaller.

Lots of meandering footpaths, water features, and ivy climbing on granite. Very French, very charming, and very big, it looked more like a hotel than a home. The kind of residence you could get lost in on a daily basis.

It was on the lake, a private multiacre estate on Lyons Bend that I could only guess the value of—six, seven million dollars, maybe more? A fortune by Knoxville standards.

Two boat docks, a saltwater pool, private helicopter pads, enough garages to hold a zillion cars, and servants' quarters.

I loved the house. Not because of its size—it was way too big. I loved it because of the views over the lake and the deer that wandered through the estate.

Hummingbirds fed from the sugared-water dispensers hanging from the back porch. At sunset, you could hear geese flying overhead. Everything about the place spoke to me of peace and tranquility, except when Chad's helicopter descended or took off.

I'd spent a lot of time here when I was married to Chad. A few friends half joked that I should I should stay with Chad even if he was cheating on me, so I could live here.

Maybe some women could. I couldn't.

But if I ever won the lottery, a place with a very similar view had my name on it. *Dream on.*

I pulled up at the private security lodge at the entrance. The guard on duty was an athletic black man named Samuel with broad nostrils and solid, muscular arms. Despite his kindly smile and diplomatic manner, Samuel was a former Navy SEAL and was always armed.

Chad once told me that Samuel was a martial-arts expert, up there with Bruce Lee, and could probably kill a roomful of aggressors with his bare hands. He doubled as one of Chad's bodyguards. Chad always kept at least six bodyguards at his home. It always made me feel uncomfortable when I lived here. Like sharing your home with half a football team. But as Chad used to say, "Dealing with foreign governments and their security forces often attracts hostile enemies. I've got to be careful, baby."

"Hey, Ms. Kath, good to see you again, ma'am."

"You, too, Samuel."

"Mr. Chad said for you to drive right on up. He's in a meeting and shouldn't be too long."

"Thanks."

"You bet."

I shifted into drive and cruised along a tree-lined avenue up to the house. I saw the company helicopter parked on the pad out back and another chopper nearby. When I reached the circular driveway at the end, one of the big double oak doors opened, and a suited butler came out. Behind him, Julie Ann appeared. My tires crunched on the gravel as I braked.

"Kath!" She waved and ran toward me.

My cell phone rang. I looked at the number.

It was my father.

I felt a powerful anger. I wanted to take the call, to confront him. But now wasn't the time. I rejected the call and let it switch to voice mail.

As I looked up at Julie Ann's approach, I glimpsed a couple of men heading toward the helicopters. They looked like pilots, and one of them climbed into the second chopper. I saw two of Chad's men along with two others who looked Middle Eastern.

I climbed out of my car, and Julie Ann came running into my arms, all smiles, and hugged me.

"Daddy said you were coming. Have you got time to go riding tomorrow? We've got a new horse, Sheena. She's really beautiful."

"Not tomorrow, sweetheart." I was still feeling the aftershocks of Tanner's revelation and Chad's announcement. Not to mention Jack's call and the photographs I'd seen. It had been an eventful day. I wasn't in the mood for a horse ride anytime soon, alone or with a thirteen-year-old.

"I miss you, Kath. I really miss you."

Julie Ann's earnestness always touched me. With her soft features and her energetic nature, she reminded me of Amy. So much so that it sometimes made me feel weak. And now, now that I held hope of seeing Amy again, her welcome sent my heart soaring. "I miss you, too."

"I saw on the news about the crash. Daddy said I wasn't to talk about it, but . . . but I don't know, Kath, I thought maybe you'd want to?"

I smiled a reply. Now wasn't the time or the place. "Not just now, sweetie."

"Are you OK?"

"Let's just say it's a difficult time."

We moved up the front steps, through the massive oak doors. From the entry hall, a vast staircase swept upstairs, like something out of a Hollywood musical. A pair of glittering chandeliers sparkled in the ceiling and on the landing.

On the walls hung rows of family portraits. Some had the kind of death-mask faces the rich and wealthy often have, where the skin looks as if it is being pulled back from behind, the cheekbones high, the lips tight. Like sentries, they seemed to line up to watch over their money and their offspring.

I could see the living room and the panoramic window that showed off an incredible lake view. I had spent some happy times here. I would take out my memories of my years with Chad every now and then, when I was feeling lonely. I didn't know if they comforted me or hurt me. Probably both.

Chad's father had lived here then. Chad still hadn't put his own stamp on the place. He had left it for the penthouse apartment he kept in Washington, which was more a mix of classic contemporary and laid-back comfortable, which always reminded me of Chad himself. He may have been driven and relentless in business, but Chad gave off a casual, easygoing aura.

When I once asked him how he managed to look so laid-back in the midst of all his frantic globe-trotting and high-powered wheeling and dealing, he rubbed his fingers together in that age-old gesture that indicates money and smiled. "That always helps."

Outside I heard a helicopter start up.

"Are your dad's business acquaintances still here?"

"They're always here. Or people like them."

Julie Ann sometimes sounded like a spoiled rich kid—she really wasn't, but right then, she almost qualified. I looked around, not sure what I was searching for.

"She's not here, in case you're wondering."

"Who's not here?"

"The woman you saw in the car."

"That's OK. Your dad is free to be with whoever he wants to be with, sweetheart."

"Daddy doesn't see her often. She's an Arab lady, from Beirut or someplace," Julie Ann said, bored. "Her dad does business with my dad."

I made no comment. It wasn't my affair.

Julie Ann said matter-of-factly, "I think she's also probably a gold digger looking for a wealthy husband, like a lot of the ladies who hang around Daddy. I wouldn't call some of them ladies, either."

I was almost tempted to smile at her precociousness. "What do you mean?"

"You know what I mean. I never hear any love in their voices. Only greed. They always want something, women like her." She put a hand on my arm. "Not like when you used to speak with him. You told him the truth."

I drew in a breath. Her maturity and directness sometimes astonished me. "Don't judge your dad too harshly, Julie Ann. He's a good man."

"He's my dad, and I love him, but sometimes he has lousy taste in women." She looked at me. "I know he still likes you a lot. I bet if he had his way and could change things, he'd like for you and him to be together again. I *know* he would. I guess I shouldn't tell you that, but he's often kind of said it."

What could I say to that? Wishful thinking on a child's part or the truth? I didn't want to go down that road, however flattering.

"He sure talks about you an awful lot," Julie Ann added for emphasis.

"How's school?"

"Except for a boy in my class who I really like, I hate it. Hate it with a vengeance."

"I think we all hated it at your age."

"I think a little more positive encouragement might be in order. Or are you trying to help create another Southern rebel?"

I heard the voice behind me and turned. Chad leaned against the doorframe. He wore a white business shirt, open at the neck, his amber silk tie loose, his shirt sleeves rolled up. The white and amber showed off his tan.

"You two are getting acquainted again, I see."

"Like you said, it's been a while."

"Way too long. You and this young madame need to spend even more time together." Chad came over, gently touched my arm, and winked at his daughter.

Julie Ann sighed. "OK, I get the message, Daddy. Time to disappear."

"We've just got some private talking to do. Thanks, honey."

Julie Ann said, "See you soon, Kath?"

"I hope so."

She kissed and hugged me, and then she was gone, like a whirlwind.

Chad's hand came up, touched my arm, and lingered there a little longer than it maybe ought to. "You coping?"

I gave a shrug.

"You seem tired."

I rubbed my eyes with thumb and forefinger. "Yeah, I'm exhausted. I'm also crazy busy, Chad. With a million things on my mind and lots to do. You said you knew why Jack disappeared. Why? Money?"

He frowned. "Why do you say that?"

"Something the FBI guy leading the case said to me."

"Who is he?"

"His name's Brewster Tanner."

"And what exactly did he say?"

I hesitated, not knowing exactly what I should be revealing, but I said it anyway. "They found a bundle of money in an aluminum briefcase at the crash site."

He frowned again. "You're not joking, are you?"

"This is not the kind of time I'd attempt a joke, Chad."

"How much?"

"A quarter of a million dollars, cash. Three million dollars in bonds originating in the Cayman Islands."

His right eye twitched with a look of genuine surprise. "Really?"

"It didn't belong to Brown Bear?"

He said nothing. "Was that all they found?"

"A priceless artifact. Some Persian mask that went missing in Iraq after the invasion."

Chad looked stunned and gave a shake of his head. "That's . . . troubling."

"What is, exactly?"

"All of it. The money, the bonds, some artifact."

"You knew nothing about them?"

"Nothing. I'm truly mystified."

I have to say he genuinely looked it, unless he was suddenly a terrific actor. Chad could have a poker face when he chose to, but usually he couldn't hide his true emotions. His face would color, his lips tighten, or his body stiffen. But I saw none of those reactions.

"What about . . . remains?"

He spoke softly, but that word still hit me like a sledgehammer. "Nothing yet. But the NTSB guy thinks Jack and the children may have survived."

Chad looked as if I had hit him hard. He reeled back and lost eye contact with me for a moment. When he recovered, he shook his head. "I'm astonished, Kath . . ."

I told him exactly what Dexter had said.

Chad reached out and touched my arm again, with what seemed like genuine concern. "I don't know what to say."

"Neither do I. But for the first time in eight years, I have a grain of hope that I may see my children again. And that's such a good feeling. Chad, I hate to press it, but what did you want to say to me?"

He seemed reluctant to talk all of a sudden. As if my news had changed the game. But after a few more seconds of reflection, he jerked his head toward his study door. It was open, an array of computers inside, walnut-paneled walls lined with overfilled bookshelves.

"Can you come with me? I need to show you something, something very private and sensitive."

I stared back at him. "Chad, I don't need any more shocks today. Really, I don't."

He was tight-mouthed, his lips barely moving, as he said, "I'm sorry, but you need to know about this. There's no other way. You need to be prepared."

"Prepared for what?"

"A big lie. A big lie Jack kept from you. And one that I've kept, too."

56

KNOXVILLE, TENNESSEE

Earlier that day, when Brewster Tanner finished shaving, he threw water onto his face, and stared at himself in the mirror.

Droopy eyes, scraggly hair that could do with a cut, and a vest that looked like it needed to be replaced. When his wife was alive, he used to look after himself. Now, on weekends or days off, he never shaved and lounged around watching TV in a size 4XL Snuggie he found on sale at Kohl's. Beware, folks, if ever there was one single reason not to retire, it was afternoon TV.

And money. Most pensions barely covered the cost of living these days. He saw that with his mom. She almost killed herself working a job all her life, retired at sixty-six, and spent a year living on a misery of a pension that barely clothed and fed her and paid the rent on an apartment the size of a garden shed. A place so small Tanner used to joke she'd get a hunched back.

Some days when he visited his mom, he knew by looking in her fridge that she probably hadn't eaten more than one meal a day. He'd force her to come out for dinner, to a local Applebee's or Shoney's, but getting her to accept the offer was hard work.

No more than she'd accept money from him. His mom would rather sit alone in her apartment and starve than be beholden to anyone. A proud black woman. He knew lots of them, doing double duty by raising kids alone and holding down two jobs. Too proud to ask anyone for help.

She went to cancer a year later, having told no one about her ailment until two months before she passed—a painful end with no health insurance worth talking about. Tanner still shivered thinking about that.

He sure didn't want that kind of miserable end to a life.

He traipsed back into his Sleep Inn motel bedroom and a plucked a fresh shirt from his suitcase. Lying on the bed were some photocopied pages from the original case file from eight years ago. He'd spent the evening reading them and was none the wiser for it. Then he left a voice-mail message for Dexter, inquiring after his progress.

His cell phone rang. It was Courtney. He picked up.

"Rise and shine, Tanner."

"I rose and illuminated thirty minutes ago. You here?"

"In the lobby."

"Breakfast?"

"I already ate."

"OK, see you in five."

He flicked off his cell. It rang a second time.

"Tanner."

"Hey, big man. It's Dexter, your friendly NTSB amigo. Got those results you've been waiting for."

"Hit me, bro."

She was waiting in the lobby, 9:30 a.m. on the button, like they'd arranged. Courtney looked smart in jeans and a pale-blue top, comfortable sneakers. She had a notebook and a pen in her hand.

"Grab a coffee? They're still serving breakfast," Tanner suggested.

"Sure."

They crossed the lobby to the breakfast area and helped themselves to two coffees. The place was empty, and they took a seat near the window.

"How's Kath doing, do you know?"

"I called her yesterday evening."

Tanner sipped from his cup. "You care about her, don't you?"

"She's maybe the best friend I've ever had. Straight, true, honest. We've had our occasional spats and disagreements over the years, but I'd put my life on the line for Kath any day. And I'll tell you this for nothing, nobody deserved what happened to her."

"You mean about her family?"

"What exactly do you know about Kath?"

"Just some stuff her former work colleagues at Bearden High School told me and whatever I found on file from the original case. I guess I need to color in between the lines."

Courtney arched a perfectly shaped eyebrow. "'Some stuff' is putting it mildly. Did they tell you her brother, Kyle, tried to kill himself nine years back?"

"No. Any reason why?"

"Kyle served in Iraq with Kath's husband and her dad. Something happened to him over there. Nobody's sure what. But he suffered from

PTSD afterward. Kath's husband Jack suffered with it, too, but Kyle was a lot worse, his head really messed up. One day, they found him hanging from a tree in Admiral Farragut Park. When they cut him down, he was barely alive. The doctors tried their best, but he wound up brain-damaged from lack of oxygen."

"You OK, Courtney?"

"Why?"

"You look . . . upset."

Courtney wiped the edge of her left eye with the tip of her nail. "Kyle and I were close. We were engaged."

"I'm sorry. I guess her mom took it bad, too? What happened there?"

"She shot herself on the afternoon of Kath's wedding. You'd think the crazy cow would have waited until her daughter's wedding was long over before she plugged herself, but no, she had to mess up everything, go out all dramatic, gun blazing, so to speak. But that was Martha Beth."

"That's tough."

"Yeah, no doo-doo."

"Kath's mom had problems, I guess."

"You can say that again. I've known people who thought she was nuts. Personally, I figured she just drank too much, which can make you crazy enough. I've no idea what went through her mind that made her put a gun to her head. Maybe Kyle's situation, maybe not. Factor in that her husband lost a foot to a grenade blast in Iraq and retired early and that she was drinking like a parched camel. I figure she was head-banged by a truckload of problems that tormented her. Otherwise, she wouldn't have drilled a hole in her own skull. Although I heard rumors."

Tanner arched his eyebrows.

Courtney said, "My mom told me that she knew Martha Beth tried to kill herself a whole bunch of times over the years. She could be a drama queen. I guess you might say an attention seeker."

"Sounds like Kath had some pretty heavy stuff to deal with."

"How she came through it all I'll never know. It got worse when her husband and kids disappeared. By rights, she ought to be in a rubber room somewhere, banging her head off the walls. But she's coped, which says a lot for her." Courtney shrugged. "Me, I'd have been a basket case, getting so much electroconvulsive therapy the lights would be dimming all the way to Idaho."

Tanner offered a nod. "You knew her mom well?"

"Yeah."

"And her father?"

Courtney nodded.

"You knew him, too?"

"Yeah, pretty well."

"What's the matter?" Tanner said. "You seemed to ball up a little when I asked that question."

"Ball up?"

"Tighten. Like a fist."

"I don't believe I did."

"So tell me about her old man."

"Nothing much to tell. It's all in the original report. You read it, didn't you?"

Tanner nodded. "But you got on OK with him? I mean, is her old man a likable guy?"

Courtney said nothing.

Tanner nodded. "Why do I get the feeling he's not a subject you want to dwell on?"

"Cut the psychoanalysis, Tanner. It's bull. He's not what's important right now." Courtney looked out the window, toward the hotel parking lot, then back again. "There's something else. Kath told me that Jack seemed a little anxious before he left on that trip and disappeared."

"Did she know what he was anxious about?"

"No, but Jack got that way now and then, with PTSD. He'd be on edge. Maybe suffer bad nightmares or bouts of paranoia."

"What was he paranoid about?"

"Kath said he'd get irrational fears that he was going to die, or he'd get distrustful of others or think that his phone was bugged. It's not unusual with PTSD. But he learned some skills from an Army psychologist he saw. It helped him cope with his problems."

"How about Kath? How's she coped since?"

Courtney took a sip of her coffee and pushed her cup away. "Are you married, Tanner?"

"My wife passed a few years back."

"When you lose a family member close to you, that's tough enough. But when you lose your entire family, why, that's a trainload of grief dumped on your doorstep. We never really get over devastating loss, do we?"

"I guess not."

Courtney paused before she spoke. "You never met a woman so in love with her family as Kath. She just adored the ground Sean and Amy walked on. She even became a teacher so she'd have more time for them in summer and on holidays. Losing the three people she loved was pretty rough on Kath. It was like she stopped breathing. I figure for a time, she wished she had."

"Survivor's guilt?"

"If you mean did she blame herself, yes, she did."

"For what?"

"Allowing the children to take the trip. She was bogged down in work, trying to get some peaceful time to write, so she let them go. She's never really gotten over that decision. I think she's always tortured herself with the question 'What if I hadn't let them go?' I don't think she's written a word since. And it took her a long time to find her way back. I mean, she never even had bodies to bury. She couldn't cope, couldn't sleep, and couldn't function."

"How'd she pull through it?"

"With a lot of pain and a lot of effort."

"You helped her?"

"As much as I could. Look, Tanner, can we get down to some real business here?"

"I got a call from Dexter at the NTSB."

"And?"

"They did a thorough search of the area using ground radar but found no remains."

"So they made it out."

"Seems likely."

Courtney considered.

Tanner said, "You look like you've got something on your mind."

"I figure Quentin Lusk didn't just drive down to the lake to admire the views. I reckon he may have had a preplanned alternative escape-route bolt hole, a backup in case things went wrong and he needed another way to get out of Dodge."

"So?"

Courtney waved her notebook. "So I took a drive out to the marina. I did some snooping in the office and got a list of boat owners."

"And?"

"Two of the berthed vessels are unaccounted for in terms of owner-ship. I checked, and it turns out the owner of one of them moved over-seas. The one that's left was berthed right at the end of the marina, only no one seems to know who it belongs to. An old Dorsett Catalina."

"Nice boat."

"I took a look on board. You need to see what I found."

57

The study looked like a command post. I knew Chad used it to com-municate with his security business's outposts abroad.

On the right wall was a plaque in polished silver: "Keep your ene-mies close but your friends even closer."

It was Chad's motto, one he often liked to quote.

In one corner, at least three computers were switched on, their screens glowing blue, leather office chairs in front of them. In the center was a lounge area with two comfortable three-seater couches facing each other. In the middle was an Arabic coffee table, carved out of walnut, inlaid with gold and ivory and delicate filigree work. An Apple laptop was open on the table. I knew Chad sometimes worked from here, alone or with several of his employees.

"You busy?"

He gave a shrug, and the brief shadow of a smile registered on his face. "Like I always say, there's a lot of insecurity driving the security business. Terrorism's made an ugly comeback everywhere. Business is always brisk when the bad boys are up to no good. Coffee?"

"No, thanks. I'm really stuck for time, Chad."

"Take a seat, Kath." He indicated one of the couches.

I sat, and Chad tugged his pants at the knee as he eased himself onto the couch opposite. That was a typical Chad move, pants tugging at the knee, along with his hands stuck in his blazer pockets. Like you see some upper-class people do—both gestures are Prince Charles's favorites.

Chad put a hand up to massage his forehead, as if he had a headache or he didn't know how to start.

"Look, I think I'm going to be straight here, Kath." He met my stare. "I know this is a difficult time for you, and I know you're stressed, and the last thing I want to do is heighten that stress. But I'm pretty sure you've got questions in your head about all of this, and I simply want to try to help answer them."

All of this? I hadn't even told him about the intruder. I wanted to but decided to leave it for now. I wanted him to get to the point.

"Yeah? Well, it's very kind of you, Chad, but why?"

He must have heard the gripe in my voice, because he said, "There's no need to let sarcasm or bitterness creep in here, Kath. I'm only trying to help."

"The way hanging out with models in New York helped?"

"All in the past and my mistake. We've been over all that. I know we've both moved on. But I still care about you. Care about you a lot."

"I guess you must like making the same mistakes."

Chad frowned, but no lines showed. A Botox moment. "If you're alluding to the woman in the Bentley, she was a client."

"Really? She's a pretty good-looking client. Better than a lot of the wealthy Arab royalty in robes I've seen you hang out with. Anyway, it's none of my business."

It was a bitchy remark, but I couldn't help it. Still, I regretted it the second I said it. "Look, I'm sorry. I'm tired and stressed out. Can you just get to the point?"

Chad made a steeple of his fingers and looked down at the tips, as if he was trying to muster his thoughts. When he looked up, he kept his fingers together. "Jack was a good man. A good man but a sick man. We both know that."

"And the point is?"

"I need to be very honest here, Kath. And that honesty may hurt you, but I don't mean it to."

"Spit it out."

He looked away, then back at me. "In the last months that Jack worked for me, I was considering firing him. I never told you. And I never told the police when they came to question me after Jack's flight disappeared. But it's true. I had some serious problems with his judgment, his performance, and his ability to do his job."

"We all know he had problems. Explain exactly."

"Do I really have to spell this out, Kath? His paranoia was getting worse. He had behavioral issues, too. He'd flare up easily, get angry and argumentative, even with customers. They'd notice and comment. Jack was becoming more troubled. Losing the plot. I put it all down to his PTSD and cut him a lot of slack. But that slack was beginning to run out."

"So why didn't you tell the police all that?"

Chad sighed. "I think I knew when the plane disappeared that it had probably crashed. As the weeks and months went by, it seemed less and less important. Besides, I reckon the police figured it out for themselves. I think they suspected, from talking to his colleagues and former comrades, that maybe Jack had purposely caused the crash. Didn't they discuss that with you?"

I had to admit that they did. It was an angle the police explored after the first few weeks when the aircraft wasn't found. Then they dropped it. I nodded.

Chad shrugged. "I guess no one wanted to tar-brush Jack. No one wanted to sully a once-good man who had mental-health problems. And he *was* good. A good soldier, a good friend. But there were incidents in the company—stuff I still can't talk about because it relates to the security of my clients—that made it clear to me that Jack was a man out of control."

"We don't know that Jack deliberately crashed the plane, in case that's where this might be leading."

"You're jumping the gun here. I never said that. Did the investigators suggest that?"

"Not to me. Not this time. At least, not yet."

"Then I may be barking up the wrong tree. But if he walked away from the crash with the children and he didn't contact you in all this time, something's not right. Something caused him to want to hide. Either his mental health was bad, or else he had a powerful motive."

"What kind of motive?"

Chad shook his head. "I've no idea. I'm just throwing it out there, Kath. Trying to make sense of all this."

"If you suspected Jack had mental-health issues, then why did you let him fly down to New Orleans in the company plane?"

"That's the thing. I didn't."

"What?"

"Jack did that without my authority. I was in Kenya on business when the crash happened, remember?"

I remembered. Chad phoned me the day after the aircraft went missing to say he was flying home at once from Kenya. He wanted to help me any way he could. I'd appreciated his concern.

"Jack took it upon himself to use the aircraft. But I never authorized it. That I did tell the police. I had to. I thought he did it because it was Amy's birthday. Just a reckless but well-meaning gesture on Jack's part. But he covered himself."

"How?"

"He arranged a brief meeting with some New Orleans city officials we did business with. It wasn't a meeting that was really necessary. It took ten minutes or less, and he was done, but it covered him if anyone queried the use of the aircraft, even though I didn't authorize it. Regarding the other stuff about Jack's mental state, I thought it best to bury it. There was no point in dishonoring an old friend."

"What about the money, the bonds, the priceless mask?"

"I've no idea. But now you make me wonder. If they were on board, maybe Jack arranged to pick them up in New Orleans and used the business part of the trip and something as innocuous as celebrating his daughter's birthday as a cover. He may not have even gotten it all in New Orleans. Offshore-banking havens like the Caymans would be ideal to stash that kind of load."

Chad tapped some keys on his laptop for quite a few seconds, then turned the screen around to face me. "Take a look."

A map came up, showing the southern U.S.A. and the Caribbean. A red arrow curved from New Orleans to a point just below Cuba. It said, "Distance from New Orleans to Grand Cayman 919 miles."

"The company aircraft was laid over in New Orleans for ten hours. Jack could have flown to the Cayman Islands, for all I know, and been there and back in six or seven hours."

"And you knew nothing about this?"

"Absolutely nothing."

"What made you mention the Caymans? And why would Jack think of flying to that location, assuming he may have?"

"Can I trust you not to speak to anyone if I tell you? And I mean no one."

"Yes."

"This is embarrassing."

"How embarrassing?"

"Sometimes I deal in cash. Clients prefer it that way. They don't want my services on the books. They want them off the radar and off-shore. I've had dealings in the Caymans. Jack was aware."

"What would the IRS think?"

"Exactly. I'd be in deep trouble. Which is why I ask you to keep that confidential."

Chad always sounded honest and truthful. Which may have been why his father wanted him to go into politics. But of course, he was a businessman, and duplicity almost went with the territory.

I looked at the laptop screen, at the red line from New Orleans to the Cayman Islands. Then I looked back at Chad. A thought hit me hard in the gut. "Offshore-banking havens. Money, bonds, a priceless artifact. I'm getting a funny vibe."

"Yeah?"

"Like, I'm asking myself, is that what this is really all about? Is that the prime reason Jack disappeared? To run off with millions?"

Chad let out a breath. "It's possible. And it gives me no pleasure to say that, Kath."

"Why is it possible?"

"Because I'm pretty sure I know where he got the money and the mask. And it wasn't from me, and it had nothing to do with my business."

I stared back at him. "You mean he got them from the Caymans or in New Orleans?"

"Jack could have gotten them from a bank vault in the Caymans or even New Orleans, for sure, but I think he had them way before then."

I looked at him, and I felt lost.

Chad saw my confusion, picked up the laptop, and came to join me. "Scoot over."

I moved along on the couch and he sat, laying the laptop back down on the coffee table. I could smell his aftershave. Eau Sauvage. I'd always liked it.

"I don't like showing you this, for lots of reasons. Mostly because it will upset you. I know it still upsets me. But there's no other way around it."

For some reason, I looked at the wall plaque with Chad's motto: "Keep your enemies close but your friends even closer."

"Get around what?"

"The truth," Chad said, and tapped the keyboard.

58

The Apple screen lit up with a media player logo.

A video started to play. Someone was holding a camera or a camera phone as a helicopter descended. The scene below looked like the aftermath of a battle and the remains of a civilian vehicle convoy.

All the vehicles were ablaze, their gas tanks on fire, and riddled with bullet holes. Black, oily smoke filled the air above the charred carcasses of several vehicles. Men in uniforms bundled out of the helicopter, and the cameraman followed, moving through the scene. Some vehicles were crashed, doors were flung open, and bodies lay inside or on the ground. Most of them were armed civilian men, their weapons nearby or still in the hands. The audio was muted or way too low to hear.

An uneasy feeling slithered up my spine. Whoever was holding the camera was walking through a scene of total carnage and devastation. There was hardly any sound, which made it even more eerie, just a few vague cries of pain and sporadic gunshots. A couple of U.S. soldiers in full battle gear ran past the cameraman, rifles aimed. Another group looked like medics and carried plasma bags. I saw more helicopters already landed in the background.

And then I got a shock. I recognized my father, leading a group of officers. He wore a helmet and was dressed in full battle gear, a holstered sidearm strapped to his leg. He was also limping, which gave me a time frame. This was sometime after he's lost his foot and gone back to active duty. He looked totally in command as he held a map in one hand and pointed, making a slicing action with the other, as he directed the officers. Another officer approached him. The camera circled so it got the officer's face in the shot.

That was my second shock. It was Jack. He looked stressed, his fatigues dusty, a shemag around his neck. He gave the camera holder a nod of recognition, and then he and my father engaged in a heated discussion. The camera scene shifted abruptly to the landscape around them.

It was flat, but I spotted a russet-colored hill in the distance. The images reminded me of some of those scenes in the early part of the first Gulf War, when Saddam Hussein's retreating army tried to escape in convoys and were blown to oblivion by the coalition forces in relentless attacks.

The cameraman kept moving through the convoy's remains. Bloodied, dead bodies were everywhere, some with limbs missing, body parts scattered. I didn't see any American military dead. A few of the vehicles were trucks and vans and looked as if they had been shredded by rocket-propelled grenades.

I recalled what Courtney and Tanner had said about Tarik. Was this the same incident? My gut told me it was. I kept my mouth shut, as Tanner told me to.

Then came another horror.

The camera zoomed in on dozens of bodies of women and children in a truck. The chassis was mangled, drenched in blood. Some of the dead women clutched their deceased infants in their arms, their clothes drenched in crimson. I glimpsed the body of a young boy, about seven. His right leg was blown off, and his torso looked riddled with shrapnel or bullets. Other children's corpses were half charred.

So many of the bodies were children. Some were half naked from grenade or bomb detonation. Clumps of them were scattered everywhere, huddled together. I recalled press photographs I'd seen of the civilian massacres at My Lai during the Vietnam War. That's what these images reminded me of. Ruthless, merciless, callous war. "I've seen enough."

Chad froze the video on the grisly scene. I averted my eyes. Horrified, I wanted to throw up.

"Have you ever heard of Babylon?"

"Yes."

"It's one of the oldest cities in civilization, four thousand years old, and the ruins lie just over fifty miles south of Baghdad."

"What's that got to do with anything?"

Chad said, "The dead were in a convoy of tribal elders, with their fighters and their families. They had decided to change sides with the insurgents and become U.S. allies. Your father had done the deal and persuaded the tribe to come over to us. They were traveling through an area south of Babylon to a new base."

"What happened?"

"Jack was in the lead. His units mistook the convoy for a group of insurgents and ambushed it, directing fire from the ground and from a bunch of choppers. The convoy returned fire; the whole thing escalated and got out of hand. Jack and his men didn't know there were women and children in the Iraqi vehicles. Not until the shooting was over."

"Jack . . . Jack killed all those people?"

"Once the target started returning fire, it was impossible to stop the battle. Jack took it bad afterward, when he realized the mistake. Your father and I arrived by chopper ten minutes after we got the call at command. I took the video you just saw."

I gestured to the grisly images on the screen. "What happened that day triggered Jack's PTSD, didn't it?"

Chad nodded.

"Kyle was there, too, wasn't he?"

He nodded again.

I shot a look at the screen and felt nausea in the pit of my stomach. I understood now how Kyle would have gone over the edge. I would, too, if I'd witnessed such carnage. I noticed the hill again, beyond the clump of bodies. It looked so unusual in the stark brown landscape. The hill's earth looked russet-brown, almost red. I pointed to the screen.

"What's . . . that?"

Chad hit a key a few times, advancing the images. I saw the hill a little sharper. "The locals called it Red Rock. A hilly outcrop just up the road from where the shooting took place. Jack mounted his attack from there. That's what we called the operation. Red Rock."

I felt a sinking feeling in my stomach. Now I knew what *Red* likely meant. I had been tempted to show Kyle's notepad to Chad, except that now there didn't seem much point. But why would my mother record those words? What did it have to do with her?

Chad looked at me. "There was an official military inquiry. The Army had been on the receiving end of a lot of bad press back then and wanted it all whitewashed. The story was, they had your father blame it on the tribe, said they double-crossed us. You get the idea. The inquiry came out along those lines. Your father and Jack and his men were cleared, and everybody moved on. Which pretty much suited everyone. No criminal charges, no jail time, no dishonorable discharges. Everything's hunky-dory."

Chad shrugged. "And that's the way it stayed. Until Jack's PTSD started to get worse. When he began to talk about the incident at Red Rock, and the Army didn't like the whispers it was hearing. Some other folks didn't like it, either."

"What others?"

"When Jack disappeared, it suited a bunch of people. He was losing it, starting to worry those with a vested interest in keeping the whole dirty business quiet. They didn't want attention drawn to the incident." Chad met my stare. "Some money that was in the Iraqi convoy went missing that day."

"What money? And what people?"

"For heaven's sake, Kath, the U.S. was doling out money to insurgents and the Iraqis left, right, and center. You knew that, didn't you? Billions of dollars. And big chunks of it went missing. It was a feeding frenzy. Pigs sticking their snouts in troughs."

"I heard eight billion."

Chad almost laughed. "Eight? I'd say that's a conservative figure. Who told you that?"

"Courtney."

"What exactly is her role in the investigation?"

"She never fully explained."

"Some estimates say twelve billion dollars vanished. And guess what? There's never been a significant government inquiry. At least, not one that sent a bunch of people to prison."

"Why is that?"

"Because there are truckloads of skeletons that lead back to the guilty. Open up one crypt, and you could open up them all."

"Who are the guilty?"

"It's a long list. Senior Iraqi government bigwigs and officials. And I could also include U.S. military brass, civilian advisers, and business-people."

I stared at the gory images on the screen. My nausea had not gone away. "I . . . I'd like a glass of water."

"Are you OK?"

"No. I feel faint."

Chad got up and moved out to the kitchen. I heard him fill a glass with ice and water from the fridge. I don't know why—or maybe I did—but I slipped out my phone, flicked on the camera, and took a couple of shots of the frozen image on the screen. It might turn out grainy, it might not, but I wanted evidence.

Chad returned with a glass of water with crushed ice. He handed it to me. I drank half of it down.

"Any better?"

"I'd like a copy of the video."

"Are you out of your mind?"

"I want it, Chad."

"No way."

"A snapshot still, then."

"What for?"

I wasn't quite sure why, maybe for the same reason I took a shot with my camera phone. I had a feeling I wanted to confront my father with the evidence. "It's personal."

"I'm sorry, Kath. I can't do it. The evidence stays in my possession."

"Chad . . ."

"I'm sorry. In the wrong hands, this could be dynamite."

Chad hit the keyboard a few times with his index finger and snapped the laptop shut.

"Are you one of those who benefited?" I asked him.

He stared back at me, looking offended. "Me? Are you kidding? Of course not."

"So where does Jack figure in all of this?"

"The convoy Jack attacked—those tribal chiefs didn't just change sides for their health."

I waited, saying nothing.

"The Army never mentioned it in the report, but those guys had just received a big payment from the U.S. government. It ensured that they switched sides to help U.S. forces fight Al Qaeda-backed insurgents. The money was supposed to be in a truck along with the convoy . . ." His voice trailed away.

"And?"

"It vanished into thin air that same day."

"How much?"

Chad didn't answer, his lips tight.

"I asked how much, Chad?"

"Maybe you need to ask your father that question."

"My father? Why?"

"He filed the report to his superiors. He tried to cover everyone, naturally. These were his men. He felt he had to stand by them. Paint them as guiltless. But I heard rumors . . ." Chad said, faltering.

"What do you mean?"

"That the whole thing was a setup. The ambush was all part of a plan to steal the money . . ." He faltered again.

"You're saying my father had something to do with it?"

"I'm saying nothing. It was a rumor I heard, that's all." He looked at me. "Kath, it was all smoke and mirrors back then. There was a lot of mistrust and a lot of double dealing. Nobody knows what the truth is or was. Things clouded it."

"Like?"

"We'd lost five men the day before in an insurgent attack."

"Meaning?"

"You want something back for it. We wanted heavy contact. Instead, we got a civilian convoy."

"What are you saying?"

"Your father's report claimed that the tribal elders had already handed over the cash to another bunch of insurgents, that they never intended to change sides, that it was all just a ruse to con us out of the money."

"So what's the truth, Chad?"

Chad sighed. "All I know is that the money was never found. Your father authorized the operation. If anyone knew what the truth was, he should have. Me, I was way down in the pecking order."

"But you were there. You mean you never spoke to him about it?"

"Sure. But the missing money was pretty much a forbidden subject. One I never revisited until you told me about Jack's briefcase. All I wanted to do today was try to explain to you what might have triggered Jack's mental problems and Kyle's. That's all. The killings that day affected us all. Maybe I should have told you the truth before now. Except I couldn't. The Army put the clamps on it, deemed it classified. But you deserve to know. It's tormented you."

His hand came across and touched my knee. Nothing sexual, but it sent a small current of electricity down my spine.

"I just want to help. To be there for you."

I said nothing.

"I kept a copy of the video in case that can of worms ever got opened up again. It's my proof that I didn't have a role in the main drama. Something like that could ruin me if I ever stayed in politics."

"You think Jack had something to do with the stolen money?"

Chad said nothing, his mouth a slit.

"Why do I get the feeling you do? You think he stole more than was in the briefcase?"

Chad shrugged, but it looked to me like a yes. "I guess he could have vanished with a lot more. A small fortune. Yeah, I guess he could have made himself a rich man."

"How much missing money are we talking about?"

Chad's hand moved away from my knee, and he made a steeple of his fingers again, touching the tips to his mouth. "We're not just talking about money. The convoy had other valuables."

"Such as?"

"The mask you saw. It belonged to the tribe, along with a bunch of other artifacts. Actually, there were supposed to be three masks. The Iraqis probably stole them in the first place, but that's beside the point."

I sat there, considering it all, and then I looked into Chad's face. "How much money?"

No answer, Chad's mouth a slit.

"I haven't got all day, Chad. For Pete's sake, how much?"

"Twenty-five million dollars."

59

LOUDON MARINA

Earlier that same day, Courtney pulled up in the marina parking lot.

She saw the restaurant nearby, Willy's on the Water, but it was empty, the lunchtime crowd at least two hours away. They walked along the marina, under the covered walkway, boats on either side, until they came to the end, where a blue-and-white-painted old Dorsett Catalina was tied up.

It had definitely seen better days, being more than a half century old, the paintwork scratched in places and the varnish worn in patches. Compared with the newer boats nearby, it was a decrepit old wreck, but it still looked solidly built, tough as granite.

Tanner looked it over, tipped the bow with the tip of his shoe. They had driven in separate cars, left them parked in the marina lot. "Used to go fishing on one of these when I was a kid. A school pal of mine, his old man had one."

"Yeah?"

"Happy days. So what did you find?"

Courtney stepped onto the boat. She moved toward the steering area. Below it, steps led down to a cabin.

"No one knows who berthed it here. Or maybe they do."

"What do you mean?"

"Someone could have slipped one of the marina staff a fistful of dollars to leave it overnight, no questions asked. Except nobody's saying. The employee I spoke with says it was just berthed here."

Tanner put a hand to his forehead, stared toward the left of the dam and the canal lock gates that enabled boats to proceed along the Tennessee River. "When was the Dorsett berthed? What's the timeline?"

"The night before Quentin Lusk arrived at Kath's doorstep."

"It often happens that folks just leave a vessel tied up here without any authorization?"

"Sometimes."

"Has the marina got security cameras?"

"Sure. And I looked at the recordings."

"And?"

"The cameras have blind spots that don't cover the end of the marina where the Dorsett was."

"Ain't that just terrific. You think somebody knew that?"

"Maybe. The canal security isn't that tight, but there are also cameras, monitored by the engineers and the coastguard. I'm going to check those and see if they turn up anything. Maybe the owner came through the gates and we can get a visual."

"Yeah, and sorry to rain on your parade, but maybe he didn't. So what did you find?"

As Tanner waited for a reply, he nosed around, lifted the cover on a storage bin. Ropes and buoys, all of them looking and smelling decades old.

"It's really all I've got. There are no ID numbers on the boat, no way to trace it back to an owner. And it looks to me like whoever left it here did a cleanup job, removing any personal items that could be traced." Courtney pushed open the cabin door. It looked narrow, too narrow for Tanner to fit through. "You think you'll fit, big man?"

"Have to, won't I?"

Courtney smiled, pushed in the door, and stepped down into the cabin.

The cramped cabin was tiny. Tanner barely squeezed in, sucking in his gut to get through the doorframe. With the two of them inside, it felt claustrophobic.

The air was hot and heavy, smelling of old wood and engine oil. Tanner's eyes roamed the cabin—the washbasin, the head, the bunk area. It all looked bare as a poor man's hovel, as if it had been stripped and cleaned.

Tanner opened all the cupboards. Bare, too—not a mug, a bottle, or a utensil in sight.

"So what's the story?"

Courtney took a pair of rubber evidence gloves from her pocket and tossed them to Tanner. "Put these on, and put your hands up."

"What?"

"One will do. Feel along the top of the cupboard on the right. You'll find something."

Tanner slipped on the gloves and did as he was told, his hand feeling along the cupboard top. He felt something papery, gripped it, and pulled it down. He was staring down at a map of some kind, the folded edges looking crisp and new.

"What kind of map is this?"

"A waterway map. Open it out."

"Be my guest."

Courtney did so, spreading it out on the cabin table. "See anything?"

"Give me a chance." Tanner studied the unmarked map and scratched his neck.

"Well?"

He looked back up at Courtney. "Naw. Is this some kind of quiz?"

"No quiz, Tanner. You give up?"

"Yeah. Hit me. I ain't in the mood for no puzzle crap."

"The boat's old. The map's new."

"So?"

"Old boat, new map. Either the boat's got a new owner, or who-ever's using it is a stranger to this part of the waterway, or both."

Tanner gave Courtney a look and then stared down at the map. "Looks fresh. Don't seem to be any marks or indications of where Quentin Lusk may have been headed. If the boat *did* belong to Lusk."

Courtney pursed her lips. "Nothing, except maybe . . ."

"What?"

"Midway down the map, there's a greasy mark, a smudge, like someone tapped a finger there. It's a stretch of waterway more than seventy miles from here, in Marion County."

"Give me a break. That's a big if. Someone could have smudged it by simply opening out the darn map."

"True. And we'll have it checked for prints."

"Meanwhile, we're nowhere closer to knowing anything more."

Courtney made a face. "You're probably right. So right now, that smudge is all we've got."

Courtney watched as Tanner drove away in his white Camry.

He gave her a wave and winked through the open window, and then he was gone. He was a handsome man. She liked his pale-cinnamon looks. A few pounds less, and she'd probably like them even more. Put him on a diet and a treadmill, and he'd be quite a hunk.

She took her cell phone from her purse and punched in a name. The call was answered immediately.

"Dexter."

"Hey, Dexter, it's Courtney from CID. How are they hanging, buddy?"

"Straight and low, as always. You doing OK?"

"Good. Listen, I just needed to run something by you."

"Run away."

"Tanner said you told him you did a thorough search of the area using ground radar but found no remains."

"That's correct. Zilch. Unless you want to count the skeletal remains of some possums, rabbits, and an adolescent bear."

"You reckon your scans are reliable?"

"First-class. Why?"

"Maybe it's the OCD in me. I wanted to be certain. And if there are any other angles you've yet to cover."

"We're going to run the radar equipment over several areas of the site again, places that seemed a little nebulous, just to be absolutely certain, but the experts tell me they don't reckon on any surprises."

"Not that I don't trust Tanner or anything. I guess I just wanted to hear it from the horse's mouth."

"You and Tanner getting on OK?"

"Yeah, why?"

"Tough about his wife. Her dying in an arson blaze. All that messy stuff in his past."

"What do you mean?"

"He didn't tell you?"

60

When I pulled up into the driveway I saw my father's blue Ford Taurus in front of the house.

A bunch of press vehicles were still on the street, as were Channel 5 and WBIR vans and a cop car. Another squad car was parked in the driveway next to my father's car, a sheriff's deputy standing by the vehicle. He tipped his hat as I got out and walked up to the front door. "Ma'am."

I had been apprehensive all through the ten-minute drive. Not only about confronting my father now that he was back but about the fact that Jack had called. I checked my watch. 4:10 p.m.—I had fifty minutes until Jack would call me back.

I still desperately wanted to tell Courtney and Tanner what was happening. But I knew I couldn't risk ignoring Jack's demands. It might prevent me from ever seeing my children again.

I felt my body quiver. It was almost violent, as if I was in meltdown, every nerve on edge, every sense heightened. The last thing in the world I wanted to do was confront my father. But I knew I had to. And I knew it had to be now. I couldn't put it off any longer.

I had the damning envelope in my tote bag, the one with the photographs that had been left on the passenger seat of my car. Part of me was scared to show it to him. Another part of me was angry, desperate for answers, to see his reaction when I confronted him.

I had never feared my father—never. He was my protector. Yet I was conscious of the fact that I had put my Taurus revolver in my bag. I didn't know how he would react.

Would I finally learn the truth after all these years? Would I learn that my father was a murderer? He was a soldier. Soldiers sometimes have to kill in battle. But I never imagined my father was capable of killing my mother.

I looked at my phone again, at the snapshot image I took of Chad's laptop screen. It was a little grainy, but I had no problem making out the pile of bloodied bodies. The weird thing is, I'd never thought of my father as capable of killing, even though he was a lifelong soldier. I guess I put that part of his life to the back of my mind.

He was my father, a man I loved and trusted, from whom I knew only love and kindness. But a brutal logic started to kick in. If my father was capable of ordering a massacre as gruesome as this—and surely there were other bloody attacks he'd taken part in during his career—surely he was capable of killing my mother?

Another thing, the twenty-five million dollars Chad mentioned. The fact that he couldn't deny that Jack was in some way involved in its disappearance unsettled me. Was that a reason Jack disappeared? The more I thought about it, the more sense it made. Twenty-five million was a lot. Or a share of it. Jack could live in comfort for the rest of his days. And it might be a motive to hide.

As I went up the patio steps, I felt my legs shaking. I opened the door quietly. The alarm was on this time. It chimed as I entered. My father's overnight case was outside his study. I heard the shower running upstairs. I stepped into his study, the same room my grandfather had used.

The smell of old books and leather and walnut was heavy in the air. My eyes moved over familiar objects. On one wall, the Irish and American flags crossed above a pair of broadswords. On another, photographs of my parents on castle ramparts high above emerald-green fields, kissing the Blarney Stone, and at the Cliffs of Moher. In a bar, their hands raised in a toast of whiskey and Guinness.

And my mother's favorite memento of her visit: a six-inch bronze cast of a legendary Celtic bird, perched on a thorn tree. I felt my eyes water as I stared at my mother's image and clutched the stiff-backed white envelope.

Anger raged through me like a tidal wave.

I heard the shower water stop upstairs. My father's voice called out, "Is that you, Kath?"

He would have heard my car from upstairs.

"Yes."

"Be right down," he called back.

I sat there, clutching the envelope, waiting for my father to appear.

He descended the stairs, dragging his foot, his wispy hair still damp as he toweled it dry. I saw very little trembling in his hands or face. He must have been taking his Parkinson's meds. Once they wore off, the trembling and other symptoms would start to affect him again.

But he looked strained, his eyes bloodshot. "I half expected some press, but I didn't think I'd see this many—or the police."

"The press will want to talk. I'm just not up to it yet."

"You don't have to talk to anyone, honey."

He wore fresh jeans, a military khaki-colored T-shirt, and Nike sneakers, and the damp towel hung around his neck. He still had that Clint Eastwood look, the confident walk of a man who kept himself in good shape. A powerhouse, despite his age.

"Are you OK?" His eyes never left my face as he came over and hugged me, kissed my cheeks. I felt the familiar rub of his chin on top of my head. My father smelled of soap and the scent of his favorite Polo cologne.

I didn't respond, just stood there stiffly.

He took a step back, sensing my unease, both his arms outstretched as he held on to my shoulders. "You look like you're still in shock."

I nodded. He squeezed my arm. I wanted to recoil.

"We both are, Kath. My mind's been in turmoil all during the drive back."

I could barely force myself to meet his eyes for more than a few moments, before I had to look away. Was my father a cold-blooded killer? I was desperate to know the truth, but at the same time, I dreaded knowing it. Instinctively, I drew myself away from him and took a few steps toward the window.

His expression changed to puzzlement. "Are you OK? What's the matter?"

I remained mute a few moments, the silence like a crushing weight. "How's Ruby?" I asked.

It was all I could muster the courage to say. The other things I wanted to discuss—the accusation written on the photograph—I couldn't marshal the strength to bring up just yet. I was distressed, couldn't get the words out that I wanted scream at my father. *Did you kill Mom?*

His expression tightened as he shook his head, slid the towel from his neck, and tossed it onto the back of the chair. "Not good."

I stood there, saying nothing.

"When they opened her up, things were a lot worse than they expected. She hemorrhaged pretty bad during the operation."

"I'm sorry," I muttered, barely able to speak.

I saw his eyes grow moist. "Look, I hate to have to tell you this, but I need to fly back up there tomorrow. The doctors are not sure Ruby's going to make it, Kath."

My eyes flicked to the kitchen clock. 5:25 p.m. I had exactly thirty-five minutes before Jack would call again.

"I know it's a quick turnaround, honey, but I wanted to be here for you. I ought to be there for Ruby, too. The doctors are not optimistic. I guess I'm caught between two stools. But just tell me to stay, and I will."

I didn't speak.

My father raised an eyebrow. "Are you OK?"

"You need to be with Ruby. I understand that."

"Are you really sure?"

"Yes."

"I'll fly back tomorrow. I've got a seat booked. With all that's been going on, I just couldn't take another twelve-hour drive. I guess you can figure it's pretty bad if I intend to fly."

"Sure." I felt as if I were talking on autopilot.

"I just had to come back, Kath. I had to see if you were coping. Are you? It's all such a terrible shock." He looked into my face, said it as delicately as he could. "Did they find the remains yet?"

"No."

"Nothing, nothing at all?"

"Some personal belongings. And an aluminum briefcase." I decided not to mention the case contents just yet.

"What belongings?"

"Some clothes of Sean's and Amy's and a PlayStation game."

"You . . . you saw them?"

"Yes."

He teared up some more and said in a kind of astonishment, "My God." He wiped his eyes with his sleeve. As always, trying not to demonstrate his pain. "That's all they found?"

"So far." I took the big envelope with the photographs from my bag. "We need to talk about some things. Personal things. They're . . . they're important."

His eyebrows crinkled as he stared at the envelope I was clutching. "What's that?"

"Something you need to see."

I felt my legs quiver. I was truly scared to show him. What would his reaction be? Anger? Denial? Fear? Puzzlement? Whatever it was, it might reveal all I needed to know. I held on to the envelope for now, didn't offer it over just yet.

My father's gaze shifted back to me. I met his stare. I needed to get the ball rolling, to spit it out. But part of me dreaded the response, whatever it would be. I forced myself to speak again as I looked into my father's face. I felt a tear roll down my cheek.

"Jack, Sean, and Amy survived the crash. They survived. Eight years ago, they walked out of those woods alive, and for whatever reason, they never came back."

61

The silence was almost total.

All I heard was my father's breathing. Deep and hard. Like he was trying to recover from a bolt out of the blue. That military term pretty much described his reaction: shock and awe.

Slowly, he wiped one eye with his left index finger, then his other eye with his right. I saw his eyes moisten, his lips quiver. "Jack . . . Jack and the kids are alive?"

"They didn't die eight years ago. I know that much. I know they survived."

My father looked as if he'd received a shot of adrenaline, his eyes widening before they narrowed with puzzlement. "Know? Now?"

"There's enough physical and circumstantial evidence to corroborate it."

"What evidence?"

I told him. About the flashlight, the first-aid kit, the bloodstains, the DNA, the blood traces in the cabin two hundred yards away.

My father collapsed into the study chair, pale shock spreading over his face like a sudden rash.

"Have they searched all the woods yet? Have they said conclusively that Jack and the children were alive?"

"The investigators can't say anything with absolute certainty yet. They still have to check the terrain with ground-penetrating equipment. But they think that if they were capable of walking out, they were in a fit enough state. They think there's a good enough chance."

As desperate as I felt the need to do so, I couldn't risk telling him about Jack's calls. The other things—the damning accusation written on that photograph—I couldn't bring myself to speak about just yet. I still felt in distress.

"I . . . I . . ." My father stammered.

That was as far as he got for a few moments, his voice hoarse, whatever words he meant to say choked in his throat. My father rarely drank during the day. For special occasions or maybe if he had a visitor now and then. But now he crossed to the liquor cabinet and plucked out a bottle of Jameson whiskey.

"What's going on, Kath? Why? Why would Jack do that? Survive with Sean and Amy and not contact you?"

"I'm guessing his mental state may have contributed. But I need you to tell me the truth. I need you to be honest with me and tell me what happened to Jack and Kyle."

He smacked a glass onto the tray and rubbed his face with a big hand. He looked trapped.

I glanced at the kitchen wall clock. Twenty-one minutes until Jack called.

"This is not the time, Kath."

"Yes, it is. It's never been the time. But now it is."

"Kath, it's . . . it's complicated." My father looked as if he were caught on the end of a hook, and he was squirming. This time, he splashed a large measure of Jameson into the glass.

I faced him. "It must be. Courtney's involved."

His eyebrows arched in a stare. "Courtney?"

"She's the lead for the CID. The feds are on the case, too."

I took out my cell phone. I selected the photo gallery and the gory image of the pile of corpses—women and children. I handed it to him. He stared at it.

"I know about Red Rock," I said. "I know there was a massacre and your men were responsible. I know a lot of money went missing that day. Is that the kind of complicated you mean?"

My father put the Jameson bottle down and stood rock-solid. The whole world seemed to come crashing down around him. For the first time in my life, I saw real fear on his face.

"Who told you all that? Where did you get this?" He looked up from my phone to stare at me, his voice a rasp.

"It doesn't matter. What matters is the truth. CID investigated Jack back then about the missing money, not just the massacre. You knew that, didn't you?"

He was silent. For a few moments, his eyes settled again on the image on the screen. Then he slowly handed the phone back to me. He raised his glass. His head snapped back, and he drank the whiskey fast. It was almost an angry gesture. He slapped down the glass.

"Yes, I knew."

"So why didn't you ever tell me?"

"Kath, what happened that day was in the public domain, but the Army kept the lid on certain details in the case. I was ordered to keep my mouth shut. Besides, why upset you? You were grieving as it was. There was no need to add fuel to the fire. No need to deepen your pain by sullying Jack's name."

"And that's your answer? That's it?"

He ran a hand over his face again. "Kath . . . things happen in war that you don't plan. Bad things. It's shifting sands, all the time. You meet action, get hit, you hit back. In the heat of battle, it's like you're fighting in thick fog. You, of all people, ought to know that. You're a soldier's daughter. No matter how well trained you are, sometimes you just can't tell the collateral damage that's unfolding until after the smoke clears. Mistakes like that get made all the time in war."

I saw my father's hands tremble as he splashed more Jameson into his glass. The man I adored, the man I always put on a pedestal, seemed to be on shaky ground before my eyes. And I hadn't even put the cherry on top yet.

He lifted his glass. "Who told you all this? Courtney?"

I saw the clock's second hand sweep around. Sixteen minutes until Jack's call. Our talk was dragging on, but I needed to know.

"It's irrelevant."

"No, it's not. I'll bet the prime reason CID is involved is to keep tabs on this, make sure it doesn't get out of control. They don't want a can of worms opened up."

"You ordered the attack on the convoy, didn't you?"

He nodded. "My intel said the convoy was insurgents. But I never knew they had their families with them in the vehicles. If I had, I would have handled it differently."

"Jack took it badly?"

"All of the men did. Soldiers are human, for God's sake. A lot of them were married men with families. So many civilian deaths traumatized us all. There were dead and dying everywhere. Children crying. Teenagers, kids, infants, badly injured. It was like a scene from Dante's *Inferno*."

"And Kyle?"

My father took another swallow of Jameson, his mouth tight, bitter. "Kyle tried to save two badly burned infants. All that was left of their mother was a clump of burning flesh. The children didn't make it, either. The whole thing affected him severely. He was the youngest soldier there and hadn't experienced battle. I could see it in his eyes. See how much it disturbed him."

His gaze never left my face. "I wanted him close to me so I could keep an eye on him. That's why Jack kept him under his wing, too. But I didn't protect him in the end, did I? I helped send my son over the edge. Caused him to be a cripple, a vegetable."

Tears escaped the corners of his eyes. They searched mine, as if my father was frantically seeking some kind of solace that he couldn't find. I didn't give in.

He picked up one of the photographs on the kitchen shelves. Of himself, in dress uniform, wearing his service ribbons and medals. But no Medal of Honor, and I always figured that rankled. He stared at the image, then held it up to show me.

"That uniform was my life. It was and is who I am. But you don't think a day goes by when I don't blame myself for what happened? That day haunts me. It's my past, my present, my future. The Army wanted it to go away. And that suited everyone. What do you think would have happened if the Army got the blame? There would be a public outcry. A trial, maybe personnel found guilty. Everyone involved would be affected. Me included. Jack. Kyle, too."

"What do you mean?"

"His care is mostly paid for through the Veterans Administration. You think that care would continue at the same level if he was deemed to have been party to a massacre? If he was branded a war criminal? Kyle could be cut adrift, lose some of his privileges. What happens then? Who's going to take care of him?"

My father's shoulders sagged. "And you don't think I'm paying the price after what happened to Kyle? Maybe even what happened to Jack and the kids? I'm paying. I'm paying in spades, Kath. War is sheer hell. There never were truer words spoken. Never."

"But there are still some causes worth fighting for, right? Like twenty-five million dollars?"

His eyes lit with fury. He vigorously shook his head. "I have no idea what happened to the money, Kath. None. You have to believe that. You think I'd be living like this if I did?"

"I've no idea."

"What have I to show for a crime like that? I've never stolen anything in my life. Look, the first I heard about the missing money was days later, when military intelligence got involved. And by then the trail had gone cold."

"What trail?"

"No one even knew if the money was in the convoy or not."

I held my ground, waited for more.

"Have you ever seen twenty-five million all at once? I have, and more, when we were doling it out to the Iraqis. You'd need a truck, maybe more than one. OK, CID suspected someone could have driven off with it. A number of vehicles escaped that day once the shooting started. Likely driven by insurgents. All of our men were accounted for. Maybe there needed to be collusion of some kind, some forward planning, but no evidence of that was ever found."

"Didn't the suspicion persist that one or more of your men were involved in the theft?"

"It could persist forever, but the hard evidence wasn't there."

"Did Mom know about all this?"

"Why do you ask that?"

"Once I overheard her talking in her sleep. She called out your name. As far as I remember, her words went something like this: 'Frank, you have to take this further . . . you have to tell the authorities. But who? Who'll kill us? No, that's absurd.' That was what she said. You don't forget words like that. When I asked her the next day, she claimed she didn't know what she'd been talking about. But I think she was lying."

He looked right at me, not a shred of fear in his face. But then, he was a soldier, so I almost expected that. "Was your mom drunk when she said those words?"

"I guess."

"Kath, we both know your mom said a lot of weird things when she was drunk or smoking a joint. Things that didn't add up."

"You have no idea what she meant?"

"None."

Why didn't I believe him? "What about the word *Red* on the piece of envelope from her safe? It meant Red Rock, didn't it?"

My father sounded exasperated. "Kath, I really have no idea. Not even the police could determine what it meant, or if it was part of a word or a name or whatever. We've been through all this years ago."

"That's a lie."

His face had deep lines now. "Why would I lie?"

"There's . . . there's an envelope. I have proof."

"What are you talking about?"

"You need to see it."

62

I grabbed my tote bag. I removed the two photographs from the envelope and tossed them onto the study desk.

My father picked them up, studied the images, and tilted the photograph to read the black-markered words. I watched his face. Not a muscle seemed to move or change at first, or maybe it just happened so subtly that I didn't notice. For a few moments, he looked unaffected, but then his face transformed.

His skin bleached white, as if a mask had slipped or he'd been slapped. His reaction made my stomach drop.

"Where . . . where did you get these?" His voice cracked.

"Someone left them on the passenger seat of my car. Don't ask me who." I told him about the intruder but held back telling him about the exact details on the dam.

He paled even more.

"The man on the bridge was a vet named Quentin Lusk. Did you know him?"

He nodded. "He was a good soldier. But . . . I believe he had some mental-health issues. He suffered serious shrapnel wounds."

"Not anymore. He shot himself in the head." I filled in the rest.

My father looked astonished. "Why would he kill himself? Why give you those warnings?"

"The fact that he'd face kidnap charges, assault with a deadly weapon, and a bunch of other charges might seem like a believable reason for killing himself. But other than that, I really have no idea, and neither do the investigators. Do you?"

"No. Why should I?"

"Lusk could have left that envelope on my seat."

"Why? What would be his motive?"

"You tell me."

"Kath, I have absolutely no idea. All I know is that I'm floundering here trying to figure out why anyone would leave the note and that this is becoming absurd."

"Absurd, really?"

He slapped the photographs angrily onto the desk. "Because it's a lie, Kath. A total lie. I never laid a finger on your mother. Never. Never harmed a hair on her head. She wasn't the kind of woman who would ever tolerate that. And you know it."

He was right about that. But I didn't budge. "The police seemed to ask you a lot of questions back then. They seemed to focus on you."

"They asked everyone who was at your wedding a lot of questions. I answered them honestly. If they'd had any real suspicions, don't you think they would have pursued them?"

"They found no proof. But that doesn't mean you didn't do it."

"Look, I'm guilty for making the wrong decision. The ambush was a mistake. I'm sorry. I'm ashamed. And I live with that shame and sorrow and guilt every day. But I'm not a thief. And I'm not a killer. I didn't kill your mother."

I looked at him, saying nothing. He held my stare, unflinching, a look on his face as if the subject or the accusation was painful. I was beginning to feel I was on shaky ground.

"You really don't get it, do you, Kath?"

"Get what?"

"Have I ever lied to you?"

"You lied about what happened to Kyle. You kept that truth from me."

"For God's sake, that was need-to-know. The Army deemed it classified. Besides, I told you, I didn't need to sully Jack's name. Didn't need to make it harder on you. Call it a lie if you want, but it was a white lie, to protect you. This is insane, Kath. Some crazy, suicidal vet with PTSD leaves a note . . ."

"I didn't say it was him. I don't know who left it."

I saw small beads of sweat glisten on my father's brow. "Whoever wrote those words is lying, Kath. I don't even know why anyone would want to make that accusation. Not unless they're deranged."

He stared at me, full on. "As for the other photo, the one of me with that money, we all took photos like that, every officer I knew. It was in the provost's office when that one was taken. You can check it out. There was maybe a hundred million dollars delivered on pallets that day. We all got our photos taken with it for a laugh. Guys were playing football with wads of it. It was just a joke. Look at me, I'm smiling. You think I'd let a photo like that be taken of me if I was stealing that money? You think I'm nuts?"

He said it with such conviction, a powerful flicker igniting in his blue eyes, as if he was trying to will me to believe him.

I wanted to. But somehow I just couldn't manage it.

Was the sweat on his brow a giveaway? Maybe. I glanced at the wall clock: 5:56. I had four minutes before Jack would call.

"I need to be alone right now. Can you leave me alone? Go somewhere, anywhere, but leave me here in peace."

"Kath . . ."

My father seemed reluctant to go. I could see it in his face. He wanted to stay, to talk it out more. So did I. It was all so inconclusive, so many questions unanswered. But I needed to hear from Jack first—and to see my children. That was more important right now.

"Please. I need to be on my own. That's what I feel. Please respect that."

He sighed, gave a reluctant nod. "We'll talk again. About your mom. About Red Rock. I'll answer any questions you want to ask. But you really do need to believe me, Kath. I never harmed her, let alone killed her. I loved your mom. You know that."

The truth was, I did know it. "Why did she write that word *Red* on the letter?"

He faltered, sighed, seemed to find it difficult to speak. "Kath, sometimes . . . sometimes the past just needs to stay in the past."

"What's that supposed to mean?"

"There's something more to all this than you know. But like I say, let's talk again."

I really wanted to talk now. Desperately. Let him tell me everything he wanted to. But I had maybe two minutes before Jack's call.

My father moved to the door. Bleached, washed-out blue eyes regarded me with . . . what? Sadness? Resignation of some kind? Or maybe he was just looking for my pity. I couldn't tell. And right then, I'm not sure I cared.

"Jack's mental state wasn't exactly first-rate back then. We both know that. But that's not really important. What matters is that we find them, Kath. Find Jack, Sean, and Amy. That's all that matters." He reached out a hand to touch my face.

I turned my face away.

"Kath . . ."

A voice inside my head was saying, *Until this is cleared up, I don't want you to touch me. Or come near me.*

I saw the shock and sadness in his eyes. And I saw a single tear trickle down his cheek. My father, the six-foot-three colonel, was crying. He just stood there, tears rolling down his face, but not moving, like a rock.

I wanted to cry, too. But I couldn't.

I knew he loved me. I just didn't know if I still loved him. It wasn't the same. It just wasn't. Something had changed between us.

And I wondered if it would ever be right again.

"I've got some things I need to think about. Please, I want you to go right now." I emphasized "now."

He looked at me with wet eyes and nodded. "If you hear anything, anything at all, about Jack and the children, I want you to call me at once. You hear?"

I nodded back.

He turned, and I heard him move down the hall and open the front door. A few moments after it closed, I heard his car start up and drive away.

On the kitchen table, my cell phone started to ring.

If Jack had told me the truth earlier, he was about to spill everything.

63

I raced into the kitchen and grabbed my cell phone.

"Hey, how are you doing?"

It was Courtney.

I didn't feel like talking, my mind totally focused on Jack's call.

"Courtney . . . I'm waiting for a call to come through. Can I call you back?"

"Sure. I just wanted you to know we're working away on some leads. I wanted to make sure you were all right, honey. Are you?"

Right then, I felt like collapsing. *No, I'm not all right. I feel like I'm ready to crack up.* But all I said was, "I'm doing OK."

Silence from the other end, as if Courtney had something else to say but was holding back.

My mind started to race. "Is . . . is everything OK? Is there something you need to tell me? Did . . . did you find more evidence?"

"No, not yet."

"What is it, Courtney?"

"I don't know. Or maybe I guess I just don't know how to say this."

"Say what?"

"I was thinking a little while ago . . . it came across my mind today . . ."

"What?"

"That stuff that happened between your old man and me, that night when you found us. I thought it had gone away."

"What . . . what about it?"

"It's been bugging me. I'd like to talk some more about that. Clear the air."

"What do you mean?"

"Not on the phone, honey. I'd rather talk in person."

What did she mean? I wanted to know, but I was also conscious of the ticking clock and Jack about to call. Right that second, another call rang in. An unlisted number. It continued to ring.

"Courtney, I have to take this. We'll talk again."

"Sure. Just take care, OK? Love you, honey." Courtney clicked off.

I hit the answer button for the other call, but when I put my ear to the phone, I heard only silence at the other end.

I waited.

I didn't want to say Jack's name and alert Tanner in case he was the one calling. The silence went on forever. Finally, I said, "Hello."

"Take a look out your window."

"What?"

"You heard me. Look. What do you see?"

I peered out. Beyond the trees, I could make out the shapes and colors of police cars and TV vans. My heart plummeted, my gut instinct telling me what was coming. "Jack, just listen . . ."

"You broke your promise."

I recognized the voice, my heart thudding. "No, Jack . . . I didn't."

"Yes, you did. You broke it. The cops are crawling all over your neighborhood."

"How did you know?"

"How do you think? You think I'm an idiot? I did a drive-by."

The thought that Jack had driven by my home creeped me out, but the tone of his voice was even more troubling. "Jack, it's not my fault. The police are here because there was an intruder."

"Liar."

"Jack, just listen, please. There was an intruder—"

"I told you, no cops, no matter what. No authorities. You were to keep them at arm's length."

I tried to speak, but he cut right across me, and I heard the vehemence in his voice and the words I dreaded.

"You broke your promise. The deal's off."

"Jack, please—"

"We're not going to meet."

"Then if not today, when?"

"Never. Good-bye, Kath."

And the line clicked.

64

WASHINGTON, D.C.

The man drove his gleaming white GM Denali toward Alexandria.

Out past the Pentagon toward the Leesburg Pike, until he reached Bailey's Crossroads. He knew that some people called this area Little Arabia. So many residents settled here from Iraq and from Iran, Lebanon, Saudi Arabia, and Egypt. He had no idea why—birds of a feather, maybe.

Rug shops flashed by, chain stores and ethnic restaurants, the streets thronged with Middle Eastern faces, some of the women dressed in chadors, their men dark and swarthy, many sporting black leather jackets and holding on to the hands of their handsome, brown-eyed children.

He passed a restaurant called the Mount of Olives, then swung off the highway until he came to a run-down, deserted parking lot. The gates were open, the chain unlocked, deliberately.

The lot was shabby, peppered with potholes, but the view was stupendous. In the distance, you could see the White House and the Washington Monument and the reflecting pool, all lit up. The lights of aircraft as they descended into nearby Ronald Reagan Airport, perilously close to the White House. The city was a sea of lights. You could almost smell the power from up here, and it was intoxicating.

He parked and switched off the engine, saw the man standing on the parapet overlooking the city. He faced toward the Pentagon, and he didn't look around as the man got out of the Denali and went to join him.

Tarik was lighting a slim cigar and staring at the Pentagon. The lighter flared, illuminating his face. He wore a padded Windbreaker to keep out the evening's chill, but he still managed to look like an undertaker, with his pencil mustache.

"You're late," Tarik said.

"A meeting with the president. I couldn't just walk out."

"You know, it always surprises me," Tarik remarked.

"What does?"

Tarik gestured with his cigar toward the Pentagon. "Why they chose the Pentagon that day in 2001 when they crashed the aircraft. The White House would have been a more prominent target, a priority for both aircraft that day, I mean including the one that went down in Pennsylvania when the passengers rushed the cockpit. The White House was a far more strategic target. And you can see it so easily. I mean, the effect on the American psyche and the world would have been profound, don't you think?"

"I'll try to remember to mention that to the president the next time I'm talking to him." The man pulled up his coat collar, shook his head.

"Don't be stupid, Tarik. The White House has protective missile systems. An incoming aircraft would be shot down."

"You really think they could have reacted that fast? With air traffic so close at Reagan, and suddenly two passenger jets come speeding like rockets toward their target? I don't think so." Tarik grunted, and it sounded like a tiny laugh.

The other man rubbed his gloved hands together. "You almost make that sound like a wish. You still hate us, don't you?"

Tarik said nothing.

The man pulled back a leather glove, stared at his watch, as if bored already. "Can we get this over with?"

"I met her. My men have been following her."

"And?"

"She's asking questions, and soon she'll start to piece things together. I'm certain of it." Tarik sucked in a slow breath. "So we need to put this to bed, once and for all, or we are all finished."

"Yeah, I get the picture."

Tarik took another drag on his cigar and stared toward the White House. "Do you really?"

"I don't like your tone, Tarik. And I don't like you. Never did. You're a conniving sleazeball, a snake in the grass. But we're joined at the hip on this one. Remember, you're here because of my recommendation, buddy. That's how you and your friends got out of that rat hole of a country of yours. You aided the U.S. military. You're a rat."

Fury lit Tarik's face. "I was fool enough to take your dollars and work for your people. But I always despised you. Your nation, your culture, your arrogance."

"Yeah? You prefer living in a mud hovel in some desert armpit of a town? I don't see you buying a return ticket back to the miserable lives you and your friends led there."

"I can never go back, never. There is nothing to go back to. You people made sure of that. Brought ruin and bloodshed to my country, all because of your lust for oil. You brought destruction, anarchy, madness."

"And it was way better under Saddam?"

"No, but at least we had a people, a country. Now we no longer have a country but a war zone, factions killing each other, a society that's spiraling down the toilet." Tarik gave a mock salute. "Thank you, America."

The other man stared at him. "What do you want, Tarik? Cheese with that whine? A violin accompaniment?"

"Don't mock me, American."

The man grabbed Tarik's arm hard. "Listen, you dirtball. You were a tribal chief's son who was as crooked as a dog's hind leg, like your father before you. You'd have ransomed your own grandmother if there was a profit in it. Save me the crocodile tears. You gladly took our money to switch sides."

Tarik shook off the man's grip. "And one of your countrymen took it back."

"The fog of war, Tarik. Strange things happen."

"I told you, don't mock me. The only reason we're talking is because you fear me. Fear what I can do to you if the truth comes out. Don't forget that."

"You're right. But it works both ways. We need each other. So the truth won't ever come out, will it?"

"Not if I get what rightfully belongs to my people."

"You're no longer one of your people, Tarik." The man grinned. "You mean what belongs to *you*."

"It was stolen from me. From my people."

"Whatever. If he's still got it, you'll have it all back." The man turned to go, heading back to the Denali.

Tarik gripped his arm. "He'd better have it."

The man gave Tarik a hard stare and pulled his arm away. "Don't ever threaten me. Not ever."

"No threat. I don't have to make threats. But you and I know the consequences if the truth comes out. For you and people like you." Tarik ground his teeth. "That's why we need to bring this whole sorry business to an end. Kill them all, including the woman. Cover our tracks."

"We don't even know where they are."

"But we will. I have a plan." Tarik grinned, his pencil mustache stretching across his face as he tapped his nose in a scheming gesture. "I have inside help."

"Meaning?"

"Someone close to the woman."

65

About a mile from DJ's home, I pulled in by the lake and let the engine idle.

It was almost 6:50 p.m. I didn't see the SUV or the van tailing me again. Maybe that was a good thing. Or a bad thing. I couldn't tell which.

Were they still out there, watching me? Not knowing was driving me a little crazy.

I was feeling apprehensive, my heart pitter-patting.

Not just about revisiting DJ. I needed to ask him about Quentin Lusk. If the intruder knew Jack, he probably knew DJ.

I was still shaking after confronting my father. Nothing seemed to have been resolved. It was all still up in the air. And Jack's refusal to see me hurt even more. Muddled as I felt, all I could think of was working on one of the only clues I had.

And I knew I had to tell Tanner and Courtney about Jack making contact and the truth about the break-in. I couldn't hide all that any longer. Just as soon as I spoke with DJ, I'd call them both.

Snow streaked the ridges of distant mountains, looking as if some giant truck had dumped tons of castor sugar over them. A ragged wind blew gray clouds across the lake.

I felt on edge, my nerves jangling, and I was barely able to muster the concentration I needed to go into Magpies Bakery on North Central Street and buy a big red-velvet cake. I had it wrapped up in a white box with a crimson bow. DJ and Vera had made it very clear that I was not to call again. But DJ was holding out, knew more than he was saying, and there was no one else I could talk to.

I figured if things got off on the wrong foot when I knocked on the door of the double-wide, I could always say I just came by to apologize and the cake was a peace offering. I'd try to wing it from there.

So long as DJ or Vera didn't blast me before I got my spiel out. Having the gun in the glove compartment definitely gave me a feeling of comfort if the muck hit the fan. But what if things turned nasty inside the home and then they found my weapon?

I began to think I was crazy to risk coming here again. DJ was suffering from PTSD and maybe volatile. And I figured Vera's belt didn't go through all the loops, either. And just like she'd hinted, they could shoot me and claim I was invading their home.

I opened the glove compartment and palmed the Taurus .38 revolver. I stared at it in my hands and couldn't decide if I was more likely to get killed by going in armed. I wasn't exactly happy about my final decision, but caution won out over fear. I slid the gun into my coat pocket.

A thin drizzle of icing snaked across the side of the white cake box. I ran the tip of my finger across it and put the icing to my lips.

It tasted delicious, and I enjoyed the sugar hit.

I just hoped Vera's sweet tooth could make a difference.

But I couldn't help thinking—actually, I was pretty certain—that I was somehow deluding myself.

Crows rose noisily into the air like wet black rags as I turned down the track to DJ's home. Sixty yards from the double-wide, I coasted the car to a halt, killed the engine, and stepped out. Fear hit me like a hard slap. I felt my legs wobble. The crows cawed as they landed on some trees. I hefted the boxed cake from the backseat and kicked shut the rear door with my foot. The noise of it slamming echoed like a gunshot.

I prayed the kids were there. That DJ and Vera wouldn't be crazy enough to let them witness a shooting. But I felt sure of nothing. It was aces wild—parents who waved guns around in front of their kids were probably capable of anything.

The mustard-colored hound wasn't around, but the metal stake in the ground was still there, the blue nylon rope discarded in the mud. A mash of paw prints blotted the lawn. I guessed the dog was inside the double-wide on a cold day. The blue Dodge van was still parked around the side.

The same junk was scattered on the lawn—the mildewed pink Barbie tricycle, the rusted old cars, the stuffed toys. As I walked up the dirt path to the front door, I felt my heart stutter. I thought I could hear the TV or shouting inside, aggressive voices muted. All the curtains were still closed.

As I carried the cake, my chest felt tight with anxiety. Another group of crows announced their arrival and landed high up on a big old white oak tree across the track. I'd hated crows ever since I was a kid. They always spoke to me of evil and death.

My eyes shifted to the rusted metal sign nailed to a two-by-four stake in the middle of the lawn. I remembered it: "Is There Life after Death? Trespass Here and Find Out."

I just hoped it wasn't a bad omen. That DJ wasn't about to validate his warning. I was about to find out.

I reached the door, sucked in a sharp breath, held it, made an O of my lips, and let it out.

I rapped hard.

66

No one came to the door.

I knocked again and tried to peer through the curtains. It was dark inside except for the TV's faint blue flickering. A ball game was playing, the volume too loud. I was sure I heard some kind of shuffling or scraping noise inside. Had anyone heard me? After a couple of minutes, I rapped harder.

"DJ? Vera? Are you home?"

No reply.

"It's Kath Kelly. I just called by to say sorry, to apologize. I wanted to leave a gift for you."

I sounded such a licker. But when someone threatens me with a 500 Smith & Wesson, I'll lick until my tongue hurts. I heard the shuffling, scraping noise again, as if someone was moving about. My pulse started to race.

"DJ? Vera?"

Still no reply.

I rapped again. Nothing. I gave it another half a minute, and then I laid the cake box down on the ground by the front door and cautiously walked around the side of the property, passing the van. Inside was the same mess. The floor was still covered in McDonald's and Burger King cartons, crushed chicken nuggets mashed into the carpet. The only thing that looked different was that the grubby, food-stained child seat was tilted over to one side.

I walked a little farther toward the rear of the home, my legs still trembling. I saw a door with some wood steps leading down. It looked open just a crack. I moved toward the door but hesitated. What if DJ was waiting to spring a trap? No, thanks.

I turned back and paused for a while when I reached the front door again. I knocked hard for at least five seconds. Even a deaf man could have heard my woodpecker rap as it echoed all over the lot.

No neighbors appeared at their windows, at least none that I could spot. The other lots looked deserted, no cars, either. I heard the noise again—it sounded more like scraping this time. It faded away and stopped. I stood there for a few minutes, curious, my ears cocked, listening, but the noise didn't resume.

I felt on edge, like one of Pavlov's dogs expecting an electric shock at any moment. I decided I couldn't linger here all day. My nerves were frayed enough. I touched the front-door handle with my thumb and forefinger, levered it open about two inches. The metal creaked like a scream.

I stood there, fear in my throat, waiting for some kind of violent reaction, for DJ or Vera to appear, screaming obscenities at me, telling me to get off their property, waving the big Smith & Wesson.

Nada.

All I saw was a TV's dreamy blue reflections, and I heard the TV, louder.

It was still too dim inside to see clearly.

"DJ? Vera? It's Kath. I came to apologize."

That's when it happened.

I felt something brush against the door I was holding, as the scraping noise started up again. I jumped back in fear, let go of the handle, and the front door creaked wide open. I got the awful stench of dog and excrement.

The mustard-colored hound appeared, pawing weakly at the door crack, trying to get out. The dog made a weird choking noise. And then I saw why. A bloody gash stained its neck with congealed blood. The animal was trying to bark but couldn't—its throat had been either shot or cut.

The pitiful creature stared up at me with pained eyes before it stumbled out onto the lawn and toward the cover of some bushes, leaving a trail of bloody paw marks in its wake. The swinging door yawned open and slapped against its stop, making me jump.

Daylight spilled into one end of the room through the open doorway.

I stared at the scene inside the home, then staggered back, clasping a hand to my mouth, my scream caught in my throat. I felt as if I was going to gag. Vera was slumped on the floor on the other side of the room, a huge gunshot wound to her skull. Her hair was strewn about her head, a lake of blood around her upper body, staining the blue carpet. I noticed bruise marks on her arms and neck, a cut under her chin, as if maybe she had been assaulted or tortured.

I felt something cold seep into me. For at least a minute, I stood there, shaking violently, my hand still on my mouth, until I mustered enough courage to step forward again. Two slow, scared steps, filled with dread.

Then I saw DJ, sprawled across the La-Z-Boy, staring up at the ceiling, one eye wide open, the other eye missing, blown away along with half of his skull, his brain matter spattering the couch and walls with bloody slime. The big Smith & Wesson revolver dangled from his hand, hanging over the side of the couch. His prosthetic leg with the silver buckles lay toppled on the floor.

There was no sign of Elvis and his sister. A split-second thought registered: murder-suicide. For some reason, that was what the scene suggested. Were the children dead, too? I stared at DJ's and Vera's bodies, put a hand to my mouth again to stifle my cry, but if it came, I never heard it.

A creak sounded as something moved behind me, freaking me out, my heart exploding like a bomb in my chest. I glimpsed a dark shadow flit across the TV-blued walls, and I spun around.

A figure stepped out from behind the door, his arm raised.

It took a split second for me to see that he had a baseball bat in his hand. And I recognized the youthful face.

It was Sean's face, my son, grown older. A mother never forgets her child, and there was no mistaking Sean's features, even after all these years—his full lips, his pale-blue eyes and high cheekbones—not even in that fraction of a second.

He struck me so hard with the bat it felt as if I'd hit a wall of steel.

Pain blossomed like a grenade going off inside my skull.

And then everything turned a dreamy black.

67

SERENITY RIDGE, SEVIERVILLE, TENNESSEE

Agnes Hatmaker checked her lipstick in her makeup mirror, twitched her lips, and blinked to examine her seriously heavy blue eyeliner. She ran a hairbrush through her thick mullet mane.

Looking good.

Well, maybe not that good.

Her hair needed doing, but her Kenny liked it that way. Kenny was a mountain man, five foot nothing, a few months off seventy, and twenty years her senior. He also dressed like a hillbilly living fifty years in the past, all plaid shirts and denim bibs—buffet pants, he called them—but you didn't want to displease a twitchy little terrier of a man who was once a tunnel rat in Vietnam.

Kenny still carried a gun everywhere. More than one gun, actually. One in his bib pocket, one in a leg holster, and another inside the pants. "One is none, and two is one," Kenny liked to say.

"Meaning?"

"Always have a spare, just in case. If you only got one and it fails, you've got none." Then he'd get that glint in his eye. "Always wanted to catch or kill me a thief."

He insisted that Agnes get her conceal-carry permit, too. Now she carried a firearm everywhere and prided herself on knowing how to use it. Kenny taught her how to shoot, plinking tin cans in the back field of his farm. "You never know"—that was always Kenny's cryptic warning. Never know what? Heck, she didn't care. For an old guy, Kenny was still a firecracker, in and out of bed.

She saw the nerdy guy come in through Serenity Ridge's entrance hall, dressed casually, carrying a metal briefcase that looked more like a toolbox.

"Can I help you, sir?"

The man noted her name badge. "Yes, ma'am. We did an online check of your video security system. Seems to be a problem with a flaky power supply."

"Flaky?"

The nerd smiled knowingly. "By that I mean the supply is intermittent, ma'am."

"Why didn't you say that in the first place?" Agnes glanced up at the TV monitor high on the wall, showing a changing feed of video streams. She could see most areas of Serenity Ridge, every patient and every room if she wanted. "Looks OK to me."

"Your system could fail at any minute. Got to check it out."

"Well, hot dog. Nobody told me."

"It's no big deal, ma'am. But we can't have the system going down, or the customer won't be happy." The man grinned and winked. "You want to keep this place tighter than a high-security prison, right?"

"It ain't Alcatraz, sonny. It's a secure-care home. You got company ID?"

"Yes, ma'am." Tetchy. He showed her his plastic-encased ID.

Agnes scrutinized the ID as if it might be a counterfeit fifty. When she seemed satisfied at last, she gave him a look. "Never seen you here before."

"Only started four months ago."

"Like it?"

"Love it." He grinned. "Just show me where the equipment is, and I'll be gone faster than a set of stainless rims at a rap concert."

The equipment was in a back room. Agnes led him in, then left him to it.

Babek checked through the system, observing the rooms and the layout, then took a copy of the hard-drive data. He tapped on the keyboard for a few minutes, scrolling through the program code, and smiled to himself. Four years at MIT on a scholarship, and stuff like this was easy cheese.

He slid a flash drive into the socket, tapped a few more keys, and waited while his program downloaded.

Babek heard talking and stepped back, peered out toward the reception area. Agnes had just wandered off down one of the hallways with a nurse, some files in her hand. He saw his chance, popped on a plastic surgical glove he took from a pack in his case, plucked the folded handwritten note from one of the case's pockets, and slid it into the "IN" tray on Agnes's desk.

He moved back into the equipment room and removed the glove, and when the download was done, he slid out the flash drive and popped it into his pocket. To make sure he'd left no prints, he cleaned everything with a couple of alcohol wipes. He was clicking his tool kit shut when Agnes came in.

"How's it going?"

"Done and dusted, ma'am."

"Gee, that was fast."

"Yeah, Speedy Gonzales, that's me." Babek regarded the woman's grotesque, out-of-date mullet hairstyle. You still saw them out in the hillbilly sticks, as if some folks believed the style—if you could call it a style—would make a comeback. It made Babek want to puke. "You get your hair done recently, ma'am?"

Agnes took it as a compliment, fluffing the back of her mullet with her hand. "Why, no, I didn't."

You really ought to think about it, Babek pondered, but then he smiled. "Looks great."

68

They say that sometimes when you're about to die, you see a tunnel of bright light.

Me, I saw a tunnel of light when I woke.

A long strip of blazing, neon-intense white light. And I heard a growling and grunting noise, like a wild animal—a dog, a bear, a hog, maybe. I couldn't tell which.

No one ever said anything about the noise or the pain at the end of the tunnel, but that's what I heard and felt as I blinked and came around. I shook my head. Big mistake. Excruciating pain stung my eyeballs like an electric shock.

It made we want to throw up. I blinked and retched.

But all I felt on my tongue was bitter-tasting bile. I hadn't eaten all day, barely sipped some coffee, my stomach empty.

I tried to wipe my lips, and that was when I realized I was tied down, lying in a bunk, my wrists and feet anchored to it with coils of blue nylon rope. I swallowed, blinked again. The pain started to ebb back into my skull. I closed my eyes to relieve it and opened them again slowly.

I still felt ill.

My white-lit tunnel turned out to be a white neon strip light overhead. I could feel its electric warmth. A weird thought sprouted in my mind, one of those almost out-of-body thoughts we sometimes have but that make no sense: Where was the red-velvet cake? Who cared.

The floor was swaying beneath me.

More rocking than swaying, and then I realized I wasn't just in a bunk—I was in a boat's cabin. It was speeding forward, waves slapping beneath the hull. The growling noise was no wild animal. I recognized a coarse engine throb somewhere to the rear.

I looked around. A bare, cramped desk and a chair, a washbasin, and another bunk. A ladder of steps led up to a worn, varnished cabin door that rattled with the engine throb. I creased my forehead, trying to clear the fog. The nauseating pain erupted again and then slowly ebbed away. The blow really hurt—it was hurting now but not as badly as the awareness that my own son had done this to me.

Sean could have killed me. But could I really be certain it was Sean in that split second when I saw the kid's face? I remembered the boy's features; he'd be about the same age as Sean. And those boyish looks were still the same, just more grown, more adult.

I tried to replay the face in my mind's eye. Pale-blue eyes. Blond hair but darker blond than I remembered. Sallow skin. A dimpled chin. A button nose, bigger now but still the same nose, I was sure of it.

Or was my mind playing tricks? Had I merely imagined Sean's face? A face I loved so much, had soothed on so many restless nights, when a toothache hurt or a fever raged. A face I loved to calm and kiss, no matter if he was loving or throwing a tantrum or too grumpy and restless to sleep.

I had my doubts, but a mother knows. A mother could probably still recognize a child she hadn't seen in thirty years—or a lifetime.

More than just an umbilical cord ties you to a child. The child is your essence, the bond that ties you to things of the spirit as much as the flesh. The very thought that Sean might want to cause me harm made me want to cry. I felt the sobs growing within me again. A kind of panic. Why did he hurt me?

I felt certain that I didn't imagine Sean hitting me. But clouded by pain, my mind began to succumb to doubt. My own son would never harm me. But my own husband had harmed me, so wasn't it possible that Sean might?

Anger and confusion gave me the strength to try to struggle to my feet. I managed to touch the bunk edge with my fingers and tried awkwardly to push myself up, but the nylon ropes bit into my skin, and I collapsed back. My strength drained from me, every muscle weak.

I heard a creaking noise. Then a bolt scraping. Above me, the cabin door slapped open. A gust of wind blew in a dagger of ice-cold air. I shivered, caught a glimpse of glittering night sky, a spray of stars in a dark universe.

A single brown boot slapped onto the first rung of the ladder, then another, and a pair of feet came thundering down the steps.

I recognized the man's figure even before I saw his face. Heavier and older, wearing a black woolen beanie, his hair graying at the sides, but there was no mistaking those sepia-brown eyes and that handsome face.

Jack.

69

I struggled to get up again.

"Stay right where you are."

Jack's speech sounded slurred. I could smell alcohol. He wore dark brown cords, scuffed black working boots, a heavy blue twill shirt. The black beanie was pulled tight down on his head, and graying tufts of hair stuck out.

He took a leather sheath from his right pocket and slid out a ferocious-looking Bowie hunting knife. I had a terrifying thought. Did Jack get drunk to muster the courage to kill me?

He laid the knife on the table, then yanked off the hat and ran a hand over his hair—longer, greasy, and bedraggled. He pulled up the chair and sat.

"We need to talk, Kath."

I saw a flash of anger in his eyes. It seemed so absurd. Jack, angry at me? My rage felt searing-hot. "Your first words to me in eight years, and you sound like we need to mend a lovers' tiff. That's got to be the understatement of the year."

"Still lippy, aren't you?" He tried to smile, seemed to struggle with it, the corners of his mouth barely lifting.

I was seething. I was looking at a man I knew but didn't know. He was older, his face weathered, his brow more deeply wrinkled. His gorgeous brown eyes and high cheekbones would always mark him out as handsome, but he looked like a man who was weary, tired of life or maybe of running.

His right hand reached out to examine the back of my skull. "How's your head?"

I recoiled. "What does it matter to you?"

"Some things never change."

"Meaning?"

"Your feisty temper."

My eyes flicked to the knife. "Are you going to kill me?"

"Now, why would I kill you?"

"I guess you did that already by taking my children from me, right?"

Jack's mouth tightened, and he gave a tired, drunken sigh.

My bound hands balled into fists. "I have no idea what you intend for me. All I know is that there are a whole bunch of questions you need to answer. The biggest one of all is why you would disappear with our children. Why, Jack? You survived the crash and vanished—you and Sean and Amy. I know that. I just don't understand why. Why you threw our lives away. Was it the stuff in the aluminum briefcase?"

His eyes widened. "How do you know about that?"

"The cops have it. They found it at the site."

"It wasn't there." His mouth creased in a grim expression. "I wouldn't have left it."

"No, I guess you wouldn't. All that money. That priceless artifact. What happened? Couldn't find it?"

His teeth clenched. "I went back to the site many times, looking for it. Never could find it. Where was it?"

"Lodged in some rocky undergrowth, about a hundred feet from the aircraft. Did you steal it, Jack? What else did you steal? Apart from my life, that is?"

He mulled that one over, but after a few seconds of clenching and unclenching his jaw, he still didn't answer.

"They found a notebook of yours in the case. And the word *Red* written on a page. The same word they found on that discarded envelope when my mom died. Or is that just a coincidence?"

No response.

"Are you going to answer my questions or just look at me like you don't care?"

"I'll plead the Fifth."

"Why?"

He shrugged and finally said, "I mean you no harm. Really, I don't, Kath."

"I hope you're telling me the truth. Because I figure I've had my fill of lies from you."

He eased the knife back into the sheath. "I had it in mind to cut you free, but I have a feeling it's better to keep you tied up for now. It'll be safer, less hassle."

"Safer for whom?"

"Everyone concerned."

"Meaning my family?"

He slipped the sheathed knife into his pocket and glanced at his watch. "It won't be for much longer. Then I'll explain."

As angry as I felt, my heart was soaring. My children were alive. I longed to see them again, to hold them. I felt my eyes become wet. Maybe because I experienced such an overwhelming surge of joy now that I knew I would see them again, my fury seemed to slacken.

"You know what I can't figure out? You sound angry, Jack. It should be me who's angry. Why are you?"

He still didn't reply, just gave me a long, unsettling stare, then turned to go.

I didn't want him to go. I desperately wanted hard answers. "I don't know what's worse. Seeing your face again or knowing Sean could have killed me. He sure has a cute way of saying hello to his mother after eight years."

"He didn't mean to. He didn't know who you were."

"My own son? It was Sean I saw, wasn't it?"

"Yeah, it was Sean. He overreacted. It's complicated. At first, we thought you were the police. I was in a bedroom down the hall when we heard you knock."

I stared at him in despair. "How could you kill them? How could you be so brutal, so despicable? And why? Were you afraid they'd talk? What about DJ's children? Are they dead, too?"

Jack just looked at me. He had that kind of faraway look in his eyes that I remembered so well, the one that told me something disturbing was going on inside his head.

"But then, I guess you did that in Iraq, didn't you, Jack? Killed innocent men, women, and children. Like that massacre at Red Rock. Did
killing just come easily to you?"

He put a foot on the stairway. His body language, his tense manner,
and his tight mouth told me he wasn't going to answer. He plucked out
a cell phone. I recognized it as mine. He tossed it onto the floor and
brought his foot down hard, grinding it beneath his boot, then stomp-
ing on it. When he took his foot away, the phone was a crushed mess.

"In case you think anyone's going to trace you, I took the battery
out as soon as I found the phone in your pocket. Your signal's dead."

"I realize something now, Jack Hayes. I didn't know you. In fact, I
really never knew you at all, did I?"

No response.

"What about Sean?"

"You'll see him after we dock."

"Why not now?"

He didn't answer the question but said, "DJ's kids weren't there.
They must have been somewhere else."

"What were you doing there?"

"I went to check on DJ. Do a drive-by."

"Why?"

"He thought some people were following him. Dangerous people.
And they were. My gut tells me they may be following you, too."

"Explain."

Jack didn't seem to want to answer that one. "Just take my word.
The likelihood is you were followed."

"Did you kill DJ and Vera?"

"Of course not."

"Someone did."

"Yeah, and made it look like it could be a murder-suicide. You saw
Vera? I figure she'd been tortured. It could have been made to look like
DJ harmed her. But I knew DJ. He wouldn't have harmed a hair on
Vera's head."

"Then who killed them?"

"Long story. But my guess is, our family is next."

I looked at him in shock.

Jack met my stare. "That's my theory, unless we stop them. And that's my plan. What I've been working on."

"Why would our family be next?"

The boat buffeted and wobbled, almost throwing Jack off his feet. He grabbed at the bunk. "Later. I'm needed up on deck. There's some chop on the water, and I don't want to leave Sean on his own." He turned, moved up the steps, and pushed open the cabin door.

"No, wait . . ."

But he didn't.

I saw sparkling stars in the cold universe again, and then the cabin door slammed, and the bolt scraped shut.

70

SERENITY RIDGE, SEVIERVILLE, TENNESSEE

Agnes was putting down the phone when she saw the private ambulance pull up by the front door and two paramedics climb out, wearing white scrubs. One of them was pushing an empty wheelchair.

They both looked kinda A-rab. She wasn't into A-rabs. As far as she was concerned, the U.S. government needed to backpedal the heck out of the A-rabs' rear ends and focus on stuff closer to home.

The men came in through the front door.

The first guy smiled, sounded real pleasant. "We've come for a patient, Kyle Kelly, ma'am. He has a medical appointment in Knoxville."

"Since when?"

"The appointment was made some weeks ago."

"Yeah? Well, it ain't on my chart. And if it ain't on my chart, Kyle's going nowhere. No way, José."

"Please check again, ma'am. The hospital doesn't usually make mistakes."

Agnes studied her chart again and puckered her face. "Ain't on the chart, like I said."

"Is there anywhere else it might be?"

Agnes searched through the "IN" tray. Sometimes documents and notes got stuck in there. She flicked through a bunch of papers, was about to give up when she found the folded handwritten note. She opened it up.

"Patient Kyle Kelly. Head scan at Park West, 12 noon. Please facilitate."

It was unsigned. A clerical error, Agnes guessed.

She looked at the paramedics and picked up the desk phone. "Looks like you fellas are in business. Let me have Nurse Deesha take you to get Kyle."

The two men were following Deesha down a hallway toward the patients' rooms, taking their time, one of them pushing the wheelchair.

Agnes watched them from the reception desk and scratched her chin. Then she stared again at the note. It was pretty irregular. There was an official form-filling process when a patient had to leave the facility and be seen at a hospital. She studied the handwriting, but it was unfamiliar to her.

She thought of phoning the manager, but she was on vacation in Florida. The paramedics disappeared around a corner with Deesha, and Agnes's eyes darted to the TV security monitor.

It was blank.

That nerdy guy was supposed to fix the darn thing. Now it wasn't working. Idiot.

She picked up the note, studied it again, and slapped the page against her palm, thinking. Something bothered her. She just couldn't figure out what. A gut feeling, maybe, certainly nothing more than that. It was the two men. What were the chances of having two A-rab paramedics. One, maybe, but two? Maybe the other guy was a beaner?

But she didn't think so. He had the same Middle Eastern look as his buddy.

She picked up the phone and called Park West Hospital. Reception put her through to a lady in X-ray appointments. "This is Agnes here at Serenity Ridge. It seems we've got a patient scheduled for a noon scan appointment. Can you check on that for me, please? The patient's name is Kyle Kelly. Thanks."

It took a few minutes, and the woman came back. "We have no appointment for a Kyle Kelly."

Agnes felt her heartbeat quicken. "You absolutely sure?"

"Real sure, ma'am. They're doing routine maintenance on a scanner right now. A lot of the appointments were rescheduled until later today and tomorrow."

Agnes looked out at the ambulance. There were a whole bunch of ambulance providers in Knoxville. But when she looked closely, she felt a shiver in her gut. For some reason, the ambulance had no identifier number on the side. Suspicion welled up inside her.

"Thanks," she told the woman at Park West, and replaced the receiver.

It sure seemed kind of strange. The two A-rabs, the security camera guy, and now the cameras not working. Her gut told her something strange was going on, but she had no idea what, except that she was having none of it. She picked up the receiver again, about to call 911, when she heard Deesha's voice getting closer, a clatter of footsteps as she returned with the men.

Agnes picked up her purse. Her Sig .40-caliber was in there, cocked and locked, as Kenny always insisted. She placed her purse on the desk in front of her. If Kenny was here, he'd love it. He loved all that gunfight at the O.K. Corral stuff. But all Agnes felt was fear and a throbbing headache.

The men returned with Deesha, one of them wheeling Kyle in the chair. The men were all smiles. Agnes felt her heartbeat race. She smiled back at the men and said, "Deesha, can I see you a second?"

"Sure. Take care, you guys."

"You, too," one of the men called out.

Deesha waved to the paramedics, and they headed toward the exit.

When Deesha came over, Agnes shielded her, pulling her behind her, and said, "Get down!"

"What?"

"Get down now!"

Agnes brought up her Sig from behind the reception counter.

"Hold it right there. You fellas ain't taking Kyle nowhere."

The two paramedics froze. A look of absolute fear ignited in Kyle's face when he saw the firearm. It was in that split second that Agnes knew she was way out of her depth. With the practiced ease of professionals, both men tore silenced automatic pistols from under their scrubs.

Agnes fired, the Sig bucking in her hands, the round hitting one of the men a glancing blow in the shoulder. He clasped a hand to his wound.

The second man aimed and fired.

The first shot hit Agnes in the chest, sending her flying back against the wall. The man fired a second time, hitting her in the head, and she was dead before she slid to the ground.

Deesha never even got out a scream. A shot hit her in the throat, and she fell back against the wall. The man who shot her moved behind the desk and shot Deesha twice more in the chest. He shot Agnes again in the head, her body twitching as the round slammed into her skull.

As the man turned away, he picked up the permission note from the desk and stuffed it into his pocket. Then he hurried toward the exit, his wounded companion already pushing the wheelchair toward the door.

The young man in the wheelchair looked wild-eyed with fear. A scream erupted from his mouth, but the second it did, the shooter slammed a fist hard into his face, knocking him unconscious.

Then both men hurried Kyle toward the ambulance as fast as they could.

71

Time passed. I had no idea how long. I guessed maybe an hour. It could have been less.

All I could do was wait, tied down on the bunk. I still felt a boiling rage, my mind a welter of confusion and mixed-up feelings. Knowing that I was about to see my children again made my heartbeat rocket, but where was Jack taking me? And why? Just to see my children, or was there more to it?

His caginess told me there had to be more. Did he have another family? And what would happen afterward? Would he simply set me free? I couldn't imagine that happening, unless he meant to vanish with my children all over again. And did he really kill DJ and Vera? My thoughts disturbed me.

As I said, it's easy to lie to ourselves. We try to preserve our illusions and not kill our sacred cows. I knew I lied to myself about my relationship with Jack, too. It wasn't all flowers.

It started out good, but in the last three years of marriage, our relationship was mediocre at best.

Arguments, anger, unhappiness, bitterness, and jealousy all reared their ugly heads. A good relationship that goes sour is always harder to deal with than one that's always been turbulent. You want the good times back. You want to be happy again and to help the boat right itself. Even if that's nigh impossible. For the last three years of our marriage, Jack was drinking and gambling, and his bouts of paranoia were getting worse.

It didn't help that a neighborhood friend of ours, Bob Seege, started trying to get a little too friendly with me whenever Jack was away. Bob was kind, pleasant, divorced, lonely, and desperate for female company. He came by our home a few times during Jack's absences but got a bit too forward after offering to help me with some jobs around the house.

There were small signs but ones that set off the panic button inside my head. Touching my arms after we shook hands or laying a palm on my back or shoulder and letting that touch linger a little too long. Making a lot of eye contact. Twice he asked me to lunch. Once I was pretty sure he followed me to the mall and "bumped into" me, then suggested we have coffee.

I made the big mistake of not dealing with the guy myself but telling Jack when he got home. He stormed over to Bob's home, and right there on his front porch confronted him and beat him badly, breaking his nose, blood everywhere. It was awful, I was mortified, and it ended with an assault charge against Jack. The charge was eventually dropped by Bob, but the whole thing didn't help our marriage.

Or our children. We often argued in front of them, even though we'd promised never to let them witness our disagreements—a pledge few couples can keep. On those nights when Jack was working abroad with Brown Bear, I'd often let the kids sleep with me, Amy in the middle, Sean on the other side. And I'd read them a story—usually Dr. Seuss or whatever they were into.

One night, the consequences of our marital disagreements hit me like a brick. The kids and I were lying in bed after turning out the light. Sean was still awake as he looked out through the wooden slats toward the clear starry night.

"Look, Mom, that's a wishing star."

"What do you wish for, baby?"

And without even a beat, my son almost whimpered. "I wish my mommy and daddy didn't argue so much."

That sad cry cut me to the bone. I was just glad we were in darkness, because right then I felt a tear roll down my face.

When Jack returned from a security contract meeting in Afghanistan with Brown Bear, I told him what Sean had said. I saw tearful emotion well up in his eyes. He called Sean and sat with him on his lap. He tenderly stroked Sean's hair and tried to explain to him that all moms and dads argued sometimes.

"But you and Mom argue a lot." Sean's voice was almost a fearful whisper.

"That may be true. But from now on, that's not going to happen, son."

He called in Amy and said the same to her, and he hugged them both, and me, and then drove us all to the Tic Toc ice cream parlor in Loudon for cones. We sat on a sun-drenched bench, and in no time, Jack had us all giggling and happy.

In the middle of it all, he looked at me, a long, deep look with those brown eyes of his, before he squeezed my hand and said, "I love you, Kath. I love you all."

He held out his two big palms, and we all put our hands in his, and he squeezed them tightly. He kissed us all. "OK, who wants more ice cream?"

That was when I knew why I married him.

But it didn't stop the arguments.

We fought the same old battles, month in, month out.

But from then on, they were fought in privacy, out of hearing of our kids.

Now, lying there alone on the bunk, I remembered those times when I knew Jack had once loved me and I knew he loved our children. I still felt I wanted to kill him. But it all was so complex and disturbing. Difficult, too. Because I was feeling an unexpected emotion. I was being torn between love and hate.

That was how it felt.

Jack was back from the grave.

And deep down, I knew that I still loved the man I had married and mourned.

72

Panera's was quiet, the lunchtime crowd departed.

"Hello, Colonel."

Frank Kelly looked up from his caramel latte and his copy of the *News Sentinel*, and his bushy eyebrows twitched with fury. Fazil Tarik stood there, wearing a dark suit and a black shirt and tie.

Kelly put down his coffee, glanced around him to see if anyone was watching, and a burst of anger lit his face.

"That idiot of yours called me on my way to Michigan. I thought I said no contact, *ever*. It's dangerous."

"We both know that this is different. That the rules are broken." Tarik looked at the newspaper in Kelly's hand. "You're reading about the plane wreck, I see. A strange twist, but then life is full of them, don't you think?"

"What I'm thinking is why are you risking your life by sticking your nose in my face? I warned you never to do that again. And I meant *never*."

But Tarik stepped in closer and whispered, "If I fall, you fall, and everyone falls. Are you prepared for the consequences if that happens?"

Kelly said nothing, but his jaw twitched and trembled.

Tarik said, "We need to fix this mess before someone puts the pieces of the puzzle together. If they do, then we're all living out the rest of our lives in a federal prison."

He paused for effect and smiled. "And we're all getting a little old to be playing the role of some three-hundred-pound convict's girlfriend, don't you agree?"

Kelly's reply was a silent stare.

Tarik sighed. "I suggest you meet me outside. Five minutes. I'll be waiting. A black Escalade, tinted windows."

"You son of a—"

Tarik smiled again. "Good to hear you haven't lost your soldier's tongue, old friend."

"We've never been friends, Tarik."

"Five minutes," Tarik repeated, and his smile faded before he turned and walked out.

Kelly stepped out into the parking lot.

A black Escalade was parked at the curb, its engine running. The rear passenger door was pushed open. He slid in. Tarik was already in the other seat.

"Do you carry a gun, Colonel? A former military man like you always carries a gun, surely?"

"What kind of a dumb question is that?" Kelly barked, and yanked the Colt .45 from inside his jacket in an instant. A soft click sounded, the hammer being cocked, and he pointed the weapon at Tarik's face. "I just hope you haven't got anything stupid in mind, because if you do, Tarik, they're going to be scraping that miserable face of yours, or what's left of it, off the windshield."

Tarik gave a humorless grin. "That's what I like about you, Colonel. You're prepared, always. I like that. It gives me confidence that you'll do what must be done."

"I'm going to take a bet you've been smoking that hookah pipe with that funny tobacco again, you dirtbag. Because us meeting like this isn't making a whole lot of sense."

"An urgent necessity. Your hands are shaking, Colonel."

"That's what rage does to you, Tarik. You know, anytime I see your ugly face, I ask myself why I didn't kill you when I had the chance. Back in Fallujah, before you sold out your own people and switched sides."

Tarik's eyes lit with a wry smile. "Those were the days, Colonel. Maybe you miss them?"

"Yeah, sure. But you were really in your element back then, weren't you, Tarik? Death and brutality were your hallmark. Roadside bombs, executions. No wonder you're an undertaker. Still get pleasure from seeing bodies?"

Tarik fell silent.

Kelly leaned in close. "Like that little flower girl who used to hang out outside our base. Remember her?"

"I remember."

"Your people used to make her take ammo to your men and threaten to kill her family if she didn't. Until one day she said no, and you personally put a bullet in her. Nice work, Tarik. Make you feel like a man, killing children? Meanwhile, I'm still waiting for an explanation."

"It will come in good time. Hold on to your gun, but point it elsewhere, please. I have a feeling you're going to need it when it comes time to deal with that former son-in-law of yours. You look shocked, Colonel."

"You know where he is?"

"No, but I will, and very soon."

And with that, Tarik touched the driver on the shoulder, and the Escalade drew away from the curb.

73

The engine slowed to a dull throb.

Finally, it growled into reverse, and I felt a hard thud as the boat hit something and shuddered. A dock, probably. The engine died. A thick silence, and then footsteps pattered across the deck.

Words drifted down, Jack's voice first. "Tie her up, then go on ahead. I'll meet you there."

"Yes, sir." A male voice. Was it Sean's? It sounded young. My heart skipped.

Feet shuffled, and the cabin door sprang open again, boots clattering down. The knife was in the sheath on Jack's trouser belt this time.

My Taurus revolver was tucked inside his waistband. The alcohol smell was stronger.

Jack managed to untie the ropes without resorting to using the knife. I expected him to drag me to my feet, but instead he collapsed in the chair opposite. As he leaned back, the wood creaked under his weight. His gritty eyes swam a little, his focus sluggish. He was definitely drunk.

"I'm waiting. Who killed DJ and Vera, and why would they want to kill us?"

"We'll get to it. There are some things I need to explain first. Important things."

I swung my legs out, rubbing my wrists where the nylon had scored red marks in my flesh. "I've waited a long time for explanations, Jack. Get to the point."

He gave a cheesed-off smile. "Yeah, just like the long time you waited to marry Chad."

"What's that supposed to mean?"

"Means what it means. Twelve months a widow, and you're seeing Chad. Twelve months later, you're a wife again. Quick enough turnaround, babe. Can't say you're a time waster."

"How dare you? How *dare* you?"

"Goes both ways, Kath."

I had no idea what he was talking about, but I lost it. My rage exploded, and I lunged at him, knowing that this was maybe the only chance I'd get. He jumped from the chair to defend himself, and I landed on top of him.

We rolled onto the floor. Jack jerked his head to the right to avoid the fist I threw. I missed him, but he cracked his head hard on the bunk. He cried out and recoiled in pain, closing his eyes tight, his body doubling up, hands covering the back of his head. I saw the gun sticking out of his waistband.

I grabbed it.

I backed off rapidly as Jack came to his senses the second he felt me grab the firearm. I squeezed the trigger. The gun exploded. But it didn't stop him, and he lunged back at me from where he lay on the floor. I scrabbled back toward the stairs, clambered to my feet. Aiming the gun at him, I cocked the hammer. "Move an inch more, and I swear I'll put a bullet in you, Jack Hayes."

His face contorted in pain as he massaged his skull. "You're just making things worse."

"Really? My husband faking his own death and my children's. A hole ripped out of my heart, big enough to drive a train through. Our lives destroyed. How much worse could things get, Jack?"

"You and Chad seemed to be doing OK back in the day."

"How dare you?" I said again.

He stared at me, still in pain, grinding his teeth.

"Take the knife from the sheath—slowly, and I mean slowly. Toss it onto the lower bunk."

He touched the knife hilt with his right hand but didn't remove it. He seemed to be playing a game of chicken. That was when I saw the blood spots on his shirt, below and to the left of his stomach. So did Jack. He blinked up at me in disbelief.

"You . . . you shot me."

He pulled up his shirt. I couldn't see where the bullet entered his abdomen, but I saw an exit would at his extreme left side. The bullet had gone clean through. I felt relieved that there wasn't much blood. Not yet, anyway. Jack grimaced, clasped a hand to his wound, and went to lunge at me again.

I aimed the revolver at him. "I've given you fair warning. Mess with me again, and I'll kill you."

He didn't move, just kept staring back.

"I'm not kidding, Jack." I flexed my grip on the gun, my finger on the trigger. He must have registered the fury in my eyes, because he slowly removed the knife.

"Throw it onto the lower bunk."

He tossed the knife.

I looked at the rope. I guessed it must have been about twenty feet long. "Pick up the rope. Tie one end around your right wrist."

He did as I told him. We were so close in the cramped cabin it scared me. I also felt a rush of concern. Jack was wounded—not badly, I hoped. He held all the answers to what happened. If he died, I might never figure it all out. I needed him to stay alive. But I also needed to make sure he didn't overpower me.

"Now, tie a loop knot and slip it over your left wrist."

"Your old man taught you well."

"Slip another loop around your neck, and turn around. Keep your back to me."

He obeyed and turned, until I was facing his thick neck and broad shoulders. Jack was still strong and muscular, a foot taller than me. The disadvantage made me edgy, my lips dry and my finger moist on the trigger.

"Now, put the rope between your legs, and hand it back to me."

It was a technique my father once showed me. It was useful if you didn't have handcuffs or tie wraps, just a rope, and you needed to move a prisoner. One end of the rope tied the prisoner's hands, and another loop went around the neck in a choke hold. The other rope end was fed back between the legs. That way, a guard could exercise some control over the prisoner.

In my father's words, when you had them by the testicles, their minds and hearts might not necessarily follow, but once you held on to the rope between their groin, there was no way captives could run away without risk of painful injury to their manhood. I searched Jack's pockets. I found a tactical flashlight, the kind you'd mount on a rifle or pistol, and a small half-finished bottle of bourbon.

"Where are Sean and Amy?"

Jack didn't answer, and his eyes slid away from me and stared down at the floor, his lip curled in a kind of defiance. I lost it again. I brought the gun down hard on his neck and stepped back. He recoiled with pain. Such savagery wasn't me, but right that second, it felt justified. And hitting Jack felt good. My animosity returned in a surge. I hated him. Hated him for what he'd done to me. Hated him with an over-powering intensity.

"If I have to ask again, I swear I'm going to put a bullet in your kneecap."

"There's a house, a few minutes' walk from here."

"Are Sean and Amy there? Was it Sean who went ahead?"

He nodded.

"Are they there? I want a proper answer."

"Yes."

"You son of a . . . You kept them from me. You kept them from me all these years and—"

Jack turned and lunged, his neck craning forward, as if he was trying to head-butt me.

He was quick, but I sidestepped. His head slammed against the wall. I brought up the gun barrel, touching it against his right temple. "Either you've drunk too much or you forgot you're dealing with a colonel's daughter."

"I could never forget that."

"Next time, the gun goes off, and you're a dead man, Jack Hayes. Now, move."

He stared at me, as if to ask where.

"Up on deck. I want answers. And I want to see my children."

74

I moved my back toward the rungs, pointing the gun at Jack and gripping the end of the rope.

"You're going to back your way up the stairs, right behind me. Turn around. Don't move until I say so."

I grabbed the flashlight Jack had dropped and put it in the back pocket of my jeans. I climbed, keeping my back to the rungs. At the top of the stairs, I kept my eyes on Jack, still with his back to me, and used my hand holding the rope to cautiously raise the hatch. Cold, fresh air seeped in. My breath fogged. I glanced up. Stars glittered.

I stepped onto the boat deck, still training the gun on Jack's back. He couldn't go anywhere except up through the hatch. I glimpsed water to my left, a wide river channel or lake, I couldn't tell which. To my right was a narrow dock. Dark landscape beyond, speckles of distant house lights.

Wherever it was, the place was kind of remote. I could just make out a pathway leading to a dim painted structure a few hundred yards away. A house, I guessed. I fumbled to take the flashlight from my back pocket but didn't switch it on.

I looked down at Jack, still in the cabin, his back to me. "Turn around and step up the stairs, like I told you."

He clattered up the steps awkwardly, almost lost his balance a few times, and had to use his elbows to right himself. In the cold, the smell of alcohol from his fogged breath was even more overpowering. I shone the light on his face, and his bloodshot eyes blinked.

"Move onto the deck, and do it slowly."

I moved farther back, still covering him with the gun. He climbed up onto the deck. I fed out a long enough length of the rope and shone the flashlight. The dock was built of weathered cedar. I stepped off the boat, and my feet hit the dock. I jerked on the rope.

"Come on. Step out."

I covered Jack with the gun as he stumbled onto the dock's cedar boards, the rope still binding him. He looked up, caught in the flashlight beam. I thought his handsome, unshaven face looked weatherbeaten and tired, as if he'd fought a lot of battles, and more than a few were inside him.

Right then, for some reason, I felt only pity for him. I didn't want to; I wanted to stay angry. Jack had harmed me so much, robbed me of eight years of my children's lives.

Once I'd loved him so much. Once I couldn't wait for him to hold me, kiss me, to feel and smell the maleness of his strong body next to mine. I could still remember how much it broke my heart whenever he left me to go overseas. My ache was always so intense I'd cry for days. A powerful anguish jolted me now like the stab of a blade.

That was in the past, I tried to tell myself, even if the rush of emotion swept back in on me like a wave, reminding me that I felt torn between love and hate. I forced myself to crush my pity, to jolt my focus back toward the house, a few hundred yards away.

My hope soared. Sean and Amy were there.

How would they react when they saw me? Would they even remember me after eight long years? Would they want to? What if Jack had a new partner who shared their lives?

What had their lives been like in this house in the middle of nowhere? What had happened to them all these missing years? I so longed to hold them, to touch them. But would they feel the same when they saw me? Amy, thirteen by now but still a child. How I longed to hold her, kiss her. Clench her body tightly to mine and never release her.

And Sean, my angel. I felt tears hot on my cheeks. Meeting Sean and Amy again—all of us together—wasn't going to be easy. There would be so much explaining to do, so many questions, so many raw feelings, at least on my part. Yet I needed to control myself. I couldn't drop my guard for a second and let Jack overpower me again. I felt overpowered already, though, by the tidal wave of emotions that ripped though me.

I wiped my eyes. "Get moving toward the house."

Jack gave me that pitiful look again. It made me almost want to hit him. *How dare you make me even consider being sorry for you?*

I kept the light shining on his face.

His tired, sad eyes locked on mine. "No matter what, I want you to know something, Kath."

I didn't answer. Didn't want to. Just waited for whatever it was he wanted to say.

"Sean and Amy. They never stopped loving you. I want you to know that."

That statement hit me with a trainload of pain. I felt my eyes become wet again. Jack looked right at me. And then it came, the most disturbing thing I'd ever heard. Something I never expected, something that sounded so absurd it sent a violent shock wave through my body, as if I'd just been in a car wreck.

"The same goes for me. I never stopped loving you, Kath."

75

We walked about fifty yards toward the house. "Keep it moving," I ordered.

I was dumbstruck, Jack's words still ringing like a fire alarm inside my head. *I never stopped loving you, Kath.*

"Don't try to play me."

"I mean it, Kath."

Jack was crazy. But crazy like a fox. Trying to distract me, overpower me again, and mess with my mind. But I wouldn't let him. I had a truckload of questions, not just about who killed DJ and Vera but about why we could be in danger.

Still, I kept my focus. What was important right now was safely reaching the house.

Then what? I had no idea. All I could envision was some kind of emotional reunion with Sean and Amy. Or was I deluding myself? My children might not remember me. Sean, maybe, but Amy was so young when I last saw her.

Beautiful Amy, how could you forget me? How could you forget the nights I held you or when you were ill and I sat up with you until dawn and your fever had passed. How did you weather all our lost years? Who held you and comforted you? Jack had been a good father when he was at home, but I could not imagine him comforting Amy the way a mother could.

Jack stumbled ahead of me, like a tethered slave. I halted, took a cautious step back, and shone the flashlight. Crimson spotted the ground behind him. He was losing more blood. He seemed to wobble, his steps less sure.

I didn't seem to care now. The closer we got to the house, all that mattered was my children. I flicked the flashlight on and off, partly to save the batteries and partly not to give myself away, in case Sean was somehow observing our approach. "Has Sean got a gun?"

"No."

"You'd better be telling me the truth. The last thing I want is to get in a gunfight with Sean."

Jack swayed on his feet, as if he was in a stupor. "Sean hasn't got a gun."

I still didn't trust Jack. I figured rural Tennessee properties like this—or wherever we were in the South—always had mini-arsenals and enough ammo to last until Doomsday. I couldn't believe Jack would get by on just a single gun.

"Don't try to play me. What other firearms have you got?"

"There's a rifle and a shotgun and a pistol locked in a bedroom closet upstairs. But Sean wouldn't use them."

"He hit me hard enough to knock me out. What makes you so sure?"

"Living out here, he's learned how to use them, but Sean doesn't like firearms. They scare him, ever since he was a kid. You ought to remember that."

I remembered—at least, Sean *used* to be that way. It was something my father couldn't fathom. The first Kelly offspring in living memory who avoided gun shows and guns and anything to do with the military. Once, my dad took Sean to the range and let him shoot his Colt .45. The powerful recoil from the single shot Sean took scared the life out of him so much that he threw down the gun and ran away.

Sean was a dreamer, a stargazer, not a soldier. Gentle Sean, who hit his momma on the head with a baseball bat. How kids change. Funny, the things you think of when you get smacked in the skull by your own son.

We reached the house. The place had a farm-manure smell. I heard a cow's distant moo in the darkness. Pale light showed between cracks in the dark curtains. I flicked on the flashlight. Next to the house, I saw a barn with peeling paint.

An old, rusted blue Chrysler van was parked on the rutted track out front. Next to it was a dented, muddied old four-wheel ATV. The property looked barren and smelled of rural poverty and decay. Was this how my children had lived for the last eight years? In a crumbling cabin? What about all that money that disappeared? In the back of my mind had been a niggling feeling that Jack may have had something to do with the disappearance of the twenty-five million and maybe cut a share of it. But this didn't make sense.

I played the flashlight over the van for a second or two, then over the house. Two fishing rods were propped against the gable wall, next to a vegetable patch, bare in winter. A withered old tree with bleached-white branches hung over it.

I focused on two things. Where were my children, and why did Jack do what he did? A million other questions buzzed around my mind, but Jack seemed dazed, in a world of his own. I aimed the flashlight and saw blood dripping down his left side, his eyes glazed.

"Are you OK?"

My pity was all gone by now. All I wanted was to make sure we made it to the door without incident.

"There's a first-aid kit in the house. I'm . . . I'm going to need it." His voice sounded weak.

It scared me. What if he got worse? "Who's inside?"

"Sean."

We were thirty yards from the front porch. The house was painted a dull apple green and almost completely camouflaged by trees protecting the back and sides. The air was syrupy with a strong scent—of flowers or fruit trees, I couldn't tell which. The track from the dock snaked away into darkness, as if toward an exit road. I saw the white twinkling lights of another house, maybe a few hundred yards away, but no sulfur-yellow road lights. The place seemed remote.

"Not Amy? Where is she?"

He didn't answer. I grazed his skull with the gun barrel. "Answer me, Jack."

"Amy's not in the house."

"Why not?" I saw a light flicker behind the curtain. Someone was moving about inside. My gut told me that getting inside without trouble could be tricky. "I asked why not?"

"She's not staying here tonight."

"Where's she staying?"

"With friends. I had to leave her with friends. I . . . I'm losing some blood, Kath."

I felt my heart sink again but not for Jack. I wanted to see Amy; my ache was unreal. But we'd solve the problem of Amy's absence later. At least my son was here.

"Where will Sean be in the house?"

"He usually hangs out in the living room or the kitchen. Or in his room upstairs."

"Describe the layout once we step inside the front door." I wanted to be prepared.

"A short hallway, with stairs on the left leading to the second floor. And be careful. There's a wheelchair stashed just inside the door on the left. Don't fall over it. I don't want that gun going off again."

"A wheelchair? What for?"

"I needed it for Amy, years back, after the plane crash."

My heart did a somersault. "Is . . . is she still hurt? Does she still need it?"

"No." Jack clammed up.

"Go on. Describe the rest."

"Living room is on the right, open plan, a kitchen at the back."

"Upstairs?"

"Three . . . three bedrooms. Amy's, Sean's, and mine. A bathroom and a closet on the landing.

We reached the front porch. "Move up the steps, nice and slow."

Jack climbed them. I didn't follow him just yet, careful not to get too close. He was on the porch now, facing the door. He looked back at me. "What do you want me to do?"

I kept the gun aimed at him. "You tell me. I figure you don't want our children put in harm's way, so we need to keep this sensible. Is it safe for you to open the door, or is Sean going to go ape again?"

"I don't believe he will."

"If he does, you'll get it first. OK, do it. Keep your hands out straight so I can see them."

Jack turned sideways as I let out the rope, and he turned the handle. The door opened a crack, a wash of light spilling out. "Sean? It's Dad. I'm coming in with the lady."

The lady? He hadn't even told Sean I was his mother. My anger returned with a surge. Seconds passed with no reaction from inside the house. I moved cautiously up the steps behind Jack. Was Sean already prepared to rush me? I had to be so careful. I didn't want this getting out of control.

"Inside. Push in the door. Go easy."

Jack moved into a short hallway. Stairs on the left, open-plan living room on the right.

I saw the wheelchair on the left. It was folded flat, propped against a wall. The place smelled of maleness and wasn't up to much, the sparse old furniture looking like it came from a thrift store. Forlorn, like some hard-up hillbilly cabin. An old TV and video player were the only modern belongings, a few stacks of DVDs beneath. No woman's touch. No flowers or photographs. And then I spotted Sean, in a corner, sunk in an old easy chair with greasy armrests.

He was twisting the crown of his hair the way he used to, twisting it into a tornado. He rose, wide-eyed, his hair falling across his forehead the way it always did, his beautiful face so much older and more mature.

My eyes felt wet. I had such a powerful need to rush across the room and crush him in my arms. I was besieged by a feeling of intense love mixed with apprehension.

"Sean, this lady . . . this lady is . . ." Sweat glistened on Jack's forehead, and he was clutching his stomach.

I felt my insides cave in, and I finished the sentence for him, said the words I desperately longed to say. "I'm your mom, Sean."

Sean reacted with a confused stare. He looked from his father to me and back again. I wanted to speak, to let him know that I loved him, but for some reason, my lips would not move.

Maybe it was because the boy staring back at me looked bewildered, in a trance, and so different from the last time I had seen him eight years ago. The silence seemed to drag on forever, until Jack said, "He doesn't understand."

"What do you mean?"

Jack stumbled and held on to the couch for support, blood seeping between his fingers. His face was white as he took his hand away and looked at the blood. He spoke without looking up. "It . . . it's complicated."

It was the last thing he said.

His eyes rolled in their sockets, his legs collapsed, and his body slumped onto the floor with a sickening thud.

Sean screamed.

76

I knelt beside Jack and felt his pulse. It was weak. He was still losing blood. I felt myself starting to panic. My feelings raged again, but this time I felt for Jack. I really felt for him. Not only that, but if he died, any answers I was looking for might die with him.

"We need a first-aid kit."

I stood and grabbed Sean's arm.

"Sean, a first-aid kit. Your father's hurt. We need to help him. The kit, where is it? Bandages, medicines—I need them now. Where are they?"

He stared at me open-mouthed, perplexed, as if rooted to the spot by panic, fear sparking again in his face.

I frantically scanned the room for Jack's first-aid kit. Being a military man, he always insisted that we were prepared for any emergency.

I hurried to a corner closet and flung open the doors. Inside smelled of men and was filled with coats, old boots, and sneakers.

"Sean, for God's sake, where's the kit? Help me here."

His expression looked vacant, so childlike. Like the little boy I'd lost eight years ago but more slow-witted. He was hardly speaking, just a few grunts and nods here and there. What was wrong with him? There had to be something seriously wrong.

I turned back and saw blood still seeping from Jack's wound. I pushed past the couch, into the kitchen. Sean came in behind me as I ransacked drawers and cupboards. Sean started to do the same. He looked more alert now, traumatized with worry. He yanked open a cupboard, hauled out a camouflage rucksack, and unzipped it. The rucksack flopped apart, revealing several MOLLE bags inside.

I realized the rucksack was a bug-out bag, the kind disaster preppers used if they needed to get out of town in a hurry, complete with emergency food packs and survival tools like a big sheathed knife and a machete. I saw that one of the MOLLE bags had a Red Cross logo patch stuck on it with Velcro.

Before Sean could hand it to me, I grabbed it and unzipped it. It contained an assortment of pill bottles, bandages, and a tourniquet, a surgical implement kit containing scissors, clamps, a scalpel, surgical wipes, and a flashlight. I found what I was looking for, sealed in a black and white pack: an Israeli army traumatic wound kit.

I grabbed the entire first-aid bag and rushed back into the living room. Tearing open the wound kit with my teeth and fingers, I knelt beside Jack. He was losing blood fast. Sean followed me, whimpering as he knelt beside me. His eyes looked moist and worried.

Inside the wound kit was a fine granular powder. I'd read about this stuff growing up on an Army base. The powder contained a clotting agent that stopped blood flow. I lifted Jack's shirt, exposing the crimson wound, and poured on the powder. In less than thirty seconds, the bleeding stopped.

It was only a temporary fix, but at least Jack wasn't still bleeding to death. I still had the bleeding exit wound to deal with. I felt his pulse. Still weak. Sweat sparkled on his brow.

I took out bandages, alcohol wipes, and hydrogen peroxide from the first-aid kit. I used the peroxide to sterilize around the wound, then grabbed the flashlight. "Hold this, Sean."

He just stared at me, wide-eyed.

"Sean, will you do as I say?"

Confusion strained his face. Some instinct made me put a hand gently to his cheek. This time, he didn't draw away. I felt the soft skin I loved to wash and kiss when he was small, but the texture was manly now. Questions rolled around inside his head, lots of them, I could tell. Who was I? What was I doing here? I could see that he was trying to figure it all out, but none of it made sense to him.

Did I see a spark of recognition when he looked into my face, or was I fooling myself? *I'm your mother!* I wanted to scream.

Reluctantly, I let my hand fall away. Tears filled my eyes. It all seemed so absurd. Eight years had gone by in the blink of an eye. Eight years, and I had lost my baby, replaced by some child-adult whom I didn't know but whom I knew I still loved.

I wiped my eyes, forced myself to focus. There was work to be done. "Hold this, Sean, *please.*"

I thrust the flashlight at him. He held it, and I showed him that I wanted him to keep his arm high and the pool of light focused on Jack's bloody waist and the bleeding exit wound.

I slipped on a pair of latex surgical gloves from the kit. "Keep the flashlight right there, like that. Try not to let it move, OK?"

I looked into Sean's eyes. He stared back, then nodded.

I wiped perspiration from my brow and went to work.

My military father was the kind of man who believed a woman needed to know how to look after herself.

He didn't believe in dependent girlies, only independent ones, and he planned accordingly. I spent three years in the Girl Scouts. On the weekends, when I wanted to play with dolls or with my friends, he'd make me do tae kwon do or take me on hunting or survival trips. And he made me learn first aid. He used to say his first-aid knowledge saved a life or two on the battlefield. He wanted me to know stuff like that and planned accordingly.

It forced me to learn how take care of myself in an emergency, things like how to shoot game and gut and field-dress a rabbit or deer. I always hated that part, the blood and gore and gristle, but later I was secretly grateful for the knowledge.

For trauma wounds, I knew the basics. Stem the blood, try to remove any penetrating objects like blades, bullets, shrapnel, or glass, then treat the wound with antiseptic and sew up if need be. Administer some pain relief if it's on hand.

I found a morphine shot in the kit but decided to leave it for now, until I knew Jack's pain level or if he was coming around again. My latex-gloved fingers carefully probed inside the grisly exit-wound tissue. It sure looked and felt as if the bullet had gone right through. I could only hope it hadn't pierced an organ. A doctor would have to decide, if I found one and if Jack survived.

Minutes later, I'd dressed the wound as best I could. I checked his pulse—it was good—and his breathing was steady. The floor was littered with blood-soaked cotton pads, and I felt exhausted. Sean kept staring down at his father. It was killing me. I desperately wanted to ask Sean so many questions about the past and what had happened to him since I last saw him—but now was not the time.

When he saw me finish sewing up Jack, he looked relieved. "Will my daddy be OK?"

It was the first time he'd actually spoken to me. His voice sounded deeper—somewhere between youth and manhood—but I could still hear the sweet and gentle childish tone that I remembered.

"Will he?" Sean repeated, eyes wet again.

I didn't really know if Jack would make it—he looked too pale and weak—but his vital signs were strong. Looking into Sean's anxious face, I knew I couldn't worry him. "Yes, Sean. Your dad will be fine. Now, help me clean up."

We put the bloodied cotton pads into a couple of plastic Walmart shopping bags and threw them in the trash. Then Sean brought a container of Listerine wipes from the kitchen and we cleaned the mess off the floor. Jack was still unconscious. The blood loss, fatigue, and alcohol wouldn't have helped. But his breathing was even. I felt his pulse again. A steady sixty-five.

I searched his pockets but found no cell phone. Had he left it on the boat or dropped it on the walk up here in the dark? I got an old blanket off the back of the couch and draped it over Jack, up to his neck. The emergency was over for now, but I needed to find a doctor.

The more I looked around the room, the more unsettled I became. This wasn't much of a home. It wasn't what I expected of a man who might have disappeared with a serious amount of money and valuables.

It was almost a hovel. It lacked a woman's touch—I saw just one vase with a few nearly withered wildflowers that I figured Amy might have put there. How had my children lived here, and in what circumstances? More important, *why* had they lived like this? And another question burned inside me, the most important one of all: Where was my beloved Amy?

"Sean . . ."

His eyes met mine. They looked so big and innocent, so childlike, that I felt overwhelmed with a powerful urge to wrap my arms around him and hug the life out of him. It was an agony not to. But I was afraid I'd scare him or he'd shun me. I knew he still couldn't figure out who I was. I fought the urge.

Instead, my fingers found his face. I touched his cheek, as if he would find comfort in it. He balked a little but stood still, avoiding my eyes. It broke my heart. I hated this. My son didn't seem like my son but a total stranger.

But right then, my focus was on finding Amy and figuring out why Jack had vanished with the children in the first place.

I looked back at Jack and felt his pulse once more. It was still good, his breathing not distressed. I knew he was stable. I needed a couple of minutes to compose myself, to figure out what I was going to do next, how I was going to find medical help.

In those couple of minutes, I could multitask, and see what I could find out. I turned to Sean.

"I want you to show me around the house."

77

Sean led me up a creaking stairwell.

The landing was as shabby as the rest of the house. A threadbare ruby carpet led off to several rooms. At the far end of the hallway, a door was open to reveal a tired avocado-colored bathroom suite that looked decades out of date.

The door on my left was half open. I pushed it and stepped into a barely furnished room that overlooked the front of the farm. More secondhand furniture. A double bed with a wooden headboard, its pine varnish worn in places. A nightstand, dresser, and mirror, all in grainy, weathered oak. A box of shotgun cartridges lay on top of the nightstand, along with a handful of coins. Jack's bedroom, no doubt.

Next to the bedside lamp were two photos in cheap plastic frames. One I recognized, a photo of Amy and Sean taken in Myrtle Beach. It was a snapshot Jack always carried in his wallet whenever he traveled. I touched the frame's cold glass, my fingertips gliding over the image, and felt a cold shiver go through me.

I picked up the second snapshot. This one was more recent, just of Jack and Sean, sitting on a muddy ATV four-wheeler. Sean was in front, and Jack had his arms around him, both of them smiling. I wondered who had taken the photograph. Amy? A lady friend?

No photos of us all together as a family, but I didn't expect that. Why would Jack want to remind Amy and Sean of me?

A man's fleece and some cotton work shirts were thrown over the back of a chair. I stepped over and peered into one of the two closets. Old clothes, some pairs of muddied work boots at the bottom. I heard a scraping noise back out on the landing, and when I turned back, I saw Sean rocking himself like an impatient child, shifting forward and backward on the balls of his feet.

When he caught my eye, he opened a door to his right and stood there, gently nodding his head, waiting for me to join him. I walked out across the landing toward a tiny bedroom.

A look of pride sparked in Sean's face as I stepped into what was obviously his room, one decorated with childish simplicity. A desk, a wall shelf with a few stacks of books, and an old CD-playing radio. A duvet cover with a football player in red and vivid-colored posters stuck on the wall behind: Transformers, Spider-Man, and Iron Man.

Some of the books looked kind of immature for Sean's age, more like those an eight- to ten-year-old might read: *Goosebumps*, *Harry Potter*, and *The Wonderful Wizard of Oz*. And then something caught my eye—an ID on Sean's dresser. I picked it up. The Tennessee state ID showed Sean, all right, his face solemn, his expression blank, but the name said "Sean Pender."

The date of birth was off by a month and a year, suggesting that he was older. The ID looked real, but it had to be fake. And it was the permanent kind that did not expire. I knew that IDs that did not expire were only issued to people with a permanent mental or physical disability. My father was issued one once he'd lost his foot.

I noticed a bunch of schoolbooks on the desk, which had two chairs in front of it. Had Jack homeschooled Sean and Amy? It made sense if he wanted to keep their true identity secret. I put the ID back down.

Sean was staring over at me, doing the nervous rocking thing with his feet. I had a gut-wrenching feeling that I didn't want to put words to yet. I don't know why I spoke, but it just came out: "I like your room, Sean."

His reaction was slow at first, but then he beamed, a beautiful, innocent smile. It was so like the Sean I remembered, the child I loved and lost.

A hurricane of emotions ripped through me—love, pain, despair, even anger for all the years when I could not witness the face that smiled back at me. His slowness, even the way he said "Daddy" instead of "Dad," the permanent ID card—they all affirmed my suspicion that Sean was in some way brain-damaged. Now that I'd admitted it, my emotions intensified and sent me into a spiral of despair. I had a desperate need to grasp my son, to crush him to my chest, cling to him, and never let him go.

It felt weird. All these years, my children were not lost but were near me and not a million miles away. Tears welled in my eyes. I felt overcome, but I knew I needed to keep this conversation unemotional in case I scared Sean. I fought the heartache and wiped my eyes with my sleeve.

"I want you to show me Amy's room."

78

Sean led me down the hall.

My heart jackhammered as he opened a door. It swung inward, and I anxiously followed him inside. I saw something I really didn't anticipate.

The room was painted in a girly pastel-pink and was so out of character with the rest of the house, like a splash of vivid color on gray walls. A single bed, frilly with lace pillows, was pushed against one wall. A typical girl's room. And then I saw something familiar, and my body jolted.

On the bed were some dolls and soft toys. Three of them I recognized as Amy's favorites, which she had brought with her on that fateful flight. A pink teddy bear named Sandy with a pink satin bow. A flesh-colored Peppa Pig character. And a blue, white, and gold cotton blanket, the kind you can buy with a silk-screen print. This one had an image of Snow White.

I remembered buying it for Amy for her third birthday. I picked it up, felt the soft cotton brush against my face, and inhaled deeply.

Every child has a scent—I was sure I recognized Amy's. A voice inside my head reasoned that if she kept these precious belongings, surely she would have remembered me. How had she coped with recalling our life together? And with the aching loss of a mother's love?

Had she been injured like Sean? I prayed desperately that she hadn't. Sean must have noticed my wet eyes, because he looked worried. "Will . . . will Daddy be all right?"

I gently let my hand fall, still clutching the blanket. "Sean, do you know now who I am? Please, try and think."

His forehead creased as if with the physical effort of thinking.

I spotted another photo by Amy's bed, a copy of the same one in Sean's and Jack's rooms, of the three of them together in Myrtle Beach. I wanted to search the house for more photographs. But I figured the last thing someone did when trying to hide their identity was to take too many pictures of themselves. Knowing Jack, he'd been careful about that.

Besides, Jack told me something once. Every digital snapshot taken generated an electronic code, which the federal authorities had access to. It was how they sometimes caught criminals and terrorists, by tracing the code back to the photographer.

Sean saw me notice the photo, and he picked it up. He stroked the picture with his fingers and smiled. "Amy . . . You like Amy, too?"

"Yes, I like Amy, too. I love her. I love you, too, Sean."

He smiled again, but my words really didn't seem to be sinking in.

"Did your dad ever talk to you about your mom?"

His face looked perplexed now, as if the effort of thinking was painful, the question too much to process.

"Don't you know me, Sean?"

He shook his head. I remembered when Amy was barely four months old, and I had to leave her with Jack when I traveled to Georgia for a weekend. The moment I returned and picked her up from her cot, Amy's eyes sparked, and she recognized me and nuzzled into me. I recalled the magic of that moment. I experienced similar moments with Sean when he saw me after an absence. But now there was no recognition, no magic.

Nothing.

My heart was breaking. I turned back to Amy's belongings. The question screamed inside me.

"Where's Amy, Sean? Where's your sister? Please tell me."

He didn't speak.

"Sean, please, I need to know. Where's Amy?"

His hand pointed to the window. I stepped over to the curtain and peered into the darkness. Sean joined me and pointed again, directing me toward the distant lights of a house.

"Amy's over there?"

"Yes."

"With neighbors? Who are they? Do you know their names?"

"Dr. Kevin."

"He's really a doctor?"

Sean nodded firmly. "Yes, it's Dr. Kevin."

I felt a surge of relief. I just hoped he was a medical doctor. Even a vet would do—anyone with medical experience. I focused on the distant lights. I guessed I was looking toward the nearest neighboring farm. Jack had probably left Amy there while he went to meet me. It made sense. The last thing he needed was a young girl tagging along. The property didn't seem that far away.

I *had* to see my daughter. I couldn't wait. I remembered the four-wheeler ATV in the barn. "I need you to take me, right now."

"Where?"

"To get the doctor for your daddy. And to see Amy."

79

I followed Sean down the stairs.

"What about Daddy?"

I could smell the scent of wood smoke in his hair as I followed him. It needed a wash. I guessed his personal hygiene could do with some attention.

Sean stopped in the hall at the bottom, and his face looked perplexed. "Is Daddy hurt real bad?"

I stared in at Jack on the living-room couch. He was snoring, his head still to one side, his lips slightly parted.

I felt those conflicting emotions rage through me again. Part of me felt no pity for him, only a burning hatred for the eight years of hell he put me through. I kept telling myself that I wanted him to pay for abducting our children.

Another part of me felt stirrings of love and concern.

And that conflict troubled me.

I led Sean into the grimy kitchen. There was an old couch in a corner with burgundy cushions, the arms badly scuffed, and one of the seat cushions was missing. I had Sean sit down and tried to take a minute to pull myself together. The kitchen clock read 1:30 a.m.

"Yes, he is. I've tried to stop him from bleeding again. We'll get him to a hospital soon. First, we'll go see the doctor."

I had to give Sean hope. I truly didn't know if Jack would make it. He looked lean and fit, but he'd lost a lot of blood and needed medical help. I couldn't tell Sean the truth, that we needed to leave his father in order to get to the neighbors' faster. I could see by the tormented look on my son's face that he would lose it if we left Jack here alone. Sean wasn't going anywhere. His entire world revolved around his father.

I could understand why. If Sean had been physically and mentally traumatized by the crash and lived such a remote life, then Jack and Amy would be the only ones he relied on.

"He'll be fine, Sean. Don't worry."

But Sean's exhausted red eyes became teary again. He took a deep breath, let it out. For moment, I thought he'd be OK, but then his fragile emotions cracked him wide open, and he started to sob like a child, his body shuddering.

I took him by the hand, hugged him, and sat beside him on the couch. The burgundy cushions smelled as if a dog had slept on them. "My poor Sean. It's OK, honey. It's OK."

I cradled his head in the crook of my shoulder and stroked his hair. He didn't stop sobbing, but he didn't pull away. This time, he buried his head in my shoulder like a hurt child.

For eight years, I thought I'd never feel Sean next to me again. I was overwhelmed. How long had it been since anyone comforted Sean like this? My eyes became teary. I couldn't focus. I wiped my face with my sleeve. I didn't want him to see me upset.

It took a few minutes until his crying ebbed away to a few sniffles and sobs. The next thing I knew, he snuggled into me and the comfort I offered. I stroked his hair.

He still looked like the child I remembered. I bet he still slept with his mouth open, a hand under his cheek. My eyes filled again. My tears dripped onto Sean's neck. I wiped them away and planted a kiss on his cheek. His warm skin no longer felt soft like a boy's but was uneven with adolescent bristles.

Feeling Sean's closeness, I desperately longed to see Amy and hold her. What would she look like now? Would she remember me? How would she react when she saw me?

I shuddered, wondering if she had been injured like Sean. Or worse. Jack had merely said she was with the neighbors. He said she'd needed a wheelchair for a while. My mind was haunted by uncertainty. What if her injuries were worse than Jack had said?

I had looked around but saw no landline phone.

I knew I had to venture out to find her, find the doctor, and call 911. I also knew it was dangerous approaching the neighbors' house alone, but I couldn't wait. I had waited eight long years to see my daughter. My anticipation raged, making me giddy with excitement, even if my exhausted limbs felt as heavy as stone.

After the stress of the last thirty-six hours without sleep, I felt as if I'd hit a brick wall. My eyelids began to flicker. But I was desperate to make my way to the neighbors'.

And finally see my darling Amy.

I grasped Sean's arm. "We'll get your daddy help, Sean. And I need to see Amy. We need to leave now."

I decided that once we reached the house where Amy was staying, I'd call the police and ask for medical help for Jack.

"Will you take me to where she is?" I gripped Sean's hand and felt his fingers, so big and adult, callused from work, not the soft, small, childish ones I remembered. He looked drowsy and lost.

I felt desperate to hug him again. It was almost impossible to hold back my affection, like trying to stem a dam that had already burst inside me, but I was afraid I'd overpower him and he'd react badly. I struggled to control my emotions.

"Sean, are the keys in the four-wheeler?"

He nodded. "Daddy left them there."

At least he was talking to me a little more. We checked on Jack, still lying unconscious on the living-room couch. His eyes remained closed, but he stirred and then settled again. Sean knelt and softly touched his father's face. He looked back up at me, fretful. "Is Daddy going to be OK?"

"He'll be OK once we get the medical help he needs."

Sean heard my words, but I wasn't sure he was convinced.

"We need to leave—fast, Sean."

I grabbed the flashlight from the table, and we moved out through the kitchen door and into the night, Sean walking behind me. This wasn't one of those Southern nights when the clammy air felt like you were walking through a film of gauze. It was darn cold. I saw the path leading across the meadow, and I guessed—hoped—it led to the neighbors' house.

I shone the flashlight on the path. But I could barely make out a distant glimmer now, the house lights masked by the woods. "Are you sure this track leads toward Amy?"

Sean nodded.

What would I tell the neighbors when I knocked on their door so late? Assuming I wasn't savaged by any guard dogs on the property or shot as an intruder. In remote parts of the South, that was a distinct possibility.

What would I do? Try to keep it calm and normal, just smile and say, "Hey, folks, I'm here to see Amy. I'm her mom. My kids have been missing for eight years. I thought they were dead, but they're not, and I've come to rescue them. I thought my husband was dead, too, but it turns out he was just hiding out. The fact is, I shot him, and he may be bleeding to death. Can I please call 911?"

They'd probably think I was some crazy woman who'd just escaped over the walls of a psychiatric facility. I'd have to pick my words carefully, but Sean was my insurance. I assumed they'd know him.

I felt a desperate flurry of excitement, mixed with apprehension and disbelief. After eight lost years, I was about to see Amy.

"Hurry, Sean."

I crossed the barn to the four-wheeler and clambered on.

The key was in the ignition. I went through the startup drill, shifted the gears into neutral, and hit the start switch. The engine gave a harsh cough and died.

I hit the switch again. Same thing. Another cough, and then the engine died. Three more tries produced the same result.

I panicked, and my hope sank.

I flicked on the choke in despair and tried once more. This time, the engine gave a noisy snarl. I revved some more, and the engine's growl exploded in the darkness.

"Climb on, Sean."

He jumped onto the back and clung to my waist. My son's embrace felt so good. I squeezed the accelerator handle, and the four-wheeler jerked about a foot, then sputtered and died again.

I swore aloud.

I checked the fuel gauge. The red pointer was below empty. "We need gas, Sean. Where's the gas?"

We climbed off, and he pointed to a couple of red plastic containers in a corner across the barn. We refilled the tank. I climbed on and tried the engine. It roared. My heart rose. I opened the throttle to keep it going.

"Come on, Sean."

Out of nowhere, a hand reached over, grasped the ignition key, and turned it off. I spun around in my seat.

"Get off."

Jack stood there, holding the shotgun, a pair of handcuffs dangling from one of the fingers of the same hand. His other palm was resting against his wound. He looked in agony, his face white. "I said get the heck off."

Crimson drenched his bandages, and he seemed delirious, his brow drenched in silver beads of perspiration.

"Jack, you . . . you shouldn't move. You'll open your wound."

"Where do you think you're going?"

"To get you help . . . and to see Amy."

"Get off. Now." He raised the shotgun.

"Jack, I have to see her. I have to see Amy. I know she's with the neighbors, Sean told me. You can't keep her from me like this, not anymore."

"Step off."

"No! You need a doctor, and I need to see my daughter."

He racked the pump action on the shotgun. I remember my father saying that the sound of a shotgun being racked was enough to scare the living daylights out of anyone. It scared me, even if at that moment I didn't seem to care whether I lived or died. But Sean looked petrified. I stepped off the four-wheeler.

Jack wrenched the keys from the ignition, and the engine sputtered and died. "Get back inside the house."

80

Cracker Barrel was busy with an early lunch crowd, most of them shrewd seniors there for the daily specials.

Tanner eased himself into the chunky wooden seat opposite Courtney. A bunch of white rocking chairs lined the patio outside. Hanging on the walls were the usual decorations—the rusted old farm implements, black-and-white photographs, and ancient tools you saw in every Cracker Barrel location across the country.

Tanner quipped, "Last time I was in a Cracker Barrel, I got a seat under a horse castrator. Had to ask to move."

"Scary."

"You've no idea." He studied the menu. "Grits and more grits. Don't you love it?"

"Don't mock, the food's OK." Courtney ordered pancakes and decaf.

"Wasn't mocking. Actually, I love 'em." Tanner ordered bacon, scrambled eggs, turkey sausage, and a double portion of cheese grits.

"But you've got kind of a New York accent."

"I lived in Louisiana until I was twelve, before my mom moved us up north. Where's Bamm-Bamm?"

"Bamm-Bamm?"

"Your partner. Reminds me of the kid in *The Flintstones*. Little Bamm-Bamm Rubble, friend of Pebbles, remember? I'd want to see an ID if he asked me to buy him a beer."

Courtney broke into a smile. "Sergeant Stone's at Fort Campbell, sifting through some files from eight years ago, seeing if he can come up with anything that might help us. And your guy?"

"Agent Breedon? I call him the Shadow."

"Why?"

"Just sticks by you and hardly says a word."

"Where is he?"

The waitress came with their coffee and left. "Adding to his air miles, being a busy boy, doing all the gofer work. First, he's interviewing the pilot Hernandez's brother down in Florida and getting a blood sample from him for a DNA comparison. After that, he's got to check to see the prints results from the aluminum case, see if we've got anything there."

Tanner tore open two blue sweetener packets and sprinkled them in his coffee. "Then he's going to see Dexter at the NTSB."

"Important?"

"Honest? I'm straw clutching. I'll let you know if my Powerballs come up."

Courtney sipped from her cup. "Anything you'd care to talk about in private now that we're alone?"

Tanner smiled. "That isn't a come-on line, is it?"

"No, Tanner, I meant about the case."

"Funny, I was probably imagining it, but on one or two occasions, I thought I was getting a vibe."

"Vibe?"

Tanner shrugged.

Courtney gave him a look that was indeterminate.

Tanner said, "Remember, it's only sexual harassment if you're *not* attracted to the guy you may think is hot for you." Tanner's smile vanished but still glinted in his eyes.

She gave him another look. Tanner spread his hands, gave a soft shrug, and said amiably, "I'm just saying."

"Lose a few more pounds, and hey, you just could be a heartbreaker."

"Couldn't we all? Straight from the hip, ain't you?"

"I'm a base brat, what do you expect?"

A spark glinted in Tanner's eyes. "Hey, I like that. Maybe if I found the right woman to motivate me . . ."

Courtney said it before she could stop herself. "Dexter told me about your wife's death, the arson."

Tanner's face tightened visibly. "He's quite the gossip, Dexter. I should have known better."

"What do you mean?"

"A little man with wiry wild hair who looks like an old woman. I told him it was confidential."

"Look, I just wanted to say I'm really sorry. It must have been tough on you."

"It was. But it's all water under the bridge."

"I don't believe that. Sounds to me like it's still hurting."

"Yeah, I guess it is."

"Can we talk about it? The arson is relevant to the case."

"Yeah, but not right now. Now is not a good time."

Courtney slid her hand across, let it rest on top of his big, meaty paw, and squeezed. "OK. And I mean that, I'm really sorry."

He nodded and squeezed her hand in return. "I appreciate it."

She took her hand away and smiled a little. "But let's stay safe for now and stick to work."

"I'm with you there. Tell me more about you and Kath."

"We're best friends since elementary school."

"So how do you feel about having to put her ex-husband away for a long time?"

"You sound pretty confident that's a given."

"We'll find him, all right, dead or alive. He's out there, and he's already left clues. And he made the mistake of showing his face."

Courtney toyed with her cup. "How do you think I feel? I'm not exactly doing cartwheels, Tanner. But I'll do my duty."

"How about Kath? How do you think she's feeling right now?"

"Her head must be so screwed up. This whole thing's a blizzard of the bizarre."

"I like that. You've got a way with words."

"You being facetious, Tanner?"

"Don't even know the meaning of the word."

"Sure you do, smarty pants."

Tanner's cell phone rang. He answered. "Tanner." He listened, said

"Got it" a couple of times, then finished with "OK, call me back if you've got anything." He flicked off his phone.

Courtney said, "News?"

"My man in Florida. He got the blood sample. Hernandez's brother was no help. Said they never really talked about his brother's pilot work, they weren't that close, and they didn't often keep in touch. A phone call at Christmas and Thanksgiving was about it. A typical dysfunctional American family."

"All families are."

"What?"

"Dysfunctional. Just some are more dysfunctional than others. So what next?"

"My guy's going to check on the aluminum case, see if they found any prints other than Jack's and Hernandez's. If anything turns up, he'll call. So we've got nothing so far. I'm starting to feel desperate."

Tanner considered, then looked over at her. "When I asked you about Kath's father, it seemed like a sensitive subject for you. Care to tell me why, or is that still off limits?"

"You don't know when to drop something, do you, Tanner?"

"I'm just curious, that's all. I sensed something wasn't right about your reaction. I wondered why."

"Not the time. Just drop it."

"If you say so."

"I do."

The waitress brought their breakfast. Courtney drizzled maple syrup on her pancakes. She sucked a wayward sugary dribble from her thumb, then pulled a notebook out of her courier bag and spread it open.

Tanner forked a mouthful of scrambled egg and swallowed. "What have you got there?"

"Some ideas about how maybe we can find Jack."

81

Jack appeared to be in serious pain. Perspiration drenched his face, and his skin was clammy. We moved back into the kitchen.

Jack lifted his shirt, examined his bloodstained wound. "What did you do?"

"You bled pretty badly. I used the trauma wound kit."

He swallowed, his Adam's apple bobbing. "You'll need to get me to Doc Borovsky. Or else I'm going to be nailed into a box."

"Sean said your neighbor's a doctor."

"That's him. He's three hundred yards down the track. He'll take care of it."

Jack looked so desperately ill, unsteady on his feet. His hand fell away, and I saw his bloodied bandages were stained even darker. "Jack, let me help."

He staggered forward, the shotgun falling from his hands. I grabbed hold of it. Jack clutched the barrel at the same time. We struggled, Jack grunting like a wild animal in pain.

Sean saw our struggle and joined in, helping Jack, pulling at the barrel. It was crazy—the shotgun safety could get knocked off, and we could all get killed.

"Jack, please, it'll go off and kill us, for God's sake! Think of Sean!"

I saw gritty determination in Jack's face. He wasn't giving in easily, but the mention of Sean did it. He gave up the struggle, and the shotgun slipped from his grasp.

"Let the gun go, son. Do as I say. Leave it be."

Sean's hands slid off the barrel. For a kid who didn't like guns, he sure held on to that one hard. I shifted the shotgun to my side, my fingers fumbling for the safety. It was still on. The last thing I needed was for the shotgun to go off inside the house and kill us all. Sean looked upset as he stood by his father.

Jack squeezed his hand. "It's all right, Sean. Everything's going to be fine."

He looked at me and grimaced in agony. "The doc, Kath. Get me to him. I've changed my mind. The pain's getting worse."

"That's where Amy is?"

He hesitated before nodding. "Give me back the gun. Please, Kath."

"No way. I don't fully trust you, Jack. The first chance you get, you're going to try to dupe me again. From now on, I don't let you out of my sight. How do we get to Amy and the doctor?"

"Get the wheelchair out in the hall. Move me into it, and we can take the van outside. It's wheelchair-accessible."

"Can Sean drive?"

"Yeah, he can drive."

"Sean, go start the van."

Sean went out, and I heard the van start up. Jack raised himself on one arm and grunted in pain.

I maneuvered the wheelchair in from the kitchen and over to where Jack lay. Sean came back in.

"Help me get your father into the chair."

Like a child, Sean looked again to Jack for approval.

Jack nodded. "Do as you're told, son."

"You think you can manage to move?" I asked Jack.

"I'll have to, won't I? Just take it easy."

"How about putting the shotgun down? It'd be safer."

"That's pretty rich, considering you could have killed me with it. I'm putting nothing down, least of all my guard."

He wheezed and coughed, put his sleeve to his mouth. I saw blood-stained mucus. "If I don't see the doc soon, I'm in trouble, Kath."

"You're in a bucket of that already. Pull your dad forward, Sean, and do it very gently."

Sean moved behind Jack. I slipped my left arm under him, and we raised him as carefully as we could, but he still gave a pained, tormented groan as we shifted him into the wheelchair.

"Easy, for Pete's sake, go easy."

"Check your wound pads. Are you bleeding again?"

"I don't know."

I checked them. They still looked OK.

Jack's agonized face was drenched. He wiped sweat from his brow. "You'll need to be extra careful," he said. "It can be a bumpy track."

"I'll do my best. Help me push your father outside, Sean."

We rolled the wheelchair out of the kitchen and eased it down the ramp into the yard. The night was alive with the sound of crickets. In the black sky above, the Milky Way spattered across the night, like the remains of the celestial explosion that it was.

I used the flashlight and opened the van's rear door, where I found the switch to raise the wheelchair. Sean and I eased the chair onto the mechanical lift, and I pressed the button. The lift whirred, and in no time we shunted the wheelchair into the rear of the van, Jack sitting in the middle.

I aimed the flashlight into his face, and he squinted. Cold sweat glistened on his brow. He didn't look well. I slid the van door shut.

"Sean, drive slowly, and try not to hit any bumps. Understand?"

He nodded, climbing into the driver's seat. I slipped into the passenger side next to him. I held the shotgun with the barrel pointed downward, my fingers making sure the safety was still on. I didn't want to risk the weapon going off as we bumped along the track. I flicked on the interior light and left it on so I could see if Jack was up to anything.

"Let's go, Sean."

He gunned the engine but looked confused as he turned back toward his father's pained face for approval. "Dad . . ."

"Drive, Sean. We're going to see Amy."

82

We would have been quicker walking. Sean snailed it like a teenager taking his first driving lesson, his eyes straining as they watched the grassy track, slashed by the silvery headlights.

To make things worse, every few yards, he tapped the brakes, easing in and out of the ruts, sending the van shaking from side to side.

Jack was subdued, chin slumped on his neck, teeth clenched in pain.

I tried to engage him. "Why did you leave Amy at the neighbors' house? Did you think she'd be safer?"

No answer from Jack, except for a pained grunt as the van lurched. He looked weak as he wiped his brow again. "Sean . . . watch . . . watch the next bend."

The van rounded a clump of oaks. Fifty yards away, the headlights revealed neat rows of fruit trees. "Where are we? Or is that still a big secret?"

"Monroe County, near the Alabama and Georgia state lines."

I saw lights appear through the trees. Were they were the ones I saw earlier? The neighboring farm Jack mentioned? A big oak tree loomed ahead. From the little I knew of it, Monroe County was mostly small farms and included part of the vast Cherokee National Forest.

Jack sounded worried. "Kath . . . there's a whole lot more to all this than I've told you. More than you can know. Sean, pull up next to the big tree."

I gripped the shotgun warily. "What's going on?"

Jack sounded almost comatose, his eyes drowsy. "The van won't make it the rest of the way. We . . . we have to cross an old dried-up creek. It's uneven, rutted."

"Then what?"

"You'll see a track to the right of the creek, just wide and level enough for the wheelchair to pass. You'll need to wheel me the rest of the way."

"You'd better not be up to no good, Jack."

He wiped his mouth with the back of his hand. "Pull in near the tree, son."

Sean eased on the brakes. I climbed out, slid open the side door, and hit the button. The chair whirred out, and Sean helped me maneuver it down off the van runners.

"Kill the engine and the headlights."

Sean did as Jack told him. When the engine died, the silence was like a force, until the chatter of crickets erupted in the darkness. I scanned the flashlight over the rows of fruit trees. House lights loomed closer now. I still didn't trust Jack. He looked anxious. What was he up to?

I clenched the shotgun, leaned in close, and whispered so Sean wouldn't hear. "Try anything, Jack Hayes, and I'll blow your head off."

In the flashlight's beam, I saw a fearful look in Jack's eyes. He put up his hands in a gesture of surrender. Was he afraid I'd really kill him if he made another attempt? His anxiety made me even more wary, my nerves in overdrive.

Jack answered quietly, "I'll keep that in mind. Let's . . . let's go."

I clutched the shotgun hard and took a few steps forward. The grassy earth felt smooth, with hardly any ruts, but my flashlight picked out a hollow ten yards ahead—an old creek. To its right, I could make out a track about a yard wide, enough for the wheelchair to pass. A pair of narrow ruts cut into the earth, as if made by an ATV.

"Push your father, Sean."

I stayed behind Jack, using one hand to help propel the chair. It wheeled along the track easily enough. "How far?"

"Seventy yards, maybe more."

I was desperate to see Amy, my heart thudding so fast I felt a pain in my chest. The lights loomed closer. I was sure I could make out a white-painted ranch house up ahead, a barn next to it. A dog barked, then fell silent.

My mind was overcome with excitement. I grunted and pushed harder.

"Keep going, Sean, we're almost there."

The moon burst from behind coal-black clouds.

The dog started barking again, and this time it didn't stop. I felt an intense fluttering in my chest that made it hard to breathe.

What would I say to Amy? Would she recognize me? How would she react when she saw me? How much had she changed? Would she remember *anything* about me? My desperation to see my daughter was like a living thing. I felt the heat of tears run down my face.

The barking dog grew louder. It was bound to wake the neighbors. I looked ahead, sure that I'd see more lights going on. I was so distracted I didn't see the wide rut as the wheelchair hit it and jumped. I felt my right foot sink—as if I'd missed a stair—and my ankle knocked hard against a rock, my leg buckling. I pitched forward, hit the ground, and the shotgun flew from my hands.

As the wheelchair righted itself, Jack grunted in pain and cried out, "Get the gun, Sean . . . get it!"

I crawled toward the weapon, but Sean beat me to it, snatching the shotgun's butt.

"Give it to me here, son."

Sean obeyed his father, handing over the shotgun. I struggled to my feet, and my shinbone felt as if it was on fire, as if it had been smacked with a hammer. Sean retrieved the flashlight.

I stared at Jack. "What are you going to do now?"

He racked the shotgun. I felt sure he was going to kill me. Instead, he aimed the weapon upright and ejected all the cartridges, one by one, into his lap. He stuffed them into his pocket, then wiped sweat from his face.

"You didn't answer me, Jack. What are you going to do?"

"Keep my promise. Let's go see Amy."

I limped on, helping Sean push the wheelchair.

I felt a strange calm. Jack seemed resigned to me seeing Amy.

But instead of heading straight along the track, Sean skewed left. "Where are we going?"

"We're almost there." I heard a tremor in Jack's voice. Was it my imagination, or did it seem he was avoiding the question? He sounded weaker. The dog's barking grew persistent. I looked back as more lights came on in the house. I was sure I saw a door open. A figure appeared in the block of light, wielding a long firearm.

But Jack and Sean paid no heed as we trundled along the track. It ended at a rocky bluff. It was hard to make out in the poor light, but it seemed as if the ground sloped away, and there was a sharp drop to a valley below. Probably stunning in daylight, but right now, it didn't feel right. It felt dangerous. What was Jack up to?

"Stop here," he said, waving a hand.

We halted.

He looked up at me. "Kath . . . I . . . I couldn't tell you the truth. I just couldn't."

His voice trembled again. I looked at him and saw tears in his eyes.

"What truth are you talking about?"

"Amy . . . Amy's dead. I'm sorry. I couldn't tell you . . . I just couldn't. I knew it would rip the life out of you."

And then it felt as if a giant, icy hand reached in and grabbed hold of my heart. I could just make out a clump of gray rocks ahead, over-looking the valley, as Sean waved the flashlight. It wasn't a clump of rocks but a half dozen gravestones scattered around a private cemetery. The light beam settled on a simple marble stone. Gold lettering inscribed the pale marble: "Amy. We will love and miss you always, sweetest sister and daughter. Until we meet again.—Mommy, Daddy, and Sean."

In that millisecond of total shock, I felt as if steel claws shredded my heart. It stopped beating. I felt the lifeblood drain from me. I stared at the chiseled words in absolute horror and put a hand to my throat, unable to breathe.

My stare shifted to Jack. He was so quiet now I couldn't even tell if he was still alive, his features a shadowed blur in the wheelchair. "No, Jack! Please don't do this to me . . . Please!"

He just looked back at me, wet-eyed, sadness etched into his face as deep as a scar.

I began to sob, burning tears that scalded my eyes. Pain blossomed in my chest, so intense that it could have been a stake driven into me. My legs buckled. I crumpled to my knees.

When I opened my mouth, an agonized scream tore from my throat, a roar so intense that it echoed around the valley like a primitive, animal cry.

"No!"

And then all my senses seemed to fade, my body pitched forward, slammed into the cold earth, and a black curtain came down over my eyes.

83

"So what have you got?"

The Cracker Barrel was still filling up with a lunchtime crowd. A bunch of elderly ladies, two on walkers, brushed past Tanner as he asked the question. He winked at one. The old lady gave him a cautious look, as if he might be a potential mugger.

"A list of guys Jack served with, whom he was close to and who live within a three-hundred-mile radius of Knoxville." Courtney leafed through the notebook pages.

"Why three hundred?"

"The Dorsett boat has a twelve-gallon tank and a one-hundred-and-ten-horsepower engine. It gives it a range of about one hundred miles in smooth water. I trebled it because there was an extra fuel store of twenty-five gallons on board. I made three circles, each a hundred miles farther apart, extending from where he docked."

"How many guys are we looking at?"

"Eleven I think may matter, but I narrowed it down to five guys he knew better than most, according to his former CO. One of them is Joe Feld. He lives in Asheville."

"What's the connection?"

"Feld was a young machine-gunner, and Jack took him under his wing. Feld was a buddy of Kyle's, too."

"Who else is on your list?"

"Two former sergeants, one living near Memphis and another in Cincinnati, Ohio. Then there's a former corporal, Dan Riker, in Cooke County. The last one's named Kevin Borovsky, in Marion County, more than eighty miles from here. By the way, all are registered as PTSD sufferers with the veterans organizations, except Kevin Borovsky, who's a qualified surgeon who specialized in head wounds. The guy also has a PhD in psychology from Vanderbilt."

"Bright dude. What's your gut telling you?"

"Joe Feld's worth trying. He and Jack were close, apparently. But Riker or Borovsky are up there, too."

"Why?"

"Remember that smudge on the map?"

"Yeah, what about it?"

"Interesting thing is it's about midway between those last two guys."

"Could still be just a smudge."

"Could be, but I figure it's too much of a coincidence."

"Anything else I should know?"

"Riker was a close pal of Jack's from the day they deployed. They always hung together. Borovsky, too, but less so. In fact, he was later Jack's shrink."

"Yeah?"

"After three tours serving in Iraq, Borovsky resigned from the military and completed his PhD in psychology. He ended up a senior partner in a chain of private medical clinics and specialized in treating PTSD sufferers. The word is it was his passion, and he had an excellent reputation, until he had a run-in with the feds."

"How come?"

"Prescribing pills, or should I say overprescribing. A medical council investigation cost him a suspended license. The feds prosecuted him, too, but the judge left it at a hefty fine, noting the suspension, which actually ends in six months."

"When did Jack become a patient of his?"

"Six months after resigning from the Army."

"Did therapy help?"

"Kath thought Jack's bouts became less extreme, but then he'd go for a while without seeing Borovsky. That's sometimes the problem, getting a PTSD sufferer to keep receiving treatment on an ongoing basis, even years afterward."

"Did Borovsky see Kyle, too?"

Courtney snapped shut her notebook. "Yes, but Kyle didn't respond too well."

"How come?"

"You'll have to ask Dr. Borovsky that question. But I reckon Kyle was too far gone to be reached."

"You loved Kyle, huh?"

"Yes, I did."

"Don't you think your role in this complicates things?"

"Because Kath and Jack were my close friends?"

"Yeah."

"My CO sees that fact more as a tactical advantage—like knowing your enemy. He also knows I'll do my duty, even if that means prosecuting Jack."

"You still see Kyle much?"

"Not as much as I'd like."

"You make the round-trip drive from Fort Campbell to Sevierville? That must be racking up more than five hundred miles every time."

"Five hundred and forty-eight."

Tanner gave a low whistle. "You never met anyone else?"

"What is this, Tanner? An audition for *Take Me Out Tonight*?"

"Just curious. You must get offers. Attractive woman like you. I'll bet you've been married or come close to it a few times."

"So?"

"But you still love Kyle?"

"You're all questions, aren't you, Mr. Investigator? You major in psychology?"

"Nope, but like I said, I'm curious. It's rare to keep a torch burning for someone when, you know, there's not much, well, fuel to keep it burning, so to speak."

"What you really mean is when there's no hope for me and him."

"You'd know the answer to that better than me."

He looked at her as she raised her coffee cup and spoke over it. "Kyle doesn't really say much, just sits there. Now and then, he'll talk a little or make a comment, like he's come out of a coma, but then, sure enough, he goes right back into that coma again. I've heard one psychiatrist call it the shell syndrome. Ever hear of it?"

"No."

"Like turtles, they stick their heads out, look around a little, and then retreat back into their shells."

Tanner gave her a studied look.

"Don't feel sorry for me, Tanner."

"I wasn't. It's more like admiration. Not many men are lucky enough to have a woman care for them like that. Am I allowed to say that, or does it sound like a come-on?"

Courtney looked at him over the rim of her cup. Tanner held her stare. Their eye contact lasted just a few beats too long.

Courtney said, "Bet you're still wondering."

"'Bout what?"

"Why I avoided your question about me and Kath's dad."

"It ain't important. Just me being nosy."

"But it is important."

Tanner didn't speak, just listened.

Courtney looked away a moment, then back again. "I loved Kyle like crazy. The day they moved him to Serenity Ridge was the day I lost any shred of hope I had. I guess to be honest, I lost it long before then, when he tried to kill himself. But it's hard to let go of someone you love, someone you put your future hopes in, someone you believed was your soul mate."

She looked at Tanner over her coffee cup. "I was still feeling low for months after Kyle moved to Serenity Ridge. One summer evening, I went to see his dad. I needed someone to talk to. The colonel understood. He'd lost both his wife and Kyle. We sat down by the lakeside dock on a blanket and talked, and we had a glass of wine. Actually, I had a few too many glasses. I was feeling teary, lost, and that's when . . . well, that's when it happened."

"What?"

"You ever see a resemblance in your family members?"

"Sure."

"Well, right then, I saw Kyle in his father's face. The same eyes, the same look and gestures, the same mouth and cheekbones. Kyle looked like his dad. I mean, I don't know where my reasoning went, but all of a sudden, I was seeing Kyle, and I was reaching out, pulling Kyle's dad toward me, kissing him, tearing at his clothes."

"How did he react?"

"He's a man. A young woman was throwing herself at him. And I guess he'd been without a woman for such a long time, and he felt lonely, too. He seemed pretty shocked, in a trance, but he kind of went with it."

Courtney paused. "We were going at it like a pair of love-hungry teenagers, kissing and stuff, until he pulled back and said, 'Courtney, we can't do this. It's not right. I know you're lonely, but it's just not right. I'm sorry.' But I was drunk and paid no heed, just kept kissing him. And that's when it turned crazy."

"What do you mean?"

"Kath came home. We never heard her drive up. She walked in on our little red-hot scene and couldn't believe what she saw—me and her old man lying on a blanket, with an open wine bottle, some of our clothes unbuttoned, me showing more cleavage than I should. I mean, what would you think if you saw your father in a situation like that?"

Tanner frowned. "Me? I wouldn't blink an eye. Used to see it all the time. My dad was a serial womanizer who was running a half dozen girlfriends at the same time he was married to my mom. She used to call him Velcro Fly. My old man went through his life with a closed mind and an open zipper."

Tanner's face became more serious. "I hated what he did to my mom. That's why she finally had enough and moved us to New York. I never saw him again after that. But I guess Kath kind of freaked out, seeing her dad and you locked in an embrace, huh?"

Courtney nodded. "I don't think she's ever gotten that image out of her head. But I told her the truth, that it wasn't her father's fault, it was mine. I was just drunk and feeling sorry for myself. I saw Kyle's face in his father's, and I guess I just lost it and wanted to be near Kyle again."

Tanner reached over and gently patted the back of her hand. "I get it."

Courtney looked at him. Their eye contact lasted just a few beats too long once again.

Tanner reluctantly let his fingers slide away. He took a quarter from his pocket change and balanced it on his thumb, ready to flick the coin into the air. "Toss you for it."

"The check?"

"Naw. Heads we see Riker first, tails it's Dr. Kevin."

Courtney's cell phone rang.

Tanner held off on tossing the coin.

She answered her phone, listened, her face drawn with concern. She nodded her head a few times.

Finally, she said, "When?"

She listened some more, nodding, and gave Tanner a long, worried look. "You're sure about all the details, Sergeant?"

A pause, and then Courtney said, "Call me right away if there's anything else." She flicked off the phone, her face ashen.

Tanner palmed the coin. "For a second there, I thought you were angry with me."

"You? Why?"

Tanner shrugged. "By the look on your face, it's bad news, right?"

"Yeah, that was Sergeant Stone."

"And?"

"As of thirty minutes ago, Kyle's missing, and two female employees at Serenity Ridge were shot dead."

84

Fazil Tarik was busy in the mortuary working on the bony, emaciated corpse of an elderly woman. A fragrant joss stick was lit, masking the stench of death.

His cell phone rang. Tarik finished applying rouge to the woman's hollow cheeks and wiped his hands on the damp towel by his side. He saw that the call was from an unknown number, and he answered. "Yes?"

He recognized the voice and listened before saying bluntly, "There can be no mistakes. You must be certain they are there."

"Look, I'm as certain as I can be. It's your best shot. Any change, and I'll let you know."

Tarik considered, then removed a notebook and a pen from his pocket. He grunted and said, "Give me the details."

The caller spoke for several minutes, and Tarik jotted down the notes he needed. "I'll send word when I'm ready to move. Call me at once if you learn anything more."

He ended the call, a kind of sexual excitement building in him, as it always did when he sensed imminent death or violence. He washed and dried his hands, massaged them with an alcohol gel, and hurried to his office, where an American flag hung limply in the corner. He picked up the internal phone. "Come here, Kiril. Bring Mehmet and Abu."

When he put down the receiver, Tarik crossed to the sturdy Centurion safe in the corner. The safe was a ploy, really. Nothing of value was kept in it except a small amount of cash. Next to the Centurion was a gray filing cabinet. He opened the bottom drawer and plucked out a black rubber suction tool. It was made of two suction pads with a release lever. He placed both pads firmly on one of the heavy gray tiles in the middle of the office floor and pushed hard.

When the sucker gripped, he heaved up the tile to reveal a combination safe sunk into the concrete beneath. He dialed in the combination and hauled open the safe door. This was where he kept his real valuables. He removed a bulky locked metal box from inside.

He placed the box on his office desk and unlocked it with a silver key he kept in his pocket. Inside the box was a green velvet sack. He loosened the sack's strings and hefted out the contents.

A centuries-old Immortals mask.

Cleaned and polished, its disturbing beauty spoke to Tarik down through the ages. The turquoise from Khorasan Province, the gold from King Solomon's mines. But it was more than that.

His Sunni father was once a curator at the National Museum in Baghdad. He was a keeper of many ancient artifacts, but the three Immortals masks he watched over were irreplaceable. Part of his genesis. The blood of Tarik's own tribe flowed back to the Immortals, so his elders always told him. The masks were under his guardianship, but the Sunni in his blood was why his tribe fought so hard against the Americans. Until the day his elders played a dangerous game that went badly wrong.

Tarik gained a fortune that day when the Americans wiped out the convoy—gained a fortune in his escape but lost so many relatives, among them his wife and two of his children.

He shifted his gaze to the American flag in the corner. Hatred sparked in his eyes. He hawked, filling his mouth, and spit across the room with such ferocity that a gob of spittle landed on the flag. It dribbled down the red, white, and blue. Tarik smirked. He despised the Americans.

The FBI had the second mask. But that was a problem to worry about later.

He wiped his mouth as he heard the footsteps out in the hall. He slipped the velvet cover over the mask and replaced it in the metal box. The door opened, and his son Kiril entered, followed by Mehmet, his bulldog face aggressive as ever. Abu stood there with muscled folded arms, like an immovable rock.

Kiril said, "Father."

"It's time. We'll know where the woman is soon." Tarik handed over the jotted notes and explained his intentions. "You know what we must do."

A steely glint flashed in his eyes as he looked in turn at Kiril, Mehmet, and Abu. "Work quickly. Then kill them all."

85

I felt a slap sting my face.

"Wake up, Kath."

Another slap, and then a pungent acid smell attacked my nostrils, hurting my lungs the second I breathed. My eyes snapped open, a fire raging inside my skull, and I gasped for fresh air. I coughed, almost choking, until I sucked life into my lungs.

A man stood over me. Mid-forties, probably, dressed in grubby work overalls. His face and arms, seared brown by the sun, gave him the look of a farm worker. A tattoo was emblazoned on his right arm, two intertwined black and red serpents.

His face was flecked with tiny pink scars, and one of his eyes was badly stitched at the far edge, giving him what looked like a permanent squint.

He screwed the top back onto a miniature brown bottle, popped it down on a desk, and sat on a chair next to me. "Smelling salts, in case you're wondering. How are you feeling?"

His accent had a hint of Chicago. I was lying on a frayed corduroy couch. My mouth felt bone-dry. I licked my parched lips, my voice hoarse. "Where am I?"

"The farm next to Jack's place. I'm his neighbor. Name's Kevin Borovsky. Just call me Kev if you want. Or don't." He fought a smile.

"I . . . I think I saw you come out onto the porch."

His fingers felt for my pulse. "Yeah. I was asleep when my dog started barking, so I grabbed my twelve-gauge. I've got security cameras all over my property."

He gestured to a TV that was turned on in the corner. The screen showed a half dozen different camera images. Two shots of a gate from different angles, another at the front of a house and a driveway. Others showed what looked like a barn and some woods.

"My early-warning radar."

"You saw me on-screen?"

"Yeah, if anything moves out there, I see it, even in darkness. The cameras have infrared. There's also a bunch of alarm sensors that trigger if anyone unwelcome shows up."

I had a vague recollection of a black curtain closing in on me at Amy's grave, right after I screamed. "Did I pass out?"

"You sure did. It happens often enough when someone experiences a profound shock."

I felt the sobs, the tears, grow within me again, the disbelief and shock. I tried to fight it, but Amy's face seemed burned into my retinas. The last day I saw her, as she helped me pack her little Barbie backpack. Her smile as she looked up at me, so excited about her trip with her father. That poignant image was not going away.

Kevin examined my wet eyes, raising each eyelid in turn with a thumb. The dog was padding about the room. A big, friendly, overweight yellow Lab.

The room seemed to serve as Kevin's office. The furniture was outdated, a man cave totally bare of a woman's touch, the walls unfinished, half-painted a pale gray, full of clutter, and lined with hideous mustard-colored laminate shelves stacked mostly with medical books.

The dog stopped right beside me and started to lick my hand. The man ushered him toward the door. "Outside, Murphy. Outside, boy."

The dog left. I wiped the wet hand on my jeans.

"Don't worry, dog saliva's often less deadly than the human kind. I guess that's why our moms always warned us about the dangers of French kissing, huh?"

"You ever think of doing stand-up?"

"Hey, those salts really perked you up, didn't they?"

They sure did. But my spirits felt so low, and my mind felt clouded, as if the blaze inside my skull still hadn't been damped down. "You're a doctor."

"Yeah, well, actually, I was. Past tense. Was doing pretty well, too, until I got disbarred five years ago."

He tossed the smelling-salts bottle into a scuffed black leather bag. On one of the unpainted walls, I noticed a graduation scroll in a glass frame. It declared that Kevin was awarded a doctor of medicine in the Harvard class of '89. Another framed scroll dated two years later said he graduated as a neurosurgeon.

"Why?"

"Disbarred? In case you're wondering, it had absolutely nothing to do with my terrific taste in interior decor."

"I'll take your word."

"More a slight misunderstanding about my prescribing too many pills."

I looked at him.

His squint became a grin. "I ran a pain clinic. Helped folks relieve their ailments, imaginary or otherwise. With Xanax, hydrocodone, OxyContin, amphetamines, you name it. The usual suspects that quell all the mysterious maladies to which the South seems especially prone—heck, the whole country is prone. We're a drugged nation. You might think it was an easy way to make money. But more often, it had nothing to do with that."

He shook his head. "I liked to think of it as a practitioner's commitment to alleviate a patient's suffering. Except the feds didn't quite see it that way, even though most of my patients were military vets with PTSD problems. Fortunately for me, the judge figured that a hefty fine, disbarment, and probation were punishment enough."

"Why the farm?"

"My alternative lifestyle by default. Raising chickens, growing organic, sitting on my porch contemplating my sins and the universe. Sometimes I reckon that judge did me a favor."

I blinked a bunch of times, my head still fogged, and noticed photographs on the shelves: Kevin in a camo Army uniform and sunglasses, wearing a desert shemag around his neck as he sat on a Humvee hood with a red cross on the side parked beside a mobile medical tent. Others of Kevin with a beautiful preppy-looking wife and two bleached-blond kids. "Your family?"

He folded his arms, snapped a nod. "After my disbarment, Cynthia hung around long enough to empty my pockets, right after the judge took the court's share. I guess good old Robin Williams got it right."

"Robin Williams?"

"His definition of divorce: ripping out a man's testicles through his wallet. Do I sound bitter? Shouldn't, really. Got a good life here, if only my kids would care to visit more often. But I guess manure and market gardening don't quite do it for teens as much as the bright lights of Nashville."

"How long have I been asleep?"

"Fourteen hours."

I stared back at him.

"Or thereabouts. A combination of shock and exhaustion. You passed out. The body's way of dealing with a truckload of distress. The brain shuts down, retreats. Seeing Amy's grave was part of it."

My eyes became wet again. I closed them tightly. I felt as if I was having a breakdown. When I opened my eyes again, Kevin handed me a tissue from a box on the desk.

I dabbed at my face. His big, meaty hand touched my shoulder but felt surprisingly gentle. "Losing a child, that's up there with the big ones we never truly get over."

"I keep thinking."

"About what?"

"What were Amy's last moments like? Were they terrifying? Did she call out my name, in fear, in pain, in desperation?"

I felt like breaking down again.

Kevin squeezed my shoulder. "You think you could try standing?"

"Why?"

"You need some fresh air."

And then it suddenly hit me. "Where . . . where's Jack? And Sean?"

"We've got some things to talk about."

86

They say people die only when we forget them. That what you remember saves you. But I never found it to be that way. What I remember cuts my soul to the quick. To me, *gone* is the saddest word in any language.

On the back patio, the sun was beginning to fade. I guessed it was six or seven. It was a simple wooden patio, long ago painted a pastel green. An ancient mosquito zapper hung from a nail in the patio beam, the cold ultraviolet bars crusted with burned mozzies. On a frayed cane coffee table stood a half-full bottle of Four Roses bourbon. A dented old silver-toned storm lamp, the kind that runs on oil, hung from a rusted nail hammered into the wooden wall by the patio door.

I could see the distant valley, but the headstones were hidden by trees. A peaceful view, but my mind felt wretched.

Amy, my beautiful Amy. Gone. I'd hoped so much, prayed so much. Tears welled up. All I kept thinking of was her grave—her angel face, my beautiful daughter, lying in the cold, unfeeling earth. Grief felt like a boulder crushing me. I wanted to lie down on the earth beside her, feel its coldness seep into my bones the way it had seeped into Amy's. I looked down at my hands. They were trembling.

The patio door opened, and Kevin came out from the kitchen carrying a cluttered tray. It clinked as he set it down. A jug of ice water, glasses, two mugs of coffee, cream and sugar, a couple of spoons. He set a bowl of ice next to the bourbon.

I saw him glance at my shaking hands. He leaned across, felt my wrist. "Your pulse is low. Drink lots of water. It'll help you rehydrate after sleeping so long."

He smiled. "I'm not suggesting you have a whiskey, because it sure won't help you rehydrate, and it may not be good for your mood. But in case you really felt like a drink, I thought I'd play the Southern host."

"Water and coffee are fine for now."

"Hey, that's a sensible gal talking." He squeezed my shoulder, then poured me a glass. I felt the shock of the ice water drench my dry throat. My hands still shook. It wasn't just hydration I needed; my nerves felt as if they'd been scoured with a wire brush.

From a round tin, Kevin took a chunk of chewing tobacco and held it between his fingers. "A dirty little habit I acquired in the South. You mind?"

I shook my head. "Where are Jack and Sean?"

He slipped the tobacco into his mouth, his right cheek filling like a squirrel's as he chewed. "Jack needed some blood. We're not the same type, but I'm O-neg and keep a few pints of mine stored in a cooler for emergencies. I gave him two."

"Don't you need to get him to a hospital?"

"Gunshot wounds attract the cops. He's doing OK for now, resting in the bedroom next door. That may change, but until it does, it wouldn't be good to get the law involved. Unless you've got other plans?"

I didn't answer the question, and I had a feeling that unsettled him. "What about Sean?"

"I looked in a little while ago, and he'd fallen asleep next to his dad. That boy lives for his father."

"So I've noticed."

"It must be weird seeing them both again after all these years."

"Weird doesn't come close."

Kevin sat back, rubbing his jaw between thumb and forefinger. "How did Sean react when he first saw you?"

"He didn't. I don't think he gets me or our relationship."

"He will. He'll get it."

"You really believe that?"

"Yes, I do. Give time time, as my old grandmother used to say."

"How long have you and Jack known each other?"

"Since Iraq. We've still kept in touch now after our duty ended. For a short while before he left the Army, I actually counseled Jack."

"He never mentioned your name."

"No surprise there. A lot of my Army buddies never want to talk much about the war, never mind meet for a beer. Want to hear my theory?"

I nodded.

He splashed bourbon into his glass, dropped in a handful of ice. "War's like a dirty little secret they shared. It can bring out the best in men—bravery, heroism, self-sacrifice. But mostly you wind up doing things you never thought you'd do—killing, maiming, destroying, you name it. The old story. You realize how paper-thin the veneer is between man and the primal beast within. That's probably why some guys don't talk much about war once they get done with it. Or hang out a lot with service buddies. They don't want to remember all the nasty crap they did."

"You knew Jack, so I'm guessing you knew my father and my brother?"

"Sure did. Your dad's Old Ironsides, tough as a jockey's hide. I was the medic on duty the night he got hit. I did his amputation. I don't recall him whining, but I do remember him screaming a bucket of swear words."

"What about Red Rock?"

"I dealt with the dead and wounded afterward at our field hospital."

"Did Jack ever talk to you much about it?"

"He didn't speak much about a lot of things, but we're veering into the tricky realm of doctor-patient confidentiality." Kevin's eyes betrayed nothing, but he had an uncomfortable look, one that implied he knew more than he was saying.

"You knew about Kyle?"

"Yes, I did, and I'm truly sorry. But at least you still have him. Twenty vet suicides a week, that's the accepted figure. It's probably a lot more."

Kevin took a swig, the ice clinking, and held up his glass. "The law says you can't walk into a bar and buy a drink until you're twenty-one. Yet you can enlist at eighteen and die for your country. How crazy is that? We romanticize war. But so many lives are ruined by its horror. We can't expect someone who lives with death and fear and horror every day, who sees it all around him on the battlefield, to return home and just pick up his life where he left off. If we send them, we must try to mend them, but we don't. Guys overdose or put guns to their heads or deliberately crash their cars, or their ill health takes care of the dirty deed."

Kevin looked right at me. "You probably heard it before—this country knows how to start a war. But it never gives much thought to repairing the cost of human suffering afterward. I saw it with my own father."

He took a long swallow this time, knocked it right back. "My old man suffered from PTSD after Vietnam. Had his skull peppered with grenade fragments. It's maybe why I became a doctor in the first place. I was always looking for the father I once had, the parent I lost. I wanted to help heal him. But it didn't work out."

"What do you mean?"

"He crashed his car one night. Drove at high speed along I-75 and smacked into a wall. Probably did it deliberately, too. Like a lot of vets with PTSD who wind up in auto wrecks. They can't live with their mental-health issues or their ghosts or both."

"How did Jack end up here?"

"Are you up to walking?"

"Why?"

Kevin grabbed the storm lamp, moved toward the patio door, and opened it on creaking hinges.

"I'll explain. There's something important you need to be aware of."

87

I followed Kevin outside into the darkness and toward the barn. "How did Jack end up here?" I asked again.

"You mean in the middle of nowhere? I was the first person he called the night his aircraft crashed."

We stopped. I met Kevin's stare.

"You're wondering why me? I directed a private clinic near Sevierville. All the latest equipment and privacy. It wasn't far from the crash site, which suited Jack because he didn't want the cops involved."

"Why?"

"I think Jack's the guy to answer that one. I just did what he needed me to do that night."

"Which was?"

"Provide medical assistance, get him and the kids to safety, check them out physically, and tell nobody."

"Why help him?"

"Because he was a buddy I cared about who needed help. There were times in Iraq when I could have died if not for Jack. He laid it on the line for me and for others."

"The investigators say there were no calls from Jack's cell that night."

"So? People use throwaway cells all the time. Jack told me he always carried an untraceable cell. And nobody knew he crashed in the Smokies."

"Tell me about Jack's phone call."

"He was distressed. He explained that his aircraft had crashed in the storm, but he didn't want the emergency services involved, no 911 calls. The pilot was dead, and he and the kids were injured. He didn't think the kids experienced any serious injuries other than being violently thrown around in the crash and suffering concussions, but he didn't want to take any chances."

"Didn't you question why Jack didn't want to call 911?"

"Sure I did. But he said I had to trust him, and he'd explain why, so I did as he asked. From his route maps, he had a pretty good idea that he was probably on the southern side of Thunder Mountain. I headed for the crash site in my four-wheel-drive Jeep. It took me a while to get the Jeep up some of the muddy mountain tracks, but Jack and I kept in touch by phone so I could locate him."

Kevin started walking again, and when we reached the barn doors, he halted and fiddled with the storm lamp. "I found him and the kids sheltering in an abandoned shack near the crash. The pilot was definitely dead from a broken neck. Jack had done some basic first aid on himself and the kids. He'd suffered several broken ribs and a leg fracture. Sean had a broken foot, and Amy's shoulder was dislocated, and all of them were concussed."

"Amy—Amy was alive?"

"Yes. She was in shock, as was Sean. I could determine no obvious or serious neck or head injuries and no serious cuts or pulverized bones, but they needed to be checked out."

I listened, mesmerized.

"We left the pilot's body, and I drove them to my clinic. After I completed some scans, it was obvious that the children's injuries were somewhat worse than I first thought. Sean sustained a serious head injury in the frontal lobe, no bleeding but internal bruising and some cranial swelling. Kind of like the blunt-force internal trauma you can experience if you're beaten senseless in a bare-knuckle fight."

I couldn't speak.

Kevin looked at me, knowing the question I was desperate to ask. "You're wondering will Sean ever recover, right?" He shrugged, displaying both his hands, palms up. "The mind and the body can be incredibly resilient and regenerative, but I figure Sean's injuries are irreversible."

I felt as if I were in an elevator and the steel hawsers had been cut. It took me a little while before I could speak. "What . . . what about Amy?"

"Jack was probably drunk when he saw you for the first time after the crash, right?"

"Yes."

"Know why? Because he knew he would have to explain about Amy. It would be painful for him and for you. He felt responsible for her death. Maybe that's partly why he could not face you. I think he had his own breakdown, too, after the crash, which didn't help matters. For a time, I know he stayed with an old Army buddy at a farm down in Florida."

The Florida connection hit me. "Who was the buddy? A guy named Quentin Lusk?"

"You'll have to ask Jack that." Kevin seemed to be avoiding saying anything he wasn't sure Jack would want me to know.

Anger braided my tone. "He's not the Jack I knew."

"He's not the Jack anyone knew. War does that to people. Changes them—and always for the worse."

The burning question kept coming back. "Who killed DJ and Vera Spears? Jack said whoever did it wants to kill us, too. Or is he being delusional? He held a gun on me. Struggled with me to wrench it back when I managed to get it from him. Doesn't that tell you something about his mental state?"

"You want my opinion? He didn't want you to have a firearm in your hands when you saw Amy's grave. He was afraid you might harm yourself once you knew the truth."

"What were Jack and Sean doing at DJ and Vera's place?"

"DJ and I kept in touch. He and Jack were once buddies. DJ visited Kyle now and then, to keep an eye on him, at my request . . ." Kevin's voice trailed off.

"That tells me nothing much."

Kevin looked away, then back again. "Look, all I know is I got a call from DJ telling me you visited him and were asking questions. Within a couple of hours, he said he noticed a couple of different vehicles drive by his house. One of them was a van with a bunch of antennas and a satellite dish on top. He said it did a couple of passes by his home. He sent Vera out at one point, and she thought she noticed another vehicle parked up the street, an SUV with dark-tinted windows. When she approached it, the SUV drove off."

Kevin paused and looked at me. "DJ was a wily redneck. He knew someone was watching him. That you had led them to him, knowingly or otherwise."

"Me?"

"He reckoned. And he was getting worried. It sounded that way when he called me. I told Jack. When we called DJ back a few hours later, there was no reply. DJ always called back. But not this time, and Jack was getting worried, too. I was going to drive over to DJ's later that day and check on him. But without me knowing, Jack decided to do a drive-by himself, see what he could find out. When he saw no activity around the trailer, he decided to head inside. That's when he and Sean found DJ and Vera dead, and your paths crossed."

"What did DJ have that these people wanted?"

"Nothing, except that whoever killed him probably figured he might know where Jack was."

"Did he? Did DJ know that Jack was alive?"

"I never told him. But like I said, DJ was a wily redneck. And once the aircraft was found and there was no mention of bodies on the news, DJ called me and started asking a lot of hypothetical questions."

I put my hand to my mouth. I felt a surge of guilt, that I had somehow contributed to the deaths of DJ and Vera.

"I reckon whoever killed DJ wanted to find Jack. My guess is you're being tailed and watched by the same people."

I followed Kevin into the barn.

There was a Polaris Ranger inside, an old one, the red paintwork muddied and dented.

I was overcome by a powerful sense of desperation. "You need to answer my questions. Who? And why did Jack vanish? Why flee with our children? And what happened to Amy?"

Kevin played statue. His eyes gave nothing away.

He moved to the end of the barn. Old farm implements and rusted chains adorned the walls. A few dozen bales of straw were piled in a corner, the floor covered in it. Kevin kicked away the straw. I saw a trapdoor. He reached down and grabbed a frayed piece of rope attached to it.

"I've waited eight years to know the truth, darn you." I felt my face go livid. "Why won't you tell me? Why? I'm begging you!"

He pulled on the trapdoor rope. "I'll tell you what I know."

88

"Open sesame."

The trapdoor yawned open to reveal blackness below, a wooden stepladder leading down. Kevin flicked a light switch that was screwed onto an upright wood joist near the trapdoor, and a light sprang on in a cavern underneath.

Kevin turned around and got ready to descend. "Jack's living on his nerves. He's felt safe here, but he's still often on edge. Afraid he might be found. Now that you've shown up, he thinks you may have been tailed, so there's a risk. That means you need to know about our backup plan."

"Where are we going?'

"There's an old coal tunnel that runs out beyond the farm. It exits a few hundred yards away in some woods nearby."

"Why are you telling me this?"

"Better safe than sorry, in case we have need of it."

He reached the bottom and beckoned for me to join him. "There's electric lighting all the way, but I always take a flashlight and a storm lamp with me just in case. Follow me down; it's safe if you stick close."

I climbed down after him.

At the bottom, I saw that we were in a cavern, the black walls obviously a coal vein. The air was chilled, almost icy, the damp black walls glistening, cobwebs everywhere. I shivered.

Kevin moved along the lit passageway, and I followed. Naked electric bulbs stretched for as far as I could see, and the ceiling was high enough to stand up under.

"This way, and mind your head, the ceiling dips a little."

I ducked my head as I stayed behind him, the chilled air prickling my skin.

I couldn't shake off the despondency of Amy's loss. It hung over me like the darkest cloud imaginable.

"Jack was prone to bouts of paranoia since Iraq. Some PTSD sufferers are totally blighted by it. No amount of reasoning or treatment can cure them."

"Don't you think I knew that?"

"Sure, but did you know that for that diagnosis to be truly valid, you have to be in fear for your life?"

"No, I didn't."

"Jack felt in fear for his life. And in his own mind, he created valid reasons to disappear."

"What reasons?"

Kevin kept moving forward, into the blackness of the damp coal walls. "Ones that a fragile mind like Jack's would find compelling, especially since the crash made his paranoia worse."

"Meaning?"

"He believed the plane crash was sabotage. That someone set out deliberately to kill him."

I stared back at Kevin in astonishment. I opened my mouth to speak, but nothing came out. I thought of the warning words from the man on the bridge. *Know what you're dealing with here? Powerful, desperate people.*

Our shadows flickered on the glistening black walls as Kevin said, "In the mind of a man suffering from paranoia, it seemed totally logical, and he therefore needed to disappear. The mind can twist anything to survive. Anything can become normal."

"But why take the children?"

"He believed that if any of you got in the way of the people trying to kill him, you'd be targets, too. In Jack's tormented mind, he decided to vanish to protect *all* of your family, you included. He figured that with him and the kids apparently deceased, those who sought to harm him would at least leave his widow in peace. That may not make sense to you, but again, we are not dealing with a rational mind."

Kevin looked at me as we kept moving. "And as unreal as it sounds, Jack meant to protect you all."

I felt a ripple of shock.

Kevin took a deep breath and let it out. "To Jack, vanishing was a better option than if he and the kids showed up alive. Or if you vanished, too, soon after the crash, to join him. That might have seemed as if the family had conspired to go on the run. So he didn't contact you. When the aircraft was never found in the months afterward and the authorities had no leads, why, that was just perfect. Jack was more convinced than ever that he had done the right thing. It also gave him time to try to figure things out."

We came to a part of the tunnel that was different from the rest. It split in two, one side leading a short way to a massive oak door set into a solid framework of rough-hewn timber that looked as if it might take dynamite to shift. The door was locked, several solid wood beams barring the way, chained and padlocked.

"What's in there, behind the door?"

"Old tools and tunneling equipment."

Kevin gave me a shifty look and for some reason didn't sound all that convincing. He moved on, a rush of fresh air wafted in, and we stepped out of the cavern past some bushes onto a small plateau. I could barely see, with the moonlight dimmed by clouds.

Kevin tilted his head toward a carpet of dark, wooded hills that seemed to go on forever. "It's why Jack ended up here. You can walk some of these trails for thirty miles without meeting a soul. Jack felt safe, until the wreckage was found."

I looked at Kevin, open-mouthed, understanding none of it. "At first I thought you were saying his fear was all in his mind. That it was paranoia. But . . . but now I get the feeling you're suggesting he vanished for a good reason."

"He did."

Kevin pointed below and led me to a pair of massive oak trees. He pulled back some undergrowth and held up the storm lamp. I saw two brown plastic tarpaulins. He lifted one, and beneath it was a blue ATV. It looked in good condition, and two spare jerricans of gas were strapped to the carrier on the back.

"There's another ATV under the second tarp." He pointed his chin toward the darkness. "We're not far from the Cherokee National Forest. A man could lose himself in those forests forever if he wanted to."

"You're saying that's Jack's plan if he has to flee."

"I guess it could be. Now, let's get back. I don't want to leave him alone for long, just in case."

As I followed him back the way we had come into the tunnel, an icy chill flooded my spine. "Who exactly would want to harm Jack?"

"The same people who killed DJ and Vera. The kind of people who want to keep a secret. The kind who'd have no hesitation about killing your entire family if they felt it was necessary. Unless we stop them."

Kevin looked at me. "That's Jack's plan. To try to put an end to this, once and for all. To stop the devil in his tracks. Jack's been a broken man for years, but now that he feels he has to protect you and Sean, he's back in the ring."

"What devil? And who are these people? What exactly happened in Iraq that caused this?"

"Simple. A guy named Fazil Tarik is the key."

"I know about Tarik. I know about the ambush." Kevin looked at me as if to ask how, but I just said, "Later. How is he the key?"

"That day near Babylon, he fled the ambush driving a truck. Not just any old truck. It contained twenty-five million dollars and a bunch of priceless artifacts from several Iraqi museums. Some said he set up the ambush in the first place, so he could steal the money and the artifacts. Knowing what I do about Tarik, I'd say that was a distinct possibility."

I said nothing, just listened as we followed the pearly string of lightbulbs along the tunnel.

Kevin held on to the oil lamp. "So Tarik flees in the confusion. When the military realize he's not among the dead or wounded, they try to track him down. They find him hiding out with relatives near Fallujah two weeks later, but the money and the artifacts have disappeared, and Tarik's claiming he knows nothing about the money. And here's where the smoke and mirrors come in."

"What do you mean?"

"A few months down the line, and Tarik's a bona fide refugee to the U.S., cleared by a military investigation, and innocent of any blame or theft."

"Who was tasked with hunting him down?"

"Your father, Chad, and Jack were part of the team. They all knew Tarik, knew his MO, and had taken part in the original deal to get him and his tribe on the U.S. side."

"You're suggesting Tarik used some of the stolen money to bribe his way out of trouble?"

"Yeah, you bet. I'm not even sure it was just twenty-five million he disappeared with. He could have salted away more. But for sure, someone helped him. Someone was on his side. And someone aided his theft."

"Who? My father, Chad, or Jack?"

Kevin didn't speak, just stared at me.

"Answer me. It was one of them, wasn't it?"

He still didn't speak. We came to the tunnel entrance again, the wood stepladder waiting.

"Which one, Kevin?"

"Look, in Jack's mind, 'they'—whoever they are—are responsible. They could be the government, the military, or whoever was in cahoots with Tarik and whatever other demons happen to be inside Jack's head at any given time."

Kevin climbed the ladder. I followed him up, and he switched off the tunnel lights.

"Are you serious—it could be the government?"

Kevin put down the lamp and dusted off his clothes with his hands. "I have no idea, even if Jack thinks he does. For eight years, he's kept his head below the parapet here, for fear that Sean and he might be a target."

He picked up the lamp again. "By doing that, he's avoided having to confront that fear too often. And that's been fine. The last thing I wanted to do was knock Jack too far off the rails by doing a forensics job on his mind. In short, we avoided talking about it until all this started up again."

Kevin took a deep, silent breath before starting to speak again.

"You've said enough, Kev."

The angry tone caught me, and I turned. A washed-out Jack leaned against the barn door for support, clutching his freshly bandaged wound. He was bone-white.

Kevin went to him. "Hey, man, you need to take it easy. You shouldn't be moving—"

"You said way too much."

"Jack, you've got to tell her. It's time, buddy. This thing can't go on forever. It's cost way too many lives. You hear me, man?"

I saw real pain in Jack's face. His lips quivered as he let Kevin's words sink in.

"You feel well enough to take a walk outside?" Jack looked at me, his voice more subdued.

"Why?"

"Kevin's right. It's time you knew the truth."

89

"You need to wait here. I'll be back in a second," Jack said, and he went into the house.

When the door opened again, Sean came down the patio steps to join us at the barn, Jack behind him.

"Why Sean?"

"Because I don't want you running off. He'll catch you if you do."

"I haven't seen my son in eight years, and you threaten to have him tackle his mother to the ground? And why would I run off?"

"I'm just protecting us all."

"But from whom, Jack?"

"You'll know soon enough."

"You've got a lot of questions to answer."

"And I'll answer 'em."

Kevin handed Jack a powerful flashlight made of yellow plastic, the blocky waterproof type you often see on small boats. "You may need this. Remember, go easy over the ruts."

"Quit playing Daddy."

We followed Jack to the barn, and he went to climb into the Ranger.

Kevin told him, "I'd feel better if Sean or Kath drove. In fact, I'd really prefer you rested and did this tomorrow. If that wound opens again, they're going to be screwing you into a box."

"It's gone on too long, buddy. It needs to be now, tonight." Jack turned to me. "You'd better drive. Sean could take all night."

I climbed into the driver's seat. Sean slipped into the back without a word. Jack eased in beside me and leaned over with a faint groan, one hand still on his wound. He made sure the gearshift was in neutral, and I kept my foot on the brake while he turned on the engine. Jack flicked the Ranger's headlamps onto full, their silver rays slashing the darkness.

"Go."

"Where to?"

"I'll answer all your questions, but first we need to go back to Amy's grave. It's important."

"I'm not sure I'm ready for that so soon."

"We need to. This story ain't done yet. There's something you need to hear."

90

My heart pounded again as I eased my right foot onto the gas pedal, my left hovering on the brake.

The Ranger growled forward, dipping into a few shallow ruts. Ten yards from the burial site, I slowed, turned in a half circle, and halted. My body was trembling, my legs weak. I still felt on shaky emotional ground. I really didn't want to see my daughter's grave again. The depth of my grief felt so raw.

Jack dipped the Ranger's headlights and flicked on the yellow hand-held flashlight. He climbed out without a word, Sean trailing behind.

The moon was bright, and we hardly needed the flashlight, but when Jack waved it, for the first time I noticed two pine-log benches off to the side of the graves.

"Sit, Kath. You, too, Sean."

Sean joined Jack on the farthest bench to the left. Jack looked grim, his face like a corpse from the blood loss. I knew Kevin's concern was real. I had a sudden, nauseating feeling in my gut that he could drop dead at any moment. It scared me. Sean would be distraught if that happened, like a child, totally lost.

Cricket sounds filled the night. It all seemed so unreal, the three of us sitting there, Jack leaning forward, his hands joined as if in prayer.

No one said anything as we faced Amy's grave, Sean staring at the ground, clasping his hands like his father.

My son was staring at nothing in particular except his grubby Reeboks, which looked sizes too big. There was something terribly sad about him. Like my brother, Kyle, he inhabited his own world, and I guessed few people were part of it, except maybe Jack. That hurt me so much.

"You said it's time I knew the truth."

"Kevin told you why I ran and hid. I know you've had your own pain to cope with since we disappeared. I know the trauma's been unreal." For a few moments, Jack seemed to falter. "Sean and Amy and I, we had our own trauma to deal with. The terror of the crash, along with everything that happened afterward."

I hated to think of that terrifying descent, the panicked horror in Sean's and Amy's hearts at the prospect of a violent death.

"We clung together before the crash. Cried and said how much we loved each other. That was really all we could do. The sheer terror seemed to go on forever, the plane buffeting and swaying wildly, until finally we struck the ground and plowed into forest undergrowth."

He went on. "I was knocked unconscious. But as soon as my head cleared and I saw the kids start to come around, I checked on the pilot. His neck was broken; he took the worst of it up front in the cockpit. After I assessed our injuries, I called Kevin."

He stood and moved to put one hand on Amy's gravestone. "Afterward was a whole other story. I tried to protect the kids and keep them safe, tried to hide. There was the constant worry that the law might find us."

"Why, Jack?"

"Because I knew the crash was deliberate. That's why I needed to keep ahead of those who meant us harm. That's why I didn't get in touch." He stared at me. "Don't you get that?"

I recalled again what Quentin Lusk said on the bridge. But I couldn't disregard that Lusk was another PTSD sufferer, maybe even a victim of the same delusions as Jack's. Besides, a part of me was so enraged that I didn't want to grasp at any reasoning. I just wanted to feed my anger.

"What I get is how crazy this is. Back then, your head was so screwed up you didn't know what reality was anymore. You were irrational, messed up from post-traumatic stress. Couldn't it all have been in your own mind?"

"You're so wrong, Kath. You don't believe there was someone out to kill me?"

"I don't know what the truth is anymore. Except that you gave no thought to how messed up I'd be, how grief-stricken. The same for our children. I didn't hear a word, not even a sign from you so at least I'd know you were all alive. You didn't care at all about me."

"Kath, I did, believe me."

"For the love of God, Jack, I don't have to believe anything you say."

Frustration lit his face. "Sure, I had a lot going on inside my head back then. But I know what happened, Kath. I *know*. And I know who did it."

"Who? I want proof."

I saw a spark of pain in his face. I wanted to believe him, but a part of me was still convinced that Jack was mentally unstable. His next words nailed it.

"Not now. All that's important right here and now is that I want you to know we're all still a family, and we always will be."

"Jack, we're dead, you and I. Don't you understand that? Finished."

The moment I spoke the words, I saw Jack's face collapse. I couldn't deny it. The life I had lived with him was still a fundamental part of me, but our relationship was over.

"I know this family is messed up, Kath. No one knows that more than me. But Sean's still your son. And he will come around to you, I know he will."

"What are you saying?"

"Like I told you. We're still a family. You, me, Sean."

I looked from him to Sean and saw silent turmoil in my son's eyes. "Somehow I really doubt that, Jack. You're a stranger to me. That's how I feel."

He nodded. "I get that. But we need to do something." Jack touched the gravestone and lowered himself into a sitting position near the granite. "I want you to come sit by Amy's grave."

I blinked, not sure how to react. "Jack, don't make this even harder on me."

"There's a reason. Trust me. Sean, sit down here, son."

Sean obeyed meekly, leaving a gap between himself and his father. Jack gestured toward the gap. "Sit here, Kath."

"Why?"

"Just sit. You'll understand why in a minute. Please."

I had no idea what Jack was up to, but I sighed and lowered myself into a sitting position between them, facing the inscribed stone.

Jack stretched out an arm. "Give me your hand, Sean."

Sean did as he was told. Jack gestured to me. "Kath, scoot in closer to Sean and me, and we hold hands."

"Jack . . ."

"Just scoot in, Kath."

"What's going on?"

"Sean's lost. He needs to know he's still part of this family. When a boy hasn't known a mother's presence for so long, it affects him."

"That wasn't my fault."

"You're right, it was mine, but this is no time for blame. We're all wounded hearts, all hurt souls. And we all need to heal."

He took a deep breath and let it out. "I know I've done us all harm, even if I did it for what I believed were good reasons. Once there were four of us, and now there are only three. But I believe that the love we once had has never really gone away. It's still there in all of us."

He met my stare. "Can I tell you something? For months, years, after I hid out, I'd still go back to Knoxville. I'd go alone, in disguise. I'd drive by our house. I'd drive by Chad's house. I'd see you, see you both sometimes. I'd see you with his child, see you happy . . ."

I could almost feel the agony in Jack's voice.

"I still loved you. Still wanted you. But I knew I couldn't come back.

I knew that if I contacted you, it would put your life in more danger—and ours, too."

Jack's words felt like a stiletto in my heart. His wet eyes met mine. "I want to tell you something else. In all the years Sean and I have been coming here, I've never truly felt that Amy's spirit has been at peace. It's like there's a discontent that floats about this grave, a powerful sense of unhappiness. Her spirit's here, Kath. It's here, and it's not at ease."

I actually tried to feel it. To feel it in the air I breathed, taking in a deep lungful. All I felt was a cool rush of air and my own discontent, my own unhappiness. Were they Amy's, too?

Jack said, "Wherever she is, she needs us to give her peace. She needs to know that we're all together, still love each other, no matter what. Sean needs to know it, too. Give me your hand."

I felt my eyes become wet. It hit me hard then. How mentally and emotionally hurt Jack was by all this trauma. Without a word, I meekly gave him my hand. Jack's callused skin felt so familiar. My spine tingled at his touch. I hadn't anticipated that. I felt something pass between us as I looked into his face. Despite everything, he was still the father of my children, still the first man I'd ever loved, the one I'd given my heart and soul to.

He placed my hand on top of Sean's. I felt the long, delicate manliness of my son's fingers. As a child, Sean always had such beautiful hands, just like my mom's—pianist's hands, my dad used to say. Their touch made me well up inside.

Jack said, "I have to be honest. Sometimes Sean asked about his mom, but I avoided talking about you in case it upset him. I only did it to protect him, to try to lessen the pain for him. Understand that, Kath. What he didn't hear or see he didn't think about. That was my reasoning."

"And Amy? What happened to her?"

"In the months after the crash, she started getting these seizures. Kevin got her to a hospital. They did all kinds of tests. He can explain better than I can. They put her on medication. It seemed to help, but within six months, she suffered a really bad seizure one night and couldn't breathe. It led to fatal complications, respiratory and cardiac failure. Kevin got here right away, but there was nothing he could do."

I felt those steel claws rip into my heart again, shredding me.

"She used to ask about you all the time. It was hard trying to steer her away from any talk of us as a family, so hard. I know how it hurts for you to know that, but it had to be done."

Jack's voice cracked with emotion. "Remember after Amy got out of the hospital that time, and we spent the evening on the hillside in the Smokies watching the fireflies? And the way we all felt, blessed and happy and together? We all need to know that kind of feeling again."

The hurt emanated from him. I felt a gash of pain in my chest. How could I forget such a perfect memory? Sean and Amy chasing a raging symphony of fireflies and the joy that Jack and I felt as parents.

Jack said, "Sean, move closer, son. Put your arm around your mom."

I couldn't speak. Wary still, Sean inched forward and put his arm around my shoulder. I felt the warmth of his breath on my cheek. He was still distant, still remote, but his father's word was law, and he seemed to relax a little, to slacken his unease around me. I wanted to weep as I felt his touch. Something primitive in me took over. I wanted to protect Sean.

We clung together, my cheek pressed hard against the headstone. In the heat of the night, it felt so cold at first, but then it warmed, seemed to become a part of us. It was strange, all of us clutching the granite as if we were holding on to a life raft in a storm.

Jack hunched us closer. I put my hand to Sean's face. This time, he didn't pull away. But then he broke down and cried, heart-wrenching sobs racking his body. Sean clung to the two of us. My heart felt as delicate as a silk thread. I heard Jack sobbing.

I wept, too, for all the joyous days we had lived together, for the love we'd known and lost. As we huddled, convulsed in tears, our emotions seemed to blend, like a deluge, and become a single, unified thing. I realized that there was reasoning in Jack's seeming madness. It was as if we completed a circle at the gravestone, Jack embracing one side of the granite, Sean the other, me in the middle, all of us clinging to the stone.

Clinging to the only solid reminder of Amy that we could touch somehow drew us together. No longer three but four.

And in so doing—as damaged and helpless, as raw and broken and lost a family as we were—we somehow became whole again.

91

Kevin half filled the glass in front of me with Four Roses bourbon.

"Help yourself to water and ice."

We were alone on the back porch. Jack had taken an exhausted Sean into the living room to settle him down for a nap so we could talk.

"How are you feeling?" Kevin asked.

"Mixed up. Stunned. Shocked. All of the above." I met his stare. "And sad. I'm wondering about the kind of bad luck my family has had. Wondering about ripples and family curses and if something bad someone in the family did is coming back to haunt us."

It was dark, just before or after midnight, I guessed. After sleeping so long, I felt disoriented. My eyes drifted back toward the trees that masked Amy's grave. I still felt crushed, the boulder still on my chest. Amy, my darling Amy. I still couldn't believe she was gone, that I would never see her again. I wanted it to be a dream, a nightmare, anything but the truth.

Kevin made a circular motion with his glass so that the ice cubes rattled. "You think it mattered, uniting at Amy's resting place?"

"Yes, I do."

"Jack always said he wanted you all to come together at her grave. To let her know you were all OK, that you loved her. He seemed to think that was important, to help you all heal."

"He was right about that. But otherwise, Jack isn't entirely right in his head, is he?"

"Probably not."

"Is he totally messed up?"

Kevin shrugged. "No, but sometimes he's better or worse than at other times. Sometimes he makes perfect sense, but other days the ghosts that haunt his head won't leave him in peace. To tell the truth, at times I really don't know what to make of him. Either way, it's not his fault. PTSD does that to you. It takes a brave person with a lot of strength and empathy to continue to love someone who suffers from it."

Kevin sipped from his glass, rattling the ice again. "What about Sean? Did you two get any closer?"

I took out a tissue and wiped my eyes. I'd cried so much the soft skin around my cheeks felt ablaze. Did I feel any closer to Sean? Yes, I did. He was the same vacant-stare Sean, but I felt more connected to him. In some small way, he acknowledged me as his mother, or at least someone connected to his life. I could still remember the tight feel of his hug, his hand clutching mine, the comforting feeling of his cheek beneath my fingers.

"Can anyone join the party, or do I need an invitation?"

I turned and saw Jack in the doorway.

"Give me a drink, Kev."

"Where's Sean?"

"Asleep."

"Better if you didn't booze."

Jack arched an eyebrow. "I'm not doing press-ups. And believe me, I need a shot of something. One won't hurt. Give me some ice."

Kevin tossed a fistful of cubes into a glass, splashed in some liquor, and handed it to Jack.

"You wanted explanations." Jack looked deep into my eyes. "Let's start with the crash. You wanted proof that it was deliberate."

"I'm listening."

"The pilot told me before we went down that the fuel feed line wasn't right, that it seemed like it was getting clogged. He'd flown that same aircraft for fifteen years, knew it like the back of his hand. He said the fuel line had been replaced only months ago and that it had been in perfect working order."

"That doesn't mean someone tampered with it. Parts can fail."

"You don't think I know that? I ain't delusional. The aircraft's fuel line was tampered with, Kath. We were meant to crash."

"Where's the proof? I don't want gut instinct, Jack, I want facts. So far, the NTSB hasn't come up with evidence of any sabotage."

"So far. But the NTSB knows nothing. Half the aircraft was shattered. They saw a wreck that was decaying in the woods for eight years. The site's been contaminated by nature and the elements. How could they ever know for sure?"

"Haven't they got experts?"

"And experts always get it right?"

"Meaning?"

"They'd never find the sabotage evidence. Not ever."

"Why not?"

"Because the people who tried to kill us are smart. The kind who could commit sabotage without leaving a shred of evidence. Who could find us no matter where we try to hide. They've got the means, the motives . . ."

"One thing at a time. How could they commit that kind of sabotage and get away with it?"

"It could be as simple as tossing a piece of rock salt into the fuel tank. It eventually causes a blockage. But salt breaks down over time, and the evidence disappears. Either in a fireball when the aircraft crashes, or it degrades to nothing over a period."

"Who are *they*?"

"The same people who'd have killed us all. Just like they killed DJ and his wife. That could have been us. They're the devil incarnate. Evil to the bone."

"Where's the proof, Jack? *Where?*" I felt so exasperated. "I don't see any proof. Can you back up what you say? Can you name names? Otherwise it sounds like madness, all of it. You're not giving me anything solid, Jack. Who sabotaged your plane? Who tried to kill you?"

He gave a lingering look over at Kevin, before turning back to me. "You need to ask your father that question."

"*What?*"

"You heard me. Ask him."

I looked at Jack, astonished at the hard, angry look on his face. "Are you saying my father had something to with your plane being sabotaged? That he'd conspire to try to kill his own grandchildren? That's— that's absurd."

Jack flung his glass across the room. It smashed against the wall, liquor dribbling everywhere, glass shards skittering all over the floor. "Kath, you haven't a clue!"

"My father wouldn't harm his own grandchildren. That's insane. He loved Sean and Amy."

"Just like he loved your mom?"

"What does that mean?"

"Kath, there are parts to this puzzle you can't even imagine. You don't know what's at stake. In war, even good people go bad."

It hit me then. "The note in my car, the photographs. It was you, wasn't it?"

He nodded. "Lusk did it for me. I wanted him to go on a recon to your place, see what he could find out, and warn you. He was an Army buddy, with me at Red Rock. I wanted to keep you away from me. I knew you'd come looking. Lusk delivered the message I asked him to. I just didn't want you getting hurt. I still don't."

"Why did Lusk kill himself?"

"Quentin had throat cancer, with months to live. I left an old boat for him at the marina in case he had to ditch his vehicle and bug out. But at the end of the day, he'd probably have put that gun to his head anyway. Saves a lot of explaining."

"If you had Lusk leave the note, you must have believed what it said. Unless you just meant to mess with my head?"

"I didn't. Your father killed your mother."

"How could you know that?"

"Call it instinct, call it gut, whatever. Why would your mother kill herself on your wedding day? You ever ask yourself that?"

"A lot."

"Unless it had some kind of deeper significance, I don't think she would have done it on such a day. And scar your life forever after with a brutal memory like that? As crazy as Martha Beth could be, I don't think that was her."

I said nothing.

Jack continued, "Maybe it was an argument that went wrong, maybe something more deliberate, but he killed her. I'd stake my life on it."

I looked at Kevin for some kind of affirmation. But he just looked back at me blankly, then stared down, eying the ice cubes in his glass, as if he wasn't sure of anything, or maybe he knew a lot more than he could say.

I said to Jack, "You know how that makes me feel?"

"Lousy. I'm sorry, but the truth always hurts."

"Are you telling me her death is tied in with the crash and the theft?"

"At a guess, she knew too much. Or threatened him in some way. But only your father can answer that. I don't trust him. I haven't for a long time."

I looked at Jack, my eyes asking why.

He met my stare. "You know what they say. If you dance with the devil, then you haven't got a clue. You think you'll change the devil, but the devil changes you."

"Meaning?"

"I think you know what I mean, Kath. You think he was the same man after he lost his foot? After the Army screwed him out of the Medal of Honor? After they shoved him out the door following Red Rock, like they couldn't wait to get rid of him?"

Jack held up two fingers, the tips almost touching. "Your father came that close to being court-martialed. He was one bitter bunny, was Frank. He tried not to show it to you, but he was an angry man, fuming. A man capable of anything. I saw that in him in his final days in Iraq. You didn't."

Jack had that faraway look in his eyes again, the look that told me something disturbing was going on inside his head. I was silent a few moments as I considered his words. I knew he was right about my father.

"You said there are parts to this puzzle I can't imagine. What did you mean?"

This time, it was Kevin who answered. "Kyle's attempted suicide, for starters."

"What about it?"

"Your kid brother was an idealist, brought up to believe in the honor of being a patriot. What he saw at Red Rock wasn't patriotism to him, it wasn't fighting for his country. Being a good soldier wasn't about massacring women and kids, mistake or otherwise. And it wasn't about being a party to theft."

"What does that mean?"

Jack said, "He knew about the stolen money. He was told to keep his mouth shut. That troubled him, caused him shame. Soldiers don't steal. Their watchword is honor. They don't enrich themselves, not even on the bodies of their enemy dead. And you wonder why he went over the edge?"

"Who exactly enriched themselves?"

Before Jack could reply, a harsh buzzer erupted, sounding like a house alarm, high-pitched, piercing our ears. The beat was so severe it made my chest thump. I guessed it was Kevin's early-warning system, because he was already grabbing a shotgun from the corner, making a dash toward the TV security monitor on the shelf.

I could make out a car halting at a wide gate. The shadowy figure of a man appeared to jump from it and pushed open the gate. Kevin grabbed a couple of black tactical flashlights and tossed one to Jack.

"Kill all the lights." Kevin started to hit the wall stitches and a lit lamp.

Jack killed the last wall switch. His flashlight flicked on, a powerful strobe at first, until he switched it to a low-powered blue beam and hurried to the window, clutching his pistol.

I watched the TV security screen as the shadowy figure climbed back into the car and drove on. A sickening feeling grew in the pit of my stomach.

Jack was watching the car, too. "You asked who enriched themselves? I think you're about to find out."

The car reappeared moments later in another camera shot that covered the farmhouse. The vehicle stopped again, and the man jumped out and started to move toward the farmhouse. As the figure came closer, I saw that he wore a hat, and his features became more distinct.

But I didn't need to see his features.

I recognized that limping walk anywhere.

So did Jack.

It was my father.

92

My father stepped toward the farmhouse.

Jack cocked his pistol. "What do you know? It seems the devil's come to us."

Astonished, I looked from Kevin to Jack, trying to figure it out "How did he know where we were?"

"I figured you were being followed, that someone might show up sooner or later."

I watched the screen in disbelief as my father moved up toward the patio.

Jack stepped toward the windows. "Kevin, keep watch on the rear."

"He's on his own. The other cameras are clear."

"I still don't trust him. Keep watch."

"Got it." Kevin hurried toward the kitchen door as Jack turned to watch from the window again.

I felt puzzlement, concern, fear, confusion, all running around inside my head like some insane circus parade. A second later, my father's voice boomed outside. "I know you're in there, Jack. It's me, Frank. I'm unarmed. We need to talk."

Jack didn't answer him but whispered to me, "I'll take a guess you'll have your questions answered soon enough."

I was tempted to call out to my father, but Jack put a finger to his lips to silence me. All the lights were still doused, except for the low-beam tactical flashlights Jack and Kevin carried. I could just about make out things in the room.

"You hear me, Jack? I'm coming in. I'm unarmed. I've got something important to say to you. We can all walk away from this without any harm being done." Silence, and then my father added, "Who's in there with you, Jack?"

Jack did not reply.

Kevin whispered from the back, "It's still all clear out here."

"What about the far perimeters?"

"I've got trip wires set up as far as two hundred fifty yards. Beyond that, I can't say."

"How do you think he found us?"

Kevin shook his head, and then Jack regarded me.

"Don't look at me like that," I said. "I never told my father you contacted me. I never told him anything."

Jack said, "Somebody did. Get back behind me. Don't make a sound or so much as move until I tell you to."

"What does he want?"

"We're about to find out. Now, get behind me, out of view in the kitchen, and keep your mouth shut."

"Why?"

"Don't question, just do." Impatience flared in Jack's voice.

I knew he was in military mode, and you didn't argue with him when he was like that, so I moved about twelve feet away, staying behind the kitchen door.

Outside, my father shouted, "You hear me, Jack? I'm coming in. Like I said, I'm unarmed. So don't go shooting. You've nothing to fear. I'll come in, and once I'm through the door, I'll lie flat on my face. You can search me."

Did my father know I was here? I heard footsteps moving up the wooden steps, then crossing the patio and stopping outside the door. The locked doorknob rattled. The it rattled some more.

"Jack? Are you in there?"

Jack reached over, flicked the lock, and called out, "Come inside. Do exactly as I tell you. Do anything I don't tell you to, and I'll shoot."

"Got it. I want no trouble, Jack."

"Open the door nice and easy. Take two slow steps inside. Keep your face forward, and don't look anywhere but straight ahead. Then don't take another step until I tell you to."

"Understood."

I heard the knob rattle again, and then the door was pushed in.

I saw my father step forward and stand maybe eight feet away. Jack's flashlight shone on him. He looked injured—his face was bruised, his right eye badly swollen.

He didn't looked left or right, just straight ahead, and he couldn't have seen me in the dark corner. "Jack? What now?"

The question was barely out of my father's mouth when Jack lunged, and the butt of his gun came down hard on the back of my father's skull.

As my father collapsed, Jack hit him again and again, furiously. I watched in shocked disbelief. My father tried to defend himself from the blows raining down, but Jack's attack was brutal and relentless, the pistol cracking into skull bone with a sickening noise. It was an abrupt attack, one that even a man as capable as my father could not defend himself against. Jack kept it up, striking my father a final blow on the back of the neck until he was unconscious.

"Jack, stop!" I screamed.

I grabbed hold of Jack's arm, but he was far stronger than me, and he pushed me aside as my father collapsed to the ground like a sack of corn.

A pair of handcuffs appeared from Kevin's pocket as he stepped in and helped Jack drag my father's limp body over to the couch. I saw blood ooze from the crown of his skull.

"Why?" I demanded.

"He got what he deserved." Rage was still blazing in Jack's eyes.

I glared back at him. "Don't hit him again. I don't want him hurt."

"Have it your way. Cuff him, Kev."

Kevin cuffed my father's hands and laid him on the couch. Jack leaned over the back of the couch as he tried to catch his breath.

Kevin laid a hand on Jack's shoulder. "Let me take a look at you, buddy. Are you OK?"

As Kevin checked Jack's wound, I saw the fury in Jack's eyes, and I figured from all the pent-up frustration on his face that it had probably been boiling up for years.

"No more exertion, Jack," Kevin said.

Then he probed the back of my father's skull. It was bleeding, the skin beneath his thinning hair cracked and gouged. Kevin felt his pulse. "He's got a head as tough as a jockey's hide, but he's out cold. He ought to come around soon. Here, give me my bag."

I handed him the black bag. He rummaged around, found some alcohol, and dabbed it onto my father's skull with some gauze, dried it off, shook on some kind of powdered antiseptic, and taped down a cotton pad on the crown to stop the bleeding.

Every now and then, Kevin flicked a look over at the TV security monitors, sweat beading on his brow. I figured he was worried, and that worry seemed to be spreading like a virus in the room. I began to feel an urgent sense of fear, of the unexpected, as if some kind of looming danger or an unknown evil was about to engulf us all. Sean was still asleep in the bedroom. At least he wasn't a witness to this, but I began to feel a growing concern for his safety.

Jack hid the light from his flashlight by pressing it against his side, then peered out the window. "I'm betting he's not the only one out there."

I was so afraid my heart was thudding "Who . . . who else is with him?"

"Every other devil in this drama, for all I know. Now, go get a bucket of cold water from the kitchen. You want answers to all those questions of yours, don't you? It's time to bring your father around."

93

Most guys dreamed about women. Babek dreamed about drones.

He was in love with them. Fantasized about them, bought magazines and books about them. As a kid in Iraq, he watched in rapt fascination as the early-version drones skimmed over towns and mudbrick villages, seeking out trouble. Sometimes they sent bombs and mortars and missiles raining down—always with deadly precision—on a threat, heavily armed insurgents about to launch an attack on Allied forces.

But sometimes they just watched, graceful, silent eyes pirouetting in the sky, gathering images and information. He was spellbound. Later, as a student at MIT, he helped design a bunch of drone projects.

In the dark warmth of the starry night, Babek stood on the edge of the road three hundred yards from the farm and started the Nighthawk's four sets of rotors, their hum a bare whisper. Then he hit the remote's buttons, and the drone lifted and hovered.

He fiddled with the remote, and the drone rose vertically two hundred feet in the air, high above any nearby trees. Babek could barely make it out against the sparkling night sky, but he didn't need to. The drone was programmed to fly in a two-hundred-yard circle, with the farmhouse at the epicenter. He could watch the camera inputs from inside the van.

He tweaked the remote again and saw the Nighthawk fly off in the direction of the farmhouse. Babek smiled, feeling pleased.

His father was once the top missile engineer on Saddam Hussein's Scud program. After the Americans invaded, he walked into U.S. military administration HQ with a treasure trove of missile blueprints, a list of all of Saddam's missile engineers, and the location of every Scud in Saddam's arsenal. A year of helping the Americans clean up the mess, and the family was allowed to emigrate to the U.S.

Engineering was in Babek's blood, and after he graduated from MIT, his dream was to start his own company. All he needed was cash. The money Tarik paid him for the occasional job sure helped, like the one at the Serenity Ridge home or bugging the vehicles Tarik told him to or following the woman's car to try to scan her cell phone's high-frequency transmissions when she was talking on it. Easy-peasy. The job he was doing now was more complex, unless you knew what you were doing. If you could afford the right equipment, as Tarik could, it was simple, really.

The Escalade SUV was pulled in off the private road. The metallic-gray walk-in Ford commercial van—Babek's communications van—was parked behind it. On top were two VHF aerials and the satellite dish. Babek was sweating as he stepped back inside the van.

"It's done."

Tarik and three men were crowded into the vehicle. They had AR-15s, shotguns, and automatic pistols. With Tarik were his son, Kiril, the bulldog-faced Mehmet, and the tall and muscled Abu. They were two heavies—literally—and the van seemed to tilt a little toward the back with their weight. On one side of the van, a laptop computer screen was on, and an ancient swivel chair was positioned in front of a dented old metal desk.

Everyone was watching the laptop's screen. Babek adjusted the hovering drone's camera angle until the infrared picture showed a bird's-eye view in the darkness, a greenish, almost ghoulish image of a man walking in the darkness toward the farm, on a road with woods on either side. Every few seconds, the drone moved forward, keeping the man's image on-screen.

Tarik said to Babek, "This equipment of yours had better be worth it. When will we hear something?"

Babek handed them each a set of headphones. "Soon enough, once he starts a dialogue. Here, put these on. You won't be disappointed, I promise you that."

They slipped on the headphones. The drone was up high and hovering, and all eyes were on the colonel's moving figure, the infrared camera working perfectly.

Tarik said, "What about the dog we heard earlier?"

Abu replied, "I took care of it. Some doped meat."

"Good." Tarik grinned at Babek. "Impressive. A silent camera in the sky, and the target doesn't even know they're being watched or listened to."

"You know Amazon is talking about using drones to speed up their deliveries?"

Kiril grinned at Babek's piece of trivia. "Yeah. I bet after the first drone arrives, another five show up bearing stuff Amazon thinks you might like."

"Shut it." Tarik was serious as he focused on the screen. "Tell me how it's all going to happen."

A glint sparked again in Babek's eyes. "You're going to love this . . ."

94

I hurried to the kitchen, found a plastic bucket, and filled it with cold tap water.

I felt a welter of confusion as I hauled the sloshing bucket back to the front room. Kevin dragged my father into a sitting position on the couch and patted him down for weapons. He found a cell phone.

"He's unarmed. All he had was this."

Jack said, "We'd better be sure. He's a wily old fox." His gaze shifted to me. "Your old man could probably still kill us all in a dozen different ways if he set his mind to it."

Jack did another check, even patted down my father's prosthetic foot, until he seemed satisfied. "He's clear. All he had was the cell."

Kevin tossed it onto the coffee table, and Jack said to me, "Step over into the kitchen, behind the door. Don't show your face when he becomes conscious, not until I tell you to."

"Why?"

"Just let me ask the questions for now. Kevin, drench him."

Kevin took the water bucket from my hands. I retreated behind the kitchen door and peered out through the crack between the door and the frame. Kevin doused my father's face and chest, two throws of water that saturated his clothes completely.

But my father was still out of it. Kevin slapped his face, and I saw my father's head jerk. He almost went under again, but Kevin gave him a few more slaps, and he came around, muttering.

"What the—"

His head arched back, and his eyes looked small and groggy. He struggled to free his hands, until he realized they were cuffed. Then he stared blankly at Jack, as if he were looking at a ghoul.

"Jack Hayes. My God. It's really you." A cry of pained exasperation escaped my father's lips. "Where's . . . where's Sean? And Amy?"

"We'll get to that. How'd you find us?"

My father didn't answer.

His silence didn't last long, though, because Jack put the gun barrel to his head. "If I have to ask again, I'm giving you a bump the size of a baseball."

"Tarik brought me here."

"Where's the conniving old snake?"

"Nearby."

"I asked where, exactly."

"Within a few hundred yards, that's all I know. Tarik told me to walk here. He wants to talk."

"I figured he might."

"All he wants is the third mask, Jack. The money, the bonds—whatever you did with them, it's all negotiable."

"What if I haven't got the mask?"

My father's face blanched a little more, and his jaw twitched.

"How did Tarik know where to find me?"

"I've no idea."

"What's in it for you, Frank?"

"Nothing. I just want everyone to walk away from this alive. There's been enough killing, enough death."

"And you really believe Tarik's going to go for that?"

"That depends on you, Jack."

Rage erupted on Jack's face. He struck my father a blow across the face, and it drew a streak of blood. Kevin grabbed Jack's hand and stopped him. "How, Frank? How exactly did Tarik know where to find me?"

"He's got the inside track. Someone's helping him."

"Who?"

"You're asking the wrong man. All I know is Tarik took a couple of calls on the way here. I figured someone was passing him information. But I've no idea who." He jerked his head to glance at Kevin. "You trust him?"

"With my life."

"I hope to God you're right."

"So what's your pitch, Frank?"

"Tarik's on his way. He wants to talk, make a deal. You know how important those masks are to him."

Jack considered, then glanced over my father's shoulder toward the kitchen door, as if trying to see my reaction.

"First you need to talk to someone who needs you to set things straight, Frank. Come over here."

Standing behind the door, looking through the crack, I heard the words and felt my pulse quicken like a drum roll.

I took slow, agonized steps from behind the kitchen door. The second my father saw me, his blood-streaked jaw dropped. I saw fear in his face.

"Kath . . ."

The sound of my name sounded like a cross between a cry of pain and a hoarse whisper.

My father looked at me, his mouth twisted, and then he turned away, unable to look at me, his eyes closed.

"You caused it, didn't you? All of it," I said.

"No, Kath, no. It wasn't all me." He took a deep, anguished breath.

Right then, I only had one question to ask, one question that haunted me. "You killed Mom, didn't you?"

This time, my father looked directly at me, his eyes meeting mine. I could decipher the look on his face before he even answered, a powerful sense of shame and grief that flooded his eyes, a look that made my blood run Arctic cold.

I saw it then, saw that I had fallen for my father's lies for years.

And that's when I really knew he killed her.

95

"It'll block any cell-phone signal. No calls in, no calls out. Including ours, unfortunately. Nothing I can do about that."

Babek had an arrogant look, the kind that the highly gifted sometimes reserve for those they consider of much lesser intelligence. He gestured to a homemade plastic control panel about six inches square. It had several switches and a dial, all connected to the laptop via a couple of USB connectors.

"Block everything except our walkie-talkies, correct?" Tarik plucked one of his slim cigars from his top pocket and lit it with a gold lighter. The stench of cigar smoke was overpowering in the van.

Babek hated smoking of any kind, but he knew better than to complain about his uncle's nasty habit. "Yes. You can use the walkie-talkies to communicate. They're on a different frequency."

"And the wire the colonel's wearing?"

"Same thing. It won't block that signal, either. He doesn't even know that the software bug is planted on his cell phone, because I downloaded it remotely. I even tweaked it so the microphone is at max sensitivity. It ought to pick up any chatter as soon as they start talking."

"What about the property's security system or any booby traps that might be around the place?" Tarik sucked on the cigar, blew out more smoke.

Babek coughed. The cigar stench was killing him. "I can't vouch for physical booby traps, like trip wires or whatever. But I did a frequency scan."

"And?"

"There's a security system in the area that's broadcasting on a few hundred megahertz. Judging by the signal strength, it probably belongs to the farm. I'm guessing there are remote sensors to pick up movement, and cameras, too."

Babek pointed to the control panel connected to the laptop. "But that will take care of any signals we want to block."

"Meaning?"

"I can interfere with the security system, including any remote sensors. Whoever's watching the input to the security cameras won't see anything on-screen except snow." Babek grinned. "So they won't see you guys coming."

"If you're wrong, we could be dead."

Babek's grin widened. "Trust me. I want to get paid."

Tarik nodded toward Babek's homemade panel. "That thing of yours won't affect the drone?"

"No. It works on a different frequency. It's all about frequencies. Once they're different, they won't interfere."

Tarik said, "What about other devices?"

Babek nodded. "You still need to watch these rednecks, they're pretty cunning, so keep a lookout for trip-wire flares and stuff like that. The gear I've seen them buying at gun shows freaks me out. Trip-wire explosives, detonators, bomb-making equipment. But I reckon if you stick to the main road once the cameras are out of action and watch the road ahead of you, you should be OK."

Tarik patted Babek's jaw with the palm of his hand. "You're a clever boy. We could have done with the likes of you when we were crippling the Americans with our IEDs."

Babek pushed one of his earphones closer to his head. "I think we've got something."

They all listened on their headphones and heard the booming voice in their ears. "I know you're in there, Jack. It's me, Frank. I'm unarmed. We need to talk."

Then silence.

They waited, but no other sound came.

Until they heard a grunt. All of them turned to look toward the far end of the van.

The young man from Serenity Ridge was lying on the floor and tied with rope. Silver duct tape was plastered around his mouth. He looked horrible. Sweat glittered around his eyes and on his brow as he became conscious, the sedative wearing off. Even his spiky hair looked wild from living too long among the depressed, the disturbed, and the eccentric. Terror lit up his eyes as soon as he saw the van's occupants and the unfamiliar environment.

Tarik sucked on his cigar, blew out a ring of smoke. "Time to go meet them. See if they take the bait. If not, we do it the hard way."

96

"Hang a right."

"You sure?"

Tanner was driving as Courtney studied the colored image on her cell-phone screen. "You don't argue with Google Maps. No point. Nobody answers back."

"How far?"

"Going by the scale, I'd reckon about five hundred yards." Courtney peered into the blackness beyond the wash of the headlights. "Hey, you think it's wise knocking on doors in the middle of nowhere in darkness? Let's pull in and take a sec to figure out what to do next."

"Sure." Tanner pulled in on a rutted gravel track.

The headlights flooded the track for about fifty yards ahead. A telegraph pole with a sulfur-yellow light on top saturated the wooden entrance gate to a property, the hinges hanging off and the gate wide open.

Courtney rolled down the passenger window and inhaled. A piney-fresh smell. Big dark spaces and the twinkle of a few distant lights. They were deep in the countryside, and even the highway they left ten minutes ago had been deserted. It had been a long day's driving.

They'd visited ex-sergeant Dan Riker's address in Cooke County, only to be met by his mother, a rake-thin elderly woman who told them that her son had attempted suicide three months ago and was in a VA psychiatric hospital in Cincinnati.

Then there was a long drive to Asheville to find Joe Feld, only to learn that he had moved to Alaska, where he was now a state trooper.

Tanner killed the engine and flicked off the headlights, and they were smothered in complete darkness until Courtney turned on the map light.

"What's wrong, Tanner? You look reflective."

"Reminds me of home. I spent the first half of my life trying to get away from crappy countryside like this. Nowhere places with minds as narrow as the back roads."

"Not so many happy memories, huh?"

"Fish fry on a Saturday night. Wearing camo when you're not even hunting. The smell of manure and the sound of crickets. The only big dream you had was of owning a truck. Need I go on?"

"Doesn't matter if you divorce your wife, she's still your sister or your cousin or whatever."

Tanner smiled and nodded. "You got it."

Courtney peered ahead again, pursing her lips in thought. "If Dr. Kevin Borovsky is here, being a veteran and a farm dweller, chances are he's going to be prepared for unwanted visitors. I don't want to charge in anywhere without some kind of plan. Let's take a look around. Keep the flashlights off for now, but leave the headlights on, dipped."

"With you on that one." Tanner switched on the headlights, and the woods around them were softly illuminated for a few dozen yards on either side.

Courtney took a flashlight but left it off as she stepped out of the car.

Tanner followed her. They walked farther along the dimly lit track. Not a sound intruded. Tanner took a deep breath. The piney smell drenched the air. "What's on your mind?"

Courtney stood with her hands on her hips, thinking as she looked around the landscape, with distant house lights visible through the trees. "A few things. You got a flasher in that car, Tanner?"

"Sure. Why?"

"Might be better if we put it on and drive right on up to the house. That way, no one's under any illusions."

"Yeah, you're probably right."

"Got a carbine?"

"Yeah, a full-auto Colt AR in the trunk and six loaded mags. In a rifle bag, with my armored vest, next to yours."

"You came prepared."

"Always like to be."

"How about you drive and I ride shotgun, just in case? Unless you want to toss for it?"

Tanner grinned. "Being a betting man, why not?"

He took a quarter from his pocket and tossed it. In the soft wash of the dipped headlights, he watched the coin spin in the air. As the quarter landed in his palm, he looked up, and his jaw went slack.

Courtney's Sig pistol was out, and she racked it, the barrel pointed right in Tanner's face.

His mouth fell open like a dead fish.

"Sorry, Tanner. We've got a change of plan, big man."

97

"Why? Why did you kill her?"

My eyes flooded. My hands tightened into fists. I saw the struggle in my father's face as he stared at me, and I imagined there was a battle going on inside him between self-preservation and honesty. It was a while before he answered.

"Kath, there's a lot you don't understand."

"You can say that again."

"Maybe you'll never understand."

"Try me."

My whole body felt cold. I wanted to ask again why he did it. But nothing came out. The words just stuck in my throat.

"I killed her. But not in the way you think." My father's eyes were moist.

"I know about the massacre. I know about the missing money and artifacts. So just tell me the truth this time. No more lies, no smoke screens. I'm done with those."

I saw Jack and Kevin look at me, register my anger. But they said nothing.

My father just sat there, his hands clasped together in the cuffs. He shut his eyes tightly. Shut them so tightly it seemed as if he was trying to shut down all his senses. When he opened his eyes again, he looked up at me.

"In the weeks before Kyle tried to hang himself, your mom had been drinking heavily. The son who went to war wasn't the son who came home. She was finding it hard.

"It didn't help that things hadn't been good between us once I was retired. I was crippled, my career gone. It all only added to your mom's woes. She had a lot to deal with. Kyle's PTSD, her own disappointments, a life squandered with alcohol. We argued a lot. And the more we argued, the more she hit the bottle. Until one night, I hit it hard, too, we had a raging argument, and the truth came out."

He met my stare. "That's when I told her what had happened at Red Rock. Told her everything. About the massacre, the money, the reasons for Kyle's disillusionment and depression. I told her the truth. That our son went to war believing it was an honorable thing to do to fight for your country. Honor was in our genes. And sure, sometimes war can be honorable. Sometimes there are still causes worth fighting for."

He shook his head. "But Kyle didn't find it so. All he found was sheer brutality like that little flower girl being mowed down, a callous gun battle that killed dozens of women and children, and a question mark over his father's integrity because I was a party to hushing it up."

"He knew?"

"Kyle wasn't dumb. He had ears. And we talked. I didn't tell him everything, I didn't tell him the whole truth, I didn't tell him about the money, but then I didn't have to. The truth was, I was ashamed. Me, I was done with the Army—they'd used me, scapegoated me, thrown me aside. The Medal of Honor was the last straw."

He sighed. "But Kyle was a righteous kid. He hadn't grown cynical like me. He still believed in truth and honor. He still believed in the code. That a good officer does not lie, cheat, steal, or tolerate those who do."

"You took the money?"

"Yes, I took it. When I heard they screwed me out of the medal, I almost felt I was owed it. If that makes any sense?"

I couldn't answer that.

My father took another deep breath, let it out slowly, as if it almost hurt. "That's war for you. It changes you. Makes you a cynic. But I knew I couldn't ever tell Kyle. I knew the truth would have been a total heart-ripper. Everything he grew up believing would have been a total lie. He'd always idolized me. But I told your mom. And that was my big mistake."

"What do you mean?"

"A while before Kyle tried to hang himself, your mom took herself a bottle and went to talk to him."

I looked at him, waiting.

"She had a little drunken chitchat."

"About what?'

"About everything. About Kyle's problems, the massacre, the little flower girl, the missing money, and his fine, upstanding father being a criminal. She told him everything I told her. In her sad, disillusioned way, she thought talking about it would help. Big mistake."

He shook his head. "It was the worst thing she could have done. Kyle didn't want to remember, he wanted to forget. It just brought it all back. Made him relive the terror and the pain of it all. It all came back and hit him like a swinging bat. And your mom telling him about me taking the money, that shook the life out of him. He couldn't believe it. Couldn't face up to that. He just couldn't. But your mom was drunk and angry.

"And when she was drunk and angry, there was never any reasoning with her or stopping her. To make things worse, she confronted Kyle, cussed him out, called him a coward for not facing up to whatever it was he needed to face up to. Kyle took it badly. The confrontation sent him over the edge. That's . . . that's why he drove to the park."

His voice softened to a hoarse whisper, and he looked me in the face. "And that's why your mother decided to end it all. Not because she could never forgive me but because she could never forgive herself about Kyle. I guess I couldn't, either, because I didn't try to stop her when she put the gun to her head."

"You . . . you were there?"

"I went looking for her when she disappeared on your wedding day. When I didn't find her in her favorite bar, I drove on home and found her in the bedroom with a gun in one hand and a bottle of pills in the other. She told me she wanted to kill herself.

"She'd threatened it before. This time, I knew she really wanted to do it, and nothing I could say or do was going to stop her. I knew she couldn't live without Kyle, and I knew she'd had enough. Of her own life, of mine, of everything . . ."

His voice trailed off, became hoarse. "And she was afraid. For all the dreams she had of wealth, she didn't want a penny of it. Tainted money, she called it. I tried to justify it. Told her lots of others had prospered doing the same. Military personnel, American businessmen and politicians. It was hard not to, there was so much money flying around. But she said I was a fool, that I'd be found out and disgraced.

"That played on her mind, too—the fear of disgrace. The fact that I might be court-martialed, our name dragged through the mud. She couldn't have handled that. She was already broken. All those high-class dreams, all those hopes that dirt-poor little girl from Temperance once had, they had all come to nothing in the end. At least, in her mind." He looked at me, his eyes wet. "You understand?"

I did.

I felt my eyes become wet, too.

I looked at Jack. He said nothing. Just stared back at me blankly. Whether it mattered to him or not, I couldn't say, but I figured he knew I needed to hear this, that I was owed it, so he kept his mouth shut.

My father said, "I walked out of the room and left her there with that gun in her hand. And to tell the truth, I didn't care if she pulled the trigger or not. Maybe I even wanted her to. Because I figured at last she'd find some kind of peace."

He was crying.

I knew then, right then, that he was telling me the truth. Real honesty tastes and smells like nothing else, has a flavor all its own.

Something else. The rock I once clung to, the solid granite that was always my refuge, my sanctuary—I felt my fingers finally loosen their grip and slip away, as if I were letting go of a ghost.

"Why didn't you tell the police?" I asked him.

"How would that have helped? If they started probing, looking into everything? God knows what they would have found." He shook his head. "I did the sensible thing and kept my mouth shut."

"The police found the word *Red* scrawled on a page from her diary . . ." I left the statement hanging in the wind.

He shook his head. "I never figured on that. She must have written it all down in her diary, everything I told her, and kept it in her safe. But before she killed herself, she must have torn up the pages and burned them. Maybe that piece of torn paper just slipped away and she didn't see it. Or maybe she left it there deliberately to cause me trouble. I like to think not. But I don't know."

"What happened to the money?"

"I never even touched a penny. Every cent is in an offshore account for Kyle, if ever he needs it."

My father's phone rang. The electronic music jangled harshly and caught everyone off guard. It kept ringing until Jack grabbed it and looked at the number. He showed it to my father. "Who?"

"Tarik."

"What does he want?"

"What I told you. But first he wants to talk."

"Why do I get the feeling that's not all there is to it, Frank?"

My father said nothing, but I sensed there was more, too, something he wasn't saying.

Jack stared at my father. "For all I know, you could be on Tarik's team, working with him, playing this out for all it's worth."

"You're wrong, Jack."

Jack hit the answer button and punched the speaker symbol. "Tarik?"

"Jack!" Tarik's voice boomed. "Welcome back to the land of the living, old friend. It's been a long time."

"Not long enough, Tarik. And if I have my way, you're headed to hell."

Tarik gave a laugh. "That's what I like about you, Jack. Direct, to the point. I'm here to tell you we can talk this out. Settle our unfinished business in a peaceful manner so that nobody gets hurt and everyone walks away happy as pigs in dirt."

"If you think I can believe that, you're nuts, you scumbag."

"I mean it. I want this settled peacefully, no trouble. That's why I'm coming in to talk. One minute. And I've taken precautions. Better hold off on any inclination to shoot. You use any guns, and you're all dead. The colonel will explain."

Tarik let his words hang. "Try to run, try to hide, and that would be unfortunate. And don't even think of trying to call 911 for help. It's a waste of time. After we end this call, your phones will only work when I want them to. One minute. The clock's ticking. Can you feel the tension, Jack? Just like the old days in Iraq, isn't it? See you soon, old friend."

The line went dead.

Kevin said to my father, "What's Tarik talking about?"

"He's got electronic equipment that can block any cell-phone signals. No one can make a call within a few hundred yards' radius without him allowing it. Same with any security system—it gets interfered with. He's also got a drone up in the air, with an infrared camera that can see in the dark. He can see everything move on the farm."

I could see the pressure was getting to Jack, and he was still grimacing with pain, sweat glistening on his face as he said to my father, "Anything else we need to know about?"

"In Tarik's mind, you're still the weak link. The loose cannon. I think he wants you gone. Gone for good. Maybe me, too."

"Why you?"

"Because he doesn't have a hold over me anymore."

"Explain."

"I don't care if this thing falls apart and we all go to hell together. Tarik knows that now. Knows he'll need leverage."

"I'm finding it hard to believe you, Frank."

"Look at my cell phone. Go to the photo gallery. Look at the last photo stored there." My father gave me a look, and something about it made my heart plummet.

His hands and jaw were trembling.

Jack fiddled with the phone. He must have found what he was looking for, because he stared at my father and then at me.

"What is it?" I asked.

He turned the screen around to show me.

I almost choked as I sucked a breath into my lungs. It was a photo of Kyle. My brother looked beaten, his face was bruised, and he was tied up, his head tilted to one side. He looked pitiful. Sweat glittered on his face, and his hair was wild. Tears streamed down his face, the skin of his cheeks raw from crying. Silver duct tape was wrapped tightly around his mouth.

"Tarik has Kyle. He abducted him, Kath. There was nothing I could do."

Outside, we heard footsteps mount the patio and move heavily across the wood, as if to announce their arrival.

Tarik.

My father looked at me, then at Jack and Kevin. "If he doesn't get what he wants, he'll kill Kyle. And then he'll kill us all."

98

The footsteps echoed on the wooden porch, and then the doorknob twisted. A second later, it was pushed in.

Tarik stood there.

I was surprised. Gone were the dark suit, white shirt, and black tie. Instead he wore a black leather jacket, a pale linen shirt, and jeans that made him look younger.

The fact that Jack and Kevin had firearms pointed at him didn't seem to bother Tarik in the least as he surveyed the room. He nodded to my father, then the others. "It's like old times again. A reunion."

"Get to the offer, Tarik. Let's hear it."

"All your guns on the floor first. Kick them forward, away from you."

Nobody did anything, and Tarik said calmly, "I have my people outside. They will kill Kyle. On the floor. Now. I will not say it again."

Kevin and Jack placed their firearms on the floor and kicked them away.

"Stand up, and turn away from me. I want to frisk you for weapons. I won't warn you again what will happen if you don't comply." Tarik looked at me. "You, too. Turn around, hands up high."

Kevin and Jack turned around. I followed. I heard a scraping noise, their firearms being swept away. I glimpsed Tarik starting to pat down Kevin and Jack, and then he snapped at me, "Look away."

I obeyed. Seconds later, I felt his hands as they slid everywhere over my body, in the area of my breasts and between my legs, leaving nowhere untouched. I recoiled.

"You can turn back around now."

We turned.

Tarik smiled, pulled up one of the chairs, and sat, taking out a slim cigar as he did so. He lit it with a gold lighter, blew a coil of smoke to the ceiling. "Sit."

"You going to get to the point, Tarik?"

Tarik smiled back at Jack. "Just as soon as our next guests arrive. Then it will be time to put all our cards on the table."

"Keep your hands high, Tanner. Right up, high as they'll go."

Tanner obeyed, his jacket far above his waist, his shirt lifting, too, showing his stomach. "You mind telling me what in the name of insanity is going on?"

"You and I need to have a talk, big man."

"You been smoking something funny? Taking any pills you shouldn't?"

Courtney raised a querying eyebrow.

"You're probably a tad young to be nutty menopausal, but you never know."

"I'm coming over to take your firearm, Tanner. You move any which way, you get a bullet. Your choice."

"I've made my choice. Go ahead and take it. All I want is an explanation."

Courtney inched forward, stretching her free hand out to flick off the thumb break on Tanner's leather holster, then gripped the Glock and removed it. She stuffed it into her pocket.

"Now do I get an explanation?"

"Open your trousers belt, loosen the buttons or zipper. All real careful and slow. Drop your trousers, then turn around. Put your hands on the hood of the car."

"I already had my prostate exam six months ago."

"You're sure a funny one, Tanner."

"Here's something even funnier. I figure there are a lot of guys who'd pay good money for an experience like this. But sister, I ain't one of them. Are you for *real*?"

"I want to make sure you don't run anywhere or make any sudden moves. Trousers down around your ankles always help in that regard."

"Tell me this ain't going to get all sexual. A dark, remote country lane, a helpless victim . . ."

"No chance."

"Lucky I'm wearing my best underwear. So me thinking that maybe you were into me was pretty much delusional?"

"I'm going to search you."

"Are you for *real*? Search me for what, exactly?"

Courtney waved the Sig in Tanner's face.

"All I can say is, you'd better have a darn good reason for this, honey. CID agent or not, you're looking at some serious court time for threatening a federal agent with a deadly weapon."

"Turn. Do it."

Tanner unbuckled his belt, opened the button and zipper. His trousers fell. He wore black-and-white-striped boxers.

"Cute."

"Thanks."

"Turn."

He turned and spread his hands out on the car's hood. Courtney moved up to him cautiously, her hands going into his pocket, taking out his wallet and his cell phone and patting him down. When she got to his ankles, she said, "No backup?"

"Hard to reach an ankle holster when you're carrying extra pounds. A man's liable to keel over and shoot himself."

"Stay where you are. Hands on the hood. Makes it easier for me to watch you."

"You're sure you're not just checking out my rear?"

"Pretty sure."

"So when do I get an explanation?"

Courtney flicked on her flashlight, put the bottom end in her mouth to grip it, and opened Tanner's wallet. She rifled through the contents, then tossed the wallet onto the ground.

Next, she looked at the cell phone, pressing a key, the screen lighting up. "No password?"

"Too fiddly."

"That's not clever, Tanner."

"What the heck are you on about?"

Courtney scrolled down through the cell. After a few seconds, she seemed to find something and looked up, the Sig still pointed at Tanner.

She smiled. "And I thought you said you came prepared. I can see all your calls and texts here. Anyone could scroll through your phone."

"Nobody does. I even sleep with the darn thing. There's nothing important there. Are we done yet?"

Courtney scrolled though Tanner's phone, her lips tightening.

She looked at the screen, then scrolled backward and forward.

"You called the same number eight times in the last seven hours. It called you twice."

"So? I took a few calls."

"It ain't your office number, and it ain't your buddy Agent Breedon. I know both those numbers. Want to tell me who it is you've been calling?"

"What's up your nose, Courtney?"

"You told Dexter your home was burned down soon after you were working the Jack Hayes case the first time around. But that isn't so. You were looking for help from Dexter, for sympathy. Wanting to get to the fifty-yard line before everyone else."

"You reckon?"

"Dexter thought so, even if he felt sorry for you. But why you wanted the inside track I wasn't sure. All I've got is my gut. And then I had Agent Stone probe around your background."

"That's the problem these days, so easy to do. You part your hair on the wrong side, and it's on social media."

"I didn't need social media, Tanner. And the parting in question didn't have to do with your hair but with your wife. Stone and I have a few fed connections we spoke to off the record. The whole wife dying thing was bull. Not so much bull as a time shift. Your wife died four years ago, and yeah, it was in a fire at your home, but there was no talk of any criminal aspect to it, unless you include the fact that the police questioned you on and off for three months, until they backed off for lack of evidence. All of which set the hairs on my neck on end."

Tanner said nothing, just raised his eyes, his lips turned down in a dismal expression.

"But then, I'm betting a guy like you would know how to take care of something like a troublesome wife. Not that I'm suggesting anything, Tanner, merely making a professional observation. Folks like us in the business, we know things, have the inside track. Either way, you lied. And if you lied to Dexter, you probably lied to me in some way. Liars can't stop lying."

Tanner almost smiled. "You finished with the insight and observations rant?"

"For now."

"You're a clever lady, ain't you? I've learned something. It hammers home an old truism."

"Yeah?"

"Never underestimate a woman. They're detectives by nature. Can I add never trust a little guy like Dexter with wiry hair who looks like a woman?"

"You want Jack, that much I'm certain of, but if it's for the right reasons, I don't know. That's just my gut talking, because something sure smells. You going to tell me the truth?"

Tanner was silent.

Courtney held up the phone. "What if I called this number now?"

"Wouldn't do any good."

"Why not?"

"Because your cell won't work."

Courtney hit the call button on the last number and held the phone to her ear. Dead. She called 911. Her hands were shaking, and the phone was still silent. Tanner just stood there looking at her, his own hands on the hood.

"You hear anything?"

"No."

"Told you."

They both heard the sound of a car. It came closer, and then they saw the headlights.

Courtney licked her lips, a strange kind of fear growing inside her. She kept her Sig trained on Tanner. "What's going down here, Tanner?"

Tanner said nothing.

"Tell me, Tanner."

"I'd be careful with that gun if I were you. There's someone wants to talk to you, put a proposition to you. If I were you, and I wanted to walk away from this alive, I'd listen."

And the sound of the car drew closer.

99

A gleaming black Mercedes GL appeared from around the bend in the track, bumping over the ruts.

It drove closer until it stopped in the twilight. Two men got out of the front, both armed with MP5 machine pistols. A man stepped out of the rear, wearing a dark Nike jacket and jeans, his black shoes polished like glassy porcelain.

Courtney recognized Chad Benton at once.

He touched his forehead in a mock salute. "Courtney."

"Stop right there. You going to tell me what's going on, or do I have to shoot someone first?"

Chad shook his head. "Wouldn't get you far. A Sig against two MP5s. It's no competition."

"I'd take one of you with me first. Maybe even two. One of them could be you."

A brief smile raked his face. "The thing is, there's no need for violence. It's highly overrated as a means of persuasion. That's what I always tell my customers. You don't go in with a sledgehammer or guns blazing. Know what you go in with first?"

"Tell me, Chad."

"A checkbook. Money always speaks louder and faster than lead."

"I'm listening."

"Take Tanner here, for example. Every man has his price. Not so much his price as his sense of what's rational. See no evil, hear no evil, speak no evil. Simple as that."

Courtney looked across. "What's your price for looking the other way, Tanner?"

He winked. "It's a lot higher than a government pension, I can tell you that for nothing."

Courtney moved nervously on the balls of her feet, keeping her eyes on the two armed men and her gun pointed at Chad. "So where does this go next? You think you've figured out my price?"

"You like the good things in life, Courtney. We can come to some arrangement. It's retirement time soon. You can make sure it's comfortable. A beach somewhere. A boat, maybe. No shortage of cash."

"What are we talking here? Millions?"

Chad gave a tight smile. "You bet. Many millions. We can get to the exact figure in a minute. But I think I know you, Courtney. You're a practical woman. You're the kind of woman I can do business with."

Courtney nervously licked her lips. "You just may be right."

"I know I am."

"And in return?"

"Any dots you connected regarding me in all of this, you unconnect. Anything I ask you to ignore, you do so. I'm doing this because we've been friends a long time, Courtney. And because killing you, or anybody else, wouldn't exactly look good. It never does. It always comes back to haunt you."

"You mean like those two women at Serenity Ridge?"

Chad's mouth twisted. "That was truly unfortunate."

"No, it was murder."

"Not me. And I hate mistakes like that."

"Tarik?"

"Yeah. His people got trigger-happy." Chad sighed. "Look, all I want is for you to listen to what I have to say. Can you do that?"

"Maybe. But I've got one condition."

"Name it."

"You tell me the truth. And I mean the truth. Tell me everything. Lay it out, no lies, no cover-ups. Then I'll know if I can trust you enough for us to come to some kind of deal."

He thought about it a second, nodded, and indicated a tree stump. "Mind if I sit?"

Courtney shook her head, keeping her Sig pointed.

Chad pinched his trousers and sat. He raised his right hand and said to the men behind him, "No need to point at anyone."

The men lowered their weapons. Courtney kept hers on point.

Chad looked at the ground a moment, deep in thought, took a long sigh, and looked up. "Here's how it is. The real deal, the full story. That day near Babylon, Tarik took off with the money. All twenty-five million."

"Let me guess. It was all a setup right from the start?"

Chad shook his head from side to side. "Well, not so much a setup as an understanding."

"Meaning?"

"If it failed, there was nothing, no deal. If it worked, there was twenty-five million in a truck, the masks, and a whole bunch of artifacts. I didn't need the money, but I liked the idea of those artifacts."

"Don't tell me. Your old man had a collection."

Chad smiled. "One of the best."

"And you've added to it?"

Chad shrugged. "Be impossible to prove. Artifacts can be stored in a bank vault halfway around the globe. Lots of ways to keep them hidden."

"So Tarik got the money and the masks, and you got the artifacts."

"That's about it."

"What about the others? Jack. Kath's dad. They got their cut?"

"Yeah. They got their cut. Kept it offshore. Safer that way, not in their accounts, no way to trace it. Doled out when they wanted it. Of course, it called for a lot of trust, but we trusted each other." Chad smiled. "At least, the colonel, Jack, and I did. None of us trusted Tarik."

"Who was in on it?"

Chad nodded. "Me, Tarik, the colonel. We all hatched the plan. Frank wasn't a happy man about the medal thing, being snubbed, and still took a little convincing until he went with it."

"And Jack?"

"He went along with it, reluctantly, I always thought. When his mind started to go from PTSD, he became a weak link. For a time, I actually thought he was going to be OK, but . . ."

Chad tilted his head to one side and shrugged his shoulders. "But I always trusted him. Trusted him enough to have him fly to the Caymans and bring me back cash when I needed it and one of the masks that Tarik had stashed there. Jack always did those secret runs for me. Except this time, something went wrong."

"What do you mean?"

"I called Jack when he got back to New Orleans from the Caymans. We had an argument, a dumb argument, and he told me he was sick of playing gofer. That he was bailing out. Didn't want to do it anymore. I figured his mind was going, getting worse. Or maybe not. Maybe it was just the stress of doing something illegal. But that's when I just knew I couldn't trust him anymore. That he was a liability."

"The plane crash was your doing?"

"Can I plead the Fifth on that?"

"Why?"

"Not saying I didn't think about it, but really, the plane crash was an accident."

"The heck it was."

"Believe what you want to. But I'd never crash a plane with Jack's kids on board. You think I'm some kind of monster?"

"I don't now. But part of me isn't convinced that you're not lying, Chad."

"You'll believe what you want no matter what I say. But it's time to make up your mind, Courtney. Are you with me, like sensible Mr. Tanner here? Are you going to win the jackpot, or are you against me?"

Chad stood.

Courtney kept her Sig pointed at him. "Where are you going?"

"To the farm. Jack's there. And Kath and Sean. The colonel. Even Tarik."

"Tarik?"

"You heard me. We're headed to a reunion."

"What about Amy?"

"I don't know about her."

"What's your plan?"

"We need to talk this all out. A reunion. See if there's a way we can find common ground. Besides, we know each other. We're friends, or we used to be. No one needs to get hurt. We've all got a vested interest. But everyone's got to be up front, and everyone's got to be honest about what they want. Can you do that?"

Courtney said nothing.

Chad said, "As a sign of my honorable intent, why don't you hold on to that gun of yours, honey?"

"Don't 'honey' me." Courtney looked doubtful. "Honorable intent? I sure wish I knew you had that in you, Chad."

"I do." Chad stood, offered his hand, "Well, have we got a deal?"

Courtney ignored his hand.

Chad's head tilted to one side again, in query. "Is that a yes or a no?"

"I've got one more condition."

100

I heard the footsteps on the patio grow louder.

The room was silent, Tarik waiting patiently, alert to the sounds outside, the front door left open a crack. Nobody moved. Jack, Kevin, and I were anxious. My father seemed in another world, dazed, his jaw slack. As if he'd just gone a battering ten rounds with a heavyweight and was facing another ten. I couldn't tell if he was deep in thought or spaced out.

He looked toward the door—we all did—as the footsteps halted outside.

Tarik stared at us each in turn, Jack and Kevin in particular, then my father and me. "I want you to listen to what has to be said. It's important. No trouble, no violence. Is everyone clear? This can be settled peacefully, unless you want Kyle hurt?"

He let his threat hang in the air. Nobody spoke.

The door swung in on its hinges. Two armed men entered, their MP5 machine pistols at the ready. They scanned the room and took up positions on either side of the door. I recognized one of them, a big guy with blond hair, from Chad's bodyguard detail.

Chad came in after them. He appeared tense, dressed casually in a dark Nike jacket and jeans. I felt a pain in my heart, sharp as a stiletto.

"Hello, Kath."

He must have seen the trauma on my face as he gave me a silent nod. I stared disbelievingly at him, and then my heart raced even faster when I saw Courtney enter the room behind him.

I didn't understand what was going on. Courtney clutched her Sig in one hand, the other bracing it for support, and she covered the room as if she was ready to shoot someone. She looked on edge.

Her eyes darted around every now and then, watching Jack and Kevin, my father, and Chad's men, before they settled on me.

I didn't get it, didn't get any of this.

Whose side was she on?

Chad said, "Tell her."

Courtney licked dry lips. "We need to talk some things out, Kath. Chad wants you to hear a proposition. I think you all need to listen."

I didn't like the sound of this at all.

Courtney swallowed. "I'm just trying to be realistic here, Kath. There's some stuff we all need to tease out. Real important stuff."

"What's that supposed to mean?"

Courtney seemed lost for words and glanced at Chad.

I met her eyes. "Whose side are you on, Courtney?"

She bit her lip, as if unsure. "Can we have some privacy, Chad?"

Chad gave a jerk of his head to his men. "Step outside, and stay by the door. I'll call if I need you."

The men slipped out onto the patio, leaving the door open. I could see them take up positions, one watching through the window, the other through the open door, ready to move back inside at a second's notice.

I turned to Courtney. "I'm waiting for an answer. Whose side are you on?"

"Kath, look, I don't know how to put this . . ."

Chad seemed to have the answer for her. "Courtney believes we all have a vested interest in being sensible. That all of us can walk away from this with our pockets full and our lives intact. She thinks it wise that you listen carefully to what Tarik and I have to say. That any bloodshed or recrimination serves no purpose. Isn't that right?"

Courtney gave a tiny nod. "You need to listen to what needs to be said, Kath."

Courtney was on Chad's side. That much was obvious.

But why?

I stared him down, feeling it all fall into place. "Walk away with our pockets full. Is that what this is really about, Chad? Money, artifacts. You were part of it, too. A big part or a small part? Which is it, Chad? How deep did your lies go?"

Chad pulled up a chair, sat, crossed his legs, and tugged at his trousers. Arrogance in the gesture. "I played a part, sure. Like your father, like Tarik, and like Jack here. We all did. It was a team effort. No use lying anymore."

His words set Jack's eyes on fire, and he seemed to lose it, his fists clenched like steel balls as he lunged from his chair. "You're a scumbag, Chad. A liar and a thief. You set it all up!"

He stabbed a finger at Chad. "You caused the plane to crash. You caused all of this . . . with your greed, your scheming. What's the matter? Didn't you have enough money?" Jack's eyes blazed at me. "He killed Amy. He killed our daughter."

His mouth was frothing with spittle, and Kevin grabbed his arm, struggled to hold him back. "No, Jack, don't lose it, man."

Jack's eyes were wet, and I knew by the wild look on his face that his mind was in overdrive, but then so was mine once I heard his words.

Chad shook his head. "No, I didn't, Jack. You're wrong there. You can claim what you want, but the crash wasn't my fault. It was simply whatever it was—engine failure, weather, a combination of events, but it wasn't me, Jack. Your mind's haywire, buddy."

I listened, dumbstruck, caught in the middle of Jack and Chad's confrontation. Jack's mind could fly wild now and then, go off the scale. Was this one of those times? Or was he right?

"How . . . how did Chad cause the crash?" I asked Jack.

"Ask him."

But before I could, a look of rage erupted on Jack's face, and he gave a snarl and lunged at Chad, grabbing him by the jacket collar. The men outside rushed in, but Tarik beat them to it, a Kimber .45 appearing in his hand. It looked like my father's gun. The hammer clicked as Tarik pointed the barrel tip at Jack's face.

"Let go of his collar. Settle down, Jack. Or your temper's going to get everyone killed. Another move like that, and next time someone is dead."

Tarik pointed the Kimber at me. "She'll be the first to go. Understood?"

Courtney calmly tried to reason. "Jack, if you want Kath, you, Sean, and your buddy"—she pointed at Kevin—"here to walk away from this alive, you really need to listen good and not lose your head. Just stay calm, and I promise you'll feel differently when you hear what's going to be said."

Jack didn't budge.

Chad's men tensed, fingers flexing on their triggers.

"Jack," I pleaded.

Jack finally let go of Chad's collar.

Chad jerked it back into place. I couldn't believe what I was hearing from Courtney. It was as if she was Chad's woman all over again and had planned this conversation out with him.

Jack's neck muscles stood out like ropes, his rage like molten lava. As Chad's men covered him with their weapons, I had a terrible feeling that this was all going to end badly. "Jack, please, do as they say."

Kevin touched Jack's arm. "Stay calm, buddy. Calm, you hear?"

I knew how unpredictable Jack could get, and I feared the worst. I thought of Sean, asleep upstairs, and my heart wrenched. I prayed he wouldn't come awake and hear, walk down the stairs, and cause anyone to get trigger-happy. If that happened, things could go very badly very quickly.

Chad patted down his jacket. He stared at me, as if insulted. "He's wrong, Kath. So wrong. It's crazy, for God's sake."

I felt my heart sink into a hole, one so deep I couldn't even begin to climb out of it. I didn't know what to believe. Could barely comprehend Jack's accusation.

"I . . . I don't know what to believe, Chad." It was all I could say.

Chad looked at a fuming Jack. "You don't believe me. I can't change what you believe. But now is all that matters. Just hear what we have to say. It costs nothing to listen. You know why you need to listen, Jack?"

Jack didn't reply, but Tarik did.

"Because if you don't, there's no way out of this, except for us all to die. We began this together, as co-conspirators. And we could all die together or spend the rest of our lives in prison."

Tarik shrugged, the .45 still pointed at Jack. "Yes, you could cut off your nose to spite your face and rat on everyone. But what would that achieve? Consider it before this gets out of hand, Jack. We all saw enough bloodshed in my homeland. We don't need to see any more. And this . . . this offer . . . allows a way out for everyone."

"That's pretty darn good of you, Tarik. A man who caused enough bloodshed and misery to send him to hell a hundred times over. And not a shred of conscience about it either. Good of y'all, in fact."

Tarik registered the sarcasm in Jack's voice, and his face twisted with a smug grin. "Well?"

Jack leaned in closer to Tarik, his fury still livid. "Like that little girl in Falluja that Kyle befriended. The flower girl. That's what really broke him, you know. You killed her, too, didn't you, Tarik? You enjoy killing. I bet you helped Chad here plan the plane crash. Was that your handiwork, too? Bet it was."

Tarik stared Jack down. "I asked you a question."

Jack didn't answer. Nobody did, and a frightening, hollow silence filled the room, like a pregnant storm cloud just ready to burst. I could hear Jack breathing heavily, his temper hanging by a flimsy thread. "What's your offer?"

Chad placed the tips of the fingers of each hand on the table, flexed them like a dealer preparing to shuffle a deck. He took a deep breath, held it, let it out fast.

"OK, listen up. Time to put all our cards on the table."

101

Babek chewed on an Atkins protein bar and watched the monitor screen.

The drone was flying in perfect circles two hundred feet above the farm. Nothing unusual, nothing odd. Zilch, in fact. Babek had watched Tarik walk up to the farmhouse and enter the front door, could hear his every word through the cell phone. Now it was a waiting game.

Babek chewed the last of the protein bar, scrunched the wrapper into a ball, and tossed it into the corner of the van. As it landed, he heard a grunt. The abducted young man, his face red, drenched in sweat.

Babek swiveled his chair toward Abu, sitting in the corner, his arms crossed, toying with his cell phone. Mehmet was busy scratching himself, looking at the drone screen.

"You think you should give him some water? He doesn't look too good."

Abu grunted and toyed with his phone.

"Hey, buddy, you hear what I said?"

A pair of dark, dangerous eyes almost cut Babek in two. "Don't 'buddy' me. I am not your buddy."

Babek didn't like Tarik's henchmen, and he certainly didn't like this guy. Dark, moody, dangerous. He sounded even more dangerous than usual. Maybe it was the tenseness of the situation, except that Babek didn't like it, felt under a cloud of threat. "But . . . he looks like he could choke. I mean, no one wants to kill anyone, right? That . . . well, that's murder. A serious business."

Abu actually smiled. "You think I care? He's dead anyway."

Mehmet gave a strangled little laugh that made Babek swallow, and a sickening feeling sank into the pit of his stomach, as if he were in a elevator in free fall. "Dead anyway? What do you mean?"

Abu's smile vanished, and he grunted. "Talk to Tarik."

A cold chill went through Babek. This guy was nuts, dangerous. So was Tarik, all his relatives knew that. Babek sometimes did things for Tarik, technical things that bordered on the edge of crime, for money. But this felt different. What if he was in danger of being killed, too?

He swallowed. What if he ran for it, just scurried to the Mercedes and drove off? But he figured there was no hiding from Tarik. He would find him, find him and maybe kill him.

He looked up at the stars, tried to think, his brain a fog. He decided then just to run. To get away from here. He didn't know where, but this whole business had a bad smell.

"I'm going outside."

Abu looked at him suspiciously.

"I need to take a leak, get some air."

"Two minutes, no more."

"Sure. Just watch the screen for me."

"It's simple. You hand over the mask and the other artifacts you took back from the Caymans. We don't care about cash or bonds. You keep them."

Jack was silent as he listened. "Yeah? What else?"

"That's it. Let's face it, if it ever comes out what happened, we're all in the same boat. Theft. Conspiracy. Kidnapping. You want that? I don't think so, Jack."

"I guess that doesn't go too well with any White House ambitions you may ever have, either, Chad."

"Not the point. That may never happen. But what could happen is that we're all looking at twenty to thirty years, depending on the judge's mood. Maybe you never see Kath or Sean for the rest of your natural. Think about that."

Something made me look at my father. His right jaw spasmed, the muscle twitching violently. But his eyes were closed, as if he was thinking hard or just trying to avoid what he was hearing, I couldn't tell which.

I felt Tanner's eyes fall on me, and I stopped looking.

Chad shrugged and sat back. "The way I see it, there are only two sides to this coin, and you've heard the first one. The other side is, if we kill you and we're found out, the stakes are even higher, so why risk it? I like to keep my stakes low. By that I mean we all agree to walk away from this, no hard feelings, no prison time."

He jerked his head toward me. "If Kath wants to, she can join you, wherever that is you all want to go. The Caribbean, the Riviera, you name it. New identities, new lives."

Jack said, "You can arrange that?"

"Sure. Either way, we all carry on as before and keep our mouths shut like nothing happened. If you hid for eight years, you can hide for eight more, or a lifetime if you want. You know that, Jack. If it weren't for the wreckage being found, you'd still be hiding out here and no one the wiser."

"True."

I said, "What about Sergeant Stone and Tanner's buddy Agent Breedon."

Tanner said, "We'll take care of them."

I gave Courtney a look. "Money makes all things possible, I guess, Chad?" I said.

Courtney didn't react, and Chad shrugged indifferently, saying, "You could be right, Kath. It sure greases the wheels."

"And if it doesn't, you kill whoever you need to?"

"Sadly, that's always a last option."

There wasn't a sound of *sadly* in Chad's voice. He uttered the remark so matter-of-factly, so coldly, that I realized right there and then that he probably had absolutely no regard for human life unless it had a meaning for him personally or he meant to gain by it. He was probably a closet psycho.

Kevin said to him, "You really believe you can get away with this?"

Chad looked pretty cocky. "If we can get away with twenty-five million and a bunch of priceless artifacts for this long, yeah, I do."

Jack's mouth tightened, a gesture that made me sense danger. "Just like nothing happened, is that what you said, Chad?"

"Yeah. Like nothing happened."

"But something did happen. You killed our daughter. You left Sean brain-damaged. You robbed me of my life. You robbed Kath's, too."

"No, you did that, Jack. And I didn't cause the plane crash. Get that into your thick skull."

I could see rage erupt again on Jack's face. Kevin said, "Jack, back down, man. Get a grip."

Chad shrugged, as if his patience was waning. "That's our final offer."

Tarik added, "Are you in or out, Jack?"

"We don't have an option, do we?"

Chad shook his head. "Do any of us? See, I don't want anyone harmed. Neither does Tarik. It complicates things immensely. This is the sensible way forward, for all of us."

Chad's gaze swept over all of us. "Well, can we cut a deal?"

102

The air was still and warm, not as stuffy as in the van.

Babek took a long, deep breath, let it out. He felt his legs shake. Fear rose up in his throat like bile. What had he gotten himself into? The Mercedes was fifty yards away. He strolled toward it. He knew the keys were still in the ignition. What if he ran for it, just drove off? But there was no hiding from Tarik. He would find Babek and kill him.

He walked back toward the van and looked up at the stars, trying to think, his brain in a fog. He decided there and then just to run. To get away. To where, he didn't know, but this whole business scared him, had a really bad smell.

He had started to flex his legs, to prepare himself mentally to take flight, when a voice whispered, "Beautiful night, isn't it?"

Babek felt his heart skip, was about to say, "Yeah, it is," when he realized the voice was not Abu's or Mehmet's or that of anyone he knew.

He felt cold metal push hard into his left jaw. His eyes skewed left. A man stood next to him in the semidarkness and whispered, "Don't speak or move. If you do that, a lot of people could get killed. You understand me?"

Babek felt as if he were frozen into a block of ice. The man pushed the gun barrel even harder into his jaw. It hurt him. He glimpsed that the barrel had a silencer. Now his legs were really shaking, felt like rubber.

"I asked, do you understand me?"

"Y-yes."

"I'm Agent Stone, CID."

The man's voice was a firm whisper. He wore black tactical gear, a bulletproof vest, black gloves. Babek heard other footsteps, soft, like a rustle of leaves, as other men in black swarmed in out of nowhere like black specters, brandishing automatic rifles, pistols, shotguns, subma-chine guns, most of their weapons silenced.

Thermal-imaging devices attached to their helmets, they moved like shadows, ghosts, wearing black, carrying firearms and flashlights like glinting sabers.

At least a dozen, and they moved everywhere at once—toward the Mercedes, circling the van, fanning out to take up positions near the woods. "CID" was emblazoned with Velcro strips on their ballistic vests.

Babek wanted to cry out, but he swallowed, managed to suppress it.

Two of the men began to pat him down for weapons. One yanked Babek's hands behind his back and placed a plastic tie wrap on his wrists. Babek stayed frozen still. He didn't want to risk a noise or ges-ture that might make the man shoot him.

"Who's inside the van?" Stone whispered. "Speak quietly."

"Abu and Mehmet?"

"Yeah? And who are they?"

"They . . . they work for Tarik."

"Are they armed?"

"Yes."

"With what? I want the truth, buddy."

"Pistols. Automatic rifles."

"What about the woman, Agent Adams?"

"I . . . know nothing about her."

"Anyone else in there?"

"A man, they kidnapped him, from a home near Servierville. His name is Kyle. He's tied up in the van."

"Where exactly in the van?"

"That end." Babek gestured to the back of the vehicle.

"Sitting or lying down?"

"Lying down."

Stone tried to digest that information and stared at the van, as if judging where to direct gunfire if needed. "Where's Tarik?"

"He went up to the farmhouse to join the others. To talk."

"What others?"

Babek told him what he knew. "I . . . I think they mean to kill everyone at the farm."

"Is Tarik armed?"

"Yes. He has a pistol."

Stone patted him on the head. "Good dog."

Stone made several gestures with his hands, two agents joined him, and he whispered to them, as others began to encircle the van, and three of the agents took up positions near the sliding side door.

Without warning, the van's side door slid open, and Abu stepped out, carrying a flashlight, Mehmet behind him, weapons in their hands.

It happened quickly.

A dozen flashlights sprang on and were directed toward the van. Shock registered on Abu's face, and his gun exploded twice, firing wildly, and that was his big mistake.

As Mehmet went to fire and duck back inside the van, he managed to get off two shots before a hail of silenced gunfire erupted, riddling the van with bullet holes, hammering both men back inside the vehicle in an obscene dance of death.

103

"So have we got a deal, Jack?"

Jack said nothing, his blank face a cipher.

Chad sat there, his leg tapping up and down, his impatience showing.

"All we want is the mask and the artifacts, Jack."

"Yeah, sure."

"You've got them stashed somewhere, stands to reason. Why dispose of a fortune?"

"Good question."

"You done being a wiseass, Jack?"

Jack was steadfastly silent, but his skin stretched tight across his cheekbones, his face white with rage, festering beneath his silence.

Chad glanced at his watch, and then, with a sweeping movement of his hand, he took out a small Sig auto and pointed it toward us.

"I told you, Jack. I don't want anyone hurt. But so help me, if you don't talk . . ." He glanced at Kevin, then at me. "Someone's going to get killed. You've got three seconds."

Jack glared back at Chad, and in that glare I recognized a hatred so intense it was ready to explode like a bomb at any second.

More silence.

Chad cocked his Sig, aimed it at Kevin. "Have it your way. Three . . . two . . ."

"There's an old coal mine that tunnels out from under the barn," Jack blurted. "A trapdoor toward the back leads down to some steps. Just kick away some hay, and you'll see it. The tunnel eventually leads to a secure storage room."

Chad gave a triumphant grin. "That's my boy. Anything else we need to know?"

"You'll find the light switch on the upright beam nearest the trapdoor. It'll illuminate the tunnel for two hundred yards. You'll come to the storage room's oak-and-metal door just before the tunnel ends and comes out onto a narrow plateau. The mask and the artifacts are hidden in the storage room."

"All of them?"

"Yeah, all of them. The door's rock-solid and heavily padlocked."

"Where does the tunnel exit?"

"Onto a small plateau."

"You planned on escaping that way, Jack?"

Jack did not reply.

"Tell me. Were you planning on escaping that way?"

"There are a couple of four-wheelers hidden behind some bushes at the tunnel mouth," Jack added.

"Once the soldier, always the soldier. Ready to bug out at a second's notice, right?"

Jack played dumb.

"You'd better not be lying, old buddy."

"I ain't," Jack said.

"Good boy." Chad held out his hand, snapped his fingers. "Keys. Hand them over. Do it easy."

"Give them to him, Kevin," Tanner said.

Kevin went to reach into his trouser pocket, and Tanner said, "Go real slow, buddy. Use two fingers, fish the keys out."

Kevin eased out a big set of chunky keys tied with steel wire onto a worn piece of old hardwood. Tanner held out his hand. Kevin tossed the keys, and Tanner caught them with a grin.

"Who the heck are you?" Jack asked.

"A party to this deal, just like you."

Jack looked at Chad as if for an explanation, but none was forthcoming as Tanner tossed the keys to Chad. "We're definitely aboveboard here, Jack? No double crosses, no pulling my chain?"

"I told you where the stuff is. Now, what about your end of the bargain?"

Chad looked pleased.

Tarik did, too, and he said, "The mask and the artifacts first. Then we finish our deal and go our separate ways."

That's when I noticed a disturbed look on my father's face. His mouth was clamped tight as steel.

"No, they won't," he said.

"What are you talking about, Frank?" Chad asked.

"You won't finish the deal," said my father. His face looked troubled, a forlorn look in his eyes, his voice flat, emotionless, as he stared at me. "I don't believe either of them. Chad's a lying crook. As for Tarik, he's a scumbag who'd kill his own grandmother if there was a nickel in it."

Tarik let out a cackling laugh that frightened me. "You were never good with compliments, were you, Colonel?"

"That's what they called you in Iraq, the Undertaker. You had a reputation for death even then, Tarik. Nothing's changed."

My father stared at Tarik as if he was a piece of dog dirt.

Chad tried to ease the tension. "We'll keep our word, so long as you keep yours."

My father's eyes shifted to me. "Kath, if I could rewind this, if I could change things, I would. I'm so sorry . . ."

I knew he meant it. But I still hated him.

"Let's wrap this up." Chad jerked his head at Tarik. "Go get the stuff. Take Tanner with you and one of the guys from outside. I'll stay here."

My father's head went down, as if in shame. That's when I saw him bend his left leg. I noticed the material of his cargo pants rise an inch or two. My father was the kind of man who always kept a weapon on hand—a gun, a knife.

Tarik had taken his gun, but I thought I glimpsed something metallic and about as long as a pencil attached in some way to my father's prosthesis. It could have been part of the foot mechanism, but I knew my father, and my instinct told me it might be a weapon of last resort. Maybe some kind of tactical blade or dagger he'd fashioned in his workshop.

Whatever it was, Jack had missed it when he searched him. I sensed trouble coming. Cold fear rose in me. My father had always been a man of action. Despite the telltale cues of Parkinson's, despite slowing with the years, he was still physically strong, still a fighter who wouldn't go down without a battle. And knowing my father, he'd wait for the right moment.

I tried to see if it really was a weapon embedded in the prosthesis, but in an instant, my father's face collapsed, as if it was melting wax, and he moaned, "Dear God . . . no!"

His cry was no distraction. It sounded real, a wail of shock and alarm, and I followed his gaze—everyone did. My heart felt ruptured as I saw Sean standing a few steps down from the top of the stairs. He looked so young and innocent. The image reminded me of when he was a little boy and sometimes came to the top of the stairs asking for a glass of water. His shirt collar was askew, and he wore an old pair of someone else's pajamas that looked a few sizes too big for him.

But he wasn't looking for water.

He was clutching a pump-action shotgun in both hands.

I saw an instant spark of recognition on my father's face, as if he'd seen the dead walk. Tears welled in his eyes, tears of joy, and fear, too, as if he recognized the extreme danger of the situation. "Sean . . . Sean, son, please, don't do a thing, son. Don't move . . . please . . ."

A horrible, frightening moment of silence. Everyone froze. It was as if all the air was sucked out of the room. Like one of those still shots in movies when the camera freezes in 3-D.

But my father's plea was wasted, because Sean was startled, and the shotgun in his hand started to rise.

"Sean, no!" I cried.

Tanner raised his gun, aimed toward Sean.

Courtney shouted, "No!" and brought up her Sig.

Tarik beat them both to it, the .45 in his hands aimed in an instant, but before he could fire, there was a burst of gunfire from outside, two rapid shots followed by two more. Not from Chad's men but from somewhere farther away. I saw the guys on the patio react, aiming their weapons out into the darkness beyond the farm.

After that, everything seemed to happen like a nightmare unfolding in horrific slow motion.

At the sound of gunfire, Sean pulled the trigger in a nervous reaction, and the shotgun exploded. The force hit Tanner in the chest, punching him backward. Courtney was caught by the blast, and she staggered back and collapsed. There was blood everywhere.

It was enough distraction for my father. His hand went down to his foot. He slid out what looked like a polished steel bolt the size of a pen. The point was sharpened.

I watched in horror as Tarik fired at Sean. The round missed him, gouging a hole in the wall to his left.

"Put it down! Put the gun down!" Tarik screamed.

Sean jumped in shock. Tarik aimed again, but this time, my father's arm swung in an arc, and he dug the metal blade into Tarik's back. Tarik went down, grunting, eyes wide, his gun going off, blasting a hole in the floor. My father yanked out the blade and stabbed Tarik again, this time in the chest.

"See you in hell, Tarik."

Chad's gun came up, and he shot my father in the face and twice again in the chest. My father reeled back, slamming into the couch.

Everything was happening so fast, all at the same time. More gunfire erupted outside, as if the men on the patio were engaged in a gun battle. Chad used the distraction to grab the bunch of keys from the floor next to Tanner's dead hand.

Jack lunged at him.

But Chad was faster. He fired two quick shots, one hitting Jack in the shoulder, spinning him around, and sending the rest of us in the room ducking for cover.

Then Chad rushed out through the kitchen door toward the back patio, the door slapping after him, and he was gone.

104

Stone shouted the order to cease fire, and the hollow thudding of silenced gunshots stopped. A stench of cordite filled the air. Stone and the others inched forward toward the van. A hand rose and twitched—Abu's—and four more rounds were fired, two into Abu's head, another two into Mehmet.

Two of Stone's men moved cautiously into the van, one of them carrying a Kevlar shield in front. Stone waited until the all-clear was shouted, and then he dragged Babek by the shirt toward the blood-spattered bodies. Abu and Mehmet were sprawled half in and half out of the van, their corpses bullet-riddled.

Babek was amazed. All the gunfire seemed accurately directed into a single space no more than three by four feet.

"These the two?"

"Yes." Babek was ready to faint at the sight of all the blood, still seeping from Abu's and Mehmet's wounds. His head spun.

Stone moved to join the other men inside the van, his AR-15 at the ready, the powerful tactical flashlight attached to it like a searchlight.

They all came out moments later with the young man who had duct tape around his mouth. One of the men removed it. The young man started to cry, convulsions racking his body.

Stone patted him. "It's OK, Kyle, it's OK. You're safe, buddy."

Two medics dressed in tactical black appeared and helped the young man away.

Babek felt lucky to be alive.

Stone waved his hand, beckoning his men to join him, and ordered two of them to remain with Babek. Stone looked worried that he might already be too late, for the sound of the gunfire volleys was still a dying echo in the woods. It gave the game away, alerting anyone in the farmhouse.

Stone snarled at Babek. "You'd better be telling me the truth about who's in the house."

"I swear."

Stone huddled his men together and snapped orders. He seemed galvanized as he punched the air with a fist. "Move out. To the farm. Prepare to engage."

He snapped at the two men remaining, "Bag him and go."

Babek thought the look on Stone's face spoke volumes—as if he knew, already knew, that they were too late. That the rattle of gunfire had given away any hope they had of surprise.

Babek watched in silent awe as Stone moved off, a trail of men in dark tactical clothes jogging behind him, like some deadly black snake slinking off into the darkness, about to seek out and strike its prey.

The next thing Babek knew, some kind of bag was thrust over his head, and everything went pitch-black.

The room looked like a butcher's shop, awash with blood.

I saw my father's body, sprawled on the floor.

My heart stopped.

I moved toward him.

His eyes were open in death and stared up blindly at the ceiling. The wound where Chad had shot him was like a drill hole between his eyes, above his nose.

That was when I noticed Kevin. He'd been hit in the side of the head, from a ricochet or deliberately, from Chad's or someone else's gun. I wanted to pass out, my head spinning with the grim unreality. What kept me conscious I'll never know, but I saw Courtney try to raise herself, a dead Tanner lying next to her, one of his legs crooked across her thighs.

She looked in agony. Blood spattered her blouse and her face; buck-shot had peppered her skin.

Jack was slumped with his back against the wall, clutching his shoulder, writhing in pain.

Sean looked on, stunned, his lips quivering like a frightened child's. He went to move down the stairs toward Jack.

I shouted, stopping him in his tracks. "Sean, get back upstairs. Stay there until I tell you. Be careful with the shotgun. Just leave it down. Leave it down, now. Go back to your room, and stay there until I call you."

"But Daddy . . ."

I saw tears in his eyes.

Jack grimaced and looked stricken, unable to move. "Go, son. Do as you're told."

Courtney tried to prop herself up on an elbow as she shouted, "Stone! Cease fire, Stone!"

But whether anyone heard her I had no idea. More gunfire erupted outside. It didn't sound as if it was from the men on the patio, or maybe they had chased after Chad.

I felt confused, bewildered. As if I'd been sucked up by a tornado and was being hurled about in a violent storm.

And I felt a powerful anger. Had Chad really done what Jack said? Caused the crash? The question raged inside me, swirled inside my head, seeking an answer. Maybe seeking revenge.

Lights flashed outside in the darkness, like silver sabers. A brief, powerful exchange of gunfire, and then it died.

A distant voice shouted, "Captain Adams, you in there?"

"Yes!" Courtney shouted back.

I went to check on Jack. He grunted as I examined his wounds.

Sweat glistened on his forehead, and he looked almost in a coma from the pain. Our eyes met. All he said was "Hang in there."

"I intend to."

Courtney flinched, tried to move, but couldn't. "Stone and the others will be here soon."

"Why side with Chad?"

"I had to stall them, to buy time, Kath. Sergeant Stone was following me with reinforcements, but he was a distance away. We didn't trust Tanner. When I couldn't keep in contact by phone, I had to play along with Chad and Tarik, hoping Stone would figure out I was in trouble and come to get me."

"Did Chad cause the crash? Tell me the truth."

"I don't know, Kath, I really don't know." She looked at me. "But he caused enough trouble."

Courtney tried to pick up her Sig, but she didn't have the strength. I picked it up for her. But I didn't give it to her. Instead, I cocked the slide, loading a round into the chamber.

"What are you doing?"

"Let's just say I have a date with Chad."

I picked up a tactical flashlight that lay fallen by Kevin's side.

Courtney grabbed at my arm weakly, looked me in the eyes. "Don't be crazy. There's help outside. They'll be in here any minute."

"Have them look after Jack and Sean. Will you be OK?"

"Kath, wait. Chad's dangerous. Wait for Stone . . ."

But I wasn't listening. Remembering Jack's accusation, I felt my searing fury burn lava-hot.

Something made me look at my father's corpse.

A trickle of blood came from the wound. I felt a rush of tears. I leaned over, and with my thumb and middle finger, I closed my father's eyelids.

I felt myself choking with pain.

And then I stood, readying the Sig and the flashlight, and raced out the back door after Chad.

105

Pitch-darkness.

Gunfire.

Flashes of torchlight splitting the blackness.

It sounded as if flash-bang grenades were going off somewhere in the night, out in the surrounding woods, but I hurried out to the barn.

I approached the open doors carefully and moved inside, keeping the Sig at the ready. The trapdoor was open, and the string of bare light bulbs in the cavern below were ablaze.

I aimed the flashlight into the tunnel and flicked it around the glistening, damp walls.

Nothing moved except the shadows made by the flashlight beam.

I listened.

I heard nothing, not even footsteps. What if Chad was waiting in the darkness to spring a trap on anyone who followed him?

I reckoned it was more likely that he was racing for the storage room before he made his escape. Get rid of the goods, get rid of the evidence. Or maybe it was just greed? Either way, with the kind of money and connections Chad had, he could disappear anytime he wanted and never be found.

I descended the steps into the cavern, jumped the last two, and my feet hit the ground.

I sucked in a couple lungfuls of chilled air, so cold it almost hurt.

That was when I heard the noise.

Running footsteps.

Chad's, I bet.

I hurried down the tunnel as fast as my legs would move.

My lungs felt frozen, as if every breath were solid ice.

Every minute or so, I halted and listened.

I heard a scraping noise, then banging.

I moved on as quietly as I could, keeping the flashlight off in case the bulbs went out and I needed it.

A few minutes later, I knew I was nearing the tunnel's end.

The noises stopped.

My heart shuddered.

I felt terrified but forced myself to go on, to cautiously negotiate the tunnel's every curve and twist.

I heard a yawning, like a door creaking open.

Then came the sound of moving feet.

Muffled noises came to me after that, so indistinct I couldn't tell what they were, but I finally came to the solid oak-and-metal door. It was wide open.

I saw no sign of Chad.

I felt scared.

My chest thudded.

And then I heard a noise, distinct and sharp.

There was a sound like a stone falling away, and Chad stepped out from a recess in the tunnel. He clutched the Sig in one hand. In the other he gripped a heavy burlap bag. I could guess what was in there.

The color was gone from Chad's face. His perfectly groomed hair was spiky, all over the place. He had the look of a hunted animal but still cocky, still confident, knowing that a few yards away was an exit onto the plateau and his escape to freedom.

"You couldn't leave well enough alone, could you, Kath?"

I brought up Courtney's pistol.

Chad laid the bag at his feet. "What are you going to do, Kath, shoot me?"

"If I have to. You're coming back with me."

He gave a nervous, furious laugh. "You really reckon?"

A thought hit me like a lightning bolt. "It's funny the things that cross your mind when you realize someone you once trusted is a liar and a cheat and a killer."

"Like what?"

"If I ever really meant anything to you. If you just stayed with me to find out if Jack was still alive and going to contact me and come back. Is that paranoid of me, or is it true, Chad?"

He didn't answer, his eyes flicking nervously toward the tunnel exit.

I moved closer to him.

"Stop right there, Kath."

"Keep your enemies close but your friends even closer. That applied to me, too? You just needed to know if Jack ever showed up, didn't you? And then when he didn't, and it was safe, you ditched me."

Chad said nothing. He didn't have to. I knew I was right.

I felt the reality of it rip open my chest.

"And the crash. That was you."

"It's not true. I'd never have deliberately harmed your children."

"Problem is, I can't believe anything you say, Chad. Not a word. But you're coming back with me. You'll answer those questions, one way or another."

Distant gunfire. Noises. They were far away, though. Too far to help me. But Chad looked nervous. He didn't need me slowing him down.

"One thing you'd better believe. If you try to stop me, I will shoot. So put the gun away and go, Kath. Go before both of us regret it and something bad happens."

He brought up his pistol.

I leveled mine. "I've got a gun, too."

"But you're not going to use it."

"Want to bet?"

"Yeah, I do." A grin flickered on Chad's face. "Tanner slipped the rounds out of Courtney's weapon earlier in the evening as a precaution. In case she didn't play along, he put in blanks instead."

I felt my heart hit the floor.

"Go ahead. Pull the trigger, Kath."

I aimed toward the exit end of the chamber, near some loose rocks, and pulled the trigger, twisting my face and my body away in case of a ricochet. A round exploded. I waited for the dull thud of the bullet striking the walls, but there was nothing. I pulled the trigger again and again. The same. The gun spewed fire but no bullets.

Blanks.

"See?" Chad picked up the bag. "Got to go. There's a four-wheeler out there with my name on it."

He went to move. I lunged after him.

"Don't. It's not worth it, Kath. Just let it go." He aimed the Sig right at my face.

I didn't know it, and neither did he, but pointing that gun at me was his big mistake.

There was a soft click, like a hammer being cocked, and I looked around.

Sean.

He stood ten yards away, in those old pajamas and in his bare feet. He inched forward into the tunnel, fear in his face.

The shotgun was in his hands. He must have followed me.

Panic lit Chad's face like a beacon, and he went to raise his Sig.

Sean said, "No . . . don't hurt her. Don't!"

Before Chad could even reply, Sean squeezed the trigger.

The shotgun exploded, the noise like a sonic boom, and the roar seemed to echo forever in the darkness of the tunnel.

106

I keep two photographs by my bed. They are my deepest wounds.

I have moved back into the cottage, into those rooms where we were once happiest.

On restless nights or when the rains pour or the winds scream, I leave my window blinds open a crack so the lunar light that washes into my room through the wooden slats falls on the faces in the photographs.

I turn my eyes toward the images, and I see Jack's face. I see the man and the love I once had and the hope of a good future that we dreamed of.

War destroyed it, as it destroys so many other dreams, with its ruinous pain. In a way, the ones who survive are the ones who suffer most—the wounded in mind and body and spirit, the bereaved, those left behind. And even those who bring courage with them to war—it kills them, or it breaks them.

It kills the good and the valiant and the brave, just as easily as it kills the fearful and the gentle and the cowardly. And those it does not kill it breaks. It breaks us all in the end, even those of us who are mere watchers from the shore, for we are broken by the same cruel tempest that destroys the ones we love.

I have forgiven Jack. What demons he had to fight within his own tormented mind I can never know, but I believe that he did his best. That he tried to protect us all. That he was a good father, despite the wrong he did. I can be kind to him. I put my acceptance down to his damaged mental state. At least, that is my excuse.

Broken by battle, wounded by war, he is not the man I married, nor do I know if he will ever be whole again or if his mind and spirit will ever find peace. All I can do is be there, try to quiet his silent screams, heal his damaged soul.

There are many questions Jack must answer in the months ahead, so many questions, but the investigators who quiz him seem to be patient. And I have sought no retribution, pressed no charges, for I know that Jack has paid the price of his own brokenness.

Sometimes I look back and see my children's faces on that beach in South Carolina, and I weep. I weep for all the irreplaceable years that we have lost, that were taken from us.

But when I see my father's face in the photograph next to my mother's, I cannot forgive him. Not yet. Maybe not ever. He was a good man, once. But goodness was no longer the master of his soul.

There is a question people sometimes ask: How do you cope with losing your family—a husband, a daughter, a mother, a father—an entire life? The answer is that you don't. When you break, you become another person. But you muddle on, the victim of a battle you never sought. For a long time afterward, you are walking dead. You cry out to God. Sometimes you curse his name. Because we never really bury our departed. They live with us, minute by minute, day by day, year by year.

And so it should be.

For as the universe conspires to soothe your pain, it allows you to embrace your deepest wounds, to realize that making pain the only recalled measure of our love is to deny love.

The music of your children's laughter, your delight at the touch of their fingers trailing like silk upon your skin, the wondrous feel of their breath upon your face—these are all part of love's price.

And it is a price that is worth all the years of sorrow past and yet to come.

Jack sleeps for now in the room across the hall.

Like cautious animals, we prowl around each other, wary of our territory, wary of offering or losing our hearts again, as if they are made of the most delicate glass.

Sean sleeps near me, in a bed that I moved next to mine. I hear his breathing. He is content here. He is no longer the bright, happy boy I once raised, but he is alive. I know that he has trouble remembering me as his mother, but I also know that he feels a vague connection to me. Some primal instinct in him made him want to protect me, and for that I am grateful.

Just as he is protected now. Safe at last.

I live in the hope that someday the closed door in his mind will open again and he will see me as I see him. I dream, and I pray, but I do not know.

Sometimes when I look at his face, I see Jack and Amy. I see the resemblance, and I hear the timbres of their voices in Sean's tone. And each night, I still read him the Dr. Seuss stories that he loved. He listens, quietly, perhaps raptly, but I do not know if I reach him or if the memories I stir are still beyond his reach.

But often, when he's sleeping restlessly, he wakes and calls out, "Mommy?"

The sound of his voice, the simple sound of my child calling my name, makes my heart soar. "It's OK, Sean. Mommy's here. Go back to sleep, my love."

And hearing the comfort of my answer, feeling the soft caress of my hand on his forehead, he closes his eyes again and falls back into the oblivion of rest.

I have started to write again.

Not much, a page or two each day, less if I'm not feeling up to it, but it is a start. And in those small hours of the morning when I lie awake, writing, for no other reason than my troubled mind or when the wind or rain whispers or claws against the glass, I often ask myself what days lie ahead for Sean and me and Jack and if they will be glorious days or dark nights of the soul.

And with Sean, will we ever truly reach each other? Find again the love we once had, the parent-and-child closeness that is nature's powerful bond. Sometimes I see in his fleeting smiles the shadow of the Sean I once knew, and it lifts my heart. On days like those, I feel we will be all right.

But again, I do not know.

Nor do I know if Jack and I will ever be all right. And although he is not the person I married, who can say any of us is? We all open doors into other rooms, and sometimes our beloved follows us and sometimes not.

All I know is that Sean is happy to be back in the company of his father and mother. And our son sleeps peacefully because of it. And so I wait patiently, hoping that Jack and I will again enter that room where we once found one another.

We do not sleep together. But on nights when I hear him call out, when his nightmares assail his sleep, I go to him and lay a damp cloth upon his fevered brow.

Will we ever love again? I can't answer that, no more than I can say for certain if there is a world beyond this one, but I know the hopeful promise of it comforts me. I hope for better days, just as I hope for better days for Kyle, but that hope is all I truly have. And although my grief for Amy is a constant ache, I would have it no other way.

Like the Celtic legend of the bird that sings just once in its life but more sweetly than any other creature on this earth, I have sought my own thorns to impale my heart upon.

As we all do.

Yet I know that the love I have had for Jack and Sean and Amy wasn't just a chance occurrence in this chaotic world but a fateful strand in the tapestry of my life. That its meaning lies far beyond my comprehension.

On those nights when I cannot sleep, I leave a lamp on in the landing. Its brilliance seeps under my door, a long strip of shimmering gold. It comforted Amy then, just as it comforts me now. Bright and shining, it glows like a spirit from another world, a fire's afterglow, a sacred flame.

It lifts my heart.

It is as radiant as my daughter was, and is, and always will be. As we all are, so long as goodness is the master of our souls.

What soothes me most is that splinter of gleaming light.

It sends a golden orb to play upon the ceiling.

On stormy nights, the orb dances. On hot nights, it is still.

But it never, ever goes away.

I call it Amy's light.

AUTHOR'S NOTE

During the U.S.-led war in Iraq, hundreds of billions of U.S. dollars were earmarked for the postwar rebuilding of the country.

At the start of the conflict, the United Nations also set aside 23 billion U.S. dollars of Iraqi money, held in overseas accounts, to be used in reconstruction projects.

An estimated $8 billion went missing in the fog of war during the U.S. occupation. Some estimates claim it was closer to $12 billion and even higher. Much of the money vanished into the back pockets and the secret Swiss and Middle Eastern bank accounts of Iraqi tribal and political leaders, U.S. military officials, and corrupt U.S. and international business contractors who benefited from the chaos and bid rigging. Notable among them were businessmen with ties to both Republican and Democratic parties.

Ironically, missing money was also undoubtedly diverted to groups with links to Al-Qaeda to help fund their war against the United States.

Iraq during this period was awash with cash. "We played football with bricks of hundred-dollar bills," claimed one U.S. Army official.

Henry Waxman, then chairman of the U.S. House of Representatives Committee on Oversight and Government Reform, said, "The money that's gone into waste, fraud, and abuse under these contracts is just so outrageous. . . . It may well turn out to be the largest war profiteering in history."

A number of high-level Pentagon investigations could not explain what happened to many billions of missing dollars or discover the whereabouts of missing records that would have shed light on the thefts. Electronic records either were not kept or disappeared.

One of the companies to profit most from the war was Houston-based engineering and construction firm KBR Inc., which was spun off from its parent, oil field–services provider Halliburton, in 2007. Halliburton was famous for its previous ties to Dick Cheney, the former U.S. vice president, who served in the Cabinet during the Iraq War.

KBR was given $39.5 billion in Iraq-related contracts over the course of a decade, with many of the deals given without any bidding from competing firms, a practice that led to a Justice Department lawsuit over alleged kickbacks. Gag orders were frequently put in place by the U.S. government in certain cases to prevent press coverage.

Also stolen during the Iraq conflict were many priceless historical artifacts from Iraqi museums and private collections. To this day, a large number of the artifacts have not been recovered.

Nor has any completely credible official U.S. government evidence been offered regarding what happened to the missing $8 billion.

Many of the thefts that occurred remain unsolved, and, remarkably, they have never been the subject of rigorous criminal investigation.

Another striking irony: while U.S. Army veterans often struggle mentally and physically to survive their lifetime wounds of war, often without much-needed medical or psychological care, stolen billions remain unaccounted for, and the criminals and war profiteers responsible for some of the biggest thefts in world history remain free to enjoy their ill-gotten gains.

ACKNOWLEDGMENTS

To all those who helped me with my research, as always, my grateful thanks. A special thank-you to Jesse Flynn, researcher extraordinaire—I will keep my promise to be there for you when the NSA sends someone knocking on your door to take you in for questioning because of all the government websites you visited, all the firearms you checked up on, and the numerous law enforcement agents you were in contact with in your relentless hunt for information. And if you do end up with a black bag over your head in some compound, I'll be there for you too, Jesse.

ACKNOWLEDGMENTS

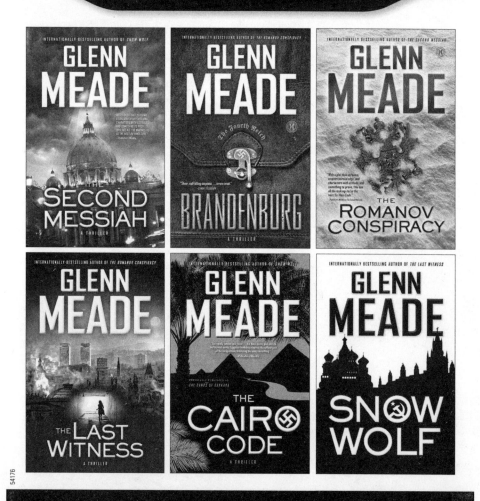